THE CALL OF THE ANCIENTS

The Chronicles Of Nadine

KIM VERMAAK

Yakhal Publishing

The Call of the Ancients

THE CHRONICLES OF NADINE - BOOK THREE

KIM VERMAAK

I dedicate this book to my parents, Denzil and Belinda.

Daddy, you once told me that while there was life in your body, you would always protect me. Thank you for being true. Mommy, thank you for your love and support that were the wings beneath that promise.

There are many people who watch a world full of suffering and sigh and shrug their shoulders. But you bring to the world a rare breed of courage that brings hope to the world of children who are broken and discarded.

For all those people who found space in their heart to love a child born into a different family, I commend your courage. Gary and Lisa, I count you as champions in bringing love to the downtrodden.

For I am LORD your God who takes hold of your right hand and says to you, Do not fear; I will help you.

Isaiah 41:13

Also By Kim Vermaak...

The Chronicles Of Nadine

A Mother's Warning

(Prequel Novella)

Last of The Silver Wings

The Fire Within The Storm

The Call Of The Ancients

SIGN UP AND DOWNLOAD THE CHRONICLES OF NADINE NOVELLA**, A MOTHER'S WARNING**, FOR FREE

Sign up for the no-spam newsletter at the end of this book and get The Chronicles Of Nadine prequel novella absolutely free.

Northern Kingdom
Holly Hill
Cave
Ruin Mountain
Tunnel
Lord Logan Territory
Holly Lake
Ancient Ruins
Medicine Woman
Nadine's Village
Forever Lake
N
E
S
W

Prologue

680 AD

Emerald Forest – Land of the Ancients

Ciommed, a high-ranking Emerald Forest Dragon, knew her last day had come. Miykaeel, of the Crafton Warrior clan, had been pursuing her for hours, with attack after relentless attack that had worn her out. When the Elders had tasked Ciommed with the protection of the eggs, they had not known that she was forming one herself. She had been gravely ill at the time, and her life force was low. The Elders could not detect the change in the Emerald Forest Dragon because of her illness. Had they known, they would never have risked sending her. The vote had been taken in her absence. No one doubted Ciommed's ability to do the task, nor her commitment. Being with egg did not make her unworthy of the task. It merely made her vulnerable. But now, with the war, there was no other that they could turn to, to assist her.

"Be safe," she had told her mate, as they went their separate ways.

"You know that you are not strong enough to carry all these eggs. Let me help you."

"But it is my sworn duty," she protested.

"Yes, and it is also your sworn duty to protect our egg. You have no sisters to help you with the task. Let me at least take the Copper Fire Dragon egg. It is the heaviest of all of them."

She handed him the egg in silence. But he pressed on. "And the Crystal Water Egg."

"No!"

"But you know the lake is closer to the caves. It will be easier for me than for you."

Ciommed looked away. He would have to fly over the battle.

"I will fly on the outskirts near the forest. I will come back for you."

"Beloved Zargo…. I love you." Ciommed closed her eyes as she made the forehead greeting.

"And I you." He lingered with his forehead pressed against hers. "Our hatchling will be the finest Emerald Forest Dragon. Just wait and see!" he said, placing the eggs in the dragon-scale pouch.

Ciommed watched him fly away until his body merged with the distant treetops.

ტ

She had been without water for hours and her throat burned. Ciommed had not told him that her egg had already begun to harden; she had waited too long. She knew that even if he survived the flight over the war zone, they would never again share one another's embrace. Even so, now she had to make her way to the hidden nesting cave.

ó

Mıykaeel's hunt did not slow. She slashed at the canopy of leaves again and again, carving a path for herself. Mıykaeel was the warlord's most trusted military strategist. It had been her plan to trap the female dragons with eggs. If she could harvest enough of them, the warlord could build an army so powerful that no one could ever defeat him. Then perhaps one day he would make Mıykaeel his queen, and they could rule together.

"Ciommed, I know you are with egg. I will find you and the egg will be mine," called Mıykaeel. "Ciommed!"

The Emerald Forest Dragon sniffed the ground, as she frantically searched for the entrance of the nesting cave. She closed her eyes and inhaled deeply. The area was so overgrown with weeds and vines that she could barely make out the scent of the sacred birthing herbs. She glanced behind her as the fragrance filled her senses. The dragon clawed at the vines that concealed the opening of the underground cave. A light emerged from within the cave as the stone rolled away. Ciommed squinted at the flickering flame. She tried to recognise the human form approaching her from deep in the shadows.

"I was wondering how long you were going to take to get here," said a familiar voice.

Ciommed almost wept with relief at the sight of her Whisperer's wife.

"Where is…?"

"He is gone," replied Nyla, her eyes brimming. "But none of that now. Let's get this egg passed."

"You are bleeding," said Ciommed. "I'm afraid most of my herbs are gone."

"It is just a scratch." Ciommed knew she was lying, but she accepted the mercy of the lie.

Nyla was a trained midwife for humans. Through her

husband's alliance with the Dragons, she had learned many of the ways of the dragon's passing of new life. She was not a dragon sister, but right now, she was more precious than a hundred dragon sisters. Humans suffered far more giving birth than Dragons. And now only this human midwife knew how to prepare Ciommed for what was to come.

"What of Miykaeel?" asked Ciommed. "She is not far behind me."

Nyla opened her palm. In it lay a crushed Yellow Spike Spider.

"I have lined the entrance with them." Ciommed recoiled in horror. One of their bites had caused her own illness. A Yellow Spike Spider could not kill a dragon. It would weaken one if the bite was near the eye. But for a human, they were lethal.

"It is not safe for you, Nyla." Nyla pulled back the covering of her tunic. Ciommed saw the spreading of a crimson mark that could only have come from an arrow. The abdominal wound was severe and Ciommed knew that Nyla must be in a great deal of pain. Nyla smiled weakly.

"You know we have very little time, so let's quit talking and get busy doing."

Nyla had prepared the cave some days before, in anticipation of the delivery. She had dug an opening on the other side of the stone entrance that Ciommed had used. The ground was covered with soft soil infused with the soothing aromatic herbs needed to calm Ciommed when the pain became unbearable.

They both knew that there could be no roars of pain. Only Ciommed's silence could protect them. Nyla tried to be strong for Ciommed, but the tears came freely when she saw how frightened the dragon was.

The pain had a searing warmth to it. While Nyla pushed to hold up the dragon's belly, her own pain radiated and pulsated through her. She closed her eyes, resisting the urge to rest.

Nyla attempted to soothe Ciommed. She rubbed herb-infused fat on the dragon's underbelly, and pushed against the dragon's strained muscles with all her strength to keep them from rupturing even more, but with each attempt Nyla winced in pain.

Ciommed was terrified. None of what was happening to her body felt natural. The pain ripped through her, as the hardened scales of the egg tore through the oviduct with each sharp contraction. Nyla saw now that she could not save Ciommed. But she would do everything she could to keep her alive long enough to pass the egg.

Dragons had no knowledge of contractions of this kind. A soft egg slipped out into a nest of its mother's choice, and her sisters and nursery elders supported her during the first days after laying an egg and when the hatchling had broken free. A mother's life force grew a hatchling. Now passing a hardened egg drained her life force. With one final spasm, the egg ripped through the end of the passage, tearing with it the last of Ciommed's strength. Her body crumpled, and she lay heaving out the remnants of her breath in painful pants. She had no strength remaining to clean the egg. Nyla covered it with a fur-lined leather wrap. The fur soaked up the excess fluid from the thorny shell. She pushed it towards Ciommed.

"What is the hatchling to be named?"

"Tagliyot," whispered Ciommed, her tears dripping onto the covered egg.

"What does it mean?"

"Discovery…" The dragon's words turned into mere vapours as her life force drained away to nothing.

Nyla etched the name onto a small stone carved in the shape of an egg and then gently placed the dragon egg with the stone into the hole she had dug before Ciommed's arrival. She dragged herself back to the spot where the Emerald Forest Dragon lay. With all her words and strength spent, she rested her head beside the Emerald Forest Dragon and the two females held each other's gaze until the light in Ciommed's eyes was gone.

Nyla lay inside the chamber with Ciommed's body, waiting for death to release her when, on the other side of the cave, she saw the shimmer of the Silver Wing Dragon's egg in the dying flame of the torch. Ciommed had dropped it when she descended into the cave, but Nyla knew she no longer had the strength to reach it.

ό

Mıykaeel's axe hacked at the roots of the tree that concealed the cave opening. The spiders retaliated against the assailant that dared to disturb their new home. Their poison made its way to her heart in moments, and the warrior's expression distorted into a grimace. Her body crashed through the opening, bringing with it an avalanche of earth, roots and stone that buried the three females and the eggs in a tomb that only the strongest of Whisperers could ever detect.

ONE

The Monastery

801 AD

The rock pillars below the monastery rose high into the air. Those who had succumbed to a fear of heights would plummet below to the jutting rocks, which showed white in the moonlight as the waves thrashed against them. Friar Watt had to admit that he was not built for flight. It unsettled his stomach. He clung to Muquin's neck and closed his eyes to another rush of nausea. As Muquin flew closer to the cliffs, the salty essence of the waves touched the Friar's face in a fine spray. It gave some relief to his assaulted senses.

Access to the monastery was deliberately difficult. Friar Watt wondered how he would explain how he had reached the long-knotted ladders. If asked, he would have to say that God had helped him. Well, it was not a lie - God had helped him, but it would not be wise to explain that the help had come in the form of a dragon.

There would be few pilgrims who would be able to question the sudden arrival of the Friar. Not many would be foolish enough to travel at this time of year.

With the constant battering of the waves and endless spray, he now pondered how long these ropes would last. In several places on the rock pillars there were the worn edges that undoubtedly sped up the passage to heaven for some unfortunate souls. He wondered how many bodies the sea had claimed.

As he could not understand Muquin, he had decided on the drop off location in advance and Nadine had interpreted his request. It was a pity Muquin could not drop him directly into the Monastery - it would raise far too much suspicion. He would have to travel a short distance on foot.

Friar Watt would also have to get there before the scheduled patrol. The treasures in the monastery made it a target for invaders who wished to plunder its inner stores. It was not unusual for mercenaries or ambitious opposing clans to create elaborate plans to claim the riches within. A lone traveller always set the guards on edge.

Friar Watt rubbed snow onto his face. The icicles stung his cheeks and produced a reddened glow. It made him appear that he had travelled for many hours in the cold.

The gate creaked open, and a guard surveyed the Friar.

"Where are your companions?" enquired the guard, peering into the darkness. Past the gate, Friar Watt saw a guard with a purple tunic covering his chain-mail. The white cross on the tunic showed him to be a personal guard of the Pope. The purple clad guard stopped and looked sharply at the Friar conversing with the gate guard.

"My companions could not make it the full way," explained Friar Watt.

"But how did you get here? With that leg of yours, you would not have been able to climb these ropes." The gate guard touched the hilt of his sword.

"God provided the way."

"Did he now?" asked the guard. "And how did he do that?"

The purple clad guard, Raguel, joined the guard at the inner gate. He stood staring down and narrowed his eyes at the first gate guard.

"What is going on over there?" he asked.

"A single Friar is asking to be let in."

"One man, traveling alone? Alert the fighting unit. There may be trouble. In the meantime, I will go see this man myself," said Raguel.

He slipped through the inner gate and moved towards the main entrance. Raquel placed his hand on the main gate guard's shoulder.

"Acacius, is there trouble?" It was unusual for a personal guard of the Pope to address a gate guard by his name.

"This Friar has arrived at the gate without companions asking to be let in," replied the gate guard. Raguel frowned. He stepped closer to the gate so that he could see the visitor.

"Friend, please forgive the guard's manner. We have had quite a few invaders pretending to be travellers. I must ask you what your business is here at the monastery," asked Raguel.

The deep rumble of Raguel's voice stirred a memory for the Friar. He pulled back his hood.

"I am Friar Watt."

"Open the gate, Acacius," ordered Raguel. "And see to it that there is a change of robes and a hot meal for this man. He shall share my sleeping quarters tonight."

"I never thought I would see you here," whispered Raguel. "It has been many years, my friend."

"You have had some trouble along the way," he observed, looking at Friar Watt's limp.

"A gift from King Radolf's men."

"Yes, he is very generous in that way," jested Raguel. "I see you have abandoned the fighting staff for a walking staff."

"It is an occupational hazard of living in the Northern Kingdom."

"You know I would take you in a heartbeat, just say the word."

"I know. But you should have realised by now that you cannot tempt me with anything you have to offer."

"Pity that. I have never met a man better with a fighting staff than you. But let's get you out of those clothes and into something better suited to this high mountain air. Then you can tell me why you are here."

When they reached Raguel's quarters, there was mead, bread and a bowl of hot stew for the Friar. He changed by the fire. His stomach felt like a black hole. The biting cold could do that. It would be weeks before the sun would strip the ground from the frosty clutches of winter.

"I must warn you, Walter, this is not a safe place." Raguel placed a small piece of parchment next to the Friar.

"It's Watt, now."

"Caution is prudent here," sighed Raguel. His voice was calm, but his eyes were never still.

The Friar bent his head to give thanks for the food, but the purpose of the gesture was to read the parchment. "The Cardinal serves the King!"

Friar Watt dipped the bread into the stew and dropped it on the table. "How clumsy of me," said the Friar as he wiped the sauce from the parchment. It smudged the words beyond recognition.

"Is it possible to get a private audience with The Holy Father?" asked Friar Watt between mouthfuls of soaked bread.

"Perhaps if the news is important enough, but protocol dictates that there always must be at least one representative from the Cardinals at the meeting. After all, there has been an attack on the Holy Father's life, so he is under constant surveillance. We cannot afford another attack on the Pope."

Friar Watt thought about the scripture in the Book of Romans: *"Their throats are open graves; their tongues practice deceit. The poison of vipers is on their lips."*

The Friar pushed his hand against his forehead. His head felt clamped with pain. Was there no safe place? A man could only endure so much. He had left the military to get away from the pain and bloodthirsty ways of man. Raguel had helped him escape the life of war when he saved his friend's leg after a battle. Raguel had recognised that the then "Walter" would serve mankind better as a healer. But to what end? He was still trapped by a corrupt world full of violence.

"Do you still get those headaches?" asked Raguel.

"From time to time, especially after a lack of sleep."

"Well tonight I will stay up and watch you," smiled Raguel, handing Friar Watt a small pouch of herbs. "I still have some."

"Oh, bless you. I have not yet found them in the wild. These will help me to get a good rest."

Raguel swallowed. There was so much he wanted to say, but that would have to wait. He watched the Friar's lips move silently in prayer. Any sign of the depth of their bond would put them both at risk.

Friar Watt prayed for the safety of Nadine and her family. He prayed for the Dragon Whisperer's emotional healing and he prayed for the Northern Kingdom.

"You are a good man, Friar Watt. It has been an honour to serve with you both on and off the battlefield. Rest well and tomorrow, we will see about getting you that audience with the Holy Father."

Friar Watt heaved his weary body, still stiff from sleeping in the cave, into the welcoming warmth of the bed. He placed his scrolls on the table next to the bed and pulled the furs up close. The Friar's body dragged his mind into the shadowy world of dreams where he played out the world of Kings and dragons. All he had to do was let go and this world would fade into darkness and he would go to meet his Lord.

Friar Watt's dreams did nothing to heal his tortured mind. Above, a falcon circled, its eyes roaming for prey. But high in the air it carried something alive. A column of scaly armour writhed and hissed in the falcon's grip. Suddenly the predator dropped the serpent, and the creature sank its poisonous fangs into something and seemed to smirk. In the dream the Friar watched in horror as the foul omen turned to look at him. Its black eyes narrowed as it spoke. "Son of Adam, now it is your turn." The hissing words that flowed from the creature's inky black mouth gripped him with terror. Friar Watt's eyes flew open. The twisted sheets upon which he lay were drenched as a testimony to his nightmare. His heart pounded and his hand trembled as he sat up and searched for Raguel's reassuring presence. Friar Watt panted out his relief as he saw his friend was stationed as promised in the chair by the fire. But something was wrong. Raguel was not moving.

Friar Watt jumped up and, grasping Raguel's arm, shook him for a response that only resulted in his friend sliding from his seated position. A pattern of puncture marks covered the Holy Father's guard's neck. In the flickering light of the flames, Friar Watt saw the winding form of a serpent on the bed in which he had lain just seconds before. The evil creature's deep pink tongue tipped in black, flicked the air to sense its next victim. Its muscular body moved in a sickening rhythm across the sheets as it locked its eyes on the Friar. The Friar picked up his staff and moved across the floor, keeping his back to the fireplace. If the creature escaped the room, who could tell how many victims it might claim. The dream had been a warning from God, but now he had to face it head on to stop the spread of death. Black eyes followed Friar Watt's movements as the serpent turned its head in his direction. The flicker of the dying fire intensified the glint of the venomous creature's gaze. The Friar matched the snake's stare as he lifted his staff to strike. Friar Watt felt the change in the serpent's movement before he saw it. The tension in the air exploded, and the creature propelled its body forward with its fangs, ready to sink into its target. The Friar lashed out, striking the serpent on the side of the head. It merely stunned the creature, but it was enough time for the Friar to grasp the tail. In a flash, the Friar flicked the serpent's body along its full length, snapping the creature's neck with a powerful thrust of his arm.

The assassin had underestimated Friar Watt's skill and the power of prayer to deliver him from danger, but now the Friar felt alone without a friend in this treacherous place. Friar Watt felt the sting of his emotions threatening to surface, which he knew he had to suppress. This man who had helped him in so many ways was the only man he could call a friend. Raguel. But now was not the time to lose control. He wondered if he had prepared Nadine enough to withstand the evil that would surely befall them if they had no allies within the church.

TWO

Nadine Returns

Nadine looked up at her new family home. It had far more space than she could ever have imagined. Although they had moved in straight after she rescued Yakhal, Nadine had left so soon for training at Holly Hill Cave that the manor still did not feel like home, despite returning most Freya's Days. How ironic that she would return home on a day that was named after the goddess of love and fertility. For Nadine there would be no love and never any children, no matter how much Nathan protested. Her shoulders slumped as she thought of entering the house and telling her father how she had almost gotten everyone in his family killed by King Radolf and his gang of thugs.

Since her last visit, her father had ordered new heraldic badges for the home. In the centre were his and her mother's and below were open areas for the three children. A local artisan was painting the colours of her mother's heraldic badge next to her father's completed one. Below, the stone worker was shaking his fist at the painter.

"Sir Nicolaus wanted this up before his daughter returned."

"Well I am sorry, but with this cold, my fingers cannot work that fast."

Nicolous was inside inspecting the records from the vigneron employed to work on the vines.

"Has the quality of the soil improved?"

"It has. We increased the slope, and we have re-planted so that the vines will get the best exposure to the sunlight when the weather turns. Drainage has improved. The pruning on the vines is complete. The yield should be good," replied the vigneron.

"Do we have a market in mind?"

"There are several vintners who expressed interest. Many of the vine growing monks succumbed to the illness. Ignorant peasants then used the wood of the vines as fuel to burn the corpses. You are lucky that these remained untouched. On his last trip, Nathan investigated markets beyond our borders. Once we have samples, he can take those on his next trade commission."

Nicolous looked up and saw Nadine standing in the doorway.

"Nadine," he said with his arms stretched out, "You are home."

Nadine walked towards him. She stood motionless as he hugged her. There was a tension in her, Nicolous did not understand.

"Nadine, this is Cayo, our vigneron."

"Good day to you," the man responded.

"Hello," replied Nadine. "I see you are turning my father into a wine merchant. I look forward to seeing your harvest."

"Cayo, can we continue with our report in the morning? My daughter is tired."

"Of course. I understand."

Nicolous took Nadine by the hand. "Where are your mother and Maireid?"

"They planned to visit Elizabeth."

"They went to Elizabeth before coming home?"

Nadine's face fell. Her eyes filled with tears and she buried her face in her father's chest, sobbing.

"Father, it was horrible. The King's men… they attacked us… I… it was… The King, he is a monster…" Her wail was more than just crying. It was the desolate sound of a person who has lost all hope. She sank to her knees.

Nicolous tried to comfort her, but she pulled away from him.

"Nadine, your mother and sister, are they…?"

"I can't do this anymore…fighting unknown people, with unknown casualties, that is one thing, but this… he hung them up. Hung them by their necks on horses and he asked me to choose which one would live. Who does that sort of thing? What kind of man does that?"

Nicolous could not bear her sorrow. His hands bunched into fists. This was why he had turned away from war. It was a senseless waste of humanity, all in the name of something that thinly disguised the real purpose, greed. Greed for power, titles and lands. He buckled under the weight of his pity for her. Nicolous had taught her to duel. To play the games of war. But he had never prepared her for this. How could he? How could he know that she would face such suffering at such a tender age? He had believed that by choosing a simple life, he could protect the ones he loved. But now he saw that war had come to him. He, who should have been there to battle with her, to protect his wife and children… he, had not been there. Nadine had never seen him fight. Not in the way that mattered. This battle she had fought alone. She faced King Radolf alone. He longed to take her in his arms and flee the Northern Kingdom. Flee with all his children. But he knew, even if he left this place, the King would find them.

"Please, Father, take me away from here. I cannot bear the cruelty anymore. I cannot watch Nathan pine for me, knowing that by loving me he puts himself in danger. I want to be far away from Maimi, Maireid and Mikael. You have travelled and can find a place for me. A place where he cannot find me, where I will be far away and then you will all live."

"Nadine, it does not work that way. You have a destiny far greater than we could have ever imagined. You have the power to bring peace. But peace has enemies and if you do nothing, do not believe that King Radolf will stop. He will never stop. No matter where you run to, he will always try to find a way to draw you out." He led her to the window.

"Do you see that tree over there in the courtyard?"

Nadine nodded, still allowing the tears to roll unchecked down her cheeks.

"When it has been cold for so long, the branches are bare. Like the souls of those who live in the shadow of King Radolf. There seems to be no ray of hope. When everything you love hangs in the balance, it is easy to give into despair. But to everything there is a season. A time to be born and a time to die. A time to plant and a time to reap. And there comes a time when that tree out there will sprout new life. In this winter season, we cut back the branches. We prune the tree. To the outside world, it may seem like we are destroying the tree. But when the sun comes, the trees that are pruned will bear far more fruit than the ones that are left to grow without cutting. To the people of our former village and to the people of this place, you are a hero, Nadine. A hero brings protection. They are the rock from which people can draw their own courage. A hero holds love in their heart. Love of family, love of what is right. It is that love that drives them to protect the weak. When you face your fears, when you have the courage to love, then you will embrace your inner hero and these people will have hope. You are God's hands and feet to help protect those who suffer at the hand of the King." Nicolous drew Nadine to his chest and kissed her forehead.

"Let's go to Elizabeth and find your mother and sister. Mikael will be back from his lessons soon." He placed his arm around her shoulders and hugged her close to him. Nadine lifted her arm around his waist and looked up at the tree. A solitary green shoot had sprouted on a branch. It was the merest whisper of the spring that was to come. She smiled and wondered where the Friar was now.

THREE

With Child

"Holy Father, there has been an incident," said the Cardinal. "Your personal guard, Raguel, is dead."

The Pope's dark brown eyes narrowed as he stared at the Cardinal.

"You assured me that this monastery was impenetrable, yet we have had two men killed within these walls in a matter of days. A candidate and his mentor are dead, another candidate was attacked and now you tell me that my guard is dead. That brings our dead to three. How did Raguel die?"

"By snake bite."

"You mean by an assassin. How can a serpent even get up here unless brought by someone?"

"The gate guard said that there was a solitary Friar who arrived last night. Raguel recognized him and ordered the guard to let him in. He must have brought it with him. However, this morning when the body was found, the Friar was missing."

A gentle knock on the door intruded on their discussion. A large woman in the final stages of pregnancy entered carrying a tray with Pope Viktor's breakfast. She was unlike any woman they had seen, roughly the same height as the Pope, which at 6 foot, would have made her quite an intimidating sight for most men. He wondered what the mother of this woman must look like. Some clans far to the north had these sorts of robust women. The Pope watched as the woman's brow knitted in pain when she lowered the tray.

"My child, sit down for a moment," he soothed. "Why have you not left the monastery yet? This child's time is upon you. Do you not have a husband to go to?"

"Thank you, Holy Father. My husband is dead. I have sent word to my sister. Once she arrives, I will travel with her to our village," said the servant with lowered eyes.

"Yes, yes! Please get to your quarters. The Holy Father and I have important matters to discuss," ordered the Cardinal as he waved the woman away.

"Cardinal, did Jesus not show compassion for all people? This woman has served this monastery well. Remember the words, *'whatever you do for the least of these, you do for me.'* We do not lose by showing a little kindness," Pope Viktor rebuked the Cardinal.

"Yes, Holy Father," said the Cardinal, his eyes dark. "This is what comes of having a Pope who is not from nobility," he thought. He wondered how long he could endure this peasant Pope. But first he had to find that Friar.

FOUR

God's Work

Friar Watt knew that he was trapped. Even if he could remain undetected behind the dark stone columns, there would be no way out of the monastery without help. His only friend within these walls lay unseeing in the upper chamber with the venom of an assassin's serpent settling in his veins. Too many guards had seen the Friar enter. When they found the Pope's personal guard, it would be natural to accuse him of being the assassin.

The words on the parchment that Raguel had penned, "*The Cardinal is with the King*," pounded in his heart. It was by faith that he had survived the archer's arrow. He had vowed to Bishop Rawlin that he would get this confession to the Pope and he had made it this far. But how could he get an audience without the Cardinal being present?

If the King could have spies and assassins even within these sacred walls, how long would it be until he found Nadine? Friar Watt would have to pass through these stone passages undetected. The speed of the boots pounding on the heavy stone floors signalled that the guards had found Raguel's corpse. His mind raced to the text from just shortly before the betrayal of Christ, '*in His anguish Jesus prayed earnestly, and his sweat was like drops of blood falling to the ground.*'

Being around this kind of relentless torment was the reason Friar Watt had decided to leave the military. He could no longer bear the sight of men so terrified by the prospect of fighting for a cause they did not believe in. Ruthless Kings and sometimes even those who professed to be champions of the faith would claim young boys from their parents' homes to fight. Not all men could deaden their senses to the suffering of war. They remained terrified all the time. The terror broke down a man's body until his sweat mingled with blood. After the constant assault of their intense fear on these men, Friar Watt could no longer find the inner peace to help them. He patched them up as best he could and moved onto the next man. Once they were declared unfit for battle, the veterans were doomed to a life of nightmares, reliving every battle every time they closed their eyes.

After he left military life, Friar Watt would care for each soul who was willing. But at first, he was too traumatised by war. He withdrew from people. He was edgy, and no longer had the desire to wake up or do everyday things. He would jump at the slightest noise, and even a blacksmith's hammering would produce such a violent trembling that his heart felt as if it was thundering through his body. For a while he was reckless, doing things that would put him in harm's way. It was only when Friar Watt met a healer from a neighbouring village that he had come to know the Lord and found a way to live, despite his experiences.

He remembered the prayer of the healer. "Father, in Your name I speak healing and restoration upon every wound inflicted upon Walter's life. Thank You for healing and binding my friend's wounds!" He remembered, too, the discovery that he could combine his gift for physical healing with spiritual and emotional healing. He changed his name from Walter to Watt and entered studies to be a monk. But the quiet life of a monk did not marry his strength and skills. Raguel had come to visit him in the Abbey.

"Friend, this place is not for you," said his battle-hardened friend.

"I cannot go back to war," Friar Watt had replied.

"That I know. But your path does not have to be one way or the other. A man like you cannot sit here under a vow of silence, forgetting what you have seen. "

"All things work for the good of those who love the Lord."

"Do you really think that you were spared for no purpose? My men are struck down by the cold indifference of death by the masses. The surviving ones either form a hardened shell which makes them savages that feed on the brutality of death or they become so dysfunctional and reckless in their quest to leave this life, that we have to cast them off lest they infect us all with their cowardice."

"Then let them go back home and be done with it."

"What has become of my friend who helped the men on the battlefield? These men are not bad men. They lack the appetite for war, but they can be good husbands and fathers. Men who will help build villages. Without help, they become wrecks and leeches, prone to drinking and lashing out at those weaker than they are. These men need a man like you. One who has known the battles of war. One who knows that healing is not just for the body, but also for the soul. I, myself, have known too many battles. I know how to lead my men to victory and through defeat. I can never leave them, but you... You can help. Do this for me, as a sign of our friendship. Do this for the men I can no longer protect, the ones who feel that God has forgotten them."

"You sound as if you are going somewhere."

"I am. They have asked me to be the personal guard of the Pope and to advise the Lord's army on matters of battle strategy. While at this post I can never marry. I will remain, for the rest of my military career, at whatever monastery the

Pope is stationed at," his friend explained. "For my mind to be at peace, I must know that you will do what I ask."

Watt had looked at Raguel, his thoughts in turmoil. Raguel had put his hand on his friend's shoulder "I feel a chill in my bones, old friend. There is something that is brewing that I cannot discern."

"What is it that you are saying to me?" Watt had asked.

"Without children I will leave nothing of me behind when I die. Some of these young men are like the sons I will never have. If you are willing to help them, I will feel my life has had purpose, that I leave behind a legacy.

When I helped you find a different life away from the military, I knew I took that risk for a purpose. Now I ask you to accept this role, for the sake of our friendship."

Watt sighed as deeply as he remembered doing that day when he had gotten up and touched Raguel's shoulder, saying, "I will do as you ask. You have my word."

FIVE

Getting the Pope Out

The chambermaid glanced behind her and slipped into the Pope's quarter.

"My name is Adira. I am here to help, but we have little time," she said as she removed her clothes, leaving Pope Viktor staring in shock at the padding concealed beneath her garments. Unstrapping the padded pouch, she stood in her undergarments.

"Quick, put this on!"

"What madness is this?"

Adira was already pulling another garment over herself.

"Unless you intend to be the next martyred saint, I suggest that you put this on and leave with me now."

"I cannot leave in this contraption."

"You can and you will. Later when you are alive and safe, I will take you myself to a member of your faith for confession."

Outside the door that Adira had bolted, the guards began to pound against the heavy oak.

"I spent months increasing the padding to prepare for this day. But you will have to adapt to the extra weight without training. Now, how good is your moaning?" Adira asked.

"My what?"

"We are going to have to walk out, past the guards. You will be me and I will be your sister - the one that you called for."

"The conversation in front of the Cardinal..." the Pope now began to see the cunning of the plan.

Adira opened a wineskin and poured what looked like water in a small puddle on the ground.

"Careful, it is slippery."

"What is it?"

"Water mixed with oil."

"For what purpose?"

"When a woman is about to give birth, this substance gets released from the body as a warning. Those guards out there will believe that you are my sister in labour. They will let us pass. We will say that you expelled the water and we now must get to a birthing chamber. With some luck, they will thrust us from the monastery."

"Now when last did you have a stomach ailment?"

"What sort of question is that?"

"Well, whatever groaning you did. Do that now."

Pope Viktor was unimpressed. He lifted his hand in protest.

"What do you think will happen to the flock if King Radolf or any of your predecessor's followers put an Anti-Pope in your place, Holy Father? You must live to face another day." She adjusted his garments and turned towards another round of heavy hammering outside the door.

"Open this door immediately!" called the Cardinal's voice sternly.

Adira took a breath and pulled back the latch. Pope Viktor clutched his middle and groaned.

"Women, what are you two doing here?" said the Cardinal, striding into the room. His foot slid on the liquid and he grabbed onto the guard, pulling him down to the floor in a heap.

"What is this? demanded the Cardinal.

"Forgive me, but my sister, she is with child. The process has begun. I merely bolted the door to examine her."

"Here? In the Pope's chambers? What pagan evil craft is this?" said the Cardinal clutching his back.

"No evil. I came to fetch my sister. I found her cleaning the Pope's chambers when her waters broke. I do not know where the Pope is."

"Get out! Get out now!" screamed the Cardinal.

Adira pulled her companion by the arm.

"You!" The Cardinal grabbed one of the guard's by the front of his tunic. "Get a cleaning lady. Get these two out of this monastery and find the Pope!"

Adira put her arm around Pope Viktor.

"Do not fret my sister. I will take care of you. Let us leave this place now," she soothed.

The open gates shot a blast of frigid air onto the Pope's face.

"What sort of cruelty is this?" screamed Adira. "Thrusting two defenceless women out into the cold." Her words were cut off by the sound of the slamming gates.

SIX

The Way

"Almighty God, I pray you stretch forth your mighty hand and help me protect the Pope," the Friar silently prayed. Despite his faith that God would deliver him, his heart pounded as his muscles flooded with life force. Now it was not the cold of the stone wall he pressed against that made his limbs quiver.

A guard opened a nearby window and looked downward. "I see no one on the ledge," he called back to his superior.

"We have a guard stationed at all the exits. He has to be here," came the reply.

The blast of cold air from the window caused a slight movement in the heavy tapestry behind which Friar Watt stood. A piece of his robe moved with the wind. Ahead, a servant girl walked in his direction. She stumbled, dropping the plates she was carrying. The sound caused the guard to pivot towards her. She fell to her knees next to the Friar's hiding place and began to gather up the broken pieces.

"It is just the chambermaid," said the superior. "Move on. We will divide the group into smaller teams and search all the rooms simultaneously. That way we will flush him out."

One of the chief guards stopped to look at the maid. She

was taller than the other servants. He squeezed the top of her arm and smiled. "You look like a fine, strong woman. The main dormitory for the guards needs cleaning. Meet me there after your shift," he sneered, noting the swell of her form.

"Yes, sir," she replied without looking up. As he walked away, she sat back on her heels, still cleaning the debris.

When the passage was clear, she whispered, "If you can make your way out towards the ledge, meet me where the decent ropes are. There are air vents in the lower parts of the center column. I will wait as long as I dare."

Friar Watt could not see her face, but he knew that he would recognize her voice. She gathered up the remains of the broken plates and made her way to the kitchen.

"Center column?" thought Friar Watt. "What center column?" Raguel had promised to show him the plans of the monastery, but he had died too soon. He had hinted that there was help. But now whoever this help was, assumed that he knew the layout of the monastery. He waited until the corridor was silent and then stepped out from behind the tapestry.

Acacius had seen the Friar earlier. He knew that to receive a promotion, his best chance was to capture the intruder. Perhaps if he proved himself trustworthy, the Cardinal would nominate him to take Raguel's place. So he did not leave when the others did, but lingered in the corridor. At each step from Raguel's chambers, he had slowed down his breathing and imagined what he would do if he were trying to escape. There were very few places the Friar could have gone.

Now he stood silently watching the corridor. One of the guards had already established that the ledge was clear. In any event, if the window had been opened before, the cold air would have left a frosty clue.

The corridor would have been far colder if someone had opened the window to go through it. No, the Friar had to be in here, but where?

He closed his eyes again, for a moment, imagining a man trying to find a hiding place. When he opened his eyes, the ceiling to floor tapestry was obvious. Most of the time he paid no attention to the furnishings.

The tapestry depicted the Divine Mercy, a larger-than-life image of Christ giving life and righteousness to the souls that dwelt in the light flowing from his heart.

"How apt for someone to hide in the Mercies of Christ," he sneered inwardly. "On this day," thought Acacius, "not even Christ will help you."

His patience was rewarded when Friar Watt emerged from behind the tapestry. Acacius waited until the Friar had just passed him, then pressed the tip of his sword into the intruder's back.

"I think it is about time that you were properly introduced to the Cardinal," said Acacius. He grabbed the Friar by the arm.

"Drop the staff."

The Friar did as he was instructed. The guard pressed the sword against the Friar's Body to keep him from running away and picked up the staff. "We would not want anyone to get hurt, now would we?"

Together they moved towards the Cardinal's chambers. Two guards stood outside and Acacius hailed them to open the doors.

"I have found the Friar. Now let me pass."

The guards heaved the dark, heavy doors with an image of Mary cradling the crucified Christ in her arms carved into the center panels.

The arches in the room were decorated with paintings of Jesus with the apostles in various settings. At the edge of the room, the Cardinal sat on a gold etched seat covered with green velvet cushions. He was engrossed in a game of chess with a Bishop. The pieces were carved from white and black marble, with such intricate detail that they had a lifelike quality. Above him was a richly coloured scene of Christ seated with the apostles on either side. It was not the last supper, but a graphic representation of Christ as a teacher.

The Cardinal looked up at Friar Watt with dark eyes, not raising his head. The deep furrows on his shaved cheeks revealed a life of frequent scowling. But his eyes brightened when he saw the Friar.

"Friar Watt," he said with outstretched arms. "Welcome to my humble chambers. I have been waiting quite some time for you."

Friar Watt looked around the chambers.

"Humble, compared to what?"

The Cardinal's eye narrowed and Acacius shifted uncomfortably as he waited for the Cardinal's orders.

"Guards, please leave us and wait outside."

The Cardinal motioned for Friar Watt to be seated. Despite his defiance, Friar Watt knew that his walk without the support of his staff had weakened him. He needed to rest to have the strength to fight if the situation called for it. He eased himself onto the chair.

The Cardinal stepped over to the fireplace. He took a key off a chain around his waist and opened a carved marble chest from which he lifted an old scroll.

"Friar Watt, I know that you think by going against King Radolf, you are protecting those you hold dear. People like Nadine and her family. This is a noble idea, but you see, the Dragon Whisperers are an abomination. God created people with dominion over all the creatures of the earth and even the sky. These Dragon Whisperers wish for these beasts to be at one with man, to converse with them. They are misled to believe that Dragons have souls and can guide us.

But in truth, we no longer have dominion over them. For us to truly control what God has set before us, we must dominate. To provide order and structure. That is all that King Radolf wants."

"No, King Radolf wants to use the dragons for his own personal power. We both know it."

"Do we now? Very well, let's test what else you know." He placed the scroll in front of Friar Watt.

"This scroll was uncovered by the monks who built this monastery. Did you know that the original structure was built on ruins of the Ancients?" The Cardinal paused to watch Friar Watt's expression.

"I believe there was a similar one in the Northern Kingdom. It is where they found this scroll, which outlines a plan to protect the dragons should there be another Dragon War. Dragon Wars have always created much devastation and destruction. Whole civilizations have perished under the fiery wrath of the dragons. This scroll tells of how each species appoints a carrier of eggs to hide them in times of conflict, so that at the chosen time the presence of a Mother Dragon or a Mother Whisperer can cause them to hatch.

If the Dragon Whisperer is female, her presence will cause the hatchlings to emerge even without a mother dragon. If you will lead us to Nadine, we can find these eggs. Then with Nadine's help we can submit them to God's ordained will."

"And what if Nadine chooses not to join you?"

"That would be regrettable. It would be a tragedy to be forced to purge the evil from a young life that has only just started. But believe me I will order it should she not willingly come to King Radolf to do his bidding."

"You and I both know that the dragon's purpose has always been to serve mankind. But all of mankind, not just the ones you deem worthy. And I believe the Pope knows it."

"Pope Viktor is a pawn. Placed by foolish peasant lovers who do not honour the authority of the old families. Those of ill-bred blood think they are equal to us, but that is an error."

"And what of the words that justice and righteousness are the foundations of God's throne? Leadership is necessary. But you cannot neglect the love of God. How is oppressing people and murdering those who disagree with you showing the love of God?"

"Who said anything about murder?"

"How many of King Radolf's opposition have disappeared or had their heads displayed on spikes?"

The Cardinal shook his head. His eyes flashed with a cruel glint.

"I can see that you have been contaminated by Nadine and her kind. We will need to purge you of this way of thinking. I have heard of your work in the healing district. Such talent. I sincerely hoped that a man of your obvious intelligence would see reason. But your soul is now corrupted, and it is my duty to purge you of it."

He removed the scroll and returned it to the box. Then he picked up a carved mahogany mallet and struck the golden shield that hung close to the chess table.

The sound of the gong brought Acacius back into the room.

"Please take our guest to the inner column. String him up by his wrists to the hook. I have a chess game to win and by then Friar Watt may have enough time to rethink my offer. I will meet with him later."

Acacius picked up Friar Watt's staff and summoned two additional guards to accompany the prisoner. A fourth joined as they boxed the Friar in and led him away.

Friar Watt resisted the urge to fight. The Cardinal had handed him a free tour to the inner column, exactly where he needed to go.

They proceeded down a corridor that led to another floor length tapestry. It was of a large cross with the inner section interwoven with silver and the outer section of the cross bordered with golden thread. Below the cross were several beasts of the ground and air. And the cream-coloured background had the family coat of arms of many of the former Popes. But at the very top there was the family coat of arms belonging to the Cardinal. It was so subtle that the Friar thought few would ever notice. But the meaning was clear. There was no sign of Pope Victor's family heritage.

Acacius pulled aside the tapestry revealing a single simple door made of the sacred oak that the Ancients had so revered.

A narrow stone staircase spiraled down into the dark. Acacius lit a torch and followed the guards. He still carried the Friar's staff.

The bottom of the stairs opened into a round room. There were several ancient carvings on the walls. The dark stains on the floor sent chills up the Friar's spine. Acacius yanked on a chain that was linked to the iron chandelier. He lit several of the aged candles and heaved the chandelier back into position. Friar Watt observed several rows of shackles lining the walls, which seemed to be a more recent addition. Acacius ordered a guard to bind the Friar's hands in front of him. He pulled another chain and a large metal hook descended from the centre of a ceiling beam. The guards slid the ropes that bound the Friar over the hook and hoisted him to the ceiling.

The pressure on his joints was immense. Friar Watt closed his eyes and tried to pull from memory a tapestry of the Christ. When the image became clear in his mind, the Friar focused his attention on the imagery.

"How long will it take for the Cardinal to arrive?" asked the first guard.

"A long time," replied Acacius. "That Bishop prides himself on being a strategist. I have guarded the room several times while they play. They can each sit staring at a piece before making a move for a half an hour. A man may easily starve to death while waiting for a game to finish. I suggest we have one man stand guard and the rest of us go for lunch. Then we can rotate. The Friar is not going anywhere."

Harlyn was the first to stand guard. He stood for a while.

But the effect of the previous night's game of dice, was now drawing his eyelids down.

He looked up at the Friar whose eyes were still closed. "What a weakling," he thought. "He has passed out before any real pain has surfaced."

The blanket of Harlyn's thoughts pulled heavier and heavier on his eyes. Soon he fell into a dreamless sleep.

As he did, Friar Watt opened his, alert immediately. Once a seasoned warrior, the Friar had kept a weekly routine of strengthening his muscles. He now swiveled his body backwards and forwards creating friction between the ropes and the metal hook. The words of Isaiah ran over and over in his mind. "*They who wait upon the Lord shall renew their strength.*" With each swing the words came again. "*They who wait upon the Lord shall renew their strength; "They who wait upon the Lord shall renew their strength.*"

Beads of perspiration dropped to the patterned stone floor. The continual movement was weakening the ropes, and he looked up to see some split and fray.

He swung harder this time, with his legs curling, and he used the momentum to hook his knees over the supporting beam. Then, using all his strength, he pulled his wrists apart, yanking on the last threads of the rope. To Friar Watt's relief, the rope split apart. He pulled his torso up and held onto the hook and dropped to the ground.

The thud jolted Harlyn from his slumber. But before he could reach for his sword, the Friar had picked up the discarded staff. He thrust the end into Harlyn's chest. The force winded the guard, stopping him from crying out. His head dropped forward, and his helmet came off. Taking advantage of the opportunity, the Friar knocked the guard behind the head, rendering him unconscious.

"Maybe that is what Isaiah meant when he said they shall mount up with the wings of eagles," he grinned, looking back up at the beam. "Now, let's find those air vents."

Friar Watt slowed his breath and closed his eyes. If he was still enough, he might feel the changes in the air. Now in a state of calm-heightened consciousness, he felt the slightest movement on the left side of his face. He turned towards a small tunnel that branched off on the side of the room. He could not enter standing up. There was a coil of rope on the floor. The Friar bound his staff to his back and got on his hands and knees. He crept as fast as he could manage down the tunnel.

His knees ached from pressing against the hard stone. But he kept moving as he felt the air move over his face. Bits of fine, aged stone that had dislodged in the tunnel dug into his palms. But he pressed forward, only stopping to rub off the grit on his robe. The prickle of goosebumps on his arms grew painful as he reached the end of the tunnel.

It opened into another room. The air vents had once just been open arches. But now they were covered with wooden slats that pivoted on hinges. He tried to open them, but the metal hinges were too corroded to move.

"Why bring me here if there is no way out?" he thought. With a crash, an avalanche of splintered wood flew past his face. As the slats exploded from the other side, he saw a woman with an axe hacking at the wood.

"It is about time you joined us," he heard the chambermaid's voice say.

SEVEN

Where Does My Help Come From

Despite the icy air, Pope Viktor had to smile. But as they walked to the edge of the rock face, he saw he had underestimated the cold. The bite of the wind caused his skin to pucker and his teeth chattered with enough violence to make his jaw ache.

Adira had turned back twice to check on the guards. But now the Monastery was ablaze with torches and shouts as they searched for the Pope.

Once out of sight of the guards, Friar Watt followed Adira and her companion to the end of the cliff.

"Holy Father, we are going to have to lower you down the edge of the cliff."

Friar Watt could scarcely believe it. It was the Pope dressed as a pregnant woman.

Pope Viktor felt his throat closing in on itself as he stared down into the blackness of the drop of the cliff. Way below small tufts of white appeared as the waves collided with the rocks. The added weight of the padding made him feel unstable on his feet. But Adira did not want to risk discarding it. If it was found, it would raise suspicion.

There was a large stripped branch suspended from ropes at the edge of the cliff.

"Please Holy Father, sit on this," instructed Adira. "We will lower you via this pulley system."

"I think my body is heavier than yours, I will surely pull us both down to the depths," said the Pope.

"Don't you worry about that. I have some assistance."

Pope Viktor squeezed his eyes shut. Time slowed down when his feet left the edge of the cliff as the log lowered down into the black starless night. His feet found nothing firm to make him feel safe. Had he survived the attack just to fall to his death from these remote cliffs?

"Lord, I am in desperate need. My enemies surround me, wanting me to fail. Only you can help me. I wait for you to work in my life," prayed Pope Viktor.

He felt as if he was already drowning with the sounds of the crashing waves reaching up to claim him.

At the top, Friar Watt and Adira strained at the rope, trying to lower the Pope at a steady pace. But the pain of the cold on their hands and the loose rocks moving at their feet made the ropes slip in their hands. The Pope descended at a startling rate with frequent jolts that terrified him. Despite the cold he was sweating with anxiety. Several times, his back slammed into the rock face, threatening to make him lose his grip on the ropes he so fiercely clung to. Loose rocks falling from above him landed with a sickening crunch below his suspended body. He wondered what his predecessor would say about a Pope dressed as a pregnant woman. He thought about the Psalm. "I lift up my eyes to the hills— where does my help come from?"

Finally, Pope Viktor's feet touched the jagged edges of the rocks and he almost laughed with relief as he saw Friar Watt and Adrira preparing to decend on their own ropes. How ironic that he would look up to the cliffs… the hills, for his help.

In his mind he recited "I will say of the LORD, "He is my refuge and my fortress, my God, in whom I trust. Surely, he will save you from the fowler's snare and from the deadly pestilence. He will cover you with his feathers, and under his wings you will find refuge; his faithfulness will be your shield and rampart."

EIGHT

Getting Down

Friar Watt stood at the edge of the cliff, trying not to look at the jagged rocks below.

"Give me your hand," Adira ordered the Friar. "Now spread your fingers apart. She wrapped some linen around the knuckles, then through the fingers, where they joined the hand and again over the knuckles and secured the linen around his wrists.

"What is that for?"

"These cliffs are treacherous. We need to protect our skin. If you slice open your hands during the descent, you won't make it."

"What about the swing we just used for the Pope?"

"It takes two people to pull the seat down and I asked him to sever the ropes when he got to the bottom."

"What! What possessed you to do that?"

"First, he cannot help us down. Second, we don't want anyone else to use it. No one will expect us to climb down."

Friar Watt hesitantly looked down at the crashing waves. "Yes, that is because it is suicide."

"And you call yourself a man of God..." jested Adira.

"And the bible states, 'A prudent man sees danger and

hides but a fool presses on and gets punished' or killed," he added. "Have you noticed that those are real rocks below that angry sea?"

"Well, if we are going to have some spiritual sparring, then I prefer the Proverb that says, 'She is clothed in strength and dignity and laughs without fear of the future'," Adira answered. "Now, back to the topic of getting down there alive. Along these cliffs are long vertical cracks and inside those cracks are places to secure your fingers and hands. We will use our bodies as grips to take us to the next level."

"How do you know this?"

"Because getting up to the Monastery I climbed these cliffs solo along those cracks," replied Adira as she crouched down to feel for the first crack. "You talk too much and listen too little. I will go first. You will follow and watch where I go."

Friar Watt swallowed and recited the verse "Yeah though I walk through the valley of the shadow of death, I will fear no evil." He looked down again. "No, Lord, there are no valleys, just sheer cliffs."

Adira eased herself down, hanging on a vine, and then swung to the right, pushing her fingers through the crack.

"Come on, Friar, remember Psalm 118 from verse 13," she called.

The guards had now made their way out of the monastery gates. No doubt the Cardinal had come to claim the Friar. Lights moved like fireflies dancing in the wind as they approached along the narrow path.

"Psalm 118, what?" thought the Friar, easing down the rock face. He could not ignore the sound of the crashing waves.

"Let go of the vine, Friar," called Adira.

"What?" Friar strained against the sound of the waves and wind to hear her instructions.

The vine snapped, and the Friar found himself falling. Falling fast. The rock face blurred past him. Pain shot through him as he landed on a branch jutting out halfway down the cliff.

"Psalm 118 - 'I was pushed back and about to fall, but the LORD helped me,' Adira called. "I believed you were scared, but now I see that you are so eager to get ahead that you attempted a free fall without instruction."

The Friar tried to breathe, but the air would not make its way through his gasps. "Short breaths" he told himself. Tiny pants of air burned their way through him, until he felt he could move again. Adira climbed closer to him. "There is another crack next to me. Stretch out your hand, I will guide you towards it. Then we can climb down beside one another."

Friar Watt reached for her and now as the air came more easily, he swung his body around and secured his foot into the bottom of the crack where she had indicated. The descent became easier, with her voice clear across the short distance between them.

At the base of the cliff, Pope Viktor abandoned all protocol and threw his arms around the Friar.

"My child, I prayed so hard for you," he cried.

"Holy Father, you have no idea what I have endured to see you. Thank the Lord that you are alive and well," said Friar Watt.

"Catch up time later. Let's move," called Adira. "Come away Holy Father. There is little time to spare."

The cold spray from the waves was unforgiving and the fabric of the dress the Pope still wore clung to his body. It was so dark he could barely see as they climbed over the rocks that led them to the bridge and the rocks tore at his hands in several places.

NINE

History

The trio clambered over the rocks that lay beyond the bridge. It was slow and treacherous, but the Friar was far more secure on this type of terrain. He helped the Pope to move through the slippery rocks.

"Can we not at least light a torch?" asked the Pope.

"I am sorry, but we cannot," replied Adira. "In this dark, just one light will be seen from all the way up there. I won't risk them seeing where we are going."

Finally, they came to some level ground, and the Pope felt secure at last.

"Now, Holy Father, I must ask that you accept this blindfold, while I open up the passage," instructed Adira.

"Young woman, I am the head of the church."

"I know, but I have been sworn by a blood oath to make sure no one ever sees this entrance."

"And what of the Friar?"

"The Friar carries with him something that allows him to pass freely without question."

Friar Watt looked at Adria. He did not understand what she was referring to. He blinked, trying to clear his thoughts. "What would that be?" he asked.

"You have the cloak of the highest order of Dragon Whisperers," revealed Adira.

The Pope shot a look at the Friar. He did not trust the word dragon, even less the legends of the Dragon Whisperers. Yet these two people had risked their lives to remove him from the Monastery and so he would have to trust that if God had brought him this far, he would not abandon him now. Pope Viktor submitted to the blindfold.

Adira slid her hand behind a few tangled vines and at once an entrance opened into a cave. She waved away the cobwebs that swayed in the rush of air. The cave smelled dusty and a little damp. The opening closed again behind them, and she fumbled in the dark for the torch at the entrance and gave a satisfied sigh when the tinder ignited the torch and a halo of warm light began to glow.

The cave was cool, but far warmer than the outside and the Pope relaxed as Adira slid the blindfold off his eyes. Now cocooned in the earth with the sturdy rock beneath their feet, the Friar and the Pope looked in awe around the cave. There were several carvings of both dragons and men.

"What is this place?" asked the Pope.

"These are the Tunnels of History," replied Adira. "At the fall of the angels, a breed of ancient warrior people emerged. They had the same jealous spirit of Cain. The warriors wanted to dominate other people without having a servant heart. They saw that by taming beasts, like the horse and donkey, men prospered. Horses allowed men to travel vast distances on land." She pointed to another set of carvings. "Here is the history of Noah, when God sent the flood to destroy the evil of mankind. The ark was massive, and it saved many species of animals. Then the warriors came up with a plan, if they could tame dragons, they could master the sky. And with beasts of the sky they could rule those who had only learned to master the land."

But the beasts they tried to control were intelligent and

had built societies of their own. They would not corrupt their purpose, which was to help mankind.

So the warriors bided their time and learned that as with all living and intelligent creatures, one can be trained to be corrupt. And the best time to do this is when the young are without the care of their mothers. When they stole the first hatchling, the Dragons rose to try to rescue their offspring. In this first war, the Warrior nations began to spread rumours about Dragons, calling them vile and evil.

We, the Guardians of History, record the deeds of mankind and dragons through these tunnels. The fear of dragons caused many to rise and slay them. The warlords used this fear to drive back dragons to try to control them. But there was a prophecy that a gifted group would rise and be the bridge between mankind and the dragons.

"Are you a Dragon Whisperer?" asked the Pope.

"I am not," replied Adira. "I am from a line of Custodians."

"What is a Custodian?" asked the Friar.

"Our purpose is to record history. It is said that history belongs to the victors," explained Adira.

"What are you implying?" asked the Pope.

"Have you seen the tapestry at the end of the hall in the Monastery? The one with the cross?"

"The silver and gold one?"

"The very same."

"I have seen it," replied the Pope. "But what is the significance of that?"

"I think I may know the answer," said Friar Watt.

"Very well, let's hear your theory," smiled Adira.

"The cross has the beasts below it, showing how we are to have dominion over the beasts of the land. Behind, in subtle hues, are woven the heraldry of all the former popes. But Pope Viktor's Heraldry is not there. Rather at the very top is the Heraldry of the Cardinal," explained Friar Watt.

Pope Viktor took a moment to absorb the implications of this.

"Are you of the faith?" Pope Viktor asked Adira.

"I do not take sides and I announce my personal faith to no one."

"Not even the Pope?" demanded the Friar.

"To no one," said Adira. "Custodians train in all faiths. We are free to choose. Once we reveal it to anyone, then those who are not of the same faith will not want to hear us. However, I think the Friar can already guess what my faith is."

"If you do not choose sides, why did you rescue me?" asked the Pope.

"Because I know that the Cardinal is with King Radolf and he plans to eliminate you. Should King Radolf win and turn a dragon, then the true history of the dragons will die. And we, the Custodians, cannot allow that."

She turned away from the carvings. "Now, I believe that Friar Watt has a confession to share with you that is of grave importance. I will prepare something for us to eat. Once you are strengthened and rested, we will take you to an Abbey that follows the true path of Christianity. After that, it is your decision where you will go."

TEN

Nadine and the Friar

Friar Watt had knelt at the cross in the Abbey before he left. He had seen the change in Pope Viktor as he had walked the distance in the tunnels. But the Pope would need friends. Friends who could protect him. For a time, he would be safe in this Abbey. For how long, only God knew. Thirty years or one year, only time would tell. But what the Friar knew was that he needed to get back to Nadine and Lady Christine quickly. He sensed great danger. The Cardinal knew the secret of the hidden dragon eggs. Perhaps not the location. But they were somewhere. Through the tunnels he had seen carvings depicting some Dragon History and customs. But these records were created by the Custodians and not Dragon Whisperers. They hinted at prophecies and methods. Now he would need the wisdom of the Silver Wings and the knowledge of the Copper Fire Dragon Whisperer to find what everyone was seeking.

Adira had given him several scrolls to take to the Dragon Whisperer. She knew that Copper Fire Dragon Whisperers were the carriers of secrets. Perhaps the new scrolls could be added to the Book of Secrets and together they might be able to find a way to get to the dragon eggs before the King's men. He sighed. More scrolls.

Was the Bishop's confession not enough? He had risked his life to make it to the Holy Father. After hearing the dying Bishop Rawlin's confession Friar Watt had escaped King Radolf's men's arrows, an assassin's serpent, a near torture and a death defying decent over the cliffs. He had watched the growing concern spread over the Holy Father's face when he read the confession.

"My fellow guardians of the faith forgive me, for I have sinned. *I*, Bishop Rawlin, confess to the sin of greed and gluttony. While many men had fallen to greed, I believe that it is this sin that has caused me to neglect my duties to uphold the moral fibre of the leaders of this land that I am stationed in. This is a dark and sinister place that tries to conceal its true purposes.

Frequently my appointments finished early, resulting in me arriving earlier than expected at the castle. Many times, as I entered, there was a man with a dark cloak who moved away. He was never introduced to me. But on one occasion I noticed the glint of metal on the side of his head. It may be my imagination, but I believe that he is masked and that his true identity remains hidden by design. On each occasion, I felt a tightening in my chest. The evil one lurks in that place. But no sooner had I felt the tell-tale signs of its source alerting my mind than the cook would arrive with trays of pastries that produced an enticing aroma that extinguished any thoughts of questioning who the man was.

There was a carved egg-shaped stone above the fireplace in the war room. The King placed it in the centre of the mantle. But as I took my seat, a servant took it away. This egg was never present when I arrived on time. But it was regularly there when I arrived early.

I have heard rumours of an army that is being bred and there are several warriors that have arrived from distant lands.

I know that evil flourishes when good men do nothing. I fear that I have fallen into the snare of the enemy by being bewitched by the lure of the King's gold. I know that the Good Book says in Proverbs that the blessings of the Lord make a person rich, and he adds no sorrow to it. But these riches… I fear, are not from the Lord. I should have eaten the dry crust of bread with a peaceful heart rather than partake of the feast in a house of strife.

By remaining silent, I have allowed the King to continue unhindered with his evil plans. All that I have left is the power of this confession. I pray that you will forgive me and use this knowledge to purge this land of its evil King and find one more worthy."

ό

Nadine climbed to the top of the tree. How old was it really? The Dragon Whisperer has told her that the one outside his cave had lived for over 100 years. But this tree was far larger. She had felt the ancient bark of the tree as she lifted her legs to climb. At the top of the tree she touched her face.

"What will I look like when I am as old as this tree? Will I be like this oak? Ancient and unyielding, or bitter and full of regret like the Dragon Whisperer?"

She looked down, and saw Nathan riding into the meadow on his horse.

Nathan, loyal Nathan. She remembered the first day that she had seen him, trying to soothe the stallion. He had been ready to race towards Lord Logan despite being alone and knowing there were at least ten bandits lying in wait. If that horse had not reared, Nathan would have injured himself by racing unprepared into the bandit's lair.

She remembered the warmth of his body as she sat close to him on the horse when they rode out to find the Medicine Woman. And she could still feel the strength in his hands the time she had removed the stings after he had outraged the bees to get honey for her breakfast. Strong hands, yet capable of such tenderness. And he had made her laugh.

But that was before she learned the truth of what she was. If things were different, perhaps she could have allowed herself to love him. Like an ordinary woman. He had grown into manhood now, in a way that still managed to stir her when she allowed her guard to drop. But with her training she had learned to manage her emotions more and more. It was one benefit of her training that she had not expected. She had even learned to close her mind to Muquin, her dragon mentor. But at times of heightened emotion, Muquin could always reach her.

Below, Muquin sat patiently on the bed of dried branches and leaves. The rich earthy smell of a world waking up after the desolation of winter filled her nostrils. Her ability to cloak her physical presence allowed her more access to mankind than any of the other kinds of dragons. It was part of what made Silver Wings special.

She watched Nathan ride past her, unaware of either her or Nadine. But she felt the girl's heart quicken at the sight of him. What would it take for the girl to change her mind? Without a mate, the line of Silver Wing Dragon Whisperers would die with Nadine.

When Megadeus chose Muquin for a mate, she too had resisted. The leader of the Silver Wings would face many challenges and tests and those jealous of their position would always scrutinize their lives. There was a time that she wanted a simple life. His long journeys to attend peace negotiations and his quests to observe mankind had made her fear for him many times.

But like Nathan, Megadeus was persistent. Her mate had

an annoying habit of sneaking up next to her and poking her belly with the edge of his tail. It had taken months of pestering to make her realise that he would never give up. He always seemed to be around. When she went with her sister to the lake. When she was hunting. Megadeus always seemed to know where she was. Eventually, her father had spoken to her.

"Muquin, I am an old dragon, and I need some peace. If you do not accept an offer of courtship, I shall never have any peace with that lovesick dragon always lurking around here."

"Father, he is elected as the next leader. I could not accept such a match. It is too risky," Muquin had replied.

"You can and you will. There are no other male dragons who can match your intelligence. If you choose another, your life will seem tedious. You were born for something higher. You have a keen mind, good humour and courage. And I know that you feel for him. There is a glow to you when he is around. Do not live with regret. Who knows how long you both may live? Do not rob yourself of years of happiness for fear, my child. I have eaten all the fish offerings he leaves for you. My belly can take no more. Your mother already complains that I have grown too big for the cave. Next time he comes with his offering, accept them and give him the forehead greeting, my child. Your mother longs for little hatchlings - as do I."

Muquin hung her head for a moment. Her parents had not lived to meet her hatchling. She was filled with regret that she had waited so long and robbed them of the joy of seeing Yakhal. Perhaps if she had not waited, Yakhal would have been born into a time of peace.

But at least she had her son. She feared so that Nadine would grow old alone and bitter like the Dragon Whisperer. Nadine might be able to live for hundreds of years, but

Nathan would not. And would Nadine then be too hard to even think of another partner?

The sound of hooves made Muquin's ears quiver. Another rider, but who? She sniffed the air. The Friar. She was only due to meet him at the pickup point the next day. Something must have happened. She uncloaked herself, and the horses reared wildly.

"Oh, dear," thought Muquin.

"Muquin! you startled me," said the Friar. "Where is Nadine?"

Muquin did not understand him, but she always recognised Nadine's name. She turned her head toward the top of the tree. Friar Watt looked up.

"But of course, she is in a tree." He glanced towards heaven. "Do you not think that I have had enough of climbing?" He pulled himself up to the first branch. "Whoever designed these robes, clearly was not a climber." It took some time before he reached Nadine.

"Friar Watt!" Nadine threw her arms around him. The Friar wobbled on the branch and narrowly avoided falling.

"I am so sorry. That was foolish," she grinned. "You are back early. What happened?"

"A lot has happened, and we need to gather everyone to plan the way forward. But before we do, how are you?"

"I am fine, I suppose."

"You are thinking about Nathan, are you not?"

"What makes you say that?"

"I don't know… It is that flushed look you get when he has been near. Followed by that grumpy look that you have adopted from the Dragon Whisperer. Come to think of it. He looks just the same when Elizabeth has been around."

"Nonsense." Nadine's cheeks blushed scarlet.

"Is it now?" The Friar's eyes crinkled at the corners.

"What do you know about love? You are a Friar."

"I was not always a Friar, Nadine."

"You weren't?"

"No, I was a soldier. Soldiers were not permitted to marry. But I did."

"Why could they not marry?"

"The reasoning was around kingdom security. The general at the time said that when his soldiers were worried about their wives left behind, they would not be able to focus on the battles. But I fell in love and asked a former childhood friend who was a Bishop to do a secret ceremony for us. My friend, Raguel, was our only witness. Although we had their blessing, we asked her parents not to be at the ceremony, as it would endanger them and us. I would go home to visit whenever I could. She had a laugh that would fill a room." He smiled at the memory.

"What happened to her?"

"She died. There had been a dreadful storm one night. Lightning had struck a branch but had not broken it. She was collecting firewood when the weight of the damaged branch caused it to snap. She was killed instantly."

Nadine's eyes welled. "I am so sorry."

"Don't be. I have many happy memories of her. You see this woven armband?" he said, extending his wrist. "Her mother made this for me, woven from her hair. With it came a letter to thank me for making her daughter happy. She asked me that I never live with regret and that if one day I chose to find happiness with someone else, I would have her blessing."

"And did you find someone else?"

"I returned to war and after all the suffering I saw, I changed. I chose to become a Friar. To serve God's people. I cannot say that I am sorry. Married life made me understand the challenges of love and marriage in a way that those who have never been in love cannot understand. I will forever be grateful for the time we had together. I think she would be proud of the man I have become.

But I do not wish to change my life to meet someone else.

There are too many who need me the way I am now. In any case, I could not imagine ever being with anyone else. There are men who can remarry as are there women who can remarry. But for a few there can be only one. Neither path is better than the other. But the greatest tragedy is, without a doubt, choosing never to love at all," said the Friar.

"Not you as well," groaned Nadine.

"Nathan is one of those who can only love once. Do not deprive either of you from a joy that is granted to us by the Creator. I will leave it at that. Now dear girl, there is much to plan." He held out his hand. "Shall we?"

ELEVEN

Lady Christine and Nadine

Lady Christine rolled over in the bed. As the warm, soft light of the new day greeted her eyes, she burrowed herself a little more deeply into the soft sheets. She wriggled her toes just to check that she was not dreaming.

"I have no nausea. Oh, thank you, Lord," she smiled.

She reached for Lord Logan, to find he had already left. A dried lavender sprig lay on the pillow. Lavender was one of her favourite scents. She pressed the delicate leaves with her fingers and inhaled its comforting fragrance. Then she felt the movement.

First, it was only a bubble. As delicate as a butterfly. Perhaps she had imagined it. Lady Christine lay very still and waited. She pressed her fingers to her belly. There was the fluttering again. The softest tap, almost as if she had pressed her fingertips under her chin. The babe! It was moving. Lady Christine's laughter erupted as a soft yet vibrant sound, like a feather dancing in the air.

Saliva filled her mouth. But this time it was not from the ever-present nausea. A smell had reached her from below her chamber. She sighed and could almost imagine the food that was toying with her senses. A picture of bacon lying in crispy waves on a sea of glistening fat, sizzling and spitting on the grill from the kitchen below called to her. But this was no ordinary hunger. It was a ravenous, lustful urge to devour whatever was before her. She leaned over and rang the bell in agitation.

The chambermaid appeared to answer her summons.

"Sarah, where is my breakfast? I must have it now," she snapped. Her hands flew to her mouth. "How rude. I am sorry."

Sarah tried to suppress a smile. "It is all right, mam, I have had three babes of my own. I recognize what it is like to remember hunger. What can I get you this morning?"

"Bacon, lots of bacon. And some of those baked cinnamon apples that the cook makes. Oh, and some soft white bread. The kind we set aside for the poor."

It felt like an eternity waiting for the meal, but when it arrived, Lady Christine layered the bacon in all its sizzling glory onto the bread and bit into it. The fat glistened unchecked on her chin. The salty crunchiness merged with the soft, buttery bread.

"Oh Lord, thank you for the gift of taste," Lady Christine sighed.

What a blessing to feel pleasure. Just the happiness of pleasure, of enjoying a good meal, and the soft bread that at that moment surpassed all other memories of joy. She was even delighted by the colour of the stained glass windows she saw every day.

The babe too, seemed revived by the food, as more stretches and bubbles emerged from her belly. But her feet felt strange, as if they were not part of her. She rolled her ankles, which made them feel somewhat better.

Even the cold water in the basin was pure ecstasy. Once she had freshened up, Lady Christine called again for Sarah. Sarah was a pleasant and happy woman, with the softened figure of a woman who was blessed with several children. Lady Christine missed Mary terribly, but the comfort of having a woman who anticipated her needs as a new mother was a blessing. She would have taken Mary back, but Elizabeth had said that Lady Christine's pregnancy might disturb Mary after the loss of her own babe.

Lady Christine had sent gifts to the family and kept Mary in her prayers. She had heard her mother had sent Mary to a nearby village to learn the art of blending herbs with cheeses. Lady Christine had sent a gift of a new goat to the family. She hoped that it would show Mary that she wished her no ill will and that it would cause a thriving enterprise for the young woman.

For their anniversary, Lord Logan had bought her a full-length polished mirror. Alone, she pulled off her nightdress and examined her figure. The softness of her belly had pushed into a hardened mound. The skin felt tight. As had the bodice of her nightdress. She drew in a deeper breath. Elizabeth had explained to her that as the babe grew, she might have some trouble breathing as the child pressed upward towards the airways of her body. Her breasts were far larger than they had been months ago. She reached for the jar of oil that Elizabeth had prepared.

"Rub this on twice a day, all over your upper body. It will help strengthen your skin, so you do not get as many of the marks that lighten the skin when a child grows," Elizabeth had instructed.

Lady Christine stared in amazement at the blossoming shape of her body. It was now that she truly appreciated the miracle of creation. Was this how God felt when he looked at what he had crafted? She felt the bubbles and tugs of the child within her again, and her belly bounced with her laughter. When she was finished with the oil, she reached for her undergarment and drew it over her head. But she could not lace up the top. Her breasts had swelled too much. Lady Christine looked in horror at her image.

"I am meant to join Lord Logan at the council this morning. I cannot possibly go out like this. I will look like one of the women from the district, trying to lure in the men," she cried. There was a knock on the door and Sarah arrived with the freshly laundered garments.

"Lady Christine, you have been crying. What is it? Is it the babe? Must I call for the Medicine Woman?"

"No! No, Sarah. I am not ill. The babe lives. It is just…" she turned to face Sarah and cupped her hands under her breasts. "It is just these…"

"Lady Christine… all women grow in that place when with babe."

"I know. I have seen it too. It is just that, well… I have a war council meeting and the men... Well, they cannot see me like this."

Sarah smiled. "Well, certainly not all men. But a husband may like the change."

Lady Christine blushed.

"Forgive me, my Lady, I forget my place."

"There is nothing to forgive. But I could do with some help."

"Well now, let me see…" said Sarah, glancing around the room. "Here, this emerald dress, it has a plunging neckline, so it will not be tight around the bosom. Then..." she said, searching for a lace handkerchief from the chest… "Yes, this will do nicely. Keep the undergarment as it is. I will remove these ribbons, so they do not show under the dress. Then, we will sew this lace over the front of the dress, which will completely cover your chest. And we won't lace up the back; we will only pull in the top and not the area around the waist."

Sarah sifted through Lady Christine's jewelry box. "And a

pretty trinket to draw the eyes to your neck... there, that works."

The servant smoothed down the dress and pulled Lady Christine's hair into an upward fashion. Her mistress's face brightened when she saw the effect.

"Thank you so much, Sarah. That is lovely and I have so much freedom to move." Sarah smiled.

"It is my pleasure. Do you have any engagements this afternoon? Perhaps I can arrange for the seamstress to come and see you for some new garments."

There was a polite knock on the door. Sarah placed Lady Christine's shawl over her shoulders and went to open the door.

"Lady Nadine!"

"Oh please, just call me Nadine. May I come in?"

"But of course," said Lady Christine. "You look troubled. Please sit and drink some tea while you are here. I was only expecting to see you at the War Council."

"That was the plan, but besides Beatrice, you and I will be the only women and I wanted to see how your pregnancy has been going." Lady Christine's eyes wrinkled with pleasure.

"That is so kind of you Nadine." She pushed out her belly. "I am getting to be a rather plump lady now. But it gives me an excuse to eat as much as I please," she grinned.

"Excuse me, my Lady," curtseyed Sarah. "I will leave you two to talk." "Thank you, Sarah. And thank you for your thoughtfulness," replied Lady Christine. Nadine looked uncomfortable.

"There is something that ails you."

"What is it like to be with child?" asked Nadine. Lady Christine paused for a moment.

"That is not the real question, but very well. For the first few weeks, I felt dreadful. But now that it has passed... Lord Logan and I waited so long that I never thought it was possible. So, it still feels unreal to me. As if I am afraid to wake up from a beautiful dream. But the babe has moved within me and now that I know that it lives, I cannot explain the joy." Nadine stared at her, unable to speak for a few moments.

"I watch my sister with the children in the area and know that she will make a fine mother. But as for me, I cannot let that happen… Do you think you will ever reclaim your Kingdom?"

"I believe I will. I now no longer have a choice. King Radolf wants all the neighbouring territories. He will stop at nothing. Once I was afraid. I still am, but it is different now. As much as I fear what may happen if I take a stand, I know it will be far worse if I do not. This child, should it be a boy, will be the last chance that my father's lineage will have for a male heir. And I have to fight for his right to rule."

"And if it is a girl?"

"Even more so. King Radolf is no respecter of women. You yourself saw that when he strung up your sister and mother. My husband is a fine man and his courage cannot be questioned. But he will need more men than those he has available. With Lord Jefferson's help, I believe we can find those men. And with your help, we will have the dragons on our side."

"Yes." Nadine looked at the patterned floor.

Lady Christine lifted Nadine's chin. "You and I, we are kindred spirits. We are both born for greatness. But for too long we have run away from our destinies. I am a Queen, Nadine, the last remaining relative of a King. And you are a Dragon Whisperer, the last of your kind. There is a purpose greater than simply our own lives. Before my father died, I was a princess, a political pawn. A breeding vessel for whoever it was, my duty to marry. But now that I have found love, this child is born of love and I intend to raise it with all the dignity that a Queen can give to a child. But I will love it as a mother who chose to conceive. I cannot tell you how that completes me. And I now know that I would give my dying breath to protect this babe and its legacy. It is my prayer that you will embrace the full blessing of being a woman and not just the title you have been born to.

Lady Christine pulled Nadine's hand to her belly. Nadine felt the flutter of life. Her eyes filled with the soft tears of joy. Lady Christine pulled her close and kissed her forehead.

"Beautiful Nadine, let's go down those stairs and show what it means when a woman rises."

TWELVE

Lord Logan's Council

Lord Logan rose to address the group inside the war council room.

"Thank you all for joining us today. I would especially like to thank Lady Christine for being here. I appreciate that she has not been well these past weeks. But I must say that today, she looks like the radiant Queen that she is."

Lady Christine bowed her head and took her seat next to Lord Logan.

"And Lady Nadine, welcome to you too," smiled Lord Logan. "And of course, Beatrice, who has brought with her Isa, Nadine's warrior tutor." Each person took their seat as Lord Logan continued.

"We have with us Friar Watt, our spiritual leader, Captain Julian, my Captain of the Guard, Lord Jefferson from the Kingdom of Ochar, (Lady Christine's inheritance), the Dragon Whisperer, Nadine's mentor and of course, her father, Sir Nicolous. Nathan has given his apologies; he has some pressing matters to attend to regarding his next trade commission. For this first meeting, we will keep this council a close group, for matters of confidentiality. As we come to an agreement on the main issues at hand, we can then invite others for their input. Are we in agreement?"

"Aye," announced the group.

"Thank you. I will hand over to Friar Watt, to report on what transpired in the Monastery," said Lord Logan.

"We have moved Pope Viktor to a safe location. However, he is still in grave danger and we will need to mobilize forces to protect him. If we do not, it is possible that the Cardinal will conspire to have himself declared as Pope. He will then be an Antipope to stand against the rightfully elected Pope. King Radolf is probably of the opinion that he can rely on the Cardinal's support. But I think the Cardinal may have a higher plan than simply to be the King's puppet.

The Cardinal is a powerful and calculating man. He knows of the King's campaign to gain the surrounding lands, with one of the most influential being the Kingdom of Ochar. It was this last territory that provided resistance to the surrounding areas. If the pressure from King Radolf is too great on the Cardinal, the Cardinal may make a move to excommunicate King Radolf and then the Lords within the territory can challenge his title. The Cardinal may even have some lands confiscated by the church. While no one would mourn the loss of the King, a land ruled by a corrupt Cardinal is not much better. We will need to have strong military minds to advise us on this. But having Lady Christine recognized as the rightful heir to the throne of the Kingdom of Ochar would be a good first move.

The Cardinal has received ancient scrolls that outline a plan by the dragons to hide eggs for the continuation of their species. There were plans to take one egg of each dragon species to a different location. This was before the last Dragon Wars. It is King Radolf's plan to find these eggs and to breed a dragon army.

"But the eggs cannot hatch without a mother," said Lady Christine.

"Not so," said the Dragon Whisperer. "You need only have the presence of a female Dragon Whisperer."

Nadine felt all eyes on her and she shifted in her seat. Nicolaus rose and stood behind his daughter.

"But Nadine is only a Silver Wing Dragon Whisperer, and there is already a Silver Wing hatchling."

"Sir Nicolous, a Silver Wing Dragon Whisperer, can communicate with all the Dragon species. Her presence will cause every kind of dragon to hatch from its egg. But for a dragon to turn, it must not bond with the mother. Or in this case, the Mother Whisperer figure. To stop the bond from forming, the King must kill the mother figure. In this case, Nadine," explained the Dragon Whisperer.

Nicolous closed his eyes and placed his hand on Nadine's shoulder.

"How do we protect her?"

"The best way is to find those eggs before King Radolf does and get Nadine to hatch them all. She will need to bond with each of the hatchlings. Once the bond is secure, they will give their lives to protect her. But during this time, Nadine will be vulnerable. The bond with so many dragons will push her to the edge of her endurance," replied the Dragon Whisperer.

"Where do you think the eggs could be?" asked Lord Logan, his eyes flicking from the Dragon Whisperer to the Friar.

"I do not know," replied the Dragon Whisperer.

"Perhaps there is a way of finding out," said the Friar, opening his pouch.

"When I was at the Monastery, I was aided by a woman who called herself a Custodian. She gave me these scrolls to give to the Dragon Whisperer," he said, placing the scrolls on the table.

"You met with *a Custodian*?" asked the Dragon Whisperer.

Excitement ran through his expression the way a lightning

bolt runs through a tree. The Whisperer's hands trembled as he opened the ancient scrolls.

"What is a Custodian?" asked Nadine.

"They are a kind of historian. They take a sacred oath to protect true history. They may follow any religion in the world. But they study all religions. They have a sworn blood oath to record history, never taking sides.

A Custodian trains in many skills, languages and customs, for to find true history, they must blend into all cultures. They never reveal their birthplace or religion to anyone, for fear it will contaminate the truth.

For a Custodian to help us, they must fear that a power seeks to wipe clean a history and overpower a nation or religion."

`He turned to look directly at the Friar. "Were you inside one of their tunnels?" he asked.

"I was," replied the Friar.

"How did you manage to gain entrance?"

"It was Nadine's cloak."

"Ah! Yes, of course," nodded the Dragon Whisperer. "A Silver Wing Dragon Whisperer's cloak can only be bestowed on someone of trust. Silver Wing Dragon Whisperers are the only ones allowed into the Tunnels of History - and then only when invited for a specific purpose. It is a great honour."

"This scroll says that an Emerald Forest Dragon named - Ciommed was tasked with the responsibility of hiding all the eggs. But at the time of the transfer it was discovered that she herself was with egg. Her mate took two of the eggs himself, as she was already in a weakened state after an illness.

The military strategist for the warlord was a woman by the name of Mıykaeel, who was rumoured to have been a favourite of the warlord, and was charged with the task of tracking down Ciommed.

The council chambers of the Emerald Forest Dragons were located about a half a day's ride from the Silk Forests.

But in times of peril, Emerald Forest Dragons would have to make a trip to their silos to extract a pouch that contained the world's most sacred herbs. It appears that would have been in the opposite direction of where she needed to go. And from the silos, she would need to travel back to the next forest to deposit the egg in safety.

Just how much strength would she have had? Perhaps - Muquin can help us to estimate how far Ciommed could have travelled.

Each Dragon species had a chosen network of lairs where they could go to for safety and each Whisperer would choose two or three of them. Should the Whisperer die, he or she would with their dying breath pass these hiding places on to their Dragons.

So now we have to find out who Ciommed's Whisperer was, in order to guess those locations. An Emerald Forest Dragon would need to have their lair underground. But as for the others... I do not know. I will need to go through my Book of Secrets and see if there are clues. Sometimes the Book of Secrets has symbols or riddles as a protection in case someone finds the book. It may be easiest for me to trace the location of the Copper Fire Dragon lairs. But, as for the others, it will take time," explained the Dragon Whisperer.

"Time is perhaps the one thing we do not have the luxury of," said Nicolous.

THIRTEEN

The Race

"We will need help," the Dragon Whisperer told Nadine. I can train you to be a Whisperer, but this treasure hunt type of quest will need special skills. One thing I do know is that the sacred herbs require someone with herbalist's training."

"Wouldn't Elizabeth be able to help? Healers often train in botany?" asked Friar Watt.

"That is true. And I believe that she trained with an Ancient. She also knows many people from different cultures. She just may be the perfect person to help," said The Dragon Whisperer.

Nadine sat staring at the floor. The impact of the Whisperer's words sat heavily in her mind, "To stop the bond from forming, the King must kill the mother figure. In this case, Nadine." Time felt like a drop of water falling but then frozen in midair as she tried to comprehend the impact of King Radolf's plan. She was to be the sacrificial lamb, but not one who was willing. A mere object for the King's brutal plan.

"Nadine, stop daydreaming and get moving," snapped the Dragon Whisperer.

"Have you lost your mind?" cried Lady Christine. "Can't

you see that this is too much for her? You wish to race off on this quest, without taking one moment to see how she feels."

"Lady Christine, how she feels is of little consequence right now. I am trying to save her life," declared the Dragon Whisperer.

The Friar looked at Nadine. "Forgive us, Lady Christine, you are right. We are racing into crisis mode without a plan."

Nadine looked up at Lady Christine. Her green dress seemed to blur and sway as she approached.

She heard Lady Christine's voice "Call for Elizabeth, tell her to come quickly."

Nadine's head slumped backwards, and she saw her father's face above hers as he eased her head down.

"I do know not that she got over the shock of the last attack by King Radolf," said Isa. "This is the trouble of being a strong woman. People always assume that you can simply cope with things which may push you emotionally past your endurance. Men can be insensitive to this. They either treat you as a damsel in need of rescue or they ignore that you are a woman, designed for a less brutal life," said Isa. "She needs some rest, wholesome food and a chance to talk about these events."

"Take her to the guest room upstairs," said Lady Christine. "Sarah will show you the way. I will be there presently."

"Dragon Whisperer, can you find Elizabeth and inform her of the threat to Nadine, it may help her to deal with Nadine's shock."

She turned to face Lord Jefferson. "As my father's most trusted friend, I ask you to outline the area of my father's lands with my husband. We will need to find a way of getting into the castle and to round up the Lords who are still faithful to my father's memory. I must attend to Nadine until Elizabeth arrives. When she does, I will return, and we can discuss the plans to reclaim Ochar. King Radolf will stop at nothing to claim ultimate power and this must not happen. Despite my current more delicate state, I will no longer hide behind those who I hold dear. I will rise up and fight alongside the people who have stood by me all this time."

"But Lady Christine, what of the babe? The Heir to the throne…" said Lord Jefferson.

"Be at peace, Lord Jefferson. I will not push myself beyond my endurance. But I have to make it known to my people that I have something worth fighting for, and that I will no longer permit men as cruel as King Radolf to lay claim to their lives."

"But Isa has returned, and Beatrice is here to help," said Lord Jefferson. "Surely they can replace you?"

"Isa yearns for her home. We do not know how long she will remain. I can only suppose she came back here because she sensed that Nadine needed her. But I can no longer let other people fight my battles alone."

FOURTEEN

Ancient Healing

Elizabeth lunged forward to catch the falling jar, as Tiber's kitten clawed frantically at the sliding embroidered cloth that the intricately carved jar had rested on moments before. But the jar shattered on the ground and dried Anise spilled in all directions.

"Can't you find a rat to chase!" she shouted. The kitten raced to Tiber, quivering in fear. Elizabeth wept when she saw the tiny dried flowers scattered on the floor.

"I can't use these now," she cried as she scooped up the seeds from the floor.

Tiber licked the kitten and looked up at Elizabeth with her large eyes.

"It's all right, Tiber. I know that when it is warmer, they will go out and explore." Tiber had belonged to Nadine, but with her regular training, she was often away. Now Tiber was a favoured companion of Elizabeth's. Nadine would visit each time she returned home.

Elizabeth kept Tiber's basket far from the rooms where she treated her patients. But every now and again, as the kittens grew older, they ventured further away from it.

"I think, Tiber," she said, rubbing the little cat behind the ears, "It is time to find some working homes for your kittens. I can think of a few barns that have a rat problem."

But that did not solve Elizabeth's dilemma. Anise brewed into tea helped clear mucus from patients who suffered with winter respiratory problems. Without the stores of Anise, she had few remedies left to cope with the increase in patients that the cold weather brought. Her hands quivered, and she placed the seeds into a small bowl. "Perhaps I can use them as a fragrance for the rooms," she thought.

A pounding on the door plucked her from her melancholy.

"Oh, not now…" She kissed the cat on the forehead. "That knock belongs to the Dragon Whisperer," she whispered. "Let's go see what he wants." Elizabeth paused at the door and lifted her shoulders.

The Whisperer peered in at the window.

"Perhaps, she is not here," he thought, although the sign she usually hung on the door to inform patients that she was away was nowhere in sight. He pounded harder. Elizabeth opened the door just as he lifted his fist a third time.

"It is unnecessary to break the door down."

The Dragon Whisperer pushed past her. "Then perhaps you should have opened it, when I first knocked."

"I was… oh never mind."

He sat down in her favorite chair. Elizabeth frowned.

"We need your help."

"With what?"

"Well, first, Nadine has fainted…" said the Dragon Whisperer.

"What happened? Where is she?" Elizabeth cried, looking up at the shelf for her shavings of hartshorn, the horn of a male deer. This, at least, was something the kittens could not reach. She did not use it frequently, but the acidic smell irritated the nose and caused the patient to inhale sharply, which brought them back to consciousness. She seized the jar and turned to get her cloak.

"Where are you going?" asked the Dragon Whisperer.

"To Nadine, as you have asked. I should hurry."

"Sit down," he said.

"I am not in the habit of taking orders, as you well know," she chided.

"Nadine is fine. She is with Lady Christine in her chambers. They can wait a few minutes. Please... Elizabeth, will you sit down, just for a moment?"

"You have but a few minutes, and then I must get to my patient."

"We have a serious situation. And we need help." The look of desperation in his eyes compelled Elizabeth to accommodate his request.

"We have learned that there are hidden dragon eggs and we need your help to find them."

"Me? What do I know about finding dragon eggs?"

"The dragon tasked with hiding these eggs was an Emerald Forest Dragon. We believe that she may have had a sacred pouch with her. It is a pouch of the herbs valued above all others. Emerald Forest Dragons kept these hidden in case we faced a catastrophic eradication of plant life in this world. If we can discover what these herbs are and where they grow, we may find where she hid the eggs."

Elizabeth rubbed her forehead. Something pricked in her memory.

"I do not know the full list of the herbs and where they grew. But I remember that my tutor from the ancients spoke of a book. The Ancients never recorded their teachings, that I understand. But they would not destroy sacred references.

Legend has it that Noah received teaching about the natural world from the archangel Raphael, who was responsible for healing. Noah wrote these down in a book and gave it to his eldest son, Shem. The Ancients found the book and hid it somewhere in their Retreat. The ruins are all that remains of that place.

If we could find that book, it may contain a list of the original sacred herbs. In the Song of Songs, frankincense, myrrh and aloes are mentioned. I use these frequently. But there are other things I do not use regularly and others I have forgotten. Perhaps a good place to start would be to go back to the valley where I met with my tutor. We will require an escort. It is far too close to King Radolf's castle for me to feel at ease.

"No harm will come to you while I am there."

Elizabeth gazed at him, momentarily drawn to a feeling beneath his words, and saw they were reflected in his expression. She swallowed and looked away.

"Can we now go to Nadine?"

The Dragon Whisperer rose from the chair. He towered over her, in a rare moment of closeness. She felt the heat rise to her face.

"Elizabeth," he said, reaching to touch her shoulder.

"Yes?" She gazed into his penetrating eyes.

"Thank you…"

Elizabeth waited for him to continue, but his hand fell to his side and he turned towards the door.

Elizabeth's heart sank. Would there ever be a time when he let down his guard? Would there always be this distance between them?

FIFTEEN

The Masked Man

"The most important part of discovery is passion," thought the Masked Man as he opened the scroll in his chambers within King Radolf's castle. "I can feel Nadine's passion. It runs wild through her. I just have to bide my time and she will lead me to the eggs."

In his solitude, he had taken off the iron mask to reveal his face. His pale skin was patchy and red along the cheeks where the iron mask rubbed. The raised scar of ownership glared hot off his skin. It stretched from the side of his eye to the start of his jaw. The close fit of the mask had led to chafing blisters, and the prolonged rubbing had darkened his skin in patches.

He ran his fingers along the mark. He could still remember the searing pain of the branding ceremony. Throughout history, warlords had pursued his kind, targeting those who were without the protection of a colony of dragons. Without a dragon to fly away with.

They had taken the Masked Man from his mother at birth. He had never had the chance to bond naturally with a dragon, although he was the son of a Whisperer. He had been used as a mere tool most of his life.

In his dreams, he could hear the sobbing of his mother as they took him away. The pleading of his father.

"But my parents had managed to save my brother," he thought bitterly. "Dragon Whisperers believe they are the bridge between humanity and dragons. But they are just pawns, in some hideous game of power."

He had come to this place when he had detected the presence of his great nephew. He had led King Radolf to believe that he could be an asset in his quest to build a dragon army. It was the only way to immerse himself in the web of deceit and power.

Now King Radolf would use Nadine in the same game. He did not think she should die. But if her death would stop the madness of this continued persecution, then he would have to be part of it. If he could just get to the eggs before she did, then he could destroy them and end the age of the dragons. Nadine could then live.

"Keep fighting Nadine," he called to the girl. "Your love for Nathan will only cause you pain. You will watch your children die. It will pierce your heart."

He sensed that she fought hard against the calling. She still refused to marry. He had worked tirelessly to keep her heart hardened to Nathan. Every time she had softened, she had opened her mind and he could get in. Probing and blocking her feelings and hardening her. His foolish brother had already given up on love. "His stubbornness has made it easier for me," thought the Masked Man! Without love, there could be no more Whisperers.

And now that he had Nabal, the Dragon Whisperer's grandson, in his control, his power grew. The young man was weak. Not worthy of the calling. Still, he was of their line. The Masked Man could not protect Nabal while the dragons lived. But perhaps in time he could teach him to blend into humanity and get away from the king.

The Masked Man's freedom had come when his warlord

was pushed back by a dragon's fire. The cruel Warlord had stumbled backwards and fallen on the very dragon spear his general had used in the wars. With the warlord gone, the Masked Man could conceal his identity. No one would know that he carried the mark of an 'owned' Whisperer.

As a younger man the Whisperer had commissioned the mask from a blacksmith four winters before that, using gold that he had plundered in a raid.

"Why would you want an iron mask to fit your own face?" the blacksmith had asked.

"My master is tired of this scar," he had replied.

"But the mask will destroy your skin," the blacksmith had argued.

"A slave cannot tell a master what to do," was all he had replied.

If his perishing skin was the price he had to pay to eliminate the dragons and Whisperers, he would gladly pay it. He knew the wrath of the King could boil up and consume him. But so be it. Whatever fate the King had in store for him could not compare to hundreds of years of suffering.

He allowed his thoughts to dissipate and set to work, cleaning the inside of the mask and applying ointment to the patches. With a noblewoman's fan that he had bought at the market, he fanned his face, cooling the burning sores.

He bolted the heavy iron door from the inside, and he had covered all the holes in the walls except for one. This allowed him to control what the guards observed in the room. He had placed pockets of fire powder at the door to detect intrusion. Several excess blankets formed a shape on the bed, with a second mask placed in the position where his face would be. He slept under the bed with his mask next to him. It gave the ointment time to work overnight, while he was at the ready to present himself, masked, should there be an intruder.

The Masked Man closed his eyes and saw Nadine's young

olive complexion in front of him. Free of the ravages of age and scars of ownership. Her blue-green eyes flashed, their passion burning bright.

"Rest well Nadine. Tomorrow you and I will play a game of search and discovery," he thought.

SIXTEEN

The Retreat

Nadine stirred in her room in the castle as she heard the knock on the door. She smiled weakly as Elizabeth entered. The healer sat on the edge of the bed.

"How are you feeling?"

"Better now, thank you."

"I heard about what happened in the war council. It must have been a big shock to hear of the King's true plans."

"All this time, I thought his sole purpose was to have me join him in his plan to turn the dragons. But now I hear he plans to kill me."

"Your fear is understandable. But you cannot focus on that. You must find a way of calming your mind. It will give you the strength to master your emotions and have a clear vision."

"The Dragon Whisperer has told me of the Emerald Forest Dragons. I believe that if we go to the Ancients' Retreat, where I received my instruction, we may find a book that will give us clues as to where the dragon would have gone to hide the eggs."

Nadine pushed herself up onto her elbow. "Where is the Retreat?"

"Not too far. It is a half a day's walk from the ruins. But we will have to ride there. Or at least some of us will have to ride," she smiled.

"When do we leave?"

"As soon as Lord Logan agrees to provide us with an escort."

"We cannot wait that long. We must go now."

"But Nadine, we must wait for an escort."

"We will have Muquin and Zairdenth with us. Muquin can cloak and Zairdenth blends well into the environment. It will be faster than horses and we can retreat even faster if there is any trouble."

"Very well, time is of the essence, and Lady Christine has returned to the war council with her advisers. If the Friar is done there, we will take him with us. He uncovered some of King Radolf's plans and can advise us."

Nadine rose. She trembled slightly, but her determination pushed through. Elizabeth reached for her to steady her, but Nadine pushed her hand away. "I am ready," she said.

Nadine checked her pouch for the dragon cloaks. Elizabeth scribbled a note for Lady Christine as a precaution. As they got to the bottom of the stairway, the Friar appeared, followed by the Whisperer.

"I came to check on Nadine," said Friar Watt.

"As did I," said the Whisperer.

Nadine smiled. Sometimes boys in the village had a better way than grown men - one well-placed punch and everyone knew who the alpha male was.

"We must leave now," said Nadine.

"Where are we going?" asked the Friar.

"To the retreat of the Ancients," replied Elizabeth.

"Elizabeth believes that there is a book of ancient healing herbs listed there. A book handed down from Noah to his eldest son, Shem. Healing lessons handed to him by the angel Raphael," said the Whisperer with a smug look.

"Archangel," added the Friar. "Some scholars believe that it was Raphael who stirred the waters of the pool where Jesus healed the lame man recorded in the book of John, although he is not mentioned by name."

"A religious sparring match with a Friar, to what end?" thought Nadine.

"Can we just go now," she said, "We can debate later."

"Then summon Muquin. You and Elizabeth can travel with her, and I will travel with Zairdenth," said the Dragon Whisperer.

"And Friar Watt?" asked Elizabeth.

"If I travel with Yakhal, Muquin can take both you and the Friar," suggested Nadine.

"No, the Friar will travel with me," said the Dragon Whisperer firmly.

Elizabeth gasped when Muquin arrived. She had previously only seen the dragon from a distance. Up close, she was a magnificent sight. Her crystal blue eyes were mystifying. And her scales shimmered silver in the light. Elizabeth was not prepared for the dragon's sheer size, either. She had seen Zairdenth several times over the years. But she had never sat upon him. Muquin lowered her neck, and the Dragon Whisperer grasped Elizabeth around her waist to help her up onto the dragon's back. He breathed in her scent as her hair brushed his face. If Elizabeth noticed, she did not comment, but her eyes shone as she eased herself into place. Her excitement stirred the Dragon Whisperer. Nadine and the Friar exchanged a knowing glance.

"She is beautiful, Nadine," exclaimed Elizabeth.

"Wait until you see the view from the skies!"

With a rush of wind Muquin rose into the sky. The air seemed to dance beneath Elizabeth's skirts, and she laughed with exhilaration. The Medicine Woman stretched out her arms and let the wind flow over her skin.

"I never dreamed it could be like this," she called to the Dragon Whisperer.

The castle below them dwarfed until it was but a spec on the ground. As trees rushed past, she wished that she could fly like this forever. The sense of freedom was intoxicating, and she knew what she wanted. To feel this for eternity.

Zairdenth's heart swelled. "She is a true Dragon Whisperer's mate," he called to the Dragon Whisperer. But the Dragon Whisperer was silent, his eyes fixed on the glorious woman who embraced the sky with wild abandon.

SEVENTEEN

Finding Myrrh

As they descended, the rich earthiness of the ground filled Elizabeth with a contented feeling of bliss. In the distance, she could smell the delicious fragrance of jasmine, her favourite flower. This place had been the retreat of the Ancients. A place where the earth welcomed all the souls who were weary. The stream's delicate movements were soothing in a way that made her forget the cares of the world. She wondered if Eden had been like this. Being close to nature made her feel closer to the Creator and her calling. It was a scripture from the books of Ezekiel that had spoken to her of her calling: *"Their Fruit will be for food, and their leaves for healing."* The Ancients had dedicated their lives to learning the secrets of the earth. It was a blessing to study with them. Her entire knowledge of herbs had come from them. She often thought that it was a tragedy that they had chosen not to write down their teachings.

Elizabeth thought of her days in the gardens. She had questioned her teacher, Paean, about it.

"Surely it will help people if you would record your teachings," she had implored.

"Child, there are many in the world who are corrupt or

ignorant. In the past, a few people did record some of our teachings, but they were incorrectly written, and people suffered because of the proportions. Some remedies, while beneficial in smaller doses, can be toxic. Therefore, those who seek knowledge can come and learn with us. In this way, we can make sure they know their craft," her tutor had explained.

In her time with them, she saw there were very few Ancients left. Many had been persecuted and exterminated. And with that destruction there followed a flood of disease that ordinary people did not know how to cure. Paean had never allowed her to roam freely in this place. He had confined her teachings to a specific area of the garden.

"In this spot, no one from the outside can see us. You will be safe here. Beyond those trees are hills. From those hills you can see directly into this garden. But this part where we teach is invisible to the outside world," he had explained.

When she was younger, her thirst for discovery had an urgency to it. Like the rebellious Eve in the garden of Eden, she had ventured into an area that was forbidden. Like Eve, it had not been to disobey, but rather a burning desire to know more. Her actions rewarded her with an arrow shot from afar. By God's grace Paean had been close at hand and had pulled her from danger, dragging her with him to one of the abandoned underground caves that the Forest Dragons had once lived in. There they had stayed for hours, waiting for the intruders to pass.

But now no one came to these parts. In the absence of mankind, the garden had grown lush and wild, with many of the herbs growing intertwined. Elizabeth looked up into the distance. Now there was no one to stop her from exploring.

"Nadine!" she called. "Come with me."

"What is it?"

"I want us to go to that section across the stream, but we need to stay close together. That way we can scan the area and protect each other in case the King's men come."

As they ascended a small hill, a puzzled look came over Elizabeth.

"Is there something wrong?"

"That tree is out of place..."

"What tree?"

"You see that short, thorny tree? It is not meant to be in this area. It is a myrrh tree."

"Myrrh tree?"

"Do you remember the three gifts brought to Mary and Joseph at Jesus's birth? Gold, Frankincense and Myrrh?"

"And Myrrh is a tree?" asked Nadine.

Elizabeth breathed. The delay caused by having to explain irritated her. But Nadine was young, and it was not fair to be annoyed because she did not have the knowledge. Elizabeth remembered that she too had once been young and reliant on others to guide her.

"Myrrh is a natural gum or resin extracted from a number of small, thorny tree species. It grows in much drier regions than this one. In fact, I only get Myrrh once a year when a merchant I know comes through our village. I often use it for toothache and joint pain for some of my patients. Myrrh was highly valued in biblical times." Elizabeth lifted her skirts to step over a fallen tree.

"Come now, Nadine, let's get up this Hill. I will explain more as we go along." Elizabeth looked at the top of the hill and wondered why she had not thought to wear riding breeches.

"Two examples come to mind. The bible tells us in the book of Esther, that she had twelve months under the regulations for the women—for the days of their beautification were completed; six months with oil of myrrh and six months with spices and the cosmetics for women.

When Jesus was crucified, they offered him wine with myrrh. The Hebrews used it as a drug for those condemned to death to decrease their sensitivity to the excruciating pain. But the text says that he refused it."

The explanation and the climb tired Elizabeth. She stood for a moment, panting, and stared at Nadine, who seemed not to be affected at all. Her endurance was far beyond Elizabeth's capabilities.

They shared some water, and Elizabeth braced herself for the rest of the hill.

"Quickly now, I want to get to that tree." she said, steadying herself with a nearby branch.

As they reached the tree, Elizabeth stopped. The range of vegetation was staggering.

"The sacred pouch," she gasped.

"Come Nadine. Call Muquin. We must get to the Dragon Whisperer."

Muquin uncloaked herself so Elizabeth could see her.

"Muquin, we need to bring the Dragon Whisperer here, and soon," explained Nadine.

"Oh, and Nadine, ask Friar Watt to get us some excavation tools." Elizabeth gathered samples of the rare herbs as she spoke, her tiredness completely forgotten.

ℴ

"Finally, you have come," said Elizabeth as she pushed away a stray hair from her eyes. The Dragon Whisperer's heart tightened as he heard the breathless excitement in her voice.

"What was the hurry, and why are we standing here at this thorn tree?" asked the Dragon Whisperer, glaring at the Friar.

"You have found a myrrh tree," said Friar Watt, walking around the tree. "Remarkable."

"Isn't it just!" Elizabeth's excitement radiated through her.

The Dragon Whisperer gritted his teeth. Elizabeth rolled

her eyes. It was intolerable being around the two of them. A reason never to marry. But they had more pressing matters.

"Dragon Whisperer, was Myrrh not one of the sacred seeds?"

"It was. Some recorded teachings were damaged in the Dragon Wars, but I still have a small scrap of the manuscript that was saved. It does not have all of them, but myrrh is one of them."

"Did you bring it with you?" asked the Friar

"Of course I did," snapped the Whisperer.

Friar Watt stretched out his hand. But the Whisperer handed it to Elizabeth, ignoring the Friar.

The Medicine Woman grabbed the scroll and laid it on a flat rock near the tree. The Whisperer was like a child fighting over a poppet. She had no time to mediate their childish battles.

She and Friar Watt poured over the contents.

Elizabeth felt a tremor of excitement. The Friar seemed to feel something too - he was almost holding his breath.

"Seven of these plants are right here," said Elizabeth with a quiver in her voice. Her euphoria was a tangible energy that annoyed the Dragon Whisperer.

"Do you know what that means?" asked Elizabeth.

"That one of the missing sacred pouches is here?" asked Nadine.

"Yes, an Emerald Forest Dragon would have protected it at all costs. For these plants to be here all together, a high-ranking dragon must have fallen in this area. The pouches were kept hidden in the silos. I see no evidence of a silo here, which means that the pouch may have been taken for safe-keeping," explained the Whisperer.

"In the Bishop's confession, he mentioned that the King had discovered that four dragon eggs had been moved in the original Dragon Wars. Only an Emerald Forest Dragon would have been given that task. I think we can assume one of the sacred pouches fell here, along with the dragon. We must rip up this tree and dig down to search for the egg," said the Dragon Whisperer.

"Rip up the tree?" cried Elizabeth and Friar Watt in union.

"How wonderful'," thought the Whisperer cynically. "Now they are even syncing their speech."

"Get a grip. They are both healers. It is natural that they think alike," intercepted the Copper Fire Dragon.

"Whose side are you on, anyway?"

"Really. Now?" Muquin glared at them. Nadine stifled a giggle. The Friar and Elizabeth stared at the group.

"Inside Dragon joke?" asked Elizabeth, with her hands on her hips. "Protecting this tree is not funny at all!"

"Why do we have to protect it?" Nadine asked the Friar

"Myrrh is very expensive. It also has a biblical history. It is mentioned about 13 times in the bible. It was one of the gifts…"

"Yes, one of the gifts given to Jesus' parents," interrupted the Dragon Whisperer.

"Can I finish, please?" asked the Friar.

The Whisperer turned away to look at the landscape so he could avoid the Friar's intense look.

"You will find it mentioned in Exodus, in…" Friar Watt hesitated, then thought the better of quoting chapter and verse. He continued, more briskly, "Myrrh doesn't usually grow in this area. But if there is a decomposing dragon here, it would have in it the nutrients this tree needs to thrive. It should not be uprooted, or damaged - it's quite miraculous!"

The Dragon Whisperer moved towards the next hill. There was a hut positioned at the top that looked intriguing. "That does not look like an Ancient's construction," he muttered to himself.

The Copper Fire Dragon intercepted the Whisperer's thoughts.

“What do you think it is?” he asked.

“I am not sure, but I want to go look at it.” Some space between him and the Friar would be worth the climb. Nadine continued her questions to Friar Watt.

“So how are we to protect the tree if we want to get to an egg underneath?” she asked.

“Trees can be damaged when their trunks or branches are scraped, if their roots are cut, or if the soil covering their roots is damaged or compressed,” explained the Friar. “If you want to save trees located around an excavation, then you must take precautions before the digging starts. When dealing with larger trees, like this one, we must form a protection zone, so that we do not disturb it. We are going to have to estimate the size of the tree’s root zone. If we can preserve at least half of the root structure, the tree should be able to survive,” explained the Friar. “Nadine, take these pebbles and place them at least ten steps away from the tree in all directions.”

Nadine saw the glint first. It was just a quick flash - some reflection a fair way off. “Get down,” she hissed to the others. ”Muquin, cloak!”

In the distance they could make out a troop of men. “King Radolf!” thought Nadine.

“Muquin! Call Zairdenth! Look, the Whisperer is within their sight. We must warn him!”

An arrow whistled through the air, penetrating the Whisperer‘s thigh. He looked around, bewildered, as the pain drove his body down.

“Nooo,” wailed Elizabeth. Friar Watt clamped his hand over her mouth, shushing her

Nadine withdrew one of the hand-painted silk cloaks from the bag she had carried since the ceremony, where she took her Whisperer’s oath.

When a Silver Wing Dragon cloaked itself, the Whisperer who rode wearing it would be invisible. The silk was a form of camouflage, allowing a Whisperer to blend in with the surroundings.

Nadine draped it over Elizabeth's shoulders.

"Go to the cave," Nadine said softly. "Zairdenth will take the Whisperer back. You can care for him there."

"No, Nadine, come with me," implored Elizabeth.

Nadine smiled. "I know my purpose. I must stay to protect this site. When you are at the cave, Muquin will come back for me and Yakhal will keep you safe."

"I must have my herbs."

"Very well, Muquin will take you to your old hut, which is closer to the cave than your new rooms and Yakhal will meet you there."

Elizabeth's heart thundered through her as she searched through the herbs at the old hut. Yakhal could feel her life force coursing through her, as took her to the cave. She began to lay out her instruments to prepare for the Dragon Whisperer's return.

Nadine slipped into her own hooded cloak. Each kind of Dragon Whisperer had, through history, prepared a cloak for a Silver Winged Whisperer. Now that Nadine was in the land of the Ancients and Emerald Forest Dragons, she needed the cloak that blended in with this area. She took out her pouch of wet soil and smeared it across her face. Then, narrowing her eyes, she prepared her shot. Nadine thought of all she had been taught as she lifted her bow.

"A warrior must have a core of love to keep her heart safe," she thought.

The bow's tautness was at one with her body. She was not yet ready to pray for the souls of her enemies. But she could protect the ones she loved.

"May the bow and I become one. Lord, make my aim true for protecting what is just. For the love of my family."

The arrow flew swiftly, penetrating the throat of the main

archer in the approaching group. He fell silently, but the horses reared wildly.

The leader of the team turned his horse in the direction of the arrow's source.

"There, by that tree!" he roared. "The arrow came from over there." The patrol turned and galloped towards them.

Nadine reloaded her arrows. She crept closer to the trees. There she would be better camouflaged.

The leader of the group was a brute of a man. But his huge form made him an easier target. Isa had taught her to aim for the throat as much as possible. It was a quick, sure way to silence your enemies. You would have to use special armour-piercing weapons to penetrate enough to make a serious torso wound. But very often the throat remained vulnerable. Isa had designed all their training to seek an enemy's vulnerabilities. Sometimes she would need to bring down one of the horses, to create chaos in the group. But Nadine could not bear to do that. Such innocent creatures were not responsible for the actions of their riders. She concentrated on the men.

The Friar had no weapons except his staff. He was skilled at hand to hand combat, but none of them was close enough for him to engage. If Nadine could turn them away, it would help their cause. They had to keep the site safe, at all costs If the men came close, he would be ready, although now he could only pray. He brought to mind Psalm 91, "You will not fear any danger at night or an arrow by day…The Lord is your protection."

Nadine's arm ached. She had never had to fire a volley of shots under this kind of pressure against moving targets. Her arm trembled, as if it was no longer part of her. Her fingers spasmed around the bow, making her hand at one with the instrument of death. Friar Watt sensed her distress and helped her to reload the arrows.

One by one, she brought the men down. Finally, as the last of them fell, the horses scattered and turned for home. Nadine sank to her knees, her hand still clutching the bow. The Silver Wing Whisperer's grip was so tight that she could still feel the sweat trapped between her fingers. Her breathing was ragged and she began to sob. She had never intentionally killed before. Friar Watt stepped forward and knelt in front of her. He pried her fingers from the bow and squeezed them to straighten her aching joints.

Even at this distance, Muquin could feel Nadine's energy, her mind wild with thoughts and completely uncloaked. She was not controlling her emotions, or even attempting to cloak herself.

Muquin tried to discern possible danger. The Masked Man! She could feel his probing thoughts nearby Was he close? Would he read Nadine?

Muquin raced back toward Nadine. "He must not find the site," she thought. "I will have to move her. Fast!"

"Close your mind" Muquin called to Nadine, over and over. It was a risk. To call her, she kept her own mind open, risking her own discovery. But she had to do it. The girl was too important to leave her to her own defences.

The Masked Man was indeed searching. Suddenly Muquin felt his presence and her mind slid shut. Would Nadine have heard her plea in time? With Nadine's hands free from the bow, the Friar placed his arms around her. He knew the girl's emotions were now uncontrollable. Her force would carry far into the distance. If the Masked Man was searching, he would find her. The Friar did not know the craft of Dragon Whispering, but he knew spiritual warfare. He would pray for protection over her. The Friar stood beside Nadine; his arms stretched wide. He prayed for her protection, calling on the God of heaven and the angels to guard her and confuse the enemy. Like Jehoshaphat he would praise his way through this, and the enemy would destroy itself.

Muquin called to her son. "Yakhal, we are under attack. Keep the Medicine Woman safe. I must go back for Nadine."

EIGHTEEN

Healing

Zairdenth lifted his wounded Whisperer and flew back towards their home. The Copper Fire Dragon worked a rhythm. His copper body glistened in the sun and he widened his wings to their full width to eliminate the need to pump them. He glided in at a low angle to keep his movement fluid when landing.

The Dragon Whisperer was half-blind with the pain of the arrow lodged in his thigh. As the Copper Fire Dragon entered the cave, the Dragon Whisperer's body arched in agony.

Zairdenth walked to the table that Elizabeth had prepared. He lowered his shoulders and moved his wing downwards to allow Elizabeth to pull the Dragon Whisperer from his body with some ease. As the Dragon Whisperer's body moved, he roared in agony. Elizabeth's hands trembled when she looked at the wound. The Medicine Woman's studies had isolated her life to one with no strong emotional attachments. Her relationship with the Dragon Whisperer was a complication that she neatly packaged into their infrequent encounters. Now her emotions trapped her in a hurricane of thoughts. She had never treated someone for whom she had feelings. But did she have genuine feelings for him? After all, they had only shared one meal together when Nadine and Nathan had flown to the ruins on Zairdenth. She thought of Paean, her tutor. What would he do now?

"Elizabeth..." the Whisperer gripped her hand. "You... have my heart..." then he slumped backwards. The Medicine stared at him in disbelief. He was obviously delirious from the pain. Elizabeth tried to steady her mind, to focus on what the Dragon Whisperer needed. First she had to remove the arrow. The Medicine Woman did not have her opium drops with her, but she had cleaned a leather strip which she placed between the Dragon Whisperers teeth. She could have used the Friar's strength, but he was still on the site at the Myrrh tree with Nadine. Elizabeth wrapped strips of fur around the Dragon Whisperer's wrists and ankles and then tied them down to the table to prevent him from thrashing out. A look of desperation captured her expression as she glanced at Zairdenth.

The dragon could see that her emotions were overwhelming her. He wished he could communicate with her to calm her.

Elizabeth used a knife to cut away the copper robe from the area surrounding the arrow. She took care in cutting the robe to salvage it for repairs. A sudden rush of wind filled the cave, extinguishing the fire below the boiling water. Elizabeth looked up in despair. But Zairdenth sensed her discomfort and blew on the pot to bring the liquid to a boil again.

The Healer tried to calm herself and, grasping the arrow shaft, she pulled it from the wound. But the shaft came away from the arrowhead and, to her dismay, the head remained lodged in the Dragon Whisperer's flesh.

She stared in disbelief at the end of the shaft. This had never happened before. Elizabeth knew some surgeons would leave an arrowhead inside the wound, so that infection would create a soft mush of pus with other putrefying flesh so that the wound would be soft enough to dig out the point. But far too many of the patients succumbed to the infection. She could not risk that. But how to retrieve the arrow from such a dangerous position was a mystery to her. She had removed an arrow from the Friar, using her forceps to clamp around the end of the barbs. But that wound had been in a far less risky part of the body. Quieting her thoughts, Elizabeth hurried to prepare a poultice of wild honey and Elderwood. She rolled tiny slithers of boiled wood to line the poultice and covered the wound with it. Elizabeth sat at the Dragon Whisperer's table with a piece of parchment and some charcoal. She drew out the image of the arrowhead and her estimation of how deep the wound was. But the Dragon Whisperer's words clouded her mind with emotion, and several times she had to pause and stare ahead. Yakhal chirped and nudged Elizabeth's fingers. She smiled at the little silver dragon. He tilted his head to the side, and his enormous crystal-blue eyes blinked at her in curiosity. The Silver Wing Dragon lifted his injured wing, showing the fine metal rods that held it in place. Elizabeth put down the charcoal and looked intently at the rods. She turned back to look at the sleeping Whisperer.

She wondered when Nadine and the Friar would return, if at all. These dragons held secrets that would help her, but she needed Nadine to communicate with them.

Yakhal called to Zairdenth. "This woman, she needs our help to save him."

"I know, but I cannot talk to her."

"Can you read human words?"

"Some of them, yes."

"If she writes what she needs, can we help her?"

"Perhaps..."

Yakhal pushed his nose against the book, onto the words. The glint of the metal rods in Yakhal's wing attracted her attention. She pointed at the rod, and Yakhal again pressed his nose into the words of the book. Elizabeth grabbed the book and flipped through the pages until she found the illustration of the dragon splints. She pointed to them.

"Zairdenth, come. I think she wants the dragon rods."

"Yakhal, they are very rare, I am not sure if the Dragon Whisperer would approve."

"Yes, he would. Especially if it could save the line. And the Medicine Woman would not ask if she did not have a reason."

Elizabeth lifted her fingers to show four. Zairdenth pulled the oilskin in the back of the cave and revealed an elaborately carved ebony cupboard. The images were of the small forest dragons and their Whisperers harvesting plants. There were a series of small metal dials on the front panels. Zairdenth pressed several of them in a sequence and a metal bolt slid back from the doors. Inside were several stacked oilskins and scrolls. Some of them showed fire damage. Elizabeth unrolled some of them and gasped as she saw the ancient Hebrew script covering the pages.

"The Patriarch Noah's handbook!" She clutched the manuscript to her chest and bent her head as if to breathe in its essence. Then she held it up and waved it at Zairdenth.

"Do you know what this is? It contains the angel's lessons to Noah to cure ailments set upon them by the watchers." She laughed out loud. "Of course. You do not understand me."

Elizabeth placed the scroll on the writing table, her hands trembling with excitement. She approached the cupboard again, but this time Zairdenth placed his claw on the bottom shelf and then motioned with his head.

"Is there something underneath the cupboard?" she asked, "Is that what you're trying to tell me?"

The Medicine Woman ran her fingers underneath the shelf and felt a small metal lever. She pushed at it and a hidden panel slid out, revealing a row of the Dragon Rods secured by leather thongs to the base. Each of them had identical markings carved into the surface. She knew instantly that they were the last of the rods that Zairdenth had created when he was a hatchling.

ό

The Silver Wing young dragon tapped on the book with his claws again.

"Words," thought Elizabeth. Yakhal tapped the page and flew to Zairdenth's shoulder and then back to the book. He repeated this several times.

"Zairdenth, do you know how to read?"

Yakhal flapped his wings, and the rods in his wing made a clicking sound as they tapped against the table.

Elizabeth grabbed the parchment. She drew a diagram describing the idea that was forming in her mind. The Medicine Woman would use two of the rods to create a fine metal sheath, with a shaft down the middle, in the exact shape and width of the bodkin arrowhead. Then a long metal spike with a screw on the other end. Elizabeth would insert the metal spike into the shaft. When the tip reached the end of the shaft, she would turn it so that the screw would drill down into the arrowhead and widen the end of the shaft around the arrowhead at the same time. The remaining rod could be melted to form a handle to facilitate the twisting action for the drill. When the tip widened, she hoped it would grip the arrowhead and allow her to extract it from the Whisperer.

"We need a blacksmith…" thought Elizabeth. She scrawled the word on the parchment. But Zairdenth could not understand. Elizabeth drew a hammer and flames and a man.

"Blacksmith… Yakhal, I think she wants a blacksmith. There is a man that the Whisperer goes to sometimes, but I always drop him off a short distance from the village and he walks the rest of the way. The village has a retired Dragonslayer, but he yearns for a kill. He wears a cloak made from the underbelly of the last dragon he killed and a pendant carved from a dragon tooth. It would be too dangerous for us to go."

"I could do it." Yakhal fluttered with excitement.

"What! No, Yakhal, your mother would feed me to the Dragonslayer if I allowed that."

"She would not need to know. I am old enough to cloak my mind from her. I have been able to cloak for several weeks now. And I could get into the village without anyone knowing I was there. I am smaller than you, so I wouldn't disturb any of the surrounding trees."

Zairdenth looked at the Whisperer. He was peaceful for now, but unless Elizabeth could remove that arrowhead, he would not survive. And Elizabeth… he could not bear to see her in such anguish. But he realised she could not leave the Whisperer in case his condition deteriorated.

"There is a leather messenger rod with a false bottom. We would need to roll the instructions into the hollow portion and then place the gold coins into the false bottom." Zairdenth looked at Yakhal and continued his thoughts. "I think Elizabeth's idea will work and we can roll the dragon rods into the centre. You would need to fly to the Blacksmith's hut. It is on the outlying part of the village, about three of my wing lengths from the horse watering hole. You must be swift. The horses will sense a dragon is close by. There is a hook outside the door. Hang the messenger rod over it and knock three times. Do not leave until he opens the door. Now we have to find a way to explain to Elizabeth what to do."

Yakhal clawed through the contents of the chest. The messenger rod had a plaited leather cord over the top that he could easily slip his snout into. He placed it on the table in front of Elizabeth, and Zairdenth placed three dragon coins next to it.

Draegon's face was minted onto the coins - The first Dragon Whisperer. Elizabeth recognised the image from a picture Nadine had shown her in the Dragon Whisperer's Field Guide. Dragons and Whisperers paid for services with these coins, and local Goldsmiths would melt them down to hide the image. Only a handful of artisans knew of the coins, and in most cases they passed the alliance between these artisans and the dragons down through generations.

When she saw the messenger-rod on the table, Elizabeth realised what she had to do. She wrote the instructions and rolled them around the dragon rods together with the diagram and pushed them into the messager rod.

Yakhal held out his forearm, and Elizabeth hooked the messenger-rod over it.

"How will I know when it is all ready?" Yakhal asked Zairdenth.

"Fly to the stream. There is an oak about six of my wing lengths from the Blacksmith's hut. In the centre of the trunk you will see several small holes which are old bark-scars from arrowheads. The blacksmith will fire a single arrow into that same spot to let you know that you can collect the order.

There is a rock about the height of the Dragon Whisperer's knee. I melted a hollow into the underside of the rock. From the outside, it looks like an ordinary rock. This is where the Blacksmith will place your orders."

"How will I recognise it?"

"There are seven rocks. They represent Draegon, his parents, and his four siblings. This is a symbol of all the Dragon Whisperers to their chosen artisans. When the blacksmith recognises the Whisperer's messenger's rod, he will stop all other work to complete this project. We chose dragon artisans for their speed, accuracy and quality of work - you will not have to wait more than a few hours."

Yakhal kept his thoughts neutral. His biggest danger now was alerting his mother - she would surely tell him not to go. He knew that once he got close to the village, the risk would be too great for her to come after him, and she would have to let events unfold on their own.

ᢦ

The young Silver Wing flew above the trees until he saw the cluster of oaks. Yakhal swooped down as he saw the horse's watering hole. "Three wing widths," Zairdenth had told him. Then he saw the smoke from the blacksmith's fire clouding the sky. On top of the hill, he saw a small stone dwelling with an enormous spear mounted to the top of a lookout inside the roof.

"The Dragonslayer," thought Yakhal. That made him think of Isa, and he wondered if they knew each other. Yakhal shuddered and focused his attention back to the blacksmith. It was rare for an artisan to have a double dwelling. The red glow of the furnace burned brightly in the workshop that flanked the house. The artisan's banner hung on a metal pole outside. It was a darkened metal with a detailed spear head to signal his speciality. Only the elite, and sometimes assassins, wanting to advertise their success, could afford such detailed spearheads. Yakhal could hear the heave of the bellows, amplifying the heat of the fire. The ping of a hammer tapping against the metal told Yakhal that the blacksmith was in his workshop.

Several spears lay in a pile near the wooden stairs that led to the upstairs dwelling. Inside, Yakhal could see a woman moving around in one room. He had to move quickly as the messenger-rod would only be concealed while it was hidden by his body, but when he reached out to place it on the hook, it would become visible and any passers-by noticing it would spread rumours about ghosts and witchcraft.

The hook, engraved with tiny wings of intricate detail, hung near the door. Yakhal slipped the messenger-rod onto it and pulled the door-knocker back three times. The hammering in the workshop ceased, and Nullah, the blacksmith emerged carrying his glowing tongs. He had a mass of thick curly black hair which he had attempted to control with a leather thong tied around his narrow forehead that gave the impression that it was permanently folded into a frown. He was shorter than Yakhal had imagined. But what he lacked in stature, he made up for in strength. Yakhal edged closer as he watched the blacksmith open the messenger-rod. It was hard to imagine the dark brow having even more of a frown, but the blacksmith's eyes narrowed as he looked around for the source of the message.

"Peberra, can you come here?" he called.

The woman looked down from the window. She had the same dark thick locks and narrow forehead, but they did not seem related.

"I have a lot of darning to do. Can't it wait?"

The blacksmith looked up the hill and squinted to see if there was any sign that Dragonslayer was at home.

"No, it can not." Peberra stomped down the stairs and stood with her hands on her hips.

"You have been complaining all week about how few socks you have and now that I have the time to mend them, you are calling me down."

"Close up the shop and join me inside," he said curtly, as he reached for her leather apron. "I need your help and we have very little time." Peberra swallowed and looked up the hill. She tossed a cloth over the Blacksmith's sign to show that the workshop was closed and then followed her husband inside, shutting the door behind her.

Yakhal could not help but look up at the hill. He wondered why they were so fearful of the Dragonslayer. The Silver Wing Dragon decided not to risk being caught by the Slayer and flew to the oak to await the blacksmith's signal.

Nullah motioned to the parchment on the workbench and held his forefinger to his lips. He tossed the three gold dragon coins into a bowl to begin the smelting process while they worked on Elizabeth's design. Peberra peered at the designs.

"Have you ever seen anything like this before?" She traced the design with her finger and then scrutinised the rods. "The craftsmanship on this is incredible. Are they made by…"

"Copper Fire…" he nodded. "I have seen none of these for at least fifteen cycles. The commission designs have come from his healer. He is made from hardy stuff, that one. If he did not write it in his own hand, then the wound must be a near-lethal one. I reckon we have very little time. But these rods are so rare that we will have to make a test model from another metal. Your fingers are more delicate. You are more likely to have success with the rods. I will keep the fire hot and do the heavy work. But you will have to create a model to practice with. We cannot risk damaging the rods."

ǿ

In the distance Nadine sat weeping at the base of the tree. The Friar felt her pain, but pity would not help them now.

"Nadine. We cannot remain here, and we cannot leave these men here. There is sure to be another patrol. We have to conceal the bodies and lead the remaining horses away."

Muquin returned from the Whisperer's cave. She saw the bodies littered over the ground. Nadine's tear-streaked face showed she had been crying, but now the Whisperer froze as she saw how many she had killed. Her face changed, and she seemed to be dead to emotion, which was in a way a good thing. The Friar had left Nadine at the base of the tree and was dragging corpses to a central point. Muquin dug a mass grave.

"Nadine, we need your help," called Muquin. "We must move these bodies. The Friar cannot do it alone."

Nadine's brow furrowed as she watched the Friar drag the bodies of the men she had killed to the hole. She pulled herself up and walked to the edge of the grave. The expressions on their faces filled her with horror. She had to find some other way to be useful. She glanced at the anxious horses, who stood snorting and stamping nearby. A group of unmanned horses would create suspicion, she thought.

Nadine's grandfather had a special way with horses. How she wished that he could be with her now, if only to hear his calming voice. She stroked the horses and whispered in their ears, soothing the animals. One by one they allowed her to remove the reins and saddles, which she threw into the hole alongside the men. Then together she and the Friar replaced the grass over the hole to conserve the excavation. A close inspection would reveal what they had done. But unless a patrol came down into the valley, no one would be able to spot the grave.

"It is time to get back to the cave. I have not heard from Yakhal for several hours and I am starting to worry," called Muquin, preparing to leave.

"Go on ahead," Nadine replied. "The Friar and I will finish up here and lead the horses away. I will call for you when we are done."

Nullah's fire had heated the room to such a degree that Peberra looked as though she had been swimming in the lake. Sweat ran down her arms and trapped between her fingers in the heavy smithing gloves. She gritted her teeth.

"Stand back", he ordered. Nullah poured a jug of water over her head to ease her discomfort. "Now, do it again. Finer this time."

It was several hours before the prototypus was done. "Get me a round of pork from upstairs."

Peberra gulped in the fresh air as she left the workshop. She glanced up the hill again and hurried up the stairs to her pantry to get the meat. Nullah loosened an arrowhead from its shaft and when he was sure that it would dislodge, plunged it into the pork "Now, we will test the device."

"You do it, Peberra." he added, "His healer is a woman, so you must test it out."

After several tries, they fine-tuned the apparatus. It was almost sunset when Nullah emerged from the workshop. There was a message on his hook from a neighbouring Lord enquiring about his order, but no other signs of visitors. Nullah removed his apron and gathered his bow and arrows.

"I will find us some game for supper," he shouted, but drew the woman closer to him and whispered his thanks. The blacksmith rode to the rock to conceal their creation. He shot one arrow at a hare and another at the oak. Nullah looked around him before picking up the hare and riding back home.

Yakhal stepped out from behind the oak. He incinerated the arrow with his dragon-fire and flew to the rocks to retrieve the device. Then he took off and flew back to the cave.

ὀ

Muquin landed near the cave. She called for Yakhal, but he did not answer. She entered the cave and saw Elizabeth at the Whisperer's side. Zairdenth had a suspicious look about him, she thought

"Where is my son?"

"Muquin, you are back so soon - where is Nadine?"stammered the Copper Fire Dragon.

"I asked you a question. Where is Yakhal?"

"Muquin, I told him not to go, but he insisted…"

Zairdenth recognised the expression of an enraged Silver Wing. What they lacked in strength, they made up in sheer cunning. A Silver Wing bent on revenge was not one to be trifled with.

"I am not in the mood for your stalling. I had to leave my Whisperer in a dangerous position and now I can see that you are up to something that you are trying to find some excuse for. Out with it, Zairdenth."

"Yakhal has gone to the Dragon Artisan Village," the Copper Fire Dragon stood his ground, but felt an odd wave of panic risein him as Muquin took a step closer.

"Have you lost your mind? That is where Deivdri lives. The most feared of all the Dragonslayers in this area. He boasts of killing every kind of dragon except a Silver Wing."

"Then you have nothing to worry about," replied Zairdenth. Muquin snarled at the Copper Fire Dragon.

"Yakhal has not yet started his battle training. He is too young. What chance do you think he has against a veteran slayer?"

"I warned him of the danger, but he says he can cloak himself. He will be fine. He is small enough to enter the village undetected. Elizabeth designed a device that will help the Dragon Whisperer and it has to be made by a blacksmith. Nullah is the best there is."

Muquin raised her tail to strike the Copper Fire Dragon, but she considered Elizabeth's haggard face, and she retracted. The Silver Wing lowered her tail, and turned away from the cave.

Muquin sat by the entrance and stared out in the distance towards the Dragon Artisan Village. She tried to call for her hatchling, but he did not answer. It was too late to follow him. She could only hope for the best. But her anger festered as her anxiety rose.

"He will return," she heard Zairdenth say.

She closed her eyes. Why were males so eager to rush into the face of danger?

"For both our sakes, you'd better be right. I have lost too much, Zairdenth, I cannot lose my son."

As the silhouette of the forest met the deep orange and red hues of the sun descending below the horizon, Muquin watched the approaching form of Yakhal making his way to the cave. Muquin almost wept with relief when she saw him descend.

"Never do that again," she scolded.

"I had to save the Whisperer."

"But you should have waited for me to go with you."

"There was no time. As it is, it took hours before the blacksmith could complete the task."

Muquin knew that she could not protect him forever. By now he would have been attending council meetings with his father and preparing for the battle strategy tests with the rest of new trainees. She so wished that she could keep him a hatchling forever. But she knew that would be selfish. She watched him hurry to Elizabeth with the device he had collected. He was so much like his father considering the fate of mankind, always making sacrifices for them.

ό

Yakhal placed the messenger-rod on the table.

Elizabeth tipped out the contents carefully in front of her. The Blacksmith had sent the results of his own tests and another set of diagrams.

She unscrewed the threaded needle tip from the inside of the instrument and examined it.

"The mechanism feels smooth. I can see why you sent it to that blacksmith. The craftsmanship is excellent and they have kept much of the engraving." Elizabeth shook her head. Why was she speaking to the dragons if they could not understand her? She tickled Yakhal under his chin and the hatchling quivered with delight.

Elizabeth re-threaded the needle into the sleeve and then prepared boiling water to disinfect the instruments.

She removed the bandage and cleaned off the honey and Elderwood flower poultice which she had applied to the wound while she waited for Yakhal's return.

Now Elizabeth lit extra torches so she could see better; as she dared not wait until morning. The medicine woman breathed in and lowered the needle tip of the sleeve into the wound. When she felt the tip of the sleeve touch the arrow head, she manoeuvred it around carefully until she felt it slip over the arrowhead. Then she twisted the screw, which lowered the needle tip through the opening and gripped the arrowhead from the inside. She pushed down onto the Dragon Whisperer's leg to get a good grip on the arrowhead. Elizabeth wriggled the instrument slightly to ensure she had dislodged the arrowhead, and then she eased the arrowhead out of the Whisperer's thigh. After washing the wound gently but thoroughly, she drenched a long thin bandage in honey and inserted it into the wound.

Nadine stood at the entrance of the cave. Her Whisperer Tutor lay motionless on the table. She was too afraid to go any closer.

"Is he…" she searched Elizabeth's face.

"He is alive. I got the arrow head out and staunched the bleeding. Now… now only time will tell."

Friar Watt placed his arm around Nadine's shoulders and led her into the cave towards Elizabeth and the Dragon Whisperer. He cupped Elizabeth's face in his hands and looked into her eyes.

"Elizabeth, you are the best healer I know. Your hand is steady and your mind is clear. He could have asked for no one better."

The Medicine Woman's lip quivered.

"He told me I have his heart… I don't know what to do with that. If he dies…"

He pulled her close and held her while she sobbed.

"Hush now, Elizabeth. All will be well. I will help you care for him. Get some rest now and I will watch over him while you sleep. And Nadine and I will pray for his strength. If God is for us, who can be against us?"

Nadine had already laid a large fur cover on the straw that covered the stone ledge. She led Elizabeth to it, covered her with another fur and sang softly, stroking the Medicine Woman's flame coloured curls from her forehead.

"There is a land where dreams are washed up by waves
No longer do our fears trap us like shut off caves.
For the Lord will carry all our worries away with the tide.
Against His will, what pain can abide.
So no longer think as if you are slaves.
For who can bind you with troubles cut by angels' blades.
Rest in the Lord and let your worries slide.
For we know when the enemy claimed the truth, he lied.
Now cast aside your fears and tell your mind to behave.
So you can gather up all your good dreams in those waves."

Elizabeth's eyes closed. The words soothed away the deep furrows of her brow. The Friar stood next to Nadine and placed his hand on her shoulder as they watched the sleeping woman.

"That was beautiful, Nadine. I don't think I have heard that hymn before."

"My Maimi wrote it. She has a way with words. Maimi would sing to me when I struggled to sleep. She told me that when she was my age, she wrote over 100 poems, but she lost them after she left her parents' home."

"It is a gift to soothe others when your own heart is troubled. May you always walk in the way of the Lord Nadine."

"But why does he allow so much pain?"

"I can not always say that I know the will of the Lord. But I know that nothing goes to waste. If you never had fears as a child, or pain or worries, your Maimi would not have penned this hymn and you would not have sung it to Elizabeth now. In my journey I have seen that women with the greatest courage often have fears and worries that others do not see. Many turn to them for strength. But these very same women also need comfort, and yet they are overlooked. Sometimes they fear that if they tell people that they are afraid, it makes them seem weak. But God places a soft heart in women for a reason. Some metals are so strong that they are brittle and you cannot work with them. To endure you must have strength, but enough flexibility to adapt when needed. When you learn that balance, there is very little that can stand in your way."

Yakhal and his mother had slipped away to go fishing, and now returned with their catch.

"Ah, just in time," smiled Friar Watt. A man can only work so long without a meal. Let's fry these up and also make a broth for the old goat over there."

Nadine smiled and looked for the pouch that the Dragon Whisperer kept his cooking herbs in.

"I am grateful for that arrow," said Friar Watt.

"What?"

"That old fool would never have told Elizabeth how he felt. When a man sees his life fade before him, he abandons his fears and reveals the secrets of his heart. Perhaps now that the truth is out, he will stop treating me as if I am the enemy."

Nadine grinned. She knew that she was stubborn, but the Dragon Whisperer had a few hundred years of additional practice in the art of being stubborn. She was grateful that the Friar was more in tune with emotions, or she was at risk of becoming too much like the Dragon Whisperer.

Nadine frowned and thought of Nathan. Was she tormenting him, just like the Dragon Whisperer was tormenting Elizabeth.

"Nadine, can you stir this sauce?" said Friar Watt, interrupting her thoughts. " I want to check on the wound."

"Of course! I did not even stop to look at it. Do you think you could teach me?"

"… what? Sorry, this is remarkable. It looks like Elizabeth designed this thing…." The Friar held up the device.

"From these diagrams, it looks like a device to remove a broken-off arrowhead from a wound. Nadine, this is what love can do. It can ignite a creativity in you that would otherwise not have been possible. With an instrument like this, a war physician could save countless lives. It could swing the balance of a battle. Injured soldiers could heal faster and be operational sooner. We should get these made up for Lady Christine's army."

The aroma of the cooking meal roused Elizabeth from her deep sleep.

"I am famished" she exclaimed, sitting up slowly.

"I can well imagine. You worked hard today. And I see that you had your engineering hat on."

"I am not an engineer."

"Well," The Friar held up the device. "I think you are a pretty good impersonator."

"It was the dragons who gave me the idea."

Nadine looked at Yakhal, his face was covered in fish scales.

"Not me," he grinned. "I just showed her the rods. She came up with the design."

Nadine wagged her finger at Elizabeth.

"Isn't that what we call false modesty?" she asked the Friar.

"I think it is time for a confession, Elizabeth. If I remember correctly, Moses brought those commandments down from Mount Sinai… what was it ?… Oh yes, Thou shalt not lie… that's the one."

Elizabeth smirked at the words, "If I remember correctly…"

"Okay, I confess. I came up with the designs. But the dragons found the blacksmith that crafted them."

"Excellent, now that you have purged the sin of lying from your heart, let's eat. It has been a long day and we have some planning to do."

Elizabeth looked at the wound. It was still red and angry, but seemed stable and the Whisperer was breathing easily.

"I must admit, he is far easier to deal with when he is asleep."

"Oh that is so mean," Nadine punched the Friar in the shoulder. The Friar pointed his spoon at Nadine.

"Watch it… or I will report you to Bishop Stephen for striking a man of the cloth," he jested, with a smile.

"I had quite forgotten about him."

"Well I certainly have not. A Bishop in the purse of King Radolf is a very dangerous one, not to mention the fact that a false prophet is a poisonous barb in the heart of a congregation. Who knows what sort of sins he will lure people into?"

"I think we need to find those eggs quickly, so that you can continue with your other work," said Nadine.

"But what about the Whisperer?" asked Elizabeth. "We cannot leave him alone…"

"It will take us several days of continuous work to move the amount of soil we need to. I will ask for Lord Logan to send some reinforcements. Then you and I can work in shifts to keep watch over the Whisperer. As long as one of us is here, there should be no problems. But I do hope you are the one he wakes up to. His glare gives me indigestion."

Nadine almost choked on the fish as she tried to stifle her laughter. She could almost imagine the Whisperer's brow furrowing in disapproval.

NINETEEN

Captain Hucchon

The messenger coughed at the entrance of the war council. "Lord Logan, I present to you Captain Hucchon."

Beatrice accompanied a weather-beaten looking knight. Although his tall body was strong and agile, the creases around his eyes showed the look of a man accustomed to long hours outdoors.

He had a short cropped dark beard, flecked with silver, and enough lines around the edges to reveal a man of good humour. His long hair was clean and pulled back with a leather thong behind his neck. But his dark eyes were serious as he walked into the heavily etched stone room of the war council.

His eyes found Lady Christine, seated beside Lord Logan. She wore a flowing bronze coloured robe that revealed the size and swell of her growing form. Its long elegant sleeves touched the ground and draped around her, as beautiful as a masterful painting. At that moment she epitomised what the pagans would have declared a fertility goddess, ripe with new life.

"Princess Christine, you are the vision of your mother," he

remarked as he bent one knee to the ground and bowed his head.

"You are welcome here, Captain Hucchon, but please call me…" Lord Logan placed his hand on hers and shook his head.

She remembered Lord Jefferson's instruction. "Let the men call you Princess Christine. Allow them to honour you. Respect, once lost, is hard to reclaim. If these men are to follow you and Lord Logan into battle, you must allow them to address you with honour."

She nodded her head in acknowledgement of his gesture of respect. "Arise Captain Hucchon and please come and join us at the table."

"And you must be Lord Logan," said Captain Hucchon, holding his fist to his chest and bowing his head.

"Please, Captain Hucchon, sit and join us for the meal. This is my Captain of the Guard, Captain Julian. And you know Lord Jefferson. Captain Hucchon bowed his head towards Lord Jefferson.

"Several of our knights are in training now. But we wanted to get better acquainted with you in a more private setting before introducing you to the rest of our team. I take it that Beatrice has already shown you the castle and where your quarters are. We thank you for accepting our invitation," said Lord Logan.

"Thank you for your hospitality and warm welcome. I believe you have Beatrice to thank for my arrival, that and the lure of seeing King Frederick and Queen Isabella's natural heir alive and well." His eyes held Lady Christine's.

"You knew my mother…" Lady Christine's voice quivered at the sound of her mother's name.

"All of King Frederick's men had the honour of knowing her. She was not like some aloof queens of neighbouring Kingdoms. She had a kind and generous heart, but her love for her subjects and her sense of honour captivated the men.

Every single one of them would have laid down his life for her."

"Where is the famous Silver Wing Dragon Whisperer that I have heard so much about?" Captain Hucchon scanned the room for the girl with the piercing eyes that so many men spoke of.

"She is on a mission with our town healer. They are visiting an ancient site searching for some intelligence that can dramatically alter the balance of power between us and King Radolf. But her father Sir Nicolous will be in attendance for this evening's banquet," smiled Lady Christine.

"Beatrice and Lord Jefferson have told us that you are somewhat of a military strategist," remarked Lord Logan.

"They flatter me. But I have been involved in several campaigns and have had the good fortune of training soldiers from all corners of the world, so one could say that I have learned a few tricks," remarked Captain Hucchon. "Perhaps you could elaborate a little more how you believe that I may be of assistance to you."

They waited while the servants brought through platters of figs, olives, wild boar, fish and pheasant.

"Captain Hucchon for much of my life, my parents managed this land in a peaceful manner," continued Lord Logan. "While I, like all men of this kingdom, have trained in military prowess, we have never had a war in these parts. The odd skirmishes, but nothing that a small group of trained men could not take care of. In contrast, King Radolf is one of the best trained military men I have heard of. I fear that we are ill-equipped to deal with a campaign of this kind."

"And what campaign might that be?" asked Captain Hucchon.

"It is our intention for Princess Christine to reclaim her Kingdom," answered Lord Logan.

"*Our* intention?" repeated Captain Hucchon as his eyes

locked with Lady Christine's. Lady Christine placed her hand on the swell of her belly.

"Captain Hucchon, when I came to this land, I was a frightened girl. I was so grateful to have escaped from King Radolf's clutches that I could not think of the future. In this place I found sanctuary, love and a home. I am not ashamed to say that I could have happily lived here and left behind all hopes and dreams of the past. Yet when I became a mother, I began to change. I remembered what my parents had always tried to instil in me. A love and duty to my country. I realised that by hiding, I was robbing my child of its rightful place on the throne. Perhaps if there had been a good and honourable man on the throne, I would have felt differently. But our true King, my father, died, and our brave Lords were slaughtered. Not by skill or strength, but through treachery and the murder of innocent women and children. It is time for a true heir to sit on the throne again and through the might of our land's brave supporters, we can offer protection to the good people of my husband's lands," said Lady Christine, holding his gaze.

"Have you approached any of the Lords within your kingdom?" Captain Hucchon glanced in Lord Jeffereson's direction as he spoke. Lady Christine noticed Lord Jefferson's shake his head just a fraction. Not enough to dishonour her, but enough to make her feel unprepared.

"No, I have not."

"Well, we must remedy that."

"What I lack in protocol, I am willing to learn. Now I call on you, Captain Hucchon, to be our guide and teach me what I need to know to help these people, our people, to reclaim our heritage. Captain Hucchon stood up, and lifted his goblet, "A toast to our new Queen… Christine."

TWENTY

The Summons

Galdolf pulled in the reins of his horse and looked at the rugged stone of Holly Hill Cave. The land had blossomed since his last visit and delicate blooms of the rock flowers had sprouted everywhere, giving the cave a much softer look.

The former Prison Master smiled, but the weight of the messenger pouch he carried reminded him of his purpose. Although he visited Yakhal, after each moon cycle, at the chance of seeing Yakhal again sooner, Galdolf's had volunteered to deliver the summons to Nadine. He missed Yakhal's boisterous play and caring for Yakhal while he was a captive in the stronghold had reignited his purpose. Now, away from the King's stronghold, Galdolf was free to train in the care of many kinds of animals and creatures. His wife had grumbled about the smell that his overnight guests produced. So Galdolf was busy planning the construction of an animal treatment shed, and with the profits from the last party they had hosted for a neighbouring Lord, they were able to make a down payment on a piece of land on the outskirts of the village. He had never dreamed that one day he would be able to escape the generational occupation of a Prison Master. But this little dragon that had landed in his care had been the catalyst that had helped propel him into a life of freedom and purpose.

Galdolf watched as Nadine emerged from the cave. Yakhal followed her and spread his wing around her shoulders. Galdolf frowned. Something was wrong. He pressed his heels in his horse's flanks and pulled the reins towards the cave. His mare who only needed gentle guidance and now sensed the urgency that rose inside him.

Nadine felt defeated. Elizabeth had fallen asleep and while the Friar insisted that they have faith, doubts still plagued her. The sound of horse hooves startled the Whisperer, and she reached for the dagger in her belt.

"Yakhal, cloak!"

"Nadine, it's just Galdolf."

"How do you know?

Yakhal shrugged. "Spend your hatchling days in the stronghold with one person who cares for you and you will surely sense them at any time."

"I guess I am being overly cautious," Nadine remarked out loud.

"That caution keeps warriors alive," Galdolf said as he entered the clearing. Yakhal flew up over Galdolf's head and tapped his helmet.

"Hey, you. I still need my brains. You are too big to play those games."

"Tell this old man that he grows soft."

Nadine laughed out loud, which served to break the tension that had held her in its grip.

"What is that little rascal saying?" Galdolf eyed Yakhal suspiciously before giving Nadine a hug that threatened to crush her ribs. Yakhal pounced onto Galdolf, flattening him, and tapped his claw onto Galdolf's nose.

"Ask him if he yields."

"He says that you are old and have grown soft. And he asks if you yield."

Galdolf wrapped his arm around the dragon's neck and rolled over, pinning Yakhal on the ground.

"Never!" he shouted.

He grabbed his dagger and pressed it against the dragon's wing.

"I shall slay thee, oh foul beast, where thou liest. Dost thou yield to Galdolf the Great?"

Yakhal strained his neck and tried to snap the blade from Galdolf's hand. But Galdolf would not release the blade.

Nadine grabbed her belly as her body shook with laughter.

"Translate, Nadine!" called Yakhal and Galdolf in union.

"I… I, I can't…

"What is going on outside here?" demanded Muquin as she lumbered out of the cave. "You are making enough noise to awaken our ancestors."

Galdolf jumped away from Yakhal and hid the blade behind his back. Yakhal jumped up and bared his teeth at Galdolf.

"The human started it."

"You'd better not be saying that I started it."

"I don't care who started it. Elizabeth has just fallen asleep. She needs the rest. Galdolf does not know of the Dragon Whisperer's injury, but you two do."

"She always takes his side," muttered Yakhal. He blew a short flame in Galdolf's direction and flared his nostrils.

"Well, he did keep her only hatchling safe in the strongholds, so she is entitled to have a soft spot for him," shrugged Nadine. Galdolf slapped at the flame that now erupted on his tunic, but Muquin did not comment.

"Galdolf is early, he must be here for a reason," said the big Silver Wing.

"Muquin asked why you have come early."

"You have been summoned to the castle, Nadine."

"What for?"

"Lady Christine's battle strategist has arrived. He wants

you and Lady Christine to gain supporters. The first must be the Pope. He needs to ratify Lady Christine as the rightful heir to the throne. And a second visit must be made to the Lords," Galdolf explained, brushing the last few cinders from his hem.

"Why do I need to be there?"

"There are still many who believe that dragons are evil. Although the Pope has been through the Tunnels of History, he has never met a Whisperer. You have been trained by Friar Watt. The Pope will want to question you and see if you are indeed of the faith. There is far too much deception around him. The Pope no longer relies on hearsay. He wants to meet you face to face. Speaking of the Friar… where is he?"

"He is gathering herbs for Elizabeth. We ran into some trouble. One of the King's patrols came past the Retreat of the Ancients and the Dragon Whisperer was injured."

"What? Why did you not call for help?"

"There was no time. I killed all the patrolmen. And we had to get the…."

"You killed them all?

"Yes, and then we had to get the Dragon Whisperer back here…

"Where are the bodies?"

"The Friar, Muquin and I buried them…"

"And the horses?"

"Will you let me finish?" Nadine glared at Galdolf.

"Sorry, yes, please continue," grinned Galdolf.

"What are you smiling at?"

"You…" Galdolf saluted Nadine.

"Quit making fun of me."

"Nadine, I am not sure if anyone has told you this, but you are becoming a fine warrior. And I am very proud of you." He hugged her again.

"Galdolf!" the Friar's voice pulled them apart.

"It is good to see you, Friar," smiled Galdolf.

They grasped on each other's forearms in the manner of old war veterans.

"Let's get your horse fed and watered and then we can speak more of why you are here."

"He wants me to meet the Pope," said Nadine.

"I see," said the Friar as he led the horse to the water trough. "Ah good, I see that Yakhal had not helped himself to all the water for the horses.

"I am going fishing," retorted Yakhal. "Galdolf feels skinny to me. It will give you humans time to babble about whatever captures your minds."

"Yakhal, don't be rude. A Silver Wing always treats visiting dignitaries with respect," called Muquin as he flew off.

"The human started it," he called back and his body cloaked with the sky. Nadine smiled at their banter. But her words were serious: "If I am to visit the castle, we need someone who will help defend the cave until I return."

"I will stay and help until you return," offered Galdolf. "If you could stop at the inn to let my wife know, I would be grateful." Nadine nodded. After the tension of the day, it would be good to see her family at the castle.

"I will make a list of what we need for the excavation and then you can give that to Captain Julian, so that we have the provisions ready when you get back." said the Friar. "The Abbey is not far from the castle, so I expect you will return within a day or so. Pope Viktor cannot risk you staying too long. None of the monks would recognise him, but an extended private visit would definitely raise suspicion."

"How will you cope without an interpreter, when I am gone?"

"We can cover the basics before you leave, but I am sure that the Dragon Whisperer will be barking out orders by tomorrow morning."

"What makes you so sure?" asked Nadine.

"Do you really think he would leave me alone with Elizabeth for more than one day? For the fastest recovery, I will just get Galdolf to whisper in his ear that I took Elizabeth to watch the sunset and he will be up in a shot."

Nadine grinned. Galdolf raised his eyebrows.

"Well, Friar, you certainly love to live on the edge. I don't think even Elizabeth could save you if you test that theory. Now let's get these lists sorted out. Those patrols are expected back within 2 to 3 days and we have already lost a day."

TWENTY-ONE

Legitimate

Pope Viktor sat in the inner prayer chamber in the Abbey where he had taken refuge. His eyes were fixed on the outstretched arms of Christ. The crimson glass that depicted the wounds in the Messiah's palms signalled the danger that surrounded the Pope. The stone walls spoke of the Lord's compassion on earth. To the left side was a scene depicting Jesus as he wept for his friend Lazarus and his sisters. To the right was a scene that showed Jesus when he asked for one of his apostles to care for Mother Mary as he hung on the cross. The Pope could almost feel the weight of the Messiah's body as the last breath burned through his tortured lungs.

Pope Viktor wore a simple friar's robe. The coarse fabric provided a measure of anonymity. Even the herbs he took did little to ease the ache in his shoulders, and his eyes bore the dark circles of a man robbed of sleep. He sighed and looked around the cold stone walls. To his right lay a dark marble sarcophagus with the faces of the Abbey's original patrons lovingly carved into the stone. He eased his aching body into a standing position and traced the lines of the carving of the dead man's face on the sarcophagus. He had long ago forgotten the simplicity of life when the cares of politics did not cloud a man of the cloth's movements. He looked at the face of the man's wife, who was immortalised next to her husband, and remembered that the pleasures of love were forever severed and his family line would not reach beyond the end of his days. Although many priests did not deny themselves the earthly pleasures that their vows demanded, he was committed to his vow of celibacy. Looking back at the husband's face, he felt the crushing weight of being entombed within the walls of the Abbey, as surely as if he was lying beneath the cold stone next to this man.

Pope Viktor had always known that the families of nobility had opposed his appointment and that he would be at risk. But he never expected the brutality that they would use to extinguish his reign. God had saved his tongue and eyes from the blade of his attacker on the day of the procession after his appointment. But his enemies had outwitted even the few friends who had taken him to the Monastery, and they had tracked him down. The Holy Father closed his eyes to block out his torment, but the bulging eyes of Raguel, his personal guard, flooded his mind. The Pope could almost see the dead man's hands stretching out to him in warning. He had insisted on seeing the body of his trusted guard, but now Raguel's face was etched into his mind.

He knew if Friar Watt had not risked his life, that the serpent would have reached his own chambers. Despite their different backgrounds, there had been a quiet respect between Pope Viktor and his guard. Raguel had served the Pope well in his short time of service. He had been a man who honoured the biblical principle of respecting all authority as if God had ordained it. But Raguel did not suffer fools. The Holy Father had seen it in his eyes. He had pressed his guard to share how he served while at the same time he questioned the heart of some of his leaders, and Raguel had left no doubt in his reply.

"I protect the church and not just one man. In time, God

will reveal the hearts of men who are not true. I obey all orders when they are just and true, but in each man there comes a time when he must do what is right and just, even if it will cost him his life. That time for me has not come, but when it does, I pray that I will have the courage to do what is right."

Pope Victor sighed and closed his eyes. He needed his time of prayer to fortify him.

His peace was shattered when the door opened and the Abbot appeared. The voices of the choir from the hall followed the

Abbot filling the prayer room with a melancholic wave that pierced his heart.

"Forgive the intrusion, Holy…"

Pope Viktor raised his hand to silence the man.

The Abbot bowed his head.

"Forgive the intrusion, but there is a visitor for you."

"Here at the Abbey?"

"She has the mark on the robe she wears. The one you told me to look for. She also has a companion."

"Send her in."

"Forgive me, but this is not the place. We sometimes have patrons who also visit this prayer room. With your permission, we have a small, private chapel set aside for visiting dignitaries. The monks know to only open it under my orders and it is in a secluded part of our grounds."

"Thank you for your kindness."

The Abbot shuffled uncomfortably in front of the Pope. He had never imagined even meeting the Holy Father, let alone having a man of this level of authority performing the most basic tasks of service as those the Pope now performed in the Abbey.

The Abbot's hands showed the darkened speckles of years of working the fields in the harsh midday sun. Pope Viktor's lips curved in a nostalgic moment as he remembered his own years of labour. It was good, simple work that satisfied a man's need to build and create.

He waited as the Abbot fumbled with the key. Although the Abbot was younger than the Holy Father, the years had not treated his joints well. Sometimes the ailments of the old visited a younger man. It was a tragedy to have a productive mind stifled by a body that betrayed a man's purpose.

They shared creases around the eyes that hinted of a life of good humour. A lesser man would have been impatient with the Abbot. But Pope Viktor waited for him to accomplish the task. The Abbot would have had countless men under his command who would have obeyed his every word. But his commitment to the Pope's safety had prompted him to complete most tasks himself, although the Pope did wonder if this practice might raise suspicions.

The aged lock released its grip, and the Abbot pushed the right-hand side of the double doors open. Although the man's joints protested, the strength of his muscles had not given in to his ailments.

To the Pope's surprise, the two women that the Abbot had spoken of were already there and he saw that they had laid out fresh fruit, bread, and cheese for the meeting. Both women wore cloaks with a hood that concealed their faces.

The Abbot reached into a leather pouch secured around his waist and drew out the Pope's ring. The Pope responded by stretching out his hand, and the Abbot placed the ring on his superior's finger and kissed the Ring of the Fisherman, so named after Saint Peter.

"Thank you. How will I let you know when we have concluded our meeting?"

"Outside the door is a small bell. Ring the bell three times, and I will know."

The Abbot looked at the two women and back at the Holy Father as he retreated, closing the door behind him.

"You may show yourselves."

Each woman lifted the hood away from her face. The Pope's eyes widened in surprise.

"You are the vision of Queen Isabella, my child." The Pope's eyes glistened with emotion.

"You knew my mother…" Lady Christine gulped and then, remembering the protocol, she approached and kissed the Pope's ring and motioned for Nadine to do the same.

The Pope had never seen eyes quite like those of the younger woman. He wondered if she was even aware of the effect she could have on men.

He watched her awkwardness at the protocol. There was a passion in her that screamed in protest at having to bow to any man, but her compliance came from her obvious respect for the Princess.

"I was at your mother's wedding," he said.

"May I present to you Nadine, the Last of the Silver Wing Whisperers?" Lady Christine stood back and gestured with an open hand.

"This is the young woman that Friar Watt has told me of. Rise my child, so that I may look at you."

Nadine held his gaze. He sensed in her the defiance of a youth who would not bend to authority for authority's sake. He sighed at her discomfort and gestured for the women to be seated.

"The Abbott has prepared refreshments for us," he said, as he broke the bread and passed it to the two women. "Why have you sought me out?"

"I have come to confess and ask for your blessing," said Lady Christine.

"There are many who would take your confession. Why me?"

"Only you can legitimize my claim for the throne and absolve me of my vows to the Northern King."

"I see. I must warn you, I am in exile, and the Cardinal

plots against me. One could barely call me a Kingmaker at this point."

"Yes, but we have some common ground, Holy Father."

"In what way?"

"Should a vote give power to the Cardinal while you are still alive, he would be the illegitimate ruler of the church. In my case, King Radolf has claimed my throne and I am the only living heir." Lady Christine waited for her words to take effect.

Pope Victor leaned forward and spread out his fingers on the table. He looked directly at Lady Christine as he spoke. "Let me be clear… you would still require a coronation and that would be risky at this time. I have no idea who I can trust, and I fail to see how I can help you.

"For now, I require only your blessing and a document sealed with your ring, legitimizing my claim. In exchange, we would offer you protection."

"From what I hear, it is you who needs protection from King Radolf. He trains his army with warriors from across our borders. And his numbers far outweigh yours."

Nadine's jaw stiffened at the diplomacy, and she gripped her fingers fiercely in an effort to keep still.

"We have something that King Radolf does not," said Lady Christine.

"And what is that?"

"We have Nadine."

"Your Whisperer…."

The Pope looked at Nadine and back at Lady Christine.

"I don't think you know what you are saying. Neither Dragons nor their Whisperers can be a Pope's protector."

"Do you think less of me because I am a Whisperer?" asked Nadine.

"I am saying that the nobles will never accept such a plan."

Nadine stared at the Pope in disbelief.

"And yet, the nobles support the Cardinal, who supports King Radolf, who is planning to use dragons to gain ultimate power." Lady Christine placed her hand on Nadine's. Her soft smile subdued the young Whisperer.

"Holy Father, I ask that you provide Nadine with protection. The corrupt have always used their power to manipulate the weak and to eliminate those who would oppose them. As you are aware, it was a false accusation against the King's mother that turned him into the man he is today. I fear that if the King fails in his plan, he will harm Nadine. Already the Cardinal plots against her. Now that you have been through the tunnels and have seen that the dragons do not mean to harm mankind, I hope that you will protect her. If you legitimize my claim to the throne, and we take back my Kingdom, we will offer you safe passage throughout our Kingdom and protect your authority as Pope."

Pope Viktor clasped his hands together and looked solemnly at Lady Christine. He was silent for several moments. The Holy Father knew of the legends of these beasts of the skies and the superstition and fear that coloured the villagers' tales of them. But he also knew what it was like to be misunderstood and attacked because he was different.

"I cannot offer an endorsement if it merely protects my life. I must do what I see as just and true. Lady Christine, you will have my letter confirming you to be the legitimate heir to the throne. But I do not know enough of this Whisperer of yours to offer her the protection she seeks. However, I will make another time to interview her myself to determine if she is deserving of that protection."

Nadine's face clouded with anger. Lady Christine gripped Nadine's wrist under the table.

"But it is not outright no, either? Is it?" asked Lady Christine.

"Certainly not! It is a deferred decision until I can learn more about her character. From what I hear from the Friar,

Nadine has several excellent qualities. But for such a bold claim on my behalf, I need to be sure. The fruits of the spirit take time to reveal themselves."

Lady Christine rose and lowered her head as a sign of respect. She retrieved a roll of parchment, quill, and ink from her bag and placed it on the table together with a stick of wax.

"You have come prepared, I see."

"My father always used to say that there is no time like the present," said Lady Christine as she rolled out the parchment and handed him the quill.

The Pope reached for the quill and penned the letter of legitimacy. By the time the ink had dried, Lady Christine had already heated the wax for the seal.

Pope Viktor opened the door and looked over the grassy plain between the chapel and the Abbey's principal building. Lady Christine and Nadine slipped out of the chapel towards the forest side before anyone could spot them. Once they were out of sight, he rang the bell three times. The Abbot hurried into the room.

"Your guests left just in time. We have an unscheduled visit from the newly appointed Bishop, so it is best I get you out of the chapel and with the monks in the fields."

"The new bishop. Is that Bishop Stephen?"

"Why yes, have you met him?"

"Yes. Yes, I have."

"Then we don't have a moment to lose, because that is his carriage, right over there."

C

"Lady Christine, I must return to the excavation as soon as possible. Do you think the team will be ready?" asked Nadine.

"They were planning to leave at the same time as we left for the Abbey. Captain Julian does not have it in him to procrastinate. By the time you return, the team will be in place and you can begin with the excavation."

"That is good news."

"You mentioned that you still need to visit the Lords. Do I need to be with you for that?"

"Absolutely. But that can wait for now. Beatrice has sent out the spies to gain intelligence, and Captain Hucchon and Lord Jefferson are preparing for the journey. I do not want to meet with the Lords until I am confident enough to answer any questions they may have. I will feel a lot better when you locate the eggs and get them far away from King Radolf. It may dilute our resources for a while, but it is a risk we must take. I will call for you as soon as I feel that I need you."

"Thank you. I will summon Muquin to take me to the site and send news as soon as we have found something."

TWENTY-TWO

Awakening

Friar Watt rubbed the back of his neck. He knew Father Stephen, or should he say, Bishop Stephen, was already conducting services at the Cathedral. There was little he could do to save the flock from the deceit, but he hoped that Nadine and Lady Christine's visit to Pope Viktor would bear fruit in their quest to purge the land of King Radolf.

But now, here he was, stuck in the role of nursemaid to the Copper Fire Dragon Whisperer, while Elizabeth supervised the excavation. There were just too many parts in this battle with the King. He knew the strategies of battle, but this was far more complex than that. There was the battle, the missing eggs and the threat against Nadine, and now he also had to deal with delusional, jealous ramblings of a man who was a constant thorn in his side.

He looked at the sun's position in the sky, eager for the change of shift. Even with his battle experience, he had to admit that he was not up for the fight that would surely erupt if the

Dragon Whisperer awoke while he was on duty. Friar Watt placed his hand on the Whisperer's forehead. It felt cool to the touch, and his inspection of the wound had equally pleasing results.

He turned and stirred the broth he had prepared. These days there was little time for quiet hours of prayer and so he had learned the art of praying during his work.

"Loving God, I pray you will comfort me in my suffering, lend skill to my hands, and bless the means used for my care of others. Give me such confidence in the power of your grace, that even when I am afraid, I may put my complete trust in you; through our Saviour Jesus Christ. Amen."

He heard a quiet moan from the Whisperer. Friar Watt raised his eyes to the heavens.

"Really Lord, why? Why me?" But he turned and scooped some broth into a bowl and placed it on the table with a hunk of softened bread.

He watched the Whisperer's chest heave as his breathing changed and his brow furrowed. Friar Watt eased his hand under the Whisperer's head.

"Elizabeth…" the Whisperer slurred as the Friar lifted his head to help ease him into a seated position. He placed the older man's feet on the ground. Pulling the Whisperer's arm over his shoulder, the Friar helped him up from the bed. He watched the Whisperer struggle to focus on the objects in the room.

"Eliz…" The Whisperer turned his head toward Friar Watt.

"What are you... Let go of me." Friar Watt tried to grab hold of the Whisperer, but stumbled back when his adversary pushed him with an unexpectedly powerful force for a man who has only recently wrestled against death. The Whisperer fell back, hitting his head against the table edge. Friar Watt gritted his teeth.

"Will you quit acting like such a scoundrel? I have little tolerance for your jealousy. If you were not half dead already,

I would beat you over the head with my staff," warned the Friar as he lifted the Whisperer again.

"Now sit here and eat your broth, so that you may build your stamina, if not your strength." The Copper Fire Dragon Whisperer snorted. in response, then lifted the spoon and sniffed the contents of the bowl. After a few mouthfuls, he dipped the bread into the broth and after devouring it, he pushed the bowl towards the Friar.

"I will have some more."

"I fail to see what Elizabeth sees in you," the Friar muttered as he scooped more broth into the bowl.

"Where is she?"

"She is at the excavation. We have taken turns to watch over you and I had the great misfortune of being here to see what kind of man you are like when you wake up. How did your previous wife ever manage?"

"How dare you speak of my late wife?" The Whisperer pointed his spoon at the Friar.

Friar Watt grabbed the spoon from his crotchety companion's grasp.

"I have filled a basin with some hot water. I suggest you bathe now before the sun lowers, as

Elizabeth shall return soon. I would offer to help you undress, but it may be dangerous to my health." The Whisperer narrowed his eyes but said nothing more, as he watched the Friar stride out of the cave and toward the lake.

"That rogue of a man, will be my undoing," muttered the Friar under his breath. "I hope you know what you are doing, Lord."

He observed the lake's glassy surface light up with the speckles of gold and orange as the sun bowed to kiss the earth good night. It was a breath-taking view and on days like this he could almost imagine God's hand tracing a brush over a pallet of colours and splashing them across the sky. He sighed as the silhouette of a dragon skimmed the water's surface, bringing Elizabeth back for the evening shift. She was a vision as she stepped off the dragon and reached for Friar Watt's hand. He squeezed her fingers lightly and smiled at her.

"How does he fare?" she asked.

"He is awake and as grumpy as ever." The Friar saw her eyes brighten with tears of gratitude.

"He is bathing now. Let's give him some more time." She nodded and looked towards the cave.

"How has your day been?" asked Friar Watt.

"Good. I believe we are very close. I keep finding fragments of some of the sacred herb plants."

The Whisperer stood at the cave's entrance watching them talk. His eyes darkened and thought of his words he spoke when his life seemed to be fleeing from him. "You have my heart." But it appeared Elizabeth did not feel the same way.

"He is watching us," said Friar Watt. "Go to him." Elizabeth nodded and walked to the cave.

"It is good to see you are up and well, at last. You had us worried for a while."

"Well, you have done your duty and now you can get on with your life." The remark cut deeper than one of her healer's blades, and she swallowed hard as she fought back the tears.

"I see you have eaten already. That is good," she said, moving the bowls from the table, grateful for the opportunity to turn her face away from him. "Now, I would like to inspect the wound."

"That won't be necessary."

"Yes, it will. I have given the men strict instructions that are not to let you on the site until I am satisfied that you being there will not rupture this wound."

"Very well," he replied, climbing onto the table. She lifted the robe and traced her fingers over the wound. The incision marks from the stitches had lost the angry red of a few days ago and the skin felt warm but not hot. Her hand trembled, and the Whisperer pushed it away and moved from the table.

"You have seen the wound. Now you may leave."

"I will stay at the hut tonight and will check on you in the morning. If I am satisfied, I will let you go back to the site. Good night."

The Dragon Whisperer felt his chest tighten, but could not draw his gaze away from the sway of her hips as she walked towards the hut.

TWENTY-THREE

Excavation

Elizabeth knew that they could no longer delay their return to the site, so she reluctantly agreed to let the Whisperer travel from Holly Hill Cave to the Ancient's retreat. With the Whisperer now settled on Zairdenth's back, Nadine brought a stool to help Elizabeth to climb up without needing to put pressure on The Copper Fire Dragon Whisperer, but the Medicine Woman touched his hand as she hoisted herself up, more out of sensitivity than need. She hoped that they would find the egg soon, so she could get back to her rooms to deal with wounds she could treat. A wounded soul was the Friar's specialty, but the Whisperer would not be a willing patient.

Elizabeth instinctively leaned back towards the Dragon Whisperer to escape the chill of the air. She gasped as the sun's first rays splashed across the morning sky and she could sense his heart beat faster as Zairdenth accelerated. The Whisperer's arm jerked as he felt her body press against his and for a moment her back stiffened, but he wrapped his arms around her waist and breathed in her scent as they soared above the trees.

The journey seemed to end too soon, and Elizabeth felt

him retreat into his own world again as the Ancient's Retreat came back into view. She saw that Captain Julian's team had already arrived, and she was pleased that she would have the company of a good humoured man for a while. Elizabeth felt the distance between her and the Whisperer grow as the dragon slowed his flight for descent. The Medicine Woman gritted her teeth as she felt the prickle of tears betray her feelings, but she looked ahead and lifted her chin as Captain Julian approached to help her off the dragon.

She could see that Captain Julian's team had already laid out the gear. She inspected the tools while she waited for the others to arrive. He had brought shovels, poles, chisels, and brushes.

"Lady Christine sent one of her kitchen hands as well, to prepare meals for the team, and the men will camp overnight so that we can resume work early in the morning," explained Captain Julian.

"And the mules?" she asked.

"To move the excess dirt away from the site. We do not want the next patrol to raise the alarm."

"Very impressive." A voice without a source startled Elizabeth.

Her heart skipped a beat.

"Really? Do you have to speak while you still have the cloak on?" asked Elizabeth.

"Sorry," grinned the Friar, removing the cloak, "But you should have seen your face."

"Well, are you going to stand around all day talking or work?" grumbled the Dragon Whisperer. The Friar did not answer, though his eyes twinkled with amusement at Elizabeth's disgruntled response.

The Friar explained to the men what their roles were as they dug around the Myrrh tree. The Dragon Whisperer relented to a time of rest in the shade. Elizabeth had placed a cushion under his foot to elevate his leg. She had added a sedative to his drink without his knowledge and after a few minutes, he had nodded off, which left the team to work unhindered.

It did not take long for them to clear a large section around the base of the tree. They kept the grass intact as instructed, and soon several piles of sods surrounded the excavation. After a number of trips, the mules had cleared away the soil. Captain Julian gave the men strict instructions to clear up as soon as they created debris. He did not want an unscheduled patrol to find them scrambling to clean up. It slowed the work, but minimised their risk of being discovered. To the outside world, they appeared to be a group of travellers setting up camp for the night.

They worked around the roots, taking care not to damage the major ones, but several of the men complained about the thorns. Elizabeth tried to ignore their comments about using the tree for firewood.

"We should have brought falconer's gloves," remarked Friar Watt, as he reapplied the bandages to Elizabeth's fingers. You could take a break from this pace." But the Medicine Woman shook her head.

"We are so close, I have to keep going."

Nadine's back ached from the long hours of bending over and removing soil from around the tree's roots. She got up and arched her spine. As she twisted her neck to relieve her aching shoulders, she closed her eyes and lost balance momentarily, stumbling on a stone. Then she felt the ground give way beneath her and she plunged downwards through the earth.

Friar Watt and Elizabeth rushed over to the spot where they had last seen her standing.

"Nadine! Can you hear me?" Friar Watt peered down the hole.

"Yes, but it is so dark here," came her muffled reply.

"Are you hurt? How far did you fall?"

"Not far. I am not injured. But I could do with some light - it's almost pitch dark down here."

"Captain Julian!" called the Friar, "We need a torch and some rope."

Nadine's fall had opened a passage large enough for two adult men to squeeze through side by side.

"Perhaps if we go down together, secured at the chest, one of us could hold the torch and the other the rope," suggested Captain Julian. He had his men bind them together, with ropes tied around their waists and chests. Captain Julian held the torch, and the Friar held tightly onto the rope while the men slowly lowered them into the hole.

The entrance was surprisingly shallow and the Friar thankfully estimated that Nadine would probably have only a few bruises.

The collapsed earth had allowed some light into the cave, and now Captain Julian's torch illuminated the gloom. As their eyes adjusted, they found Nadine standing near a mound of overgrown plants that reached up to the very top of the cave.

"The sacred herbs… they are all here." The Friar marvelled at the column of greenery in front of him. "I think we could use more light."

"Well, if you care to untie these ropes, I can hand you the torch and get more help?" prompted Captain Julian.

"Right… sorry." The Friar fumbled with the torch. "Nadine, a bit of help, please. Nadine took her blade from the harness.

"No, don't cut the ropes! We will need them," said Captain Julian, handing her the torch. "Hold this." He detached himself from the Friar, then tugged on the lead rope, and was hauled back up to ground level. He spoke to Elizabeth, barely able to contain his excitement.

"Elizabeth, we have found the site. You are going to want to see this. And I suggest you bring something to store these herbs in. Look - there are so many that in a few days you could surely start a business as a herb merchant." Captain Julian gave her a handful of herbs he had grabbed from the column inside the cave.

"Incredible..." Elizabeth gazed at the bundle of herbs in astonishment.

"I never dreamed I would see some of these sacred herbs again after the Ancient Gardens were destroyed."

"I thought so. Here, you go first." He handed her the rope. "I will wake the Whisperer. We have to get a pulley system to remove the dirt from the site. And there is also a lot of plant life that will need to be moved."

"Yes, this would be a good time to wake the Dragon Whisperer. We could really do with his knowledge now."

TWENTY-FOUR

The Find

The Dragon Whisperer eased down the hole and made his way to the column of plants.

"This is where she would have slipped into eternal sleep. You see how the plants grow up from this point and the surrounding area has very little plant life? Her body is returning the gift of life. She may have died to save the eggs, but her death gives life to others."

He walked to the side of the column of herbs. It was wider down the middle and tapered near the end of the cave.

"I think this smaller section here is where the dragon's tail was. Elizabeth, salvage what you can from the sacred plants. We must harvest the seeds to rebuild the silos, although we will require the cold fire of the Emerald Forest Dragons to stop the seeds from germinating. Let's hope that we find the egg before the weather warms too much. A hatchling must first learn to control its fire before it can breathe the cold fire."

Elizabeth asked for one of Captain Julian's men to work alongside her, packing each of the plants she harvested into its own container. Each precious sample had to be carefully sealed - they could not risk light and air from above reacting with the herbs to cause their seeds to germinate. For now, they gathered the sacred herbs and would keep them safe until they had time to sift through them in detail.

The Friar joined the clearing team. They had to work very carefully and progress was slower than they had hoped, but eventually, the bones of the dragon began to emerge as they brushed away the layers of plants and soil.

Once Elizabeth felt confident that they had harvested and catalogued all they could, she joined the others in the excavation of the dragon bones.

Their quiet concentration was broken by her gasp.

"Come and look," she called, "See what I have found." She brushed away more soil. "These look like human hip bones - a woman. "

"A woman? How can you tell?" asked Nadine, leaning over to peer at the bones.

Do you see this joint?" asked Elizabeth. "This is where the two front bones near the male or female parts lie. In a woman these bones form a much wider triangle than in a man. A man's bones form an angled join, but for a woman to bear a child, this area must be wide. The full area between the top of the legs is much deeper and wider than in a man."

The team kept scraping and gently brushing away more and more of the soil around their find. Finally, the full form of the bones was visible..

"Look, she is lying right next to the dragon here..."

"Indeed, she is," said the Whisperer as he leaned in. "A female dragon, curled around the human female. I think they died comforting each other."

"How can you tell that?" asked Nadine.

"The human female's hand bone is extended towards the dragon's abdomen. This could mean one of two things. Either the dragon was injured, or she was with egg."

"The woman was injured. You see this clean break through the rib? Probably pierced with an arrow or spear, but the break is low, so there may have been some other injury that caused her death," continued Friar Watt.

"Look here!" cried Elizabeth. "An Ancient's healer's ring - a Life Bearer's ring." The Dragon Whisperer leaned in even closer.

"May I?" The torchlight illuminated the curves of Elizabeth's face, as she nodded and handed it to him.

"Look, Nadine," he said, holding the ring up to the light. "You see this marking?"

"I recognise the mark of a midwife... but not this symbol..."

"She was indeed a midwife. But a high ranking one, allowed to interact with dragons. Possibly a Whisperer's wife. They could have allowed no one else this close to a dragon," said the Dragon Whisperer.

"Over here," called one of the helpers. "Another set of bones."

"What is this hollow in the jawbone?" asked the Friar, moving across and crouching over these new bones.

"It looks like some sort of hole. The jaw is not crushed and has no other breaks. It seems burrowed out..." said Elizabeth. A movement from the ground startled her, and she fell silent. She lifted her hand towards Nadine.

"Move away slowly, Nadine. Everyone, back away from this side." The broken earth from the excavation seemed to come alive, and a stream of yellow bubbled to the surface of the skull.

"Yellow Spike Spiders," shouted the Friar. "Get away now."

Nadine scrambled up the side of the excavation towards the pulley system. The Dragon Whisperer hoisted Elizabeth in a single sweep. They stood panting outside the cave.

"Elizabeth!" screamed Nadine. "There is one on your garment."

"Quietly now - try not to alarm it," said Friar Watt. He

opened his healer's pouch and selected one of the herbs, which he dusted over a twig and ignited with the flame of his torch.

Elizabeth closed her eyes with a shudder as the spider began to crawl up her bodice. But Friar Watt continued his quiet commands, as though completely unmoved.

"Captain Julian, please secure Elizabeth's arms. You must by any means keep her still and prevent her from thrashing out. Nadine, when I call, you are to throw water onto the area straight away." Captain Julian hesitated.

"Just do it," said Elizabeth.

"Everyone, stand back!" instructed the Friar. "Lord, make my aim true and protect Elizabeth."

Then he plunged the burning twig onto Elizabeth's bodice just below the spider. The fabric began to smoulder. Elizabeth cried out as the flame took hold, but Captain Julian held her fast. Excruciating seconds passed while the fabric continued to burn. Nadine's jaw tightened. She tried to look away but could not. Her throat closed as the tears stung her eyes, but she had to remain strong for Elizabeth. A shriek emerged from the spider as it sprang off Elizabeth's bodice, its body bursting in the air and splattering yellow venom in all directions.

"Now," cried the Friar.

Nadine threw the water at Elizabeth, dousing the flames.

"Have you lost your mind?" cried Nadine as she tried to cover the areas where the dress had burned away.

"Put her over there on that soft patch of grass so that I may inspect the wounds," instructed the Friar, without missing a beat.

The Dragon Whisperer's hands were bunched into fists.

"Can you not see that she is exposed? Get away from her," he seethed. "I cannot leave a burn untreated. I have to see if the spider has pierced her skin, and besides, there is the risk of infection," retorted the Friar.

Elizabeth's face had drained of colour. Pain washed over

her. Nadine knelt next to her and reached for her hand. The Medicine Woman smiled weakly and squeezed Nadine's hand in return.

Friar Watt worked for a few minutes and then sat back on his heels.

"I don't think it pierced the skin," he said. "We will have to give you herbs for pain while the burn heals. It is deep, but small, so I won't be saying any final passage prayers."

The Friar smiled and turned to find a snarling Dragon Whisperer glaring at him. "And you can be thankful for that indeed," he growled.

"We must burn the nest now, to prevent further attacks," said the Friar, pushing past the Whisperer, "and to allow us to continue the excavation safely."

"What are those hideous creatures?" asked Nadine.

"That, Nadine, was a Yellow Spike Spider. They are highly venomous. Once the venom immobilizes the victim, the spider's spike will burrow into the site of the wound, drilling a cavity into the closest bone. It then lays eggs and the young feed off the flesh of the victim. Sometimes the victim remains alive for days, waiting for the tiny spiders to hatch and begin feeding.

The herb I used disturbs them momentarily. It gives us only a few seconds and then the heat of the flames causes them to release their grip on whatever they are holding onto. They can jump far distances. So, when you thought it was flying, it was really the spider jumping away from the heat of the flames. The heat ruptures the membranes around its body. That is why it exploded. But even the flying venom can cause severe damage if it lands anywhere soft - like eyes, mouth, nose or an open cut. If we are to continue our work on this site, we must find the nest and burn it." Nadine nodded, but gave an inward shudder, hearing just how close they had been to grave danger yet again.

Friar Watt mixed a powerful blend of herbs, which sent

Elizabeth into the abyss of sleep. He thought back to the time when Elizabeth had saved him from certain death when she lanced and disinfected his wound. He knew that she would have done the same in this situation, but still he did not enjoy having to administer the burns. In time, he felt the Dragon Whisperer would understand. But for now, he would have to absorb the old man's anger. Having a choice between the painful burn and death, the choice was obvious, but difficult. No man can endure to witness the pain of a woman he loves.

The Friar had often prayed that the Dragon Whisperer would find a way to admit his feelings for Elizabeth. It was obvious to everyone that she would return his feelings. But for now, they circled warily around each other, never stepping fully into one another's emotional space.

Yakhal had volunteered to burn the spider's nest; what young dragon could resist a chance to practice fire-breathing? After a few hours, the team felt safe to begin their search again.

Elizabeth woke and insisted that she continue to be part of the team, despite her burn. The others agreed only if she promised to take it slowly and rest often.

They worked until they had uncovered most of the bones. But where was the egg? A small shard of a thorny scale was found among the bones, but the actual egg had not yet been unearthed.

"I think I understand how this dragon died," said the Dragon Whisperer, after much thought.

"What do you mean?" Nadine stared at the bones as a sense of sadness settled in her spirit. Her eyes glistened as she gently ran her fingers over the dragon bones.

"This shard is from a protective casing for an egg. Females usually pass their eggs while the casing is soft, and then the egg would harden on the outside. But if a female was not able to pass her egg early enough, it would harden inside her. That means that when the egg came out, it would rupture the internal organs as it passed through her. I believe that this piece of shell broke off as the egg was being passed through the oviduct."

"These bones over here are from a human warrior. Based on what is left of the armour, this was a warrior from one of the ancient warlords who rose against dragons. It is possible that she was pursuing the dragon, and that all three of them died here. From the chin bone I can see that it was indeed a yellow spike spider that killed this warrior." He walked slowly around the side of the excavation.

"But the egg? The midwife would certainly have concealed the egg. It must be somewhere on this site, but it may be further away from the body. So we must keep digging around a wider area," instructed the Dragon Whisperer.

"We must find it before nightfall," panted Elizabeth, trying to breathe through her pain using the old technique that midwives taught new mothers. She had tried to stretch out the time before taking more herbs for pain - she felt that they dulled her senses, but now she was almost at the end of her endurance.

"Do not be discouraged," said the Dragon Whisperer, touching her back only for a moment. She wished for just this once he could hold her, and she closed her eyes as he moved his hand away. Nadine and Friar Watt exchanged a glance.

"It will be close by, Elizabeth." The Dragon Whisperer's tone softened. But still, he could not bring himself to hold her.

"With this kind of injury, the dragon would not be able to move much. Her caregiver would have moved the egg for her. Eggs are heavy, so the injured caregiver would not have been able to move it very far. She would have hidden it out of sight of the cave's entrance. We need to look further away from the body, but not too far."

Elizabeth and the Friar split up the team, moving them in different directions.

"We must hurry, we lost half a day because of the spiders," said Friar Watt.

They worked from dawn to dusk.

Friar Watt was a mess. His head felt as if he had burrowed into a molehill and his skin itched. He had to sit down for a while. In the torchlight he could see a cluster of stones he thought the team had moved to one side. "Ah, a place to sit for a moment," he smiled. As he eased his aching body down, something sharp pierced his skin.

"Ouch," he cried. The Friar put out his hand and felt around the rock in the center of the pile. Feeling more sharp barbs, he held the torch closer, and saw a soft green hue in the light.

"Elizabeth! We found it, we found it," he called out.

"What? Move aside, Friar," the Dragon Whisperer answered gruffly, and pushed the Friar aside to get the egg. He ran his hands over its surface.

Elizabeth and Nadine stared in amazement. The tiny barbs that looked very much like rose thorns snagged the Dragon Whisperer's skin. There was a definite green shimmer. He placed his open hand over the egg and felt the energy that lay beneath the shell.

"It is an Emerald Forest Dragon egg, isn't it?" asked Nadine. She felt a well of protectiveness build inside her, as she did when her brother Mikael fell and scraped his knee.

"Is it alive?" she whispered.

"There is life inside it," nodded the Dragon Whisperer. "Here, place your hand just above the egg and close your eyes. Do you feel anything?"

"I feel a tingling… almost as if I had fallen asleep on my arm and my sensation had just returned… and... ouch!" Nadine pulled her arm away.

"What is it, Nadine?" Elizabeth frowned as she inspected Nadine's arm.

"It feels like tiny thorns stabbing me all over my forearm."

"I don't see anything." Elizabeth ran her fingers over Nadine's skin.

"She is not injured," explained the Dragon Whisperer. "It is a life-force surge. The hatchling inside the egg feels a Mother Dragon Whisperer's presence. Nadine has broken the dormancy cycle. We must move the egg to a safer place quickly."

"But how? It is covered with spikes," asked Nadine as she rubbed her arm. She did not want to tell the Whisperer how afraid she was, but Elizabeth recognised the look. New mothers often looked this way when the first pains of childbirth tore through their young bodies. She squeezed Nadine's hand, but she had no idea how to prepare her.

"We will need a lot of cloth to wrap the egg and somehow build a crate around it," replied the Whisperer. He looked intensely at Nadine for a moment, but she looked away. Now was not the time to have her wretched emotions cascading all over the place, beckoning to their enemies.

"I only have bandages," said Elizabeth, stepping in front of Nadine. Her eyes flashed a warning to the Dragon Whisperer not to chastise his student now.

"We will require more than that. Those barbs are very sharp. There must be some other way to lift it," said the Friar.

"Perhaps if we could fashion a harness, perhaps a sled, or a crate and then hoist it with the pulley system," suggested Nadine, still avoiding the Dragon Whisperer's stare..

"That might work..." The Friar looked hard at the egg, trying to organize his thoughts.

"No crate building," warned Captain Julian. "This area is swarming with King Radolf's men. A patrol passed this way around noon, reported by one of my men out gathering firewood. We can't have the men hewing wood and cutting and hammering. It will raise suspicion."

"Then what do you suggest?" asked Nadine. "We can't just carry it out. Those thorns are razor sharp."

"Nadine, your first idea is brilliant," exclaimed the Friar. "A harness or a sled. In the war we moved our injured with harnesses and sleds made from cowhide and sticks, secured with rope or vines. Two layers of cowhide will offer enough protection from the thorns and cowhide won't raise suspicion."

"I have three with my camp supervisor. How many do you think you will need?" asked Captain Julian.

"About four per egg. That is, if there is more than one egg," replied Nadine. The Dragon Whisperer looked impressed, and Nadine's eyes flashed with pride as her crooked smile spread over her face.

"What? Did you think that I had no skills before my apprenticeship? How do you think I hauled all my equipment towards Forever Gone Lake when I started my quest? My father taught me how to make sleds and even basic shelters using cowhide, sticks and vines." Captain Julian bowed to Nadine.

"Cowhides, you shall have, my Lady," he grinned. "I will send one of my men straight away."

Nadine rolled her eyes and shook her head. The Dragon Whisper gave his usual grunt, but even he could not dampen Nadine's spirits. After the men arrived with the extra cowhides, Nadine and Friar Watt began to show two of the team how to cut holes into the cowhide to thread the vines through to secure the pieces together. The Dragon Whisperer checked the tension of the vines and the pull against the cuts in the cowhide several times.

"I think we are done," announced Nadine after comparing the measurements of the hide to the egg with a piece of vine.

"Roll the egg onto the hide, with your boot," instructed the Dragon Whisperer, as he sat to rest his leg. "We have to get it to Holly Hill Cave.

"My men will take it and stand guard until you return."

"I will not have your men rummaging through my belongings..."

"They are well trained, I assure you..." Captain Julian felt his usual good humour draining from him.

Elizabeth stepped towards Captain Julian.

"What the Dragon Whisperer is trying to say is that he is "The Keeper of Secrets" and protocol dictates that no one is permitted unaccompanied into the cave."

"What about our training lodgings? There are no secrets there... except for the smuggler's hatch I built under the flooring," added Friar Watt with a grin.

"An excellent place to hide an egg." Captain Julian slapped the Friar on the back. "Now let's get it out of here," he said, tugging on the rope to signal the men to pull the harness to the surface.

TWENTY-FIVE

Stronger Together

"This is an Emerald Forest Dragon egg. As a guardian, she would surely have had other eggs with her?" questioned Nadine.

"There must be something more here." Muquin moved as she sniffed the ground, pausing now and then with a raised claw.

"I feel it. I can feel its energy. A Silver Wing egg! It is close by. She would have not hidden the two eggs together, so that if someone were to find this egg, they might feel that it is the only one.

Look... Near the site where the Yellow Spike Spiders nested. The Guardian must have lined the cave opening with spiders, knowing that whoever entered this cave would be exposed to them. And if she knew she was dying from her battle wounds, she would have been willing to risk it. She may have hidden it close to the entrance of the cave. Here, dig here."

As they dug, a shiny silvery light appeared, and Muquin sighed as the dirt fell away from the egg.

"Another hatching! Oh, my… There is another of our kind."

Muquin blew away the dirt. This egg had no thorny spikes. It was satiny to the touch and had a sponginess on it. "This egg with the silver hue to it. It is one of us…" Muquin passed her claws over the egg and closed her eyes.

"It lives," she breathed. "Nadine, it lives. We have another of our kind. The line of Megadeus will continue." Muquin looked towards the heavens. She could almost feel her mate smile as she bowed her head in the forehead, greeting to the memory of her mate.

"My love. I hope it is female. Yakhal may have a mate of his own and that he may grow to have love, as I have known it," said Muquin, resting her head against the egg.

"Nadine, the time is close, but it is so for the other egg, too," urged the Dragon Whisperer, breaking the magic of the moment with practicality. He eased himself onto the stone as the ache in his leg throbbed in protest to the work.

"Close? Close to hatching? What do we do now? Can we hatch them in the same location?"

"We will have to separate. Muquin and Yakhal will take the Silver Wing egg," explained the Dragon Whisperer, wincing for a moment. Elizabeth moved to help him, but he held up his hand to stop her. "I need only to rest for a bit."

"And the Emerald Forest Dragon egg?" asked Nadine.

"The eggs cannot be together. Nadine, you must hatch the egg yourself."

"Why me? What do I know about hatching eggs?" asked Nadine. "You never included that in your training."

"You are the highest ranking Dragon Whisperer. It must be you. You represent the mother figure. Although you have not married and have not had children, that does not matter. The Life Force in you will stir the egg to hatch. But I must ask for one thing - and that is, that you summon Nathan, to be with you in this," said the Whisperer.

"Nathan? I thought I made it clear that I will never marry."

"What you want right now, is of little consequence. What is important is that this egg is hatched successfully. That requires two parties, male and female. While I know that you do not want to marry, we need the life force that will come from you and Nathan together."

"But he is not my husband."

"I am not asking you to mate. I am asking you to help protect this dragon. When the egg hatches, you would need to stay with the hatchling, while Nathan goes out to do the first hunt."

"The Hatchling must be fed a first meal of live prey. In this case, it must be fish. This hatchling comes from a line of herbivore dragons. The only time they eat any animal food is when they hatch.

There are certain herbs that you must take, which are now growing in abundance in this area because of the sacred pouch. You will place them according to the instructions in the scroll. Once the egg hatches, you must remove any evidence that you were there."

"How will I know when it is ready to hatch?"

"You will feel it. We will keep the egg at Holly Hill Cave until the time is close. And I will prepare you for the hatching."

"Why can't it be Muquin?" She looked pleadingly at Elizabeth.

"It will be alright Nadine," said the Medicine Woman reaching out for her hand. "All new mothers have fear. Although this is a hatchling and you have had no training, your inner strength along with Muquin and the Dragon Whisperer's instructions will equip you for the task."

The Dragon Whisperer frowned at the interruption.

"Nadine, protocol for post-war hatching is that the eggs must be hatched in different locations. Those locations must remain secret to keep everyone safe. Until both eggs are hatched, you and Muquin will have to sever your bond."

"Muquin? No, I couldn't do that," protested Nadine.

Muquin felt Nadine's pain. To be without a sister for a first hatching was a sorrow she knew too well. She had no desire to abandon Nadine, but there were no other sisters to help and so Nadine would have to endure what would come without a dragon sister by her side.

"And if we find other eggs? Am I going to hatch all of them?"

"What is this?" asked the Friar, picking up a small egg-shaped stone covered with intricate carving.

"Give me that," demanded the Dragon Whisperer, grabbing the stone from the Friar. "I haven't seen one of these for a very long time." He turned it over carefully in his dusty old hands.

"It is a messenger pod." He reached into his garment and produced a small chain with a gold amulet. The end of the amulet had a claw with several notches in it. The others watched in amazement as the Dragon Whisperer inserted the claw and a clicking sound came from the pod. The top of the stone opened, revealing a message carved inside the stone. The Dragon Whisperer squinted inside. "Nadine, the text I taught you to read. Do you remember the symbols?"

"I think so…"

"Then come, read what it says inside the stone egg." Nadine took the stone and peered at the tiny etchings inside.

"This dragon.. I can't quite make out the name... Her... I think this may be the symbol for mate…" she showed the Dragon Whisperer the symbol.

"Yes, you, that is correct… move along."

"The dragon's mate took a Crystal Water Dragon egg and a Copper Fire Dragon Egg and was meant to fly across the warpath to hide them... I am sorry, I do not know what all these other carvings mean." She handed the stone back to the Dragon Whisperer.

"Across the warpath... Where would that be?" asked Friar Watt.

"I do not know, but there is this," said the Whisperer as he drew a tiny scroll that was curled inside an inner wall of the stone egg. He laid the parchment onto the cleared rock.

"This scroll says that there is a Book of Secrets that has the clues for the routes the Guardians would have taken to secure the eggs."

The Copper Fire Whisperer sighed.

"What is wrong?" asked Elizabeth.

"Over 80 moon cycles ago, there was another great sickness. A group of fanatics believed that Emerald Forest Dragon Whisperers' herbs were used for Witchcraft potions. They accused them of causing the great sickness and slaughtered a small surviving group of Emerald Forest Dragon Hatchlings and their Whisperer Guardians. They burned the forest and the scrolls of the Guardians were destroyed. If we are to stop the war, we must hatch these two eggs safely and then go and find the remaining eggs. And we must do it before King Radolf does."

In the Northern Kingdom, King Radolf had plans of his own. It was time for his secret weapon to enter the game.

TWENTY-SIX

New Beginnings

Meira's hand went limp in the clutch of her guardian's hand as they walked through the village towards the merchants' quarter. Everything was new. She had one moment been an indentured servant and the next she was being fitted for dresses like those the nobles wore.

Her parents had never taught her to read or write. But the work master had said that a nobleman had taken pity on her and that her life was about to change.

She was shorter than the other girls of her age. The sparse rations had stunted her growth.

When she arrived at the tailor's house, there had been a meaty broth with bread waiting for her, but she struggled to ingest it.

"Never have I fitted such a wreck of a girl," announced the tailor as he lifted her arms and roughly moved her around. "She smells awful!" he added. "Where did you find her?"

He had summoned a seamstress. "Sarah, get this foul child cleaned up at once. I won't have her stench contaminating my textiles."

"Very well," her guardian had agreed. "Let your seamstress bathe her, while you and I discuss what she will require to fit into a noble life. And best you do not deceive me. I know how to spot a liar and a swindler. I have much experience in that regard."

The tailor eyed the coin pouch his new patron carried. "I have never cheated anyone," he griped.

"That remains to be seen," sneered the guardian.

The tailor thrust Meira into the back room, where the seamstress was to wash her soot covered body. The child's ribs had shown painfully through her skin, and Sarah's eyes welled up as she rubbed the scaly patches on Meira's body. Little skin infections decorated Meira's limbs, where her filthy fingernails had scratched the parasite's bites into raw, bloodied patches. The girl had stared listlessly into the distance as the seamstress scrubbed and scraped. This was not a bathing room, and the seamstress fretted at the rise of goosebumps on the shivering girl's body. The tailor did not permit fires in his rooms for fear of losing his stock of fine fabrics. She tried to work quickly, but the layers of grime seemed relentless in their hold on Meira.

Sarah called for a chambermaid to bring her a bed-warmer filled with hot coals from a neighbour, a privilege given to only the wealthiest customers who dressed in the tailor's rooms. At the very least, she thought, the girl should be able to dress in warmed undergarments. Meira had stared listlessly into the distance and even further, coaxing her to eat did not seem to interest her.

The hourglass had already been turned by the time Meira was presented to the tailor. She stared nervously at the two men.

"I thank you," said the girl's guardian while his eyes lingered on Sarah's bodice. He bowed his head slightly. "Are there any problems in her form that may need a healer's attention?"

The seamstress averted her eyes, her hand rubbing her own arm. Customers never addressed her.

"Answer the customer," instructed the tailor.

"She has several sores on her body, which she has scratched open. And she is very thin. Her eyes are quite dull. I am surprised she lasted the winter," she replied, her gaze moving from the patron back to the floor.

"No one asked your opinion," retorted the tailor sharply. The guardian held up his hand.

"I asked, and she answered. I am not in the practice of inspecting naked young girls, so I am grateful for your apprentice's help. She is an honour to you," he said, smiling at the young woman.

"May I speak privately, with your seamstress?" added the guardian, his eyes never leaving Sarah's body.

"Suit yourself. I will measure the girl," grumbled the tailor.

The guardian held out his arm to show Sarah should join him and went to the back room. "Thank you for your help. I know the girl was filthy, but I could not send her to a bath house alone. I do not know men like your employer for their generosity. So, I would not feel comfortable in giving you this token of my gratitude in front of him," he said, holding out a week's worth of wages in his hand.

Sarah's feet shifted uncomfortably. She stared at the coins. The guardian had done nothing dishonorable, yet she felt as if he had the cunning of a cat about to pounce on a mouse. She glanced towards the door that led outside.

"I see I frighten you," he smiled. "I understand. This is a dangerous world for an unmarried maiden. There are many who would take advantage of you. But I assure you, I am not one of them," he added, placing the coins on the table. "I only came to the back to make sure that this token of gratitude is seen by you alone. You may tell your employer that I asked about finding a healer who is used to helping a new male parent to better understand the physical needs of a young girl." He bowed more deeply this time and left the room.

"Did you get what you were looking for?" asked the tailor with a knowing smirk. The guardian looked at the tailor with disdain.

"I have never been in a position where I felt I had to force a woman to do anything. With the correct words, they always come willingly - a fact that men like you can not comprehend. Now, when can I expect these dresses to be finished?" asked the guardian.

"I will have all five of them finished at the end of the month," said the tailor.

"How about tomorrow?" suggested the guardian.

"Sir, have you gone mad?" complained the tailor. "In one day?"

"I think you will find that there are a fair number of seamstresses in this village who are, in fact, without work. If you hire some of them, you may well finish on time," replied the guardian.

"These are lean times, Sir. How could I afford to employ extra seamstresses?" he said, staring at the guardian's coin pouch.

"I shall double the price of each garment if you find the ladies to finish the work. And I will need one garment for her to wear with me to the market - today," said the guardian.

The tailor looked around the shop. There was an unfinished garment on the workstation that required only the embellishments to be attached.

"If you will take only a basic ribbon sewn onto this one, I could let you take it within the hour," suggested the tailor.

The guardian looked at the little girl's green eyes. He pulled a roll of silk embroidered ribbon from his pocket. I think you may find that this shade will do the trick," he smiled.

After the tailor sewed the ribbons, the guardian held out his hand.

"Come little Meira, let's find something to put some meat on those bones of yours and then purchase a few things that you will need for our trip." He left the tailor with a curt reminder that he would collect the other garments the next day. Then he walked with Meira to the covered marketplace at the other end of the street.

The guardian's first purchase was a small poppet. The plaything had a red patchwork dress, with small lace trimmings and a tiny soft wig made from real human hair. He knew he could not use his usual persuasions on a young child and that she must miss her mother. So, the poppet would have to do. It would give her some comfort. There must have been so many uncertainties in her young life that he would need to make sure she had something she could trust in.

"For you, my Lady." The guardian bowed as he handed the poppet to Meira. Despite her fear, a small smile threatened to emerge as she touched the soft hair of the poppet.

They wandered on through the market, but the stench assaulted the guardian's senses. Human waste littered the open streets. As Meira stepped forward, he saw that he had neglected to buy shoes appropriate for her outfit. Her shabby footwear was worn through at the soles and her right big toe peeked out of the aged boot.

"No, Meira." The guardian pushed her back. "Do not walk there."

Tears welled up in the little girl's eyes.

The guardian stared down at her. "Do not cry, Meira," he said, taking a handkerchief from his pocket. He pressed the cloth to her eyes. "You must not fear me. I meant only to stop you from getting filth on your feet and dress. I will have no other clothes for you until the tailor finishes your new dresses."

He looked up and saw the seamstress, Sarah, making her

way across the courtyard. The guardian lifted Meira and hurried to catch up with her.

"Sarah!" he called out. She stopped and looked around her.

"Where are you going in such a rush?"

She smiled at the little girl being carried by her guardian.

"I see you have a new poppet, pretty girl." she smiled.

She faced the guardian. "I have to get new ribbons and thread for the tailor."

"Surely, a tailor would have enough in stock, not to have to send you out," frowned the guardian.

"Yes, but we have a sudden order for five new dresses," she dared to tease.

"I see," he smiled. "But before you run off, may I ask you something? I have neglected to find a suitable tradesperson for shoes for my… ward," he said, setting the girl down. His old duelling injury sometimes hurt if he carried a heavy load for too long. Honour duels were an occasional occupational hazard for a man like him.

"Our shoemaker is away, but his merchant has some stock and I think there are a few children's shoes. It is very close to where I am going. I will take you there. But we must be swift, or there will be trouble for me when I get back."

"I would not want you to get into trouble," he smiled. "Show me the way."

The walk was too brisk for Meira, and she stumbled over a loose rock. Her lip quivered as she tried to regain her footing.

"Oh, you poor thing," cried Sarah, touching the girl's face. She looked up at the guardian. "We are pushing her too hard."

"It is not long to go, Meira," said Sarah.

"I will carry her the rest of the way," said the Guardian, lifting her up again, despite his discomfort.

Sarah could not hold back her curiosity, and although it

was not her place to enquire, she blurted out her question. "How did you come to be with this child?"

"I was looking for a servant for my new home. I heard that there were workhouses close by. Many families are forced to sell their children in times when there is a great debt. I usually 'buy' one of these indentured servants, by paying off the family's debt and then enabling that young person to earn money and help their families. I mostly take on strong youths. But on that day, I saw this tiny whelp of a girl with exquisite green eyes and my heart was filled with pity for her. Workhouses are places of terrible suffering.

I have no children of my own. I have always wished for a daughter and on the day that I saw Meira, something in me softened and I decided to make her my ward. It is my intention to have her educated and allow her to lift her station in life."

TWENTY-SEVEN

Into Lord Logan's Lands

Meira's words would not come. Her guardian gave her a troubled look.

"When you are ready, you may call me Papa Zee," he said, straightening Meira's cloak. He tucked a blanket over her legs and checked the saddle to make sure it was secure.

"Today we will make enquiries about a home. We will find loggings for us in Lord Logan's lands. I have heard that he has prospered and that he has several manor houses available, as the sickness claimed many of his people. I also hear that he and his wife favour children and have hired tutors to teach any children whose parents wish for them to be educated. I have little patience or time to teach you myself. I must regain the fortunes I lost in the fire," explained her guardian.

Shortly before sunset, Lord Logan's castle came into view. There was a knot in the guardian's stomach as he looked up at the castle walls. "This is Lord Logan's castle," he said. "Do you like it?"

Meira looked up at the stone walls towering over the village. Scattered around the castle were manor houses of different shapes and sizes. She pulled Emma, her poppet, a little closer, but still she did not speak. Her guardian put his palm gently against her face.

"You are cold. It is time to find you a meal and a warm bed." He eyed the village as the horse slowed.

Captain Julian himself led the patrol that evening. It was a practice his wife disliked. She preferred him to be within the fortifications of the castle. But only a small handful of Lord Logan's men had any experience of King Radolf's men, and Captain Julian felt that it was his duty to protect his village in this way.

Galdolf was training the healers and stable boys in a more formal understanding of anatomy and healing herbs. Animals at the castle sometimes had ailments similar to those of humans. He had always had a love for animals and since his arrival, more villagers had asked for his help with their livestock. But as the only other man who had been on active duty in King Radolf's castle, Galdolf also headed the patrols twice a week, as he knew the inner workings of the King's army. Every other week, he took a trip to Holly Hill Cave to visit with Yakhal. The Dragon Whisperer had even invited him for a brew inside the cave. Granted, it was only the once, but it was more than anyone else had achieved.

Captain Julian and Galdolf often joked that they would rather face King Radolf than a worried and angry wife. Captain Julian smiled now at the memory. He squinted into the setting sun at a figure moving towards him. His jaw set as he waited for the traveler to come to him.

"Halt!" called Captain Julian. The guardian raised his hand in greeting.

"Greetings, my name is Lord Zayne," said the traveller.

"From whence do you come?" asked Captain Julian.

"A remote area just west of here."

"Where is that?"

"I doubt you have heard of it. But I have a map of the

area and my patents of nobility with me," replied the guardian, presenting the scrolls.

Captain Julian nodded and took the scrolls. He unrolled them and glanced over the contents.

"You are a long way from home, Lord Zayne," he said, handing back the scrolls.

"We had a fire which destroyed most of my manor and fields. When my cargo arrives in the summer, I will have enough to rebuild some of what I have lost. But in the meantime, I have come seeking sanctuary. I have enough to hire a manor for myself and my ward."

"Your ward seems a bit thin and timid," said Captain Julian, who was unsettled by the child's look. He eyed Lord Zayne suspiciously.

"I do not speak of it much, so as not to embarrass the girl, but I rescued her from a workhouse."

"I see. Forgive me."

"I seek a place to stay for the night. A place that is not attached to the tavern. My ward is tired, and she needs a warm meal and a good night's rest."

"I know of such a place. The innkeeper is a woman, and she has built a section of rooms well away from the noise of the tavern, for families traveling with children. Perhaps she will have a room for you. Then in the morning, you can report to the castle and we can make enquiries as to a vacant manor for you."

"I thank you," replied Lord Zayne. "Come, Meira, let's get you out if this cold and fed."

It was but a short ride to the inn.

ↄ

Sophie, Captain Julian's wife, was visiting her sister at the inn. "I like what you have done with this section," she said.

Aisha gave a satisfied smile. She tugged at Sophie's veil,

saying "Sister, you no longer need to wear this. The oils the Medicine Woman gave you are working well. The scars on your face are almost gone." Sophie pushed her sister's hand away.

ↄ

Aisha yanked at the veil again. "Our father left his country so that we would not have to wear these. Why do you hide your face?"

"Leave it. I am not yet ready," replied Sophie.

"Forgive me. I push too hard. Father always tried to teach me that by forcing my opinions on others, I am just like the men who tried to force me into a life not of my choosing." Aisha touched Sophie's face again. "You are so beautiful, sister."

The sound of horses' hooves broke the moment.

"I see you are standing around doing nothing, as usual," said Captain Julian, with a devilish grin at his sister-in-law. Aisha folded her arms and narrowed her eyes at him.

"You know better than to bait her," scolded Sophie.

"I know, I know," replied Captain Julian, reaching down to kiss Sophie's hand. "I thought I had dysentery that time she laced my ale with that herb," he grinned. "But by way of apology I have brought you a new customer." He indicated where Lord Zayne and Meira should dismount.

"While you ladies get your guests settled, I have a small errand to run. I shall be back in time for the evening meal."

TWENTY-EIGHT

Bully

The morning brought no relief to Captain Julian and his mood grew worse as he kissed Sophie goodbye.

His meeting with Beatrice the night before troubled him. She was as cagey as ever. Her penetrating stare revealed nothing as she listened while he spoke. But the Spymaster had offered to meet with him again today.

He was headed to the inn to check on the new arrivals. Captain Julian arrived to find Meira dressed, with her hair tied back in the fashion of the school and holding a bag with bread, cheese and preserved fruit. She stood quietly as her Guardian took her hand and led her to the schoolroom.

"Children, let's welcome Meira to our classroom," announced the tutor.

Most of the children wore the simple wool or linen tunics that were the mark of peasants. Meira's tailored dress set her apart from the other children. She was also by far the smallest child in the class. Meira bit her lip and glanced over her shoulder. Two of the girls glared at her. They were definitely not smiling.

As the tutor began to speak, the children reached into

their bags and took out their wax covered wood slates. They also had a wooden stylus each. When the tutor saw that Meira had neither, he took his own tablet and stylus and gave them to his new student.

Most tutors concentrated on teaching Latin, but Lady Christine insisted that some lessons be taught in the language spoken by the local children. It made the lessons bearable, but soon Meira's head began to ache. She had never been in a schoolroom before, and did not understand the work. Her eyes began to droop.

A loud crash jolted her out of her slumber as the tutor slammed his rod on the table where she had slumped onto her arm. He slammed his rod again and the children burst out laughing. Meira's lip quivered and she looked down at the tablet to hide her humiliation, but her crimson cheeks betrayed her as her tears splashed onto the wax.

When the gong sounded for the break, Meira waited until all the children had left the class before she joined them, but as she stepped out of the room, she tripped and spilled the contents of her meal all over the ground. The courtyard hounds raced up to the unexpected treats and devoured them.

Meira began the cry. Her dress was a mess and her hands were grazed.

"What are you doing here, you babe?" said one of the older girls who had been sitting at the back. She rolled her eyes and kicked Meira's bag away.

"Where is Meira?" asked the tutor when the group walked into the schoolroom to begin the next lesson.

"She hurt herself and ran back home," said another of the girls.

But Meira had not gone home. Home was too far away, and she would never know how to find her way back even if she wanted to. She sat just outside the class waiting for her guardian to come and fetch her.

From the castle Captain Juilan and Beatrice watched what had happened.

"There is something that bothers me about this child and her relationship with her guardian," said Captain Julian.

"Where are they from?" asked Beatrice.

"To the West of the Northern Kingdom. He has presented a map and patents of nobility."

"Being of noble descent, does not mean that he is noble of heart," replied Beatrice. "What is she like when she is with him?"

"She does not seem afraid of him, just afraid," said Captain Julian.

"But of what?" pondered Beatrice.

"I sent Nadine into the town square today to observe people. I think that tomorrow, she should be stationed outside the school," suggested Beatrice.

TWENTY-NINE

Meira

Meira picked up the poppet as she sat inside the Manor Lord Zayne had secured for them. Her fingers moved through the silky smoothness of the doll's human hair. Her blank expression shifted ever so slightly, and her eyes grew moist for a moment. How she had loved her Maimi's hair. She remembered the summer days when Maimi had washed her hair and how the light had shone off the curls. Her father had carved a comb for her mother from the horn of a deer that had broken off during a stag fight.

She lifted the poppet to her face and rubbed its silkiness across her cheek. Then Meira closed her eyes and thought about the sound of her Maimi's voice singing the tavern song that her father had sung to her on the day that they met. Maimi always said that he had been a crazy fool who seemed way too drunk to notice anything at all. But he had put his tankard down, gone down on one knee, and belted out the song to her. She had been a waitress at the time.

When the great sickness came, the tavern owner had become ill and the town's people had nailed wood across all the doors and windows, trapping the owner and his family inside to die of the sickness. Maimi and father had fled to the countryside and tried to make a living off the land.

She remembered her father's unshaven face rubbing against her Maimi's cheek.

"Stop it, that prickles," her Maimi would scold, giving him a playful punch on the shoulder.

"Come on, love, don't be like that, can't you see Meira needs a baby brother or sister to play with?" Then he would grab her Maimi's arm and swirl her around the room in a boisterous dance that threatened to knock over the chairs he had carved.

Meira would giggle, and the sound would bring her father roaring towards her like a giant, ferocious bear. She would squeal and run around the table as he chased her, and when he caught her, he would tickle her until she pleaded for mercy. Then he would hoist her onto his shoulders, grab a hunk of the bread cooling on the table, and march out of the door.

"What about breakfast and the prayer of thanks?" her Maimi would cry.

"We will have breakfast in the fields and the Lord's ears are big enough to hear our thanks out there," he would shout back.

Meira did not know that her mother secretly took herbs to stop a new babe from coming. It was a trick she had learned from the prostitute who frequented the tavern. The taxes were too high, and Meira's father was not skilled enough to work the lands to raise enough to feed the family as well as the King's appetite for taxes.

A look of despair replaced her last memory of her father's mischievous smile as the soldiers had dragged her away. His hands hung loosely by his side. His roughened hands, that were so tender when he touched her cheek, were powerless to protect her.

Meira stared down at her own hands. She had nibbled the nails down to the quick. There were calluses where her hand met her fingers. She tried to hide them under the long sleeves of the new dresses, but in the classroom, there were few opportunities to keep them covered. The tutor had raised one disapproving eyebrow when he saw the fresh flecks of red on her fingers that had appeared after the lunch break the previous day.

Meira's heart tightened as she thought about going back to the school. Her fingers had learned to work with small items in the workhouse, and so she had mastered the quill quickly. But her fingers hurt from the self-inflicted wounds of her gnawing and the tremor of fear that was her constant companion made the letters messy.

Nesta, an older girl with a tendency to steal other children's lunches, was the first to notice Meira's rough hands. She had looked down at Meira, her lip curling.

"With all this finery," she said, touching the fur at the cuff. "You think you are now better than us," she said and knocked the jar of ink all over Meira's dress.

Her guardian had been furious. "This is a serf's full year's wages," he cried. "Now look at it, ruined. No better than a kitchen rag". But the dress had returned. Although now it was as black as night, with a dark grey fox trim around the cuffs.

"My mother was a seamstress," explained her guardian. "She taught me that a dress could change colour. Now if we must attend a funeral, you will have something to wear."

Nesta had returned to the schoolroom the next day with a look of venom in her eyes. She spent most of the day glaring at Meira under her lashes. Nesta had winced when the Tutor had touched her shoulder, and she had not gone near Meira that day.

Meira's face seemed never to change. Except for the stolen moments when she chewed her nails, Meira seemed not to be of the world. She ate her meals with the guardian in silence. Her refusal to speak unnerved him and she was frequently left alone with the servants, who always seemed to stop whispering when Meira entered the room.

It was clear that her guardian had been at the tavern when he returned that night. Lord Zayne had some of the jovial spirit that her father had sometimes displayed when he made his own brew. Her guardian stopped and stared at her; his smile disappearing. She was so innocent. So fragile. Her large green eyes held no expression, but as he stared into them, he felt something of her sorrow.

He ran his fingers through his hair. "What am I doing here?" he thought. "She is just a child." His training had not prepared him for this. But he thought of the spikes outside King Radolf's castle, and realised he could not change his chosen course of action.

"Get to bed," he ordered. Meira had dutifully padded down the corridor to her room. Chewing her thumb, she pulled at a bit of skin that had not yet healed. She winced as the skin pulled further back along the fleshy part of her finger. It was only then that she stopped.

Meira took the poppet from its hiding place beneath the cloth that covered the table next to her bed. Hiding the plaything somehow made her feel safe. She undressed and put on the nightgown with the embroidered flowers. With the poppet's hair resting against her cheek, she crept into bed.

Meira did not understand why she was here. But she remembered the hardness of the King's face when she was presented to him. It gave her a sinking feeling. Like the time when her foot was caught in the hot, sticky mud near the bog close to their home. Her father had pulled her from it, his brow creased with worry, but there was no one who would come for her this time. She did not even know if her father was still alive. Meira cried herself to sleep that night.

THIRTY

Beatrice and Captain Julian

Beatrice, Lady Christine's spymaster, stood as mute as the pitted stone walls of Lord Logan's castle. The one thing she could recognise in others was fear. For some it was roaring and obvious, but for others it was a quiet gnawing of the spirit that ebbed away joy. She saw it now as she watched the little girl below in the courtyard outside the school.

Her companion on the wall was different. Captain Julian had never lost his joy. Even in times of battle and great sorrow, his boisterous nature and good humour were the balm that lifted the spirits of the men with whom he served.

"What does he truly know of the sorrows of women?" thought Beatrice, as she looked at him. Yet even Beatrice could not extinguish the curve of the smile she tried to suppress when she watched some of his tactics. But today Captain Julian was uncharacteristically silent as they stood together on the battlement of the castle.

"I cannot shake the feeling of danger. Yet none of my enquiries have produced results," he shared. "But Lord Zayne's eyes are never still. He appears to be silently gathering stores of information."

"The secret lies with the girl," said Beatrice. "But from what I hear she is mute."

"When we went with Nadine to rescue the hatchling, there was a girl taken from her parents for a tax debt. We were too far away to get a good look, but she reminds me of that child. Yet that little girl was wailing for her mother and father."

Beatrice turned to look at him. She knew the king took the tongues of those he wanted to keep silent. She hoped that was not the case.

"In times of great trauma some children stop speaking," she said. "Let us hope it is for that reason only that she does not speak."

"Do you think he beats her?" asked Captain Julian.

"I do not. But there is a defeated spirit that comes from too much suffering over too long a period. I have trained very young girls to reclaim their power. But some will always remain victims," she said. Her eyes were guarded and her emotions never reached her face.

Captain Julian marveled at this woman. Over time he had come to trust her judgement, but she was never an easy woman to talk to. He preferred working with Nadine. True, Nadine was impulsive and prone to outbursts. But her emotions were obvious to read, and he always knew where he stood with her. It made strategy easier and if he had logical explanations for her, she would come around to his way of thinking. But Beatrice kept her own counsel - a natural approach for a spymaster. Yet, he always felt ill at ease with her. His skin would crawl under the cloak of her stare.

They watched as Lord Zayne walked the child to school and then left in the direction of the Medicine Woman's rooms. Captain Julian's jaw set as he saw a girl far larger than Meira shove her forward. The force of it sent the little girl sprawling on the ground. He lurched forward, but there was nowhere to go except over the end of the battlements.

He turned to see Beatrice's expression had remained unchanged.

"How can you stand to watch her without… feeling?" he demanded.

"Captain Julian, the saviour of women's virtue…" she smirked. "If this is the girl you mentioned before, why did you not save her, then?"

Captain Julian knew she was baiting him, but the question could not remain unanswered.

"There were too many of the King's men nearby, and…"

"And what?" Beatrice's voice was like a serpent slowly circling its victim with soft caresses, waiting for the moment to squeeze any logic out of protest.

"It would have jeopardized our mission…" his voice trailed off.

"I do not have the luxury of planning great daring rescues. I must bide my time and extract intelligence, as time allows events to unfold. I must observe tendrils of truth leak out until they paint the picture of what lies inside our enemy's mind. Time lulls our enemies into thinking they are safe, and then when they relax, they make mistakes," said Beatrice.

"The child is not a pawn," said Captain Julian.

"She already is one. I did not make it so. But believe me, should I find out that the true purpose of Lord Zayne is to harm this land, Lady Christine, or that child, at the right time I will liberate them of him with my own hand," she said with a smile as beguiling as one of the exotic hunting cats he had encountered on his travels.

Captain Julian's mind forgot to squash the instinct to shudder. He turned to leave.

"I will meet with you later. But now I have another matter to attend to," he said, a little too quickly. "I bid you a good day."

"And I to you," said Beatrice.

The Captain descended the stairs, his boots clipping the

edge of the stones. He heard Beatrice call behind him, "Oh and Captain Julian, Happy Birthday."

The Captain stumbled. "Happy Birthday?" he thought. "It can't be. I have not had a birthday celebration since…"

A slow smile crept over his face. "Sophie," he thought. He knew of no other wife that celebrated a husband's birthday. But Sophie always did.

Now Beatrice had destroyed Sophie's birthday surprise for her husband, and Captain Julian knew he would have to feign ignorance to at least keep the illusion of surprise for Sophie. An almost impossible task with her advanced sense of female intuition.

He rubbed his hand along his jaw. "Think man, think," he muttered. If Sophie knew that Beatrice was responsible for ruining the surprise, there would be hell to pay. Sophie was seldom angry, but if anyone interfered with the birthday surprise, he would never hear the end of it. A small bead of perspiration trickled down his forehead. Captain Julian laughed as he leaned over the trough of water to splash his face. When he looked at his reflection, he grinned.

"I am a grown man. A seasoned warrior, and here I am shaking in my boots." The sting of the icy water cleared his thoughts. "No, a man is in charge of his own home." He straightened his back. He would go to his sister-in-law's tavern, sit there for a short while, and then go home. It would be a little later than he had promised her. But the delay would add to the surprise.

As he approached the tavern, the sound of a fallen jar startled him, and he turned to see where it had come from. As he turned, he bumped into Teafa, who was carrying a jar of perfume across the square. He stumbled forward, taking them both to the ground in a heap with the jar crushed beneath them. The door opened and his sister-in-law stared down at the two of them.

"And what, may I ask, are you doing?"

THIRTY-ONE

Another Year

The smell of perfume clung to a discouraged-looking Captain Julian as he trudged towards his home. Galdolf had lent him one of his own tunics, but even the change of clothing did little to cover the smell and there was no time for a thorough bath.

"Would you like me to get you an apple?" Galdolf asked.

"An apple? For what?"

"To cram into your mouth, so you look like a real stuffed pig, when your wife gets a whiff of that perfume," laughed Galdolf.

"Jest all you want, BROTHER. You are going to be my witness that I did nothing wrong. Or else..." Captain Julian shook his fist at Galdolf.

"Well, that depends..."

"On what?"

"If you can get a replacement for my shift. There is a dragon ceremony I have to attend," grinned Galdolf.

"You would extort your own brother," snapped Captain Julian.

"Well, in truth, you are not my actual brother. Only my brother-in-law," grinned Galdolf.

"Only… so, is that how it is going to be," said Captain Julian, tugging at the ill-fitting tunic. "Fine, I will cover your shift. But if I get sent to the inn to find a bed tonight, then our deal is off."

Galdolf leaned over and sniffed Captain Julian's shoulder. "I will have to ask Nadine to send my apologies to the Dragon Whisperer," he laughed.

"Couldn't you just tell her you were buying her a bottle of perfume and dropped it?"

"Now I know you were a Prison Master for too long. You are as demented as some of your former inmates. This is sandalwood. Sophie prefers rose," sulked Captain Julian. "Besides, your wife saw me with Teafa."

"True that," pondered Galdolf. "Suppose this truth is like drawing out an arrow. It hurts like the fires of hell, but only when it is out, then the healing can start. Friar Watt would remind us that the biblical verse is 'The truth will set you free'.

"Or have me sleeping at your inn for a week," said Captain Julian. His steps slowed as he neared his home.

Several passers-by threw him some surprised looks and hurried by. But only one stopped in mid-stride. A single word came to mind "Teafa." And in the distance sat a silent observer.

Captain Julian and Galdolf pushed open the door of the house. They were greeted by a silent house devoid of evidence of the merriment he assumed he would find.

"Could she have forgotten my birthday?" he thought. He shook his head. If Beatrice had said it, she must know something. Then perhaps she had heard about the incident with Teafa. "Oh Lord," he thought. He threw a panicked look at Galdolf who was sorting through his clothes.

"What are you doing?" asked Captain Julian.

"Getting you another tunic. If I do not, I will never get that stench out. Besides, you are bulging out of mine."

"Can I help it, that you are so puny?"

"Are you looking for another wrestling match?" asked Galdolf.

Captain Julian smiled. His wiry brother-in-law had a sinewy strength that had rendered many a larger man helpless once caught in his grip.

"Let's get to the castle," said Galdolf. "I need to make enquiries to see if our plans for extensions have been approved. If my wife makes any further extensions without the permit, I will have to pay penalties and heavier taxes forever. One thing I like about Lord Logan is that he has no favorites. The thing I dislike about him is that he has no favorites," grinned Galdolf.

"Very well. I will go with you to the castle. But only because I cannot afford to have Sophie find me alone without my witness," grumbled Captain Julian.

"You are going the wrong way," said Captain Julian. "The treasury office is on the east wing. You are going to the great hall."

"Am I? I must be confused," replied Galdolf. "Where are we now?"

"You are at the great hall," said Captain Julian.

"Really, can I have a look?"

"What are you - a woman on a tour? Let's get to the treasurer, so that I can go and find Sophie."

"Come on, it will just take a second," said Galdolf. "Help me with the doors."

Captain Julian felt a shiver of fear. The guards that usually opened the doors were not there. He drew his sword and glanced around. "Galdolf, this does not feel right."

The great doors swung open, and a blast of fire flew past as a Jester started a series of tricks. The smell of roasted boar flavoured with spiced wine filled the air and Minstrels played a merry tune.

"You took long enough," said Sophie, walking towards her

husband. She gave him a curious sniff and kissed him on his cheek. "It appears that I have to keep a closer eye on you in this place," she said with a wink.

THIRTY-TWO

Not Worthy

Meira stared at the cracked stone and wax tablet, damaged after her fall in the courtyard. Would she be punished for this? Was it her sinful nature that caused these things to happen? Perhaps, if she had not demanded so much time from her parents, then they would have made enough money for taxes. Then she would not have been sent away. She knew what she must do. She would get up earlier and do her lessons. She would work harder. She would pray that God would take away the selfish desire to play. She would endure the sufferings in silence and make sure she did not cry out. Meira knew she could do better. She could pray harder. She could find ways around the manor to help. Perhaps the cook could give her some vegetables to peel.

The little girl lifted the tablet. There was a chip off the corner of the stone of the tablet. The wax had a dent in it. But that was easy to remedy. But the wooden stylus. Where was that? She checked all around her. But it was gone. Had it rolled away? Tears spilled over her cheeks, already pink with cold.

"Maimi," she thought. "I miss you. I am sorry that I was

bad and had to be taken away,". The sound of approaching footsteps made her brush away the tears. Only babes cried.

"Are you looking for this?" came a soft voice. Meira saw a hand reaching down with a stylus. "It is a little wet. But a day out in the sunshine will take care of that."

Meira looked up at the blue-green eyes of a lovely young woman. "My name is Nadine. What is yours?"

Meira wanted to answer, but the words would not come. Her eyes lowered towards the ground, waiting for the reproach.

Nadine placed her hand on the little girl's shoulder.

"Come, I will walk you to class. Sometimes I grow tired of endless words. I hear them all the time. Friar Watt always teaches about God. The Whisperer with his anatomy lessons and protocol. Isa never seems to think I work hard enough. Then there is my Maimi. She always tries to teach me about how to see things from someone else's perspective. So many words. Sometimes I just need a rest. Well here we are," said Nadine.

She kneeled in front of Meira. "Let's straighten this dress a little." Nadine brushed a little dried mud off thc child's shoulder.

"I can't tell you how many ripped skirts I have. It was all that tree climbing. She winked at Meira. Only Captain Julian ever comes up after me. I will introduce you to him one day. He is a true champion. Every girl needs to have a hero that she can trust to save the day."

Meira looked up at the door of the schoolroom. It took all her strength to walk through it. She was late again, and the children lifted their heads from their letter practice to stare at her.

THIRTY-THREE

The Quest for Words

Lord Zayne approached the door of the Medicine Woman. He could no longer bear the silence. It gnawed at him every time he thought of the girl's eyes. Silent reproach tugged at his dreams. If she would but speak, he could feel a little better. Each night he withdrew to the tavern. He craved some feminine comfort, but his true purpose had not yet revealed itself, so he denied his longings.

Elizabeth's smile turned as she opened the door and saw him there. "How may I be of help?"

"I am Lord Zayne," he announced.

"Yes, I have heard of you. You are young Meira's guardian," she said. "Please come in."

A curious looking collection of bones lay on the worktable. Elizabeth quickly covered them with a cloth.

"What is your ailment?" asked Elizabeth.

"It is not I, but the girl." Elizabeth smiled softly when she looked at Meira peeking out at her from behind her guardian. She invited them in and showed Meira where to find the chest of poppets for her to play with while she spoke to Lord Zayne. There was something about Lord Zayne that unnerved Elizabeth. His eyes seemed to take in everything. Although his eyes seldom left hers, he would make small gestures that allowed him to divert his gaze and despite the mere moments his eyes left hers, she had the feeling that he had filtered some new knowledge when they returned.

"Please tell me what her ailments are," instructed Elizabeth.

"I rescued her from the workhouse. I believe that they took her because her parents did not pay taxes," he explained.

"Then why did you not return her to her parents?"

"I very much doubt they are alive. But even if they were, the Pope has imposed a secondary tax on the people of the Northern Kingdom to raise funds for a war. Few of the peasants can raise the money for the new taxes. So, by returning her to her parents, it would simply continue the cycle," said Lord Zayne.

"A valid point. But have you asked the girl or tried to find her family? Perhaps there is another way?"

Lord Zayne turned away from Meira and whispered to Elizabeth.

"Some guards watch for rescues. Then, if they trace them, they use the children's trauma from the workhouses to further exploit the impoverished family. Believe me, this seldom ends well."

"I have to believe that there must be some other way."

"In time I may offer her family employment, so they can be close to her. But after the fire, I had to let many of my trusted servants go. I kept Meira because I feel responsible for her. When my next shipment comes in, things will be different, but for now, I do not want to give her false hope."

Elizabeth peered at Meira chewing the vanilla cookie the Medicine Woman had placed on the plate for her. She smiled at Lord Zayne's ward while she examined her, but she fretted at the thought of such a young child having so much trauma at such a tender age. After the examination, she mixed a tonic for Meira and watched sadly as the little girl held out her arms for Lord Zayne to lift her onto the horse.

THIRTY-FOUR

Night Terrors

Lord Zayne asked the servants to bring his evening meal and an extra blanket to the child's room. The rich, meaty aroma of the dish held no appeal for him. He watched Meira as she slept, the soft whimpers that accompanied her dreams tearing at his heart. She was just a child, a mere whisper of a girl. Despite her poor appetite, he had watched the colour return to her cheeks, like a wilting bloom revived by a drink of rain. And he had felt the faintest increase of pressure as he held her hand on the way to school. Meira had not yet called him Pappa Zee, as he had offered, but he sensed a softening in her eyes when he called her name. When she shivered, he offered his cloak for extra protection and when she dropped her poppet; he picked it up, cleaned off its dress, and gave it a small kiss on the forehead to ease the poppet's pain. His soothing of the poppet always brought a hint of a curve to Meira's lips, but never an actual smile.

Lord Zayne always chose just the right colour dress to show off her beautiful green eyes, and he promised extra coins to servants if they could get her hair to shine like a polished mirror. He knew she would be a rare beauty when she reached womanhood and, despite his mission, he felt a protectiveness towards her that went against his better instincts. Lord Zayne told himself that it was to protect his asset. But he wondered about the future.

He thought about his boyhood home. His mother had favoured the soft white blooms of jasmine which had grown outside her window. It would be several weeks before the lingering fragrance would permeate through the corridors of his manor. Perhaps, if he could leave the girl with his oldest sister, but Lord Zayne knew he could never go back to his home. Too much time had passed. He had seen too much and done too many things.

Just one wrong acquaintance could take a man down a path from which he would never return.

But to take advantage of a child, that was an unspeakable cruelty. It sat heavily with him how children were mere pawns to the decisions of adults. This was a distasteful assignment, but he knew what became of men who crossed King Radolf. Again, he thought about the spikes on the castle wall and shuddered.

One wrong turn.... His thoughts returned to the day that he met his tutor. He was an inexperienced boy, crying on the side of the road next to his father's body.

The bandits had stripped them of all that they had, and he could not save his kin. It had been his first trip with his father, a merchant. But he had ignored his father's endless ramblings along the way, and after the bandits left, he had no clue of which way to travel to get back home. The bandits had left the boy without so much as a crust of bread, half naked, weeping in the cold as he clutched his dead father's hand.

A traveller had found him and offered bread and clothing if he would drop off a message at a Lord's manor nearby. He was to wait for a returning message and when he had delivered it, his rescuer had smiled.

"You have brought a traitor's message and now, boy, you

can never go home. You belong to me, and your trade will forever be that of a spy."

C

Meira's cry ripped Lord Zayne from his thoughts, and her hand flew up to her chin. He reached for the calming herbs and mixed them into the milk on the table.

"Meira," he said softly. "I am here, you are safe."

But the child continued to thrash and cry out with her eyes closed. He tried to subdue her, but she lashed out, kicking him in the stomach. Lord Zayne groaned at her strength and he thought that she must surely be awake, but her eyes remained closed as she continued to scream.

The door opened, and one of the girl's attendants raced into the room.

"She won't stop screaming," said Lord Zayne. "I did not hurt her."

The servant glared at him.

"I know Lord Zayne. It is a night terror. She is trapped in a bad dream. We must wake her." she said as she tried to grasp the girl's limbs. "Please, can you give me the fur. We will have to wrap her, to protect ourselves from her."

"Meira," she called. "You must wake up now."

Meira's limbs escaped from the covering and kicked the servant with such ferocity that it stunned the woman.

"It is alright. Go back to bed. Now that I know what it is, I will take care of her," said Lord Zayne.

"But Lord Zayne, it will take a long time to soothe her," she replied.

Lord Zayne gathered a fur blanket from the trunk. He wrapped Meira and gripped her body as he climbed onto the bed. He held the child and rocked her rigid body. Lord Zayne sang a song that his own mother had soothed him with.

He held her until her limbs lost some of their force and

she slumped in his arms. When the servant sneaked into the room in the early hours of the morning, Lord Zayne's chin lay on his chest, with the girl's head resting in his arms. The servant smiled at the sleeping pair, removed the dinner dishes, and went downstairs to check on the morning's meal.

C

A look of concern came over Lord Zayne as he woke and eased Meira off him. His arms were stiff from cradling her through the long night. He did not know how long he could continue with this plan. He never expected to have a child with him. The spy specialised in procuring secrets from women. Women understood the rules of engagement. Being with a man they were unmarried to was considered a sin. So being involved with him was a woman's choice, even though he manipulated and seduced them. But a child was a different story. Meira was innocent.

He ran his fingers through his hair, over the back of his head and down his neck. His neck ached after the long night of watching Meira. Lord Zayne walked to the stone balcony and looked out over the horizon. He filled the cages he kept there with new seed and water. A nearby cooing sound jolted him into awareness, and he looked up to see a slate-coloured pigeon with a faint shimmer of green and purple on its neck feathers.

But the beauty of the feathers did not stir him. His heart pounded like the thundering of stallion's hooves racing through a muddy river. Splashing around through his fear.

The thin cord wrapped around a tiny roll of parchment secured to the bird's leg signalled that the time was now upon him to report to the king. Now there was no turning back. He could no longer protect Meira. He had to report. Lord Zayne unrolled the slither of parchment and closed his eyes before reading the contents. He turned to look at his ward. The night terror was behind her for now. But for Lord Zayne, it was just starting. A faint tremor ran through his fingers as he scrawled the message his mind screamed against.

Meira wrapped her arms around his leg and squeezed.

"It's all right Pappa Zee. You are safe now," she smiled. He realised she had heard the words he had spoken while the night terror gripped her. He lifted her into his arms and held her small body close, squeezing a little too hard. She flinched, but did not pull away. Meira reached up and touched his wet cheeks and traced the beard with her small fingers.

"I am being rather foolish this morning. But I think the big breakfast that the cook has made for us will make me feel much better," he smiled.

Lord Zayne lifted Meira onto his shoulders and turned one last time to look over the horizon before descending the stairs that led to the dining hall.

"After the meal, I will walk you to school."

THIRTY-FIVE

It is Time

Meira stared at her fingers, as she stood in the school courtyard. She thought of her Maimi's welcoming arms and her warm smile. Maimi was always there to comfort Meira when she hurt herself. Her eyes grew thick with tears now. Children all around ran, jumped and laughed. But no one came to call Meira to join in their games.

She could almost hear her father's laughter. Just the memory of it created a knot so heavy in her throat that she could not swallow away her grief. Lord Zayne was kind to her, but he was not her Pappa. If only she could have run faster, perhaps the soldiers would not have taken her. If she had played fewer games, perhaps she would have helped Pappa more in the field. Maybe then they would not have taken her because her Pappa would have had enough coin for taxes. Perhaps one less mouth was better for her family. Maybe her Maimi's fingers would not be so swollen and red from all the hard work. Maybe her parents were better off without her. Could all the children in the class be right? She did not fit in. Meira watched as a mother arrived with a forgotten lunch sack for one child. She remembered her own Maimi running through the field after them the day before King Radolf's men had taken her, when she had forgotten her lunch. Her Maimi's work-weathered fingers had traced a line from Meira's mouth to her eyes on that day.

"When your smile reaches your eyes, you show your beauty," she would say. No matter how much work her mother had, she would never scold Meira for playing. Her soft body was a place Meira could bury her face when she was hurt. There was always love for her at home.

Lord Zayne had tried to make a home for Meira. There had never been this much food in her hut in the forest. But no amount of tasty gravy, thick woollen dresses or fur-lined boots could cover the sorrow in her heart.

C

Nadine stood at the corner of the schoolroom. She watched the young girl as the tears flowed unchecked down her face, and she remembered Meira all too well. There was no mistaking whose child this was, and Nadine recalled the impotent despair of a father who knew he was too weak to fight off the soldiers. She tried to squash the memory of the day she had witnessed them pull the girl from her weeping mother. The blood that flowed from the father's forehead and the way he stared at his impotent hands had filled Nadine with loathing for the King.

She sniffed away her own tears, but her jaw set into a line of determination. King Radolf thought he could take whatever he wanted. Lives were meaningless to him. Nadine felt the frustration of that day fill her lungs with a scream that she could not give life to. Instead, it churned within her and made her feel like tearing at her hair. She had heard of young women who clawed at their faces as an act of utter despair. While she knew that Lord Logan had outlawed the practice, in some primal part of her, she understood their instinct to tear away their flesh as an attempt to eliminate the inner pain they felt.

"Nadine," called Muquin, "Calm yourself. The Masked Man will feed on your anger and you can not help the girl like this."

Nadine closed her mind. How could they expect her to squash every feeling? It was impossible. No one was that strong. But Meira was of the same age as Mikael. She tried to imagine what she would say to her brother if he suffered, as Meira had.

Nadine breathed out and closed her eyes for a moment. She flexed her cramped fingers to relax her muscles.

"Hello Meira," she said. Meira rubbed her nose on the back of her fur trimmed sleeve.

Nadine straightened her back. Muquin was right; she could not help Meira by allowing her to wallow in her loss. She held out a handkerchief to the child.

"I was there the day that they took you," she said.

Meira looked up, her eyes filled with yet more tears.

"No Meira. Do not cry. The King seeks to weaken everyone. Now is the time to gain strength. Men like King Radolf are bullies. They take what is not theirs. They breed fear and rely on their victims' fear to keep them weak. I have seen what he is capable of. He may have been able to take you from your parents. But there is one thing that he can never own. And that is your heart. You may not yet have the full strength to fight, but you can never surrender your heart. One day, we will reunite you with your parents. For now, we will work with you to reclaim what is only yours to give way. No one has the right to take your dignity.

You have the full right to defend yourself against bullies. Let no one tell you that turning the other cheek is the way to go. Friar Watt tells us that while it says to turn the other cheek, there are places in the bible where defence is the only way. Like in Nehemiah, the men rebuilt the walls. They built, but they also held a sword and kept watch against those who would destroy their plan.

Now is the time to stand up to your bullies. Do not fight them with anger, it will only bring a stronger attack. But let them know that their time to conquer your heart is over. A skilled and deliberate strike to stop the bully will earn you respect. But before you learn to fight a physical fight, the fight is in your heart where you declare you will no longer be a victim. In time, when this battle for these lands is over, we will seek out your parents.

That time is not now, not with the threat of King Radolf's attack. But the time will come when we will be free of his clutches and I myself will help you find your family. But for now, I need you to wipe away those tears and to find the courage that I know you have in your heart. Here take my hand, let them see you are not alone."

Meira looked up at Nadine. She had never met a girl like her. Fierce, yet beautiful. Nothing like the other girls she knew. Already some students were talking about Nadine. The girl who defied a king, rode dragons and had rescued Lord Logan. Maybe there was still some hope. Nadine squeezed Meira's hand and winked at her. She pulled back her cloak so that her dagger sheath was displayed to the other students.

Then the Silver Wing Dragon Whisperer turned her head, glancing over at each of them. A stunned silence filled the cobbled play area as Nadine walked Meira back to class.

THIRTY-SIX

Retaliation

Nesta waited in the courtyard for Nadine to leave. She had endured the beating by her father in silence after someone had paid a visit to their hut. Nesta did not know who it was, but she would find out. She had bided her time, but now her need for revenge could not be silenced. The older girl had played the scene out in her mind. As soon as the smaller girl lifted her skirts to avoid the puddle, Nesta would slide her boot under Meira's foot.

Nesta's efforts were rewarded as Meira collided with the ground. The younger girl's chin crashed into the courtyard and her teeth rattled with the impact. The jagged white edge of her jawbone shone through the angry scarlet rivers that ran down her neck and onto her dress. Grit and dirt from the courtyard was embedded in the scraps of skin that flapped below her chin.

Nadine had just returned to check on Meira when she saw the girl fall. There was no time to chastise Nesta. Instead, Nadine rushed forward to help Meira. The little girl rose to her feet and stared at her hands, which throbbed with fresh beads of red oozing between the bits of gravel that littered her palms. For a moment she looked at Nadine with terrified eyes, but darkness claimed her as she collapsed again. Nadine scooped up Meira's limp body and ran through the courtyard to Elizabeth's cottage.

"Elizabeth, Elizabeth!" she called, cradling Meira in her arms.

"What happened?" asked Elizabeth, as she opened the door with a look of shock replacing her usual calm demeanour.

"That older girl in the classroom - she tripped Meira. There is a gash in her chin," blurted Nadine.

"Quickly! Let's get her on the table," ordered Elizabeth.

The medicine woman lifted the little girl's chin and inspected the large flap of skin that hung ominously from her face. The Medicine Woman added more logs to the fire and moved the boiling pot into the heat of the flames. She added lashings of salt and dropped several strips of linen into the scalding liquid. Then she laid a large ceramic tile on the table and wiped it clean with a salt solution.

"Nadine, use these metal hooks to lift the boiling linen from the water and place them over the cooling rack," she instructed. The steel rack was a row of blunt metal blades on a stand that the blacksmith had made under her guidance.

"We must try to keep her still," she said as she dropped small amounts of opium oil onto Meira's tongue.

Lord Zayne had seen Nadine run off with Meira. He followed and pushed open the door to find Meira bleeding on the table. Elizabeth glanced up at Lord Zayne. A look of fear passed over her as her eyes darted to her studies table. Both Nadine and Lord Zayne followed the movement. The dragon bones lay exposed. Nadine pulled a crumpled sheet over the bones and busied herself moving jars of herbs around. She hoped that she had been subtle enough.

"Speak to me, Meira! Child, why will you not speak?" lamented Lord Zayne.

"Do not press her. She is in pain, and this is not the time. I need to clean the wound. I need you to keep her still, Lord Zayne," instructed Elizabeth.

"Nadine, hand me one of those linen strips and give me my pincers. Lord Zayne, there is a sheep's bladder on the table with salt water in it. I need you to squeeze droplets of the water onto the wound. I will then pick out the gravel from her chin."

C

"Lord Zayne, I must stitch up this chin," said Elizabeth as she pulled together the flaps of skin. "If we are lucky, this will not scar her face."

They both knew that it would not take long before she went into shock. Elizabeth stitched the wound with delicate stitches as quickly as she dared. When she was finished, Lord Zayne moved to pick Meira up.

"No. Let her lie here for a while. I have to see how she reacts. And there is also another tear that needs to be stitched," said Elizabeth.

"Nadine, I would be grateful if you can keep that water boiling and keep replacing the boiled linen for me. Put the soiled strips in that jar. We will clean them and reuse them after we have boiled them in salt water," instructed Elizabeth.

The Medicine Woman looked out of the window. She could see by the shadows that Lady Christine would be arriving soon. Lord Zayne, too, recognised the time of day.

"I have an urgent errand to run. I will come back," he said as he dashed out the room. He bumped into Lady Christine just as she reached the door.

"Forgive me, my Lady," he said, with a low bow. Then he ran off before she had time to acknowledge his apology.

Lady Christine clutched at her growing belly as a shiver ran down her spine. She glanced at the back of the man who had just passed her.

"Elizabeth, who is this child that is here? And who was that man?" she asked as she rolled her fists into her lower back.

"This is Lord Zayne's ward, Meira. And that was Lord Zayne who just left. What ails you?" asked Elizabeth with a look of concern.

"My hips ache terribly. I have spent a long day listening to endless complaints from villagers who have all sorts of claims. The hearings are necessary, but they exhaust me. And I'm tired of sitting. I thought I could come and have some tea with you," she explained. "But I see that you are busy."

"You are always welcome. Come! Can you hold onto Meira's hand? I need to clean the wound, and find her something to change into," said Elizabeth. "I would welcome the help; Nadine is already busy with the linen strips and Lord Zayne has left."

Lady Christine gasped when she saw the bloodied scraps of linen and the mutilated face of such a small child.

"What happened to her?" she asked.

"She fell at the school, but I don't think this was just a clumsy moment," said Elizabeth.

"Whatever do you mean?"

"Nadine says there is an older girl who has been deliberately hurting her," replied Elizabeth. She picked up the sliver of bone with a hole in the end that served as her needle.

"Within our school?" lamented Lady Christine.

"No, no, do not blame yourself. It is not your fault at all… Can you pass me that ceramic slab, with those thin strands on it?"

"What are these?" asked Lady Christine, peering curiously at the straw-coloured thread-like strips.

"They are catgut suture strips," replied Elizabeth, as she threaded the bone sliver.

"Made from cats? Like Tiber?" quizzed Lady Christine. Elizabeth looked up from the needle.

"No, of course not. That would be a very dangerous occupation, catching cats. Too many people still think cats are used for witchcraft. So, handling them would condemn some poor innocent," she smiled.

"Perhaps the name comes from the fact that they look fine, like the whiskers of a cat. But in truth, we make them from the twisted strands of part of the intestines of cattle, sheep and goats." Elizabeth talked while she worked, gripping the edges of cleaned skin and sewing them together with the threaded bone. "This is the last bit, and then we are done." Lady Christine reached up to touch the wound.

"Rather, do not touch it. We need to clean it around the stitches and then bandage up her head to keep her from moving her jaw," said Elizabeth as she measured out the linen for Meira's head.

C

As the herbs wore off, Meira opened her eyes and looked up at Lady Christine. Lady Christine saw the most beautiful green eyes gaze back at her. She was just considering what an exquisitely lovely child she was when the little girl began to weep.

Lady Christine ran her finger down Meira's cheek.

As Meira cried out, she said a single word, "Maimi."

"Lady Christine, Meira is the child we saw when we were travelling to the Northern Kingdom to rescue Yakhal, the Silver Wing Hatchling. The one I told you who was taken by the King's soldiers for unpaid taxes," explained Nadine.

"Yes," said Elizabeth. "Her guardian has told me about it. He mentioned that they took her from her parents as an indentured servant."

"What is she doing so far away from home?" asked Lady Christine.

"I do not know. Lord Zayne said that he found her in the

workhouses and that he rescued her and needed to pay the taxes for her family to take the girl," replied Elizabeth.

"But then surely he knew whose taxes he was paying and how to find her family," said Nadine.

"Why did he not take her back to her parents?" asked Lady Christine.

"He said that he did not want the cycle to continue. Perhaps when the special tax collection for the Pope's army is over, he can return the child to her kin," suggested Elizabeth.

"She misses her Maimi," said Nadine. "There is something not right about the situation. I cannot quite discern what it is."

"We will make enquiries," offered Lady Christine. "Let us ask Beatrice to see if her network can find out more about this child. Look at her. She's such an exquisite little thing. Like a little porcelain statue." Lady Christine groaned again as her back arched.

"Please sit down," instructed Elizabeth.

"I feel as if I'll be sitting forever," groaned Lady Christine. "Lord Logan only wants me to lie down and to sit. But I needed to move so that I could build up my strength again."

"Well, I think we have all indulged you for long enough. I'm afraid that I will be exactly like Lord Logan. I need you to sit down and put up your feet. We will get you some soothing tea so you can relax a bit," she said as she settled the soft cushion behind Lady Christine's back.

"Now what to do about this child's mental health?" she said, looking at Lady Christine and Nadine. "Meira, has Lord Zayne harmed you in any way?" asked Elizabeth. Meira shook her head.

"I have a terrible feeling of foreboding," whispered Nadine.

"There is something not right. Why have I never seen this man before?" asked Lady Christine.

"I don't know. Perhaps because you were in the castle for

so long, you seldom interact with all the people every day. Maybe that is the reason, as he has no reason to meet with you," said Elizabeth.

"I suppose you're right. But I feel that we're missing something and just don't know what - only time will tell," she said.

Nadine smoothed the hair from Meira's face.

"Let's see if you can get up," she said.

Nadine gently lifted Meira off the table. Despite being a bit wobbly, Meira held onto the side of the table and took a tentative step. Meira's eyes were fixed upon the studies table. The little girl walked over and pulled back the cloth that covered the bones.

"No," said Elizabeth, and not as gently as she had hoped to.

"This is not for children to look at. Let's keep that covered." But Meira had seen something shimmering under one of the bone fragments. She reached in her hand and pulled out a single emerald coloured scale. It was hard. As if it belonged to something that was once living. But why did this have colour? She had seen bones before, and they were always grey. She ran her fingers along the scale and then slipped it into the pocket of her dress, unnoticed by the others.

When Lady Christine had finished her tea, she touched the little girl's face and bid her farewell.

"I hope that I will see you again soon, Meira," smiled Lady Christine, before she left for the castle.

A few moments later, Lord Zayne returned for Meira.

"How is she?" he asked.

"The procedure went well. The wound will hurt for some days. It must be cleaned every day. I am taking a short trip, but I will give you some ointment. If I show you how, would you be able to change the dressing and clean the wound?" asked Elizabeth.

"Of course," said Lord Zayne, "I will do anything to make sure that she is well. Where are you going?"

There was an uneasy silence as Elizabeth looked at Nadine.

"I have some customers from my previous practice that I visit regularly and I need to take them some remedies. But I shall be back soon."

"Very well," smiled Lord Zayne. "I await your return. Thank you for taking care of Meira," he said as he touched her hands for the briefest moment.

Elizabeth worked with Lord Zayne, giving him the instructions to clean the wound. There was a sinewy strength to his body and his hands worked in a steady flowing way that oozed sensuality. Lord Zayne had a way of unnerving Elizabeth, and he stood a little too close to her for comfort. Although his voice sounded kind, his eyes seemed to take in all of his surroundings in swift glances, but never lingered on one thing for more than a fraction of a second. She could feel the warmth of his forearm as it brushed against hers.

Nadine's eyes narrowed as she watched the heat on Elizabeth's cheeks spread across her face and neck. But Elizabeth hurried to the other side of the table.

After the Medicine Woman wrapped up a bundle for Lord Zayne, he bowed. "I thank you so much." His eyes wandered over her form and then gazed into Elizabeth's eyes and smiled. It was a rich yet gentle smile that seemed to penetrate her core.

"I think there are few men that could appreciate what a remarkable talent and heart lies beneath your extraordinary emerald eyes," he said. Elizabeth felt an odd stirring, and she lowered her dark lashes as she blushed under his gaze. A stray fiery red curl fell over her left eye, and Lord Zayne lifted his hand as if to move it, but dropped his hand as she quickly brushed the curl away.

He turned his attention to Meira and carried the child outside. Her guardian lifted her onto the horse and fussed over her, adjusting the straps for her height. Instead of climbing up behind her, he patted her hand as he walked alongside her. His voice was soothing as he reassured her that everything would be all right.

Elizabeth stood, watching them leave. Lord Zayne's presence had unsettled her, in the way the mesmerising flicker of a lethal flame draws in a moth. She felt a quiver run down her spine.

"I do not trust that man," said Nadine, watching the blush fade from Elizabeth's neck.

The Medicine woman touched her burning cheeks in dismay.

"I agree with you, Nadine," she said as she tried to slow her breathing. "Let's clean up this mess, shall we," she smiled. But she could not look Nadine in the eye.

Lord Zayne pushed open the manor door and entered with Meira. He ordered the servants to bring through a thin, but nourishing gruel, so that Meira could rebuild her strength. Elizabeth had explained to him that the child would have difficulty eating and that her meals needed to be thinned down so she could drink them, as chewing would cause much pain to the child. Meira sat quietly as Lord Zayne gently spooned small sips of the gruel into her mouth. He was careful not to let the gruel trickle down her chin.

After a few spoonfuls, Meira's eyelids drooped and her head dropped onto her arm at the table. Lord Zayne lifted her into his arms and carried her up to her room. He drew back the covers and laid her gently on the bed. Meira sighed in her sleep as her head touched the cushion.

He did not change her clothing, for that would not be proper, but he tried to arrange her clothing in a more comfortable way so that there would be no folds to bunch under her skin. As he smoothed down her dress, something fell out of her pocket. It looked like a piece of green bone. Lord Zayne pulled the soft fur over his ward and reached down to pick up the fallen fragment. His brow furrowed as he rubbed his thumb over the surface.

"This cannot be bone," he thought. "Dry bones are not green. They are grey." The tip felt a little like a broken off thorn. He placed it on the table next to her bed and stared at it for a moment before returning his gaze to Meira. He leaned over to smooth her hair to the side. Without knowing why, he bent over and gently kissed the child on the forehead. As his lips touched her skin, a memory of his own father rose to the surface of his mind. A faint smile teased the corner of his mouth, but then his eyes darkened and he quickly left the room.

THIRTY-SEVEN

Sins of the Past

Teafa read through the scrolls Elizabeth had lent her. The former prostitute had taken over one of the hunting huts near Holly Hill Cave. The hut provided a peaceful refuge for the girls who would come to her. Elizabeth had given her many lessons in anatomy and healing. But because of the hunt for the eggs, Teafa could not spend a great deal of time with the Healer, so they had devised a 'library method' of instruction. Now Teafa had learned how to cleanse the body and purge it of many of the elements that came from the work these women performed in the District's squalor. She had also learned to heal wounds, so that there was minimal scarring.

Dalila had fallen asleep in front of the fire. Teafa lifted the child and carried her to the bed. Her beautiful skin was as smooth as silk. But inside Dalila's mind lay the troubles of the past that still jolted Teafa from her sleep as Dalila thrashed and cried out at unseen assailants. Teafa kissed her forehead and wished for her night to be filled with the healing balm of sweet melodies.

But something was bothering her. She couldn't place it. Perhaps it was the disease of letting go of the past. But frequently when she had travelled to Elizabeth, she felt a sense of foreboding she could not explain. Perhaps one could call it a woman's intuition?

Over the years that Teafa had worked in the District, she had seen many men come and go. They had all left a mark on her in some way, by spirit, in other ways, or more physical harm. She wrapped her shawl around the old scars on her arm, where she had fallen after a beating. No more would men have power over her. But for the child's sake, she could not allow bitterness to remain in her heart. Elizabeth taught her to help minimise the scars of physical injury, but the inner healing took much longer. She looked around the cottage and smiled. Who would have believed that she could live like this, away from the tyrants and the evils of the District?

Tomorrow, she would go back to the village and take the little girl with her.

Dalila could not read and write, and felt intimidated by Lady Christine's school. But once a week they went to the schoolmaster, who would prepare lessons for them both. She packed up a bundle for the trip, softly humming to herself.

Her small smile became a chuckle as she remembered Captain Julian's earlier discomfort. Of course, his wife had known all along that nothing would have happened between them. But that sandalwood was a strong perfume, and it had spilled all over him.

The sandalwood scent was what Teafa used to mask the scent of the men. She could always smell them. In the smell of their sweat, what they ate seeped through them. For some men it was the spicy scent of eastern foods on their bodies, some were rich in the herby fragrances of a plant-based diet, and she could definitely smell when they drank excessive ale. It seemed to seep from their skin when they were with her - a sickening sweet smell.

She knew so many of these things. When a man sweated, the essence of the life that he lived came from him, whether he was clean or dirty, and she could smell it. Again came the nagging worry in the recesses of her mind. What was it she feared? She just could not catch the thought. She looked back at the child who lay beside her.

Beatrice had told her of another little girl who had come to the village. Meira, they told her, was a timid little creature who did not speak. Teafa knew it was from the traumas in her young life when she had been taken away from her parents. But she now had a guardian who cared for her. By all accounts, he had bought her clothing and he had cared for her in a beautiful home. When she was injured, he had apparently hurriedly taken her to Elizabeth, who had treated her. What more could a young girl wish for than to have the protection of a man? A man who had means could care for her.

Teafa was relying on her new patron, Lady Christine, to protect her and provide for those who would seek sanctuary with her. But there was always fear. She had chosen to live away from the District so that she could protect the child and those who would come to her. But it was an isolated life. Lady Christine had asked her to remain in the village because of the war they were preparing for, but Teafa had declined.

"I know that war is coming. But these children that you have put into my care, will not be accepted by the villagers. They must grow healthy and strong away from people. And once they can embrace their identity, away from the sneers and the remarks of villagers which will surely come, that is when they can be released back into normal society. But for now, they need solitude. And the care of someone who knows their past but loves them for who they are and not for what they have endured."

"You are right," said Lady Christine. "But they are all such fragile little creatures. And I would not want any harm to come to them. Already we have heard that the patrols of the king come further and further into our territory. And there is little we can do to stop them."

"Why can you not stop them?" Teafa had asked.

"Because this entire territory, Lord Logan's land, lies within the Northern Kingdom's territory. Lord Logan did not mean to enrage King Radolf.

He has lived his life away from the King's ruthlessness, as Lord Logan's territory always pays its taxes, and the King does little to interfere with a territory that is peacefully run and profitable. But he defied the king by offering sanctuary to me and Captain Julian. The king knows this castle is well fortified. And it frightens me to think what would happen if we left you and the women and the children that you care for unattended.".

"I understand, Lady Christine. But I cannot see any other way to make them feel safe. We will pray that we remain undetected.

"You do not know King Radolf, the way that I do. He will use any means that he can to gain his advantage. And I fear for your safety. Call it a woman's intuition. I feel when things are going to go wrong. I feel when there is trouble. Perhaps we can devise a communication plan so that we can alert you to danger. I will discuss it with Beatrice."

C

Later that day, Beatrice had listened to the plight of the women that Teafa was charged with protecting, and it appeared she was very much in agreement with Lady Christine

"I cannot leave you now, Lady Christine. And I cannot send more reinforcements to your halfway house, Teafa. The wisest decision is for you to stay within these castle walls, where you can be protected," Beatrice had said.

"I have already discussed that with Teafa, and she has refused," Lady Christine had replied.

"Then I cannot help her if she will not allow me to protect her. Because I cannot leave. I must stay with you," said Beatrice.

"Is there nothing that can be done?" Lady Christine had pleaded for Teafa.

Beatrice sat in silence for a moment.

"We can set up a training camp for young women. I cannot train the girls myself, but I can call for my warrior sisters from the Phoenix Pass. My father sent me to them when I showed my first moon flow. And I fled to them after he drowned. They will send me their most seasoned trainers. We will prepare the girls in case of an invasion, on how to defend themselves," said Beatrice.

"It is a good plan. Let me know what you need, and I will make the arrangements," offered Lady Christine.

"Perhaps…"

"What is it?" asked Lady Christine. "I see a plan brewing."

"There are not enough men in the land for Lord Logan's army. And we need every able-bodied man that we have to join. While away to your father's Kingdom the drain of men will leave this castle vulnerable. If we make a formal training camp for women, we can double our resistance," said Beatrice.

"But we won't have enough women who will want to fight," said Lady Christine.

"With respect, that is where you are wrong. They will want to fight, they just need the right motivation. I have seen women claw, kick, bite and hack at a man wanting to claim them as spoils of war. They do not lack the will to fight - only the techniques and confidence.

"The two best kinds of warriors are those who are fighting for what they love and those who have nothing left to lose.

There are many women and girls who have been orphaned or committed petty crimes or are forced into prostitution. Offer them a way to create a better life for themselves and they will come. I will need someone to build dormitories for them and we will need to provide them with at least two full meals a day. We can teach them to make bows and arrows for our army, to defend themselves and how to train others.

Then I suggest that every woman in the land who has a child receives at least two hours of training a day. We will explain that if the King does invade, the chances of the soldiers raping the women and children is high. If a mother knows that she can stop this, she will fight. I have claimed several women from the clutches of a warrior who has a taste for preying on those weaker than himself. Some of them I would only get to after the act. Those women who have suffered the brutality of war will be the best trainers to make the women fear what is to come," explained Beatrice.

"I do not want to instil fear into my people," said Lady Christine.

"Fear is meant to propel us. What is better? That they live in quiet ignorance or that they prepare for the fight and stand a better chance of winning?" asked Beatrice

"Lady Christine, I too have seen how a brutal man can crush a woman's will to live. Many of the girls of the District were forced into the life of prostitution. I know that they would have welcomed the chance to learn how to defend themselves beforehand," explained Teafa.

"Very well. Decide what will be your best position and I will arrange to have timber cut and have the dormitories built for the women. I will send for my scribe so that he can make up the notices to be nailed in the courtyard," offered Lady Christine.

"The women will need to work together. Create a roster. When one woman leaves her family fields, another woman will need to tend to them. This way we will not interrupt the supply of food. We will issue weapons and a horn so that all women working in the field will have a weapon and a method of alerting the neighbours if there are soldiers coming or that she is in distress," instructed Beatrice.

And thus the plans for the training of the women were put in place.

THIRTY-EIGHT

Discovery

When the little Dalila woke at the sanctuary, Teafa prepared for the trip to Elizabeth for her next treatment lessons. She laid out a dress for Dalila. It was one of the garments Lady Christine had sent for the child.

Teafa had prepared the hot water for washing. Dalila took off her nightgown and stood in the basin of water. Teafa began to soap her body. Elizabeth had sent two beautiful lavender fragranced soaps which were Dalila's favourite. Teafa washed the child from head to foot. But as she went past the child's private areas, she stopped - a little sore, no bigger than the tip of her baby finger...Teafa began to tremble.

"What is it, Teafa?" asked Dalila.

"It is nothing. Just a little indigestion. I fear I might have eaten my last meal too quickly. I suppose it's an old occupational hazard," she smiled weakly.

"Come on, let's get you dressed. Put the coat on."

Let's eat and then we will go to the Medicine Woman and get our lessons from the schoolroom as well. Dalila dressed swifty. But there was a silence that stretched between them. Unspoken words of something that Teafa knew she could not tell a child. They rode in silence to the village. Teafa's expression brightened as she saw the castle walls come into sight.

"Perhaps they'll be selling some of those little spicy sausages that you like. And some sweetmeats. I have heard Elizabeth say there is a man from across the seas who has set up a store in the village, and he sells sweets that are pink and chewy. Those are the ones that you like," said Teafa. "How are you feeling?"

"My throat is a little sore, and I feel tired, but it is just because of the cold. Life is so different at the cottage, don't you think?" she replied.

"Yes, but isn't it so much better?"

"It is better, but just a little colder, than in the District, I think. So many of the ladies used to have big warming fires outside their rooms so you could easily walk from one to the other and feel perfectly warm."

Teafa smiled. "Yes, it was much warmer. So many people around and so many fires. But we're glad to have that behind us."

"Yes," said Dalila.

"So many things have changed. And even though there are a few of us. I do feel happier," she said.

They did not speak of the time. Speaking of it again would mean defiling Dalila again. At only 12 years old, she had lived through things that no child should ever have to experience.

C

Elizabeth heard the curt knock and opened the door, pausing in her work cleaning up after her last patient.

"What happened here?" asked Teafa when she saw the discarded, soiled linen strips. She felt the acrid smell of blood assault her senses.

"One of our new residents, Lord Zayne's ward, was here.

She had fallen and cut open her chin. I had to give her a good few stitches.

"Really?" said Teafa as she sniffed the air. Yes, there was the smell of blood, but there was something else that she sensed. She wondered what it was.

"You say the man's name is Lord Zayne?"

"Yes, he is a Noble from another place. He lost his home, through a fire, and he has come to seek sanctuary with Lord Logan until his next shipment comes through," said Elizabeth, observing intently as Teafa inhaled the scents of the room.

"You look disturbed."

"It is nothing much," shrugged Teafa. "I need you to have a look at Dalila. She has a little sore and I would like to ask if there is some ointment we can use to eliminate it. I think she might need to disrobe.

Elizabeth felt the cold hand of a dread pass over her as she listened to Teafa.

"Elizabeth, Dalila was such a frail little thing. And her body had been exposed so many times. I would not ask if it was not necessary," added Teafa.

Elizabeth nodded. She understood - although she hoped she was mistaken.

"Come, little one. I am going to look you over to see that you are in good health."

"Is there something wrong?" asked Dalila, her eyes darting between Teafa and Elizabeth.

"Well, Teafa thinks you may have a skin infection. I need to decide what sort of remedy we will need to give you," Elizabeth smiled and placed a small plate of vanilla cookies next to Dalila. The child's eyes brightened and she bit into one of them.

"These are good," said Dalila. After Elizabeth had completed her examination, she washed her hands and spoke to Teafa.

"Teafa, there is a little shrub outside that has got rather

large thorns that I need to get some leaves from. Would you mind coming with me to help? I find that if I try to pull the leaves off myself, I get nasty scratches on my fingers. But if you could pull back the branch and hold it firmly, I can pluck the leaves I'm looking for without getting scratches."

"Of course."

As Teafa drew the branch back, Elizabeth whispered her fears.

"It is as we feared. I will need you to bring her to me several times, but I must confess that there are few remedies that will treat her. I can try to make her comfortable. And we need to keep the sores as clean as possible to slow down the spread of the infection. These symptoms usually last about three to four weeks and then the next stage will come. You're to expect a rash. It is highly contagious. I will need you to administer the ointment and make sure that anything that you touch after that is burnt.

The lesion on the throat… could get far worse - in the bodies we have dissected, we have found deformation in the bone. I have even seen cases where there were holes in the skull…"

"So, it is syphilis?"

"I'm afraid so. I have not yet seen it in a child. Usually it's adults who have had many partners where I see the disease from time to time. You do not often find it in a pious community, but it is easily transmitted by prostitutes to their customers, and from the customers to other prostitutes." Teafa's eyes closed for a moment.

"Dalila is just a child," she said, finally allowing her tears to flow unchecked.

"But she is strong. We need to give her very good nutrition and plenty of sunshine. Let's see if she can help try to fight off that infection herself. And I will give you treatments for the sores. The back of the throat will be more difficult. Perhaps she can rinse out her mouth with salt water. But for the rest of the body, you can administer the treatments.

There are some experiments where people have used a metal-like substance which they crush into tablets and vapours. But I have never seen them produce good results. And very often the patients die later, from poisoning, which I think is due to the treatment.

We must try to find another remedy to ease her suffering. But you know, as I do, she should never have children, and never have a husband."

"I understand," said Teafa. "I will try to make her as comfortable as possible. But it is such a cruel injustice that an innocent child would get this disease."

"Yes, Elizabeth. A child defiled by men of greedy and perverse appetites. These are the two victims of prostitution. Those whose bodies are defiled by others and who must sacrifice the unborn. Some ignorant and superstitious men believe that having physical intimacy with an innocent will magically take away their disease from them. But it only serves to spread diseases to the innocent."

"Oh, my dear Teafa, I'm so sorry," said Elizabeth.

"There is nothing to feel sorry about. It's not your fault," said Teafa. "It is just the life we were thrust into. I had hoped that in time she would find a husband and have the joy of children and put the past behind her. But I know that many women who have the disease will have deformed or stillborn babies. And now all that I can do is pray that God will be merciful to her."

THIRTY-NINE

Away

Nesta's dull eyes followed Lord Zayne as he placed Meira on the horse. The injury was serious enough for Meira to have spent several hours at the Medicine Woman's cottage. Nesta felt an icy ball of fear rise inside of her. She flinched at a sudden noise in the courtyard. In her mind, an imaginary fist crashed into her arm. She rubbed her father's favourite impact spot.

She had to ensure the sleeves of her tunic always covered the bruise. Her parents argued constantly. Her mother insisted that Nesta attend the school. She wanted Nesta to have a better life. But Nesta's father's disapproval always loomed below the surface.

Lord Logan had endorsed the school and passed a decree that no parents could prevent their child from going to school once enrolled. The school was not compulsory but withdrawing a child invited questioning by the officials.

Nesta sighed. But officials were not inside her home. Her father's domain was his to control, and no school decree would stop him. She could hear his words ringing in her ears.

"You think you are better than me. Do those letters on that wax thing of yours feed this family?" he had shouted.

Nesta clenched her own fists as hot tears streamed down her face. She wiped them away and kicked one of the withered shrubs in front of her. She felt trapped. Her thoughts and emotions collided inside her head. There was her father's rage, her mother's expectations and the school tutor making her feel as if she was inadequate. She never wanted to be in this place. It brought a misery she could not understand or control. Her mother's fatigued face and her father's fists seemed to be a constant companion. Being at the school robbed the fields of her labour and added to her mother's misery.

Out in the fields tending the crops. That felt real, she thought. That brought food to her belly. Nesta thought she may go mad if she could not silence the voice inside her head.

ტ

Meira was as fragile as that precious poppet that she sometimes carried in the village. Her hair was brushed to shining glory like the human hair on her plaything.

Nesta had to wait for the merchant that Lady Christine had appointed to feed the peasant children to get her daily ration, but Meira carried with her a parcel of food each day that her guardian had sent. Meira thought she was better than them. But she was just lucky. Below those fine noble clothes, she was just an indentured servant. A peasant playing noble pretend games. Nesta squeezed the painful spot on her arm and gritted her teeth. It hurt when she practiced her letters on the wax tablet. It was no accident that her father always chose her writing arm when he used his fists. Each movement reminded her that he never wanted her at the school.

The bitter cold of the mornings that forced him to get up early left fresh bruises on her mother's frail limbs. But the warmer months had ground his resentment into a fragile, polished shell that contained his volatile emotions. It meant that she could at least do a few chores before she had to run the distance to the school. Each serf child in the school had been given a new pair of boots along with their bag and wax tablet, so Nesta's feet had sturdy protection against the rough stones her calloused young feet had endured for so long.

Now she stared at her fingernails. Each morning she stopped at the oak tree just before the last guard station near the castle to scrape out the dirt with her stylus. She used a sharpened twig before, but her father had snapped it and thrown it into the fire. The school master inspected the children's fingernails each morning as he checked their letters. Dirty hands and faces were frowned upon. There was a bowl of water with enormous bars of hardened fat infused with salt and lavender scented oil. On the first day she had enjoyed the simple pleasure of the luxury of hand washing. But the beautiful scent outraged her father.

"You think you are better than your mother," he had sneered.

It was the first time his fists had found her face. But the day away from school to ease the bruising had brought questions from Lady Christine's school guards as they sought the missing child's father.

Since then, Nesta had two rituals. The first was to scrape out her fingernails in solitude before school. The second was to rub her hands with soil on the way back. She never touched the lavender cleaning bars again.

But now, that girl Nadine, the one that Lady Christine favoured, had seen her trip Meira. There would surely be brutal consequences for her actions.

Her father had once told her of the practice of a whipping boy. The tutors of noble and royal families used this method to control their students. A tutor could not strike the child of a noble family. They would bring a peasant child to be the companion to the noble boy, to sit in on the lessons. The two children would form a bond. Then if the noble child transgressed, the tutor would beat the peasant boy in front of the noble boy as a way of managing the noble boy's behaviour. The bond between the boys would often deter the noble boy's future transgressions. For the peasant the role of whipping boy brought pain, but also brought an education that he would otherwise not have received.

Her father had met such a man who explained how they made the whips and had fashioned one from a thin strip of young sapling cut from a growing tree near the river. It made a hissing sound as it sliced the air, and the exquisite sting on the flesh produced an angry long welt that stung for hours after he inflicted it. The flesh would be so delicate afterwards that several of these lashes would bring a rush of blood to the surface. One beating was enough to produce a horrid, enduring fear that would rise at the mere sight of the reed.

Nesta and her mother both had scars from this punishment to remind them who was lord over their home. Her father had explained that it was essential to witness the beatings so they could understand how their defiance of his will would affect the other members of his household.

The sight of Meira's bandaged face called to Nesta's darkest memories. She could not endure another "whipping boy" lesson. If her mother remained with such a man, it was of her own choosing. But Nesta felt she had to get away.

The words she had learned from her struggles with the wax tablet were enough for her to follow signs and read the parchments hammered into the town square posts. She had seen a call for able-bodied women who wished to train in one of the warrior camps to prepare for the threat of war.

No brutality from the camps could ever be worse than the belittling cruelty of her father, she reasoned. It was a day's walk from the castle, one that she could endure with ease as her years of gruelling field work made her fitter than many other youths in the village.

Nesta had heard that villagers who had committed petty crimes could work off their debts to society in the training camps. A recruit needed only the clothes on her back and the will to fight. Perhaps she could wash away her sins against Meira in the glory of battle. She looked back toward her family home and prayed to a God she didn't know existed to find a way for her mother to gather the courage to leave her father.

FORTY

Camp

Nesta's leggings were soaked as she ran through the early morning dew drenched grass. The tiny seed-like flowers clung to her garments as she pushed her way through their reed like stems. In the distance, beyond the tall trees that reached up towards the blinding early morning sun, she could hear shouts and the ring of swords clashing drift through the surrounding silence. The camp had to be close by.

There was a narrow gap between the dense clusters of trees. Nesta squeezed her way through. Below in the valley she saw a group of young women lined up for inspection. To the right were twenty women in neat formations with leather and metal chest armour and mid-thigh-length skirts with leather strips hanging from a thick metal belt. Despite the early morning cold, their garments were sleeveless.

In the middle was a line of shivering women and girls stripped down to thin linen undergarments. Two women issued uniforms to the group. Nesta heard the shrieks of a handful of girls who bathed in a frigid stream on the other side of the border of massive coned trees.

"Keep it down!" called one of the female guards. "Do you

want to wake the entire regiment of King Radolf's men? Can you imagine what they would do if they found a river full of half-naked untrained women?"

Nesta stared at the group. She had never imagined that there would be so many of them. Nesta felt the prick of icy steel on her back. She spun around to see a youthful, ebony skinned woman with cold eyes that belied her gentle smile.

"Did you come to enlist?" she asked.

"I... think so," muttered Nesta, eyeing the woman's sword.

"Well, is it yes or no? A warrior has little time for indecision," said the woman.

"Yes, I have," replied Nesta as her eyes hardened at the woman before her.

"Good, well I will escort you to the admissions bench," she replied. The woman slapped Nesta on the back. "Welcome to camp."

Ten girls sat on the bench, waiting for their turn to speak to the woman seated at a small table with a stack of parchments. She recognised one or two of them, all daughters of serfs. Nesta swallowed hard. She had not expected to see anyone she knew. When her turn came, she stepped up to the table.

An aged, wiry woman with slanted eyes and pepper coloured hair with traces of silver gazed at her. Nesta looked back at the woman, whose eyes seemed not to release her. A moment stretched between them, and Nesta felt seen for the first time in forever.

The woman's words drifted through the space between them as she asked, "Name?"

"Nesta" The name sounded foreign in Nesta's ears.

"Have you had your first moon flow?" she asked, considering Nesta's form.

"Yes," replied Nesta as she glanced over her shoulder at the other girls.

"When was your last moon?" asked the woman. Nesta stared puzzled at the woman.

"In this camp, we train all women and girls. We never extinguish the life flame inside. But girls and women with children cannot endure serious physical training without risking the babe. So, they are camped separately and only complete defensive training. We must make special arrangements for their food and training.

Our questions are merely to place you in the best type of training," explained the woman.

"Fourteen days ago," answered Nesta.

"You will be required to complete a physical examination. It will be conducted in private behind that screen," said the woman.

Nesta looked at the screen but did not move.

The woman looked up at Nesta and put down the quill.

"Nesta, I can be with you during the examination. I am not a physician, but I can watch over it if it would make you feel safer."

Nesta's eyes brimmed with tears, and she nodded.

"Calisa," called the woman. "Please, can you question the rest of the girls? I must assist this trainee. Nesta walked in silence with the woman to the screen and undressed. The woman held her breath as the overlapping pattern of long thin welts was revealed when Nesta's clothing fell to the ground. Nesta wrapped her arms around her shivering body and clutched the bruise on her shoulder.

The woman pulled her own cloak from her shoulders and wrapped it around Nesta after the examination.

"Come, bathe in another part of the river," she said as she gathered some salted, scented fat and something to dry the girl.

Nesta stepped into the water and gasped - the cold felt like icy needles. She dipped her hand in the rich scented fat and rubbed the rough texture all over herself.

"My name is Shuo," said the woman as she held out the linen undergarments Nesta had seen from her viewpoint earlier.

"Except for the occasional inspection by Lord Logan's captains, there are no men here. No one will hurt you. The scars you bear show that you are a survivor. Here we will make you strong, so that no man will ever harm you again. But you will have to fight harder than the other girls against yourself." Shuo's words were calm and held no sense of accusation or blame.

"Fight… har…der." stammered Nesta, her body trembling with cold.

"For those who have endured much cruelty, there is a temptation to feel stronger by making those weaker than themselves suffer. But to do this gives your tormentor power over your soul. Then you will always remain a victim," said Shuo.

Nesta hung her head in shame.

"I have already failed," she sobbed.

"As so many of us have," said Shuo, as she lifted her leather skirt. Nesta saw the repeated white scars of a branding iron on the yellow-skinned upper thigh of the older woman. She dropped the skirt. "In time you will find a way to make it up to those you harmed while you were suffering. Now come, we must join the others."

Nesta turned to look at the girls lined up to receive their training weapons.

"Come quickly, Nesta. You must receive your weapons and join the others for their morning meal before training starts."

FORTY-ONE

The Lords of Righteousness

Lady Christine drew her cloak around her and swallowed hard against the dryness of her mouth. She stared into the distance of the darkened forest. The stars above glistened in the sky, but the woods were silent. It seemed as if the leaves of the trees held their breath as the night sounds evaporated around her. Even the long-eared speckled owl that watched her from above appeared like a statue in its silence. She meandered along the pathway, as instructed on the scroll she had received, desperate to obey Beatrice's commands.

"Remember to breathe," her champion had told her as she had rubbed the fragrant oil over Lady Christine's hardened belly before she dressed her for the night. Lady Christine wished she could feel the warmth of Lord Logan's protective arms, but they both knew why she had to journey alone.

The trail of white pebbles patterned over the path was a beacon in the darkened forest, but they lead to an unknown future. A quickening in her womb provided a reminder of her purpose, but it took all of Lady Christine's courage to keep moving. She clutched the small embroidered cross Lord Logan had ordered for her. It was soft enough for her to squeeze and squash in her rising anxiety. A small group of warriors spread around her to scout the area for danger, but even they were silent. Above, Lady Christine heard a rush of air as the soaring dragons covered the moonlight. As the pebbles tapered away, a simple wooden door came into view. She hesitated at the door and counted out the four torches that were secured on aged wooden poles flanking the entrance.

Her warrior companions separated and left her alone to light the third of the four torches. She could not see Beatrice, but knew the Contron was watching with her spear, ready for Lady Christine's defence.

Christine waved the torch in the air with three steady swipes. At the third swipe, the door swung open to reveal the stone stairs that Lord Jefferson had spoken of. Her father's secret war council rooms. She had never seen this place, and her heart pulled at her chest as she looked down into the darkened passage. She squeezed the cross as a tremor threatened to overtake her hands.

"Breathe," she heard Beatrice whisper, as the warrior lit the next torch and walked ahead of Lady Christine.

After the ordered steps, they stopped in front of four doors. This time they took the first door. An oval room revealed itself in the torchlight's flicker, and Lady Christine felt the heat of the fire in the hearth soothe the prickle of the cold on her skin. The women staggered their approach, surveying the room for an ambush.

A table stood in the centre of the room. Artisans had carved it from a single giant fallen bark from the ebony volcanic forests. Locals said the wood was harder than stone, and shone with the lustre of the black diamonds that were unique to the area.

The 11 Lords of Righteousness sat along one side of the table. There were 12 ornately carved chairs, but they had left the 12th chair vacant. It represented the fallen Judas, one of the 12 apostles of Jesus. The empty chair served as a constant reminder that betrayal was a genuine threat. Her father had abandoned the practice, but since King Frederick's death Lord Jefferson had reintroduced the 12th chair as a gesture to the Lords that he would never again allow the house to crumble from within.

Christine felt the babe move inside her. She walked to the carved gilded wood chair. She imagined her father seated with his back tall and proud against the delicate and intricate carvings inlaid with silver. She ran her fingers over the wooden armrests, polished with age, as she sat on her father's throne. Alongside stood Lord Jefferson.

Lady Christine held her posture in the manner that Lord Jefferson and Beatrice had trained her. The Lords had risen to their feet as she approached to signal their honour for the last day of the king. But they did not kneel in submission. Lady Christine knew that it was a test. A test which she had to pass.

She took her turn to look at each man and named them, just as Lord Jefferson had coached her for weeks before the meeting. Each day she had studied the features from original portraits of each Lord and recited their lineage, lands won and lost, and the battles they had fought in her father's armies. But now she could no longer rely on Lord Jefferson. She had to stand her ground.

"My Lords," she said. "Please be seated."

The Lords sat, staring at her. The silence of the room was overwhelming, and fear gripped her. This was the time she simply could not show any sign of fear.

She spoke Psalm 91 in her mind. "The Lord will be my rescuer." And she steadied her heart.

"I stand before you today. The only remaining heir of the King. The true King of these lands. What King Radolf stole from you, I will restore. But I ask you now to stand with me. This land that we call home is meant to be free. Our birthright was taken through treachery and murder. Tonight, I call upon you to rise and claim what is rightfully ours." One of the Lords cleared his throat.

"You have something to say, Lord King Jankin?" asked Lady Christine. "Present your case before your future queen."

"All these years, we thought you were dead. But instead you left our lands unattended and made no move to claim them. How do we know that we can trust you, that you will not run away? As you did before?" he asked.

"I understand your corner, but you are mistaken in believing that I ran away. King Radolf captured me. He murdered my parents, your King and Queen. I had no way of making the journey home, and I was too young to know who to trust. Lord Logan helped me and gave me sanctuary. While he falls under the command of King Radolf, his heart is true, just like my father's was, and he is every bit as noble. His allegiance comes at great personal risk. Lord Logan has declared his promise to grow this army. He will champion our claim as rightful heirs to these lands and mine to the throne. I ask for courage from each of you to take a stand so that you may live with honour.

I know that I will need much guidance and much courage, but I ask each of you present, will you be the man to stand here and declare upon your oath that you will stand for this house, and follow this house?"

"Princess Christine, you are a woman and have no experience in battle. Yet you expect us to stand with you," said another of the Lords.

Lady Christine stood and lifted the spear sceptre she carried with her. She hammered the base of the spear on the stone floor. Two female warriors stepped in, flanking her.

"Who are these women?" asked Lord Dugald. The women remained silent but glared at the Lord. He could feel the penetrating heat of their eyes upon his face.

Then Beatrice stepped forward.

"I am Beatrice of the warrior clan, Contron. I have

pledged my life to protect the honour of Princess Christine. And now I will show you to whom you owe allegiance," she said.

She bowed before Lady Christine and unhooked the velvet sleeves from her shoulders. Upon each arm below the shoulder were the fire forged amulets of a warrior Princess of The Tribe of Argon.

Then she pulled the sash from below Lady Christine's bodice. The covering from her belly fell away to reveal taunt skin where the sign of her fertility heralded a new line. Lady Christine resisted the urge to cover her vulnerability. Only the heave of her chest hinted at her humiliation. While modesty was a virtue which her mother had trained her for, she knew that only the most rebellious Lords would openly defy an heir who had proved the ability to fortify the house through a blood lineage.

"How do we know that this child is not the seed of King Radolf, forced upon her while in captivity?" enquired Lord Dugald. The challenge was a blatant breach of Christine's honour.

Lady Christine's dagger hissed through the air and impaled the Lord's cloak to the chair. It hit the exact mark that Beatrice had trained her for. The forged clasp of Lord Dugald's lineage lay shattered on the stone floor.

The Lord bent to gather the remains of the symbol. He walked unsteadily towards Lady Christine, bent down on one knee and laid the fragments at her feet. Then he drew his sword and held it across his extended hands before her.

"You have my honour," said Lord Dugald, his eyes not leaving the ground. The heat on his face lingered as Lady Christine placed her hand on his shoulder.

"You may rise, Lord Dugald. Beatrice, summon the marital witnesses."

Two blindfolded witnesses were led into the room: the first

the chief midwife of Lord Logan's lands and the second the family's spiritual representative.

Lord Jefferson addressed the witnesses.

"Were you present on the night of the consummation of Lord Logan and Lady Christine's marriage?"

"We were my Lord," they announced.

"And what were your findings?"

The midwife spoke first.

"We examined Lady Christine at the time of betrothal and on the day of her wedding and found her to be pure."

"And you, sir?" asked Lord Jefferson, turning to the other witness.

"It is customary for me to be present at the inspection and I found Lady Christine to be pure. This child was conceived within the confines of marriage," said the man.

"Princess Christine, what of the rumours of King Radolf having a dragon in his army?"

There ran a murmur amongst the men.

"Call for Nadine," ordered Lady Christine.

Nadine stepped into the room with her Silver Wing cloak covering her head. She removed the hood, and her eyes glinted in the flickering light of the torches.

"I am Nadine. The last of the Silver Wing Whisperers, highest order of all the Whisperers. I have trained under an elder whisperer, a warrior tutor, and a spiritual leader. I have under my command two Silver Wing Dragons, and an alliance with a Copper Fire Dragon. We will fight alongside Lady Christine to reclaim her rightful place."

"Are there any other claims or disputes," asked Lord Jefferson.

"No," replied the men.

"Then you may swear your allegiance to your future Queen," said Lord Jefferson. Each man rose and laid his sword before Lady Christine.

Beatrice stepped forward.

"My Lords, the hour is late and Lady Christine must return to the castle before the guards change. We bid you goodnight," she said as she bowed her head to the Lords.

Outside, Reginald stood watch over the horses. While Nadine had offered to return Lady Christine on the Dragon, many of the Lords were still suspicious of dragons and uncertain of Lady Christine's bravery.

She would have to ride as they did. Reginald had strapped sturdy leather thongs at intervals along the side of the horse to help Lady Christine with extra grips to mount the horse. He had practiced with her several times over the last few weeks, and now she knew where to place her feet, even in the dark. But he felt a moment of panic as he saw the quiver in her arms as she paused before throwing her leg over the mare. He had chosen a gentle mare for the trip, one that would not easily bolt.

Reginald had placed a fur cloak around Lady Christine's shoulders. Beatrice had commissioned a special saddle with extra cushioning. As with many women with child, Lady Christine's joints had softened, making it easier for her to lose her footing. A fall could put the babe at risk and lose them the ground they had gained in allegiance from the council of Lords.

It sickened Beatrice that the woman she had grown to love had been reduced to a mere breeding vessel by this patriarchal society. But it was the way of men. Men were honoured above women and they only saw a Queen worthy if she fulfilled her duty to produce an heir.

Although the saddle was soft, it still pressed against Lady Christine's thighs. The unyielding design made her feel unstable, and she felt a buzz in her ears. She leaned to one side to relieve the pressure.

"No! Keep your back straight," whispered Beatrice. "It will balance you and you must not show weakness." She could not allow herself to steady Lady Christine, although her instincts were screaming at her to help her employer. She exchanged a nervous glance with Reginald.

Lady Christine nodded, but she felt the prickle of tears burning her eyes. She closed them briefly and then straightened her back and raised her chin. She was grateful for the dark, it would camouflage her fear.

Her seated position pushed the babe up and against Lady Christine's lungs. She inhaled deeply to steal what little air her lungs could contain. She gripped the reins and gritted her teeth. They rode at a steady pace away from the council and towards the forest.

Despite the gentle sway of the mare's body, Lady Christine felt as if she was staring over the edge of the cliff, ready to topple over into a dangerous ravine. The babe pressed harshly against her, reducing her breathing to pants like that of a thirsty hound after a boar hunt.

At the pace that they were travelling, the densest part of the forest seemed to be hours away, even though its shadows told her that it was just a short ride. By the time they arrived at the trees, Lady Christine's body screamed out at her for relief. Reginald tried to steel himself against her plight, even though he felt his feelings threatened to overwhelm him. His wife had often jested that his sense of compassion would lead him into trouble.

As the first trees shielded them from the view of the council, Reginald dismounted. From behind the trees, a woman dressed identically to Lady Christine stepped out from the shadows. She ran her hand across Reginald's cheek and smiled; she felt the wetness of his face. She squeezed his hand in silence, and he returned the gesture. Reginald reached for Lady Christine and eased her off the saddle. He removed the fur and draped it over his wife's shoulders. He gave her a playful prod in her cushioned belly and lifted her onto the mare.

From behind another of the trees, Nadine stepped forward

and unrolled a silver cloak. This she wrapped around Lady Christine and led her a short distance to Muquin. The dragon lowered her neck to the ground, so that Lady Christine could easily mount. The dignitary saddle was far larger and this time Lady Christine could feel the cushioning that Nadine had prepared. Together Nadine and Reginald secured Lady Christine with silken cords to prevent an accidental fall. Satisfied, Reginald returned to the others and set off to the castle.

Lady Christine gasped as the force of the wind rushed over her body as Muquin pumped her wings to gain sufficient force to lift herself. Normally she would run for a short while to ease the liftoff with an untrained passenger, but there was too little space in the forest. Muquin would have to jump into the air with her wings still beating. Lady Christine could understand why the restraints were necessary as she felt her body sway in the saddle.

The future Queen kept her eyes tightly shut as Muquin launched into the air, but after the dragon's body settled into a gentle glide, she opened them to see the world turn into a miniature celebration of the night. She felt cocooned between the glistening silver of the stars and the dark shadows of the trees below. The rush of the cold night air made her eyes feel dry and tired, but she could not bring herself to close them for more than a second. In the distance she could see the sprawling lands of… she gasped in recognition. Her own home lands, the Kingdom of Ochar. She had never seen them from the air, but she knew. The curve of the mountain flanking the castle and the beautiful Sapphire Lake in the distance. Her heart tightened as she remembered her father tracing the line of her face with a bud of the new white roses that her mother had planted.

"Christine, you are more beautiful than a thousand white roses. One day you will make a fine queen and I know that you will always make your mother and me proud."

Her mother had scolded him. "You best find a husband

for her that is as well trained in flattery as you are or she will never be happy when she compares him to you."

"What nonsense, you speak, wife," he had said, bending down to kiss her. "Any man with any intelligence, can see that I have the most beautiful daughter in the world."

She had returned his kiss and smiled. "Yes, a man of intelligence may know that. But a husband who affirms it so openly is a rare find and I do not want her to have false expectations."

Her father had snorted. "You have so little faith in the hearts of men."

"And you, perhaps, have too much," her mother had replied as she picked up her basket of roses.

Her father had tucked his arms into theirs as they strode away from their favourite picnic spot in the royal gardens.

"We will know soon enough. Our match maker has a list of suitors for us to look over," the King had replied.

He had frowned for a moment as he looked at Christine. "Don't fall in love with someone who lives too far away. I fear that my heart would cease to find joy if I could not visit often."

Christine closed her eyes at the memory and felt the steady flow of tears for her precious parents. How she missed her father's gentle touch and the glow of pride wherever she presented some new achievement. From mud pies to inedible pastries, she had attempted to make herself when the cook was not around. He even found joy in a stain on her dresses. He had told her that a good Queen is more concerned with helping her people than keeping her clothes tidy. He was the only King to conduct a full war council with a silk clad princess on his knee.

FORTY-TWO

The Scent of a Man

As Teafa went back into Elizabeth's rooms, she sniffed the air.

"Teafa, what is it?" asked Elizabeth.

"I recognise a smell."

"There are many familiar scents in the room."

"No, it is something else. Elizabeth, ever since I was a child, I have been sensitive to smells. I can pick up a scent much in the way that a hunting hound can. And when I was in the district, I could tell which of my customers was close by.

I worked in Lord Teebald's spy training camp. Our purpose was to train men about the ways of women so they could use them to gain intelligence. But I noticed that I had a gift to discern scents and odours. Sometimes the gift is difficult, as the scent of someone can trigger painful memories for me...." Teafa stopped and sniffed again, quite deliberately. "Yes...One of Lord Teebald's men has been in this room."

"That can not be true, I have had no..." Elizabeth's voice trailed off.

"Who was the last man to enter this room?"

"It was Meira's ward. Lord Zayne."

"I know this is a strange question, but did he seem charming? Well mannered? Was there something alluring in his speech?" A pink hue spread over Elizabeth's cheeks and neck. She touched her face and brought her hands down in horror.

"Teafa, what are you saying?"

"I am telling you, Elizabeth, that one of King Radolf's spies has been in this room with you."

"But Lord Zayne is Meira's guardian. He cares for her. I know it. I have seen them together."

"The child is one of his tools, Elizabeth. They are trained in the ways of women. There are few things as alluring as a man who cares for a child. It calls to our maternal instincts."

"But the child's injury is genuine. Nadine witnessed it."

"I do not doubt you. But I know that the spies that Lord Teebald recruits are opportunistic. They will use any means to gain information."

"Who is Lord Teebald?"

"He is King Radolf's spymaster. He is the one who commissioned the training camp in the District.

These spies seek women who have little opportunity to find love. Either because they are plain or because their work keeps them so busy that they have little time for frivolity."

Teafa's words rang through Elizabeth's mind. She remembered Lord Zayne's smile. But she also remembered how quickly he had left the room as Lady Christine approached. She had thought nothing of it at the time. But his hasty retreat, almost bordering on ill manners, had not been like his previously calm and composed approach at all.

"Some time back, a man called Zacchaeus, a spy trained by Teebald held Lady Christine captive in the castle. He seduced one of Lady Christine's attendants and she showed him a back-way into the castle. But from her description, it surely could not be the same man."

"Lord Teebald has methods of altering a man's appearance." Elizabeth closed her eyes and breathed in as she tried to blot out what Teafa was trying to tell her. She could not believe that Lord Zayne meant Meira any harm, but she could not ignore Teafa's warning.

"Calm yourself, Elizabeth," said Teafa, with more resolve than she felt. "I will speak with Beatrice myself about my concerns before I return to the sanctuary. I only ask you to be cautious. "

"If King Radolf has planted spies, then we need to find those eggs and find them now. I will tell our team that we must return to the site first thing in the morning."

FORTY-THREE

Why

Teafa sat alone in the darkness. She could no longer bear the suffering. Dalila was asleep in the other room.

"What am I doing here?" she asked herself, not for the first time.

The suffering of those around her was becoming too much to bear. She had lost her own child, but now to watch little Dalila fade away seemed a cruelty too much to bear. She felt as if she had given too much of her life to the District.

Each day there were new arrivals at the refuge - women who had been rescued from the District. Their suffering tore at her heart. Now at night, she imagined picking up her meagre personal belongings and walking. Walking until her feet could carry her no longer. Walking to a place where no one knew her. She craved a place where the brokenness of those around her could no longer reach her.

Each time she closed the door of the hut, the path beckoned to her, and she could feel her heart begin to soar as she imagined the first steps of freedom away from this place. In her mind she could run and then as she ran faster and faster she could spread her arms and as they spread, her feet would lift from the ground and she would fly. She would fly in the sky with the birds who knew what a life of freedom was. The sun would kiss her skin and the sound of her laughter would fill her ears and the world would pass her. Trees and huts would fly past, racing faster and faster until she was so high that no pain could ever touch her. Her soul could rejoice the way it had when she was a young girl and believed in hope and love and joy.

But then what would become of those who so needed a lifeline of hope? Her dream of being free brought her sinking down to the earth again, spiralling slowly to the ground as the outstretched arms of the lost beckoned to her. They looked at her as if she was an angel descending from the sky. In her mind, she saw the guardian angels of all the lost standing behind her. Above their heads were the names of all the lost souls of the women and children who passed through her life in the District. And she remembered the verse "To those whom much has been given, much will be asked."

But Dalila was so young. She had never known the tender love of a man. Even in Teafa's relationship with her child's father, she had known the tenderness of physical love. But Dalila was still a child. Her virginity had been stolen in the District by customers of the vile man who ran the child prostitution camp. And now, with her young body diseased through syphilis, she had lost every chance of finding love.

Women with syphilis were far more likely to lose the child before the full term of pregnancy, but carrying the child to full growth was almost worse. The disease deformed the children into creatures no one wanted.

She had watched how the disease ate into the minds of those cursed with it. When the children raised in the district grew their first teeth, they had notches on them. Sometimes they would have seizures. For some there would be blindness.

She knew girls from poorer communities who saw an older man as a way to gain favours, pretty dresses and sometimes coin. But this often came at a price that far outweighed the temporary joy of their gifts.

She did not have the heart to tell Dalila of these troubles. But on quiet moonlit nights, Teafa would sneak out and let the tears overtake her. What she needed would never come. No matter how much she sought it, peace never came. She could not work her way out of it. There was no path to success. There was just pain and noise and more pain.

Teafa heard the door creak open. She angrily brushed away her tears. It was Dalila, holding tightly to her small rag poppet.

"Teafa, I woke up, and you were not in your bed," she said.

"I came to look at the moon."

Dalila looked into Teafa's eyes and touched her cheeks.

"Does the moon make you feel sad?" asked Dalila.

"A little," smiled Teafa.

Dalila shifted the fur she had around her shoulders to cover both of them.

"It's okay, Teafa, I will sit here with you, so the moonlight does not make you feel so lonely. I will protect you the way you protected me. I know God sent you to be my guardian angel," she said.

"Your what?" sniffed Teafa as she stared at Dalila in disbelief.

"My guardian angel," repeated Dalila. "Jesus told me in a dream. He told me he sends some special people with really big hearts to help the lost ones. And he told me he would send another one to help other girls that you do not know how to find. He told me that a man called Luke wrote what you need to know in the big book. He said to whom much is given… or something like that."

Teafa put her arm around Dalila's shoulder and kissed her cheek. She realised that her act of kindness in helping Maireid and Nathan find the lost girl, Mary, had taken her on a path that brought her here. Without Maireid and Nathan, she would never have escaped the District. And she would never have had the opportunity to share her freedom with Dalila.

Teafa knew she must find the purpose in her pain - she had been given so much and now she had to honour that gift and protect those who were every bit as much God's children as she was.

FORTY-FOUR

The Mission

"You need me to do what?" Nathan asked Elizabeth. He had just returned from a trading commission when Elizabeth arrived with the guards from the excavation site and visited him. She smiled when she saw the home he had built. Much had changed since Lord Logan first made him a stable boy. Now he was the trusted trade adviser for the region, and the treasury had grown substantially under his leadership.

"Nathan, we need you. Nadine cannot hatch the egg alone. You must act as her mate for this event," explained Elizabeth.

"But I am not a Mother Dragon Mate. Do you not remember that Nadine rejected my proposal? She told me she would never marry."

"I know, but even though you are not married, you are able to complete this duty. The Friar will be close by. We need only for you to make the first hunt for the hatchling. Nadine can not leave the egg unattended."

"You do not understand, Elizabeth… I cannot be near her right now. I… she still …" He broke off, shaking his head and averting his eyes.

"She moves you... Yes, I know. I understand that. But there is a time when we must do what is right even if it pains us."

"It does not pain me. It tears out a piece of my soul every time I see her. I gave my word of honour to Lord Logan that I would be part of the defence of the Kingdom. But that does not imply that I can be matched to an unwilling Dragon Whisperer."

Elizabeth touched his shoulder.

"I am sorry Nathan. It is not my intention to hurt you. I know that you love Nadine and that I am asking a lot. But have you considered the consequences of not offering your help?"

"Very well, I will take the bait… What are the consequences of not being the mate?"

"King Radolf needs a female Dragon Whisperer's presence to cause the egg to hatch. After they have hatched, he will need to break the bond. The only way to do that is by…"

"By killing the Dragon Whisperer…" Nathan sighed. "Can't you ask Muquin to fetch me when the egg is ready to hatch?"

"There may not be time. Yakhal was snatched just minutes before his mother came back from the hunt and we have no idea how Nadine will react to the hatching process. You say you love her… You surely do not want her to be vulnerable at the time when the Masked Man can sense the new life force?" Nathan narrowed his eyes at Elizabeth. He felt manipulated, but could not deny the logic of the Medicine Woman's words.

"Very well. I will help. But you better bring a year's supply of those vanilla cookies for me, so that I may find some solace in those buttery bits of heaven."

"We have an accord," smiled Elizabeth.

"We will have to ask Lord Logan's permission as I am meant to attend the training camp every day."

"Of course. When can you ask?"

"Tomorrow, after I present the trading reports. You should have my answer by midday."

ὁ

Lord Logan rubbed his hand over his jaw as he watched Nathan's discomfort at presenting his request. They were in the great hall of the castle going through the trading report when Nathan blurted out that he needed to take a leave of absence to help hatch the Emerald Forest Dragon Egg.

"I see the merits of you going. If King Radolf gets those eggs, the consequences would be disastrous. But I also cannot risk you staying away from training. Because after the last attack, King Radolf knows who you are. That puts you in danger."

"I will go with him," offered Nicolous. "I can train him and also show him what will become of any man who wishes to steal my daughter's virtue."

Nathan's cheeks turned scarlet, and he shuffled his feet as a distraction.

"A wise plan," Lord Logan grinned. But tell me Sir Nicolous, how will you manage if your leg is not fully healed?"

"Much of the movement has returned. And training Nathan will improve my strength and endurance. I do not need endurance to teach him the skills, but I can build my stamina while we train.

If the Friar goes with us, he can help train Nathan in stick fighting, which will be a valuable skill should he lose his sword in a skirmish. Nadine is also quite an accomplished archer. Her competitive nature will give him a worthy opponent to hone his archery skills."

"Of course, there is only one adversary to this plan that I must still conquer," said Nicolous.

"Your wife," said Lord Logan and Captain Julian in unison.

"Why is it only the married men who understand this?" grinned Sir Nicolous.

Lord Logan placed his hand on Sir Nicolous' shoulder.

"Shall I call the Friar to pray for you?"

"That may be prudent," said Nadine's father as he moved towards the door.

ϭ

Nicolous watched his wife move around the room, checking the linen for moth holes. He smiled as he thought of the day they first met. He had not yet known what a formidable woman she could be. He had seen her pretty smile, but knew little of how she could thrive in adversity. She was the kind of woman that he could always count on to do what was needed for the protection of the family. But it was that same fierceness that made him fear what he now had to tell her.

"Dorothea, how has your day been?"

"My day? Why did you ask? What is wrong?" Dorothea eyed him suspiciously.

"Can't a man ask his wife how her day has been?"

"A man can, but my husband? You are preparing me for something that you don't quite know how to tell me. What is it? Is it Nadine?"

"Why do you assume that it is about Nadine?"

"It is, isn't it? What is it now?" Her hands were on her hips and she looked ready for battle.

They were both quite accustomed to Nadine's daredevil exploits as a child. But ever since Muquin had taken the villagers hostage, Nadine's adventures had taken a dangerous turn. One which had swept them all up in its consequences.

Nicolous sat heavily on the chair. It was true that his leg was more mobile now, but after standing for long periods of time, it felt stiff.

"Where is my armour, Dorothea?".

"Your armour? Nicolous, no. You are not battle ready."

"It is just a precaution. I must accompany Nadine and Nathan to help them hatch the Emerald Forest Dragon egg."

"How do you help them hatch the egg? Surely it must hatch itself?"

Nicolous shook his head. "Just let me know where you have put my armour."

"The tunics are next to the garderobes."

"What? You know I hate that smell."

"I know, husband," she said, planting a kiss on his forehead. "But you also know that the smell of the urine keeps the moths away. Had I known that you needed them, I would have transferred the garments to the airing room with lavender and rose to dilute the odour. I will have the armour sanded and then oiled for you. Now tell me about this quest."

"A female Whisperer's presence can cause a dragon egg to hatch. But the father figure must complete a first hunt in order to ignite the life force in the hatchling. In the case of Nadine, Nathan is her mate."

"Not yet, he is not."

"My point exactly. Which is why I will accompany them, to ensure that they remain pure. But I will also train Nathan as he cannot attend training camp."

"You mean to say, they will be leaving the castle walls?"

"Yes." Nicolous braced himself for what was coming.

"Nicolous. No! The last time Nadine left the protection of the castle, look at what King Radolf did. Tears threatened to reveal themselves just at the sound of King Radolf's name on her tongue."

"Dorothea, I know it is a risk." Nicolous held his wife close. "But the alternative is far worse. If we do not claim these eggs, King Radolf will. And then…"

"Do not say it Nicolous. Do not say the words…"

"Dorothea, please help me prepare for the trip. We will leave at dawn's first light.

"Oh Father, God," prayed Dorothea silently. "Protect my child." She rested her head on her husband's chest and allowed her tears to roll freely down her cheeks.

FORTY-FIVE

The Calling

Nadine rolled out her sleeping mat next to the egg. Her father had brought straw and lined her side of the cave. She heard an owl's soft hooting outside. In the top of the cave the rocks shone with an iridescent light that made it feel as if there were stars gazing down on them.

Together Nicolous and Nathan had layered the bottom of the cave with the moss that they harvested from an underground cave nearby.

After Nadine told of the horror of the Yellow Spike Spiders they had decided not to hatch the egg underground, but in a converted cave that they transformed into a forest sanctuary. Nicolous had tucked soil into the pockets of rock lining of the cave and Nathan had spent the morning placing the plants that needed little sunshine around the entrance of the cave. The sanctuary cave had the soft fresh smell of earth drenched in rain.

The Copper Fire Dragon had forged thin funnels through the rock where they could channel water from the entrance through the inner plant sanctuary.

Nicolous had fashioned a small handheld harp with twisted cord. Although he was not an accomplished player, he could make music. Emerald Forest Whisperers were great lovers of music and the Dragon Whisperer said that regular music might help rekindle the life force of the dormant egg.

"When is your next moon flow?" asked the Dragon Whisperer.

"What sort of question is that?" asked Nadine.

"About two weeks before your flow, your body will release its own eggs before your moon flow. This will make your body ripe for making a child. The hatchling will sense the life force surge in you. It is the best time for the egg to hatch. At this time, you must be close to the egg," explained the Dragon Whisperer. "However, it is also a time when most women are in a heightened state of emotion. And at that time the Masked Man is most likely to sense you."

"Nicolous, you must be ready to protect Nadine and Nathan. You must have chosen and checked your route to get to the river and back again. You will need to work as a team and with nature to protect this egg."

"I understand," said Nicolous.

"Nadine, Knowing your moon flow cycle will help us prepare," said the Whisperer. "When the time comes, we will need the Friar. I worry that Nadine may not be able to contain her emotion when the egg is ready to hatch. The Friar will help protect Nadine. He is a man connected to the healing herbs of the earth and is a true spiritual warrior."

Nadine cleared her throat and turned away from Nathan's stare. Her fertility was not something she wanted him to hear about.

For Nathan, the thought of Nadine's femininity stirred him in a way that filled him with sorrow and longing all at the same time. He remembered the touch of her hands, the time she had tried to remove his bee stings when they first met. His mind swirled with the thought of the warmth of her body pressed against his when they rode together, and the exhilaration that had drawn him in when they had first flown on a dragon.

He turned away so that she could not see the emotion in his eyes as he tried to control his feelings. It was going to be an arduous few weeks.

"Where is the best fishing spot from here?" he asked, trying to keep his voice low and even.

"I will take you tonight," said the Dragon Whisperer. "Nicolous, will you watch the egg for us? I will need Nadine to see where Nathan will be fishing. She must be connected to him. As a Dragon Mother she must know how long it takes for him to get back, so she can pace herself. If she is worried about how long he will take, her anxiety will reach the hatchling and break the sense of harmony that it must have to thrive."

C

As the last rays of the sun began to colour the cave with its crimson hues, the Dragon Whisperer returned to Nadine and Nathan.

"Remove your shoes."

"For what purpose?" asked Nadine.

"To feel the earth beneath your feet. Emerald Forest Dragon Whisperers are at one with the earth. They seldom wear shoes. They wear them only for travelling, inside the forest they are barefoot."

Nadine felt the softness of the delicate moist moss under her soles. She spread her toes out and felt the green sponginess of the moss press between them and sighed at the pleasure of the gentle cushioning beneath her feet. She looked over at Nathan, who stood in stony silence with his bare feet on the damp moss.

Nicolous sensed their discomfort with each other. But the

Dragon Whisperer seemed to be immune to the young people's raging emotions.

When the silence became crushingly heavy, the Dragon Whisperer turned and led them out of the cave.

Nadine felt the small, hard crunchiness of the fine bed of crushed stone outside the cave and hobbled slightly as her feet found a way to balance the weight of her body on the stones. The earth felt cool under her feet as they followed the Dragon Whisperer down the path to the stream.

They walked in silence, as the Dragon Whisperer had instructed. Nadine and Nathan felt each caress of the night air on their skin and the different textures of the path under their feet. The damp soil reminded Nathan of his boyhood home, where he helped his father sow seeds in the cool of the evening. They soon arrived at the stream.

"Sit on the bank and listen to the sound of the forest."

The zing of the night insects buzzed in harmony with night sounds, and a soft peacefulness began to roll over them.

"Now take off your cloaks and pull up the sleeves of your tunics."

Nadine felt the prickle of goose flesh emerge on her body.

"Breathe out slowly until your body welcomes the new temperature on your skin. Now step into the stream."

Nadine gasped as the cold seemed to rush from her toes all the way up her body.

"Keep still and keep breathing until your body calms."

Nadine trembled all over and could barely contain the chattering of her teeth.

"Breathe, Nadine…Now stretch out your hand and feel the caress of the water flowing over your palms."

As Nadine's breathing slowed, she began to feel the movements of the forest. The gentle rush of the water and the hum of the night's insects.

"When you are still, the fish will come. Do not attempt to

grasp the fish. Just let them flow over your outstretched palms."

After a few minutes, Nathan sensed, rather than heard, a gentle movement of the water as a curious fish made its way towards him.

He could feel the water respond to the pressure of the fish's body as it sliced through the water. He steeled his mind to force his fingers to remain outstretched.

The Dragon Whisperer waited until several fish had passed over Nathan's hands before he instructed Nathan to open and close his hands.

"Keep the slow pace until the fish feel at peace with you."

Nadine and Nathan both flexed and closed their fingers in a gentle rhythm, as the fish began to circle around their hands.

"Now time it, so that when the next fish is just about to pass the edges of your fingers that you close your hand around the fish."

Nathan curled his fingers under the fish as it touched his fingers and he slowly covered the fish with his other hand.

"Now, pull the fish out of the water." Nathan grasped for it, but the fish slipped away.

"Do not be discouraged, we will try again tomorrow night, " said the Whisperer.

Nadine and Nathan stepped out of the stream. They shivered as the cool air passed over their skin and their wet clothing clung to their bodies.

"Now we will return to the cave." Nadine made a move to run back to the Sanctuary Cave.

"No! Nadine! Do not run. Embrace the cold. Feel how your skin responds to its touch."

By the time Nadine and Nathan returned, their muscles were rigid with cold. Inside, Nicolous had built a fire. Nadine stepped into the cave.

"No, do not enter. Stand here and let the heat of the fire

grow from within the cave and reach you. Remember to breathe."

Nadine could feel her body relax as the gentle sway of the fire's heat as it reached her. When Nadine and Nathan had wiped their feet, the Dragon Whisperer allowed them to enter the cave, where Nicolous handed them each a bowl of steaming pea and shredded pork pottage. Sleep came easily at first, but the proximity of the egg kept Nadine's senses alert and soon the night sounds pulled her from her dreams.

Nadine slapped at the high-pitched zing of a mosquito in the dark cave. But the disappearance of its shrill sound did not lull her back to sleep. Instead, she sat up and absorbed the sounds of the night. The rhythmic clicking and croaking of the frogs drifted across the night air along the riverbanks as they sang back and forth to each other. Nadine felt the prickle of the cool air as she searched for the crimson flames that had bled out into the night. She pulled her cloak around her and slipped past her father's sleeping silhouette.

The young Dragon Whisperer padded through the spongy moss cloaked in the softness of a thick fur. She stepped out into the cool night air and absorbed the surrounding sounds. It was a symphony of clicks, buzzes and the occasional squawk of birds she did not yet know the names of. Each one called across the forest floor to its own kind amidst the din of the hundreds of emerging pre-dawn creatures. Nadine looked out over the shadows of the trees to the light that was hidden just beyond them and thought of Muquin.

The Silver Wing Whisperer wondered if they were looking at the same starless part of the sky. She breathed in the cool air and the chill sent a river of quivers through her. Nadine somehow felt more alive than she ever had. A movement behind her startled her, and she saw Nathan step out from the shadows of the cave.

"Please do not speak," she thought, as her eyes remained fixed on some unknown point in the sky. But Nathan did not invade the solitude of her mind. He stood in silence beside her, enveloped by his own furs.

For a moment the sound of his breath invaded the symphony of sounds in her head, as her senses welcomed his scent and life force into her space. But he seemed to blend into the sounds that danced around her. Nadine's blood slowed in her veins as she breathed in the peacefulness of the night. Then she felt Nathan's hand slip into hers. Her breath was sharp as she felt the strength of his hands surge through hers. This time she did not resist him, and he knitted his fingers between hers. Nadine felt a tremor run through her core, and she did not pull her hand away.

In the cool air, the warmth of his touch made her feel safe. They stood in silence for a few moments, and Nadine turned to look at his face. His firm jaw was outlined by the hidden moon's gift of light.

Nathan felt her eyes on him and moved his arm around her shoulders. She leaned in and pressed her head onto his chest. The sounds of the forest seemed to melt into a soft blanket of music. Nadine only heard the thundering of his heart. The Silver Wing Whisperer felt stirrings unknown to her. But the piercing whistle of a bird in the distance pulled her senses away and she felt a hook of panic tug at her heart.

The hum and hiss of the night insects rose from a gentle background sound to a growing frenzy.

Nadine felt a sharp sensation inside her body. From Elizabeth and her mother, she knew that it was the time when her body was at its ripest for making a child. But this pain had an unknown intensity to it. The sounds of the forest grew until they screamed at her pounding head with their songs. And her mind was filled with a screeching that ripped at her sanity. She crumpled to the ground, clutching her stomach.

"Nathan," she wept. "It hurts." Nathan scooped Nadine up in his arms and carried her into the cave.

"Sir Nicolous! Nadine needs you," called Nathan. Nadine

lay quivering in Nathan's arms as wave upon wave of pain surged through her body. The tears ran unchecked from her eyes. Nicolous clasped Nadine's hand.

"Nadine, what is it, child?" But Nadine could not speak. Her hand stretched forward towards the egg, and Nicolous turned to see the egg quiver. Then he knew. He had seen this look on Dorothea's face with each child she bore. The panic as the pain of birth clawed at her sanity.

"Nathan, it is time for the egg to hatch. Go now, boy, to the river and get the fish. I will take care of Nadine."

Nathan stood and stared at Nadine. His heart burned as he watched the woman he loved writhing in pain.

"Go now! And also bring back some clear spring water for Nadine," roared Nicolous. Rivers of sweat poured from Nadine's brow. She whimpered again.

Her father carried her to the egg and frantically placed the flowers in the pattern that the Dragon Whisperer had instructed. He knew nothing about dragons, but he knew about childbirth. And somehow Nadine's body was responding to the hatchling as if she was birthing it herself.

He stretched over and grabbed her pack with his free hand. Nicolous held onto Nadine's hand with the other. He kissed her forehead and then shook the contents of the pack out onto the floor of the cave in front of him. There he found the book he needed. He prayed that he would find the right page. They had been caught unprepared. He should have sent for the Friar days before, but none of them had known the signs.

A surge of power shook Nadine, and she pulled her head back as another wave of pain ripped through her. Nicolous grasped her hands and lifted her body up and into a seated position. He placed the egg in front of her.

"Father, the Masked Man, he calls!"

Nicolous scanned the cave and, letting go of his daughter's hand, he hurried over to the extinguished fire. He found two charred sticks of wood which he fashioned into a cross with some loose vines.

Nicolous returned to Nadine's side and placed the cross in her hands.

"Hold on to this and look into my eyes!" He scanned the book again.

"Heavenly Father," he prayed, "In the Book of Samuel, you showed us how you protected David from Saul. Saul relentlessly pursued David, a man after your own heart. But you distracted Saul with the threat of the Philistines. And so, I pray now that you protect my child from the Masked Man.

Protect her, protect her, protect her…"

Nicolous held onto Nadine's shoulders, whispering God's protection over her again and again, as he

held her gaze.

Nadine's eyes never left his as he steadied her against the pain.

The egg wobbled, and they heard a crack as a tiny talon emerged from the shell.

"Nadine, the hatchling, it is coming," Nicolous smiled as he sensed the end was near.

Nadine nodded through her tears and groaned again as another wave of pain seared through her.

Nathan stumbled over the rocks close to the river. He plunged into the water and searched frantically for the fish he needed. But the fish darted away into the pockets of rocks below the icy morning depths of the river. Nathan felt a sense of despair. Then he remembered the Dragon Whisperer's instructions.

"Be still and be at one with the river."

Nathan fought to control his erratic breath. He closed his eyes and opened his palms in the water.

He tried to concentrate on a single species of animal. A bird called to its mate from a tree nearby. Nathan forced his mind to hone onto that one sound. His breath was laboured as he battled to calm himself. Visions of Nadine's face contorted in pain flickered back into view.

Nathan growled at his impotence. He knew that focusing on despair would do little to help Nadine now. He tried again to calm his mind and heaved in a shaky breath until he filled his lungs to the brim. Nathan held onto the breath and pushed it out.

As he exhaled, a calmness entered him, and he inhaled again. Time seemed to fight against Nathan, but he breathed in again, focussing on the breath leaving his body. Slowly Nathan's body relaxed until he felt part of the river. He repeated the words the Friar had told him.

"Be still and know that I am God."

Nathan felt the rise of the gooseflesh, but instead of fighting it, he let it pass as the Dragon Whisperer had instructed and he repeated Friar Watt's phrase again as he settled his mind.

The first kiss of the morning sun pierced the water's surface and danced over the satiny silver scales of the fish that approached Nathan's form. He let them circle his ankles and swirl around his legs.

Then they sought his hands, which formed an arc in the clear water. He resisted the urge to grasp the first one and waited patiently for the curiosity of the fish below to mature. Nathan felt them swirl around him and as the first fish moved away, he sensed it was time and closed his hands around one of their floating forms and pulled it into the open air.

Nathan thrust the fish into a watertight pouch already filled with stream water.

"I thank you God for your gifts."

As the prayer left his lips, he turned and saw a bush of the berries that Nadine so loved. He grabbed a few handfuls and placed them into his pouch, and secured the river water Nicolous had requested. Nathan prayed for Nadine with every step as he ran back to the cave.

ⴰ

Nicolous wiped Nadine's brow as her body arched into a spasm again. But by now they could see the soft sheen of the hatchling's pale green scales as it clawed through the egg.

Nicolous hoped that once the head of the hatchling had emerged that Nadine's pain would subside, as it had when Dorothea had birthed their children.

His daughter's head hung in exhaustion as she still clutched the cross that he had made for her. She peered at Nathan through swollen eyes as he entered the cave.

She tried to form a reassuring smile when she saw the look of horror on his face, but her eyes only creased to squeeze out more tears. Nathan approached slowly as he saw the egg wobble and fall over.

The tiny hatchling, no bigger than a newborn kitten, stumbled out of the ruptured egg and chirped as its talons flexed to find something to grip onto.

Nadine's body slumped in exhaustion.

"Nadine!" shouted Nicolous. "The hatchling, it lives. Nathan, bring the fish. We must turn the hatchling so that the fish lies between it and Nadine, and then we must step away so that she is the first thing it sees when its eyes open."

Nathan positioned the fish, and the two men moved to the side of the cave.

"You did well, Nathan." Nicolous embraced the younger man.

Nathan nodded, but his eyes never left Nadine as she picked up the hatchling. She pressed her forehead to the tiny creature and pushed the still flapping fish towards its snout. Sniffing the fish, the hatchling slowly opened its eyes. It chirped and gazed at Nadine's swollen face. The pale scales of its body radiated with energy, and a golden light formed a halo around its body. The tiny dragon grew as the life force of the bond between Nadine and the hatchling burst forth. The little dragon turned its head to the side as it gazed at Nadine's shining blue-green eyes.

She smiled as it pushed the fish towards her. The hatchling's tiny teeth sliced into the fish, absorbing nature's offering to the new Emerald Forest Dragon's life force. Another growth spurt surged through and its body swelled to the size of one of the small dogs that some ladies at court kept as pets.

"Come, Nathan," called Nadine, as the hatchling clambered into her arms.

Nathan turned to Nicolous, who was paging through the book.

"Go, it says here that you must both whisper its chosen name to the hatchilng. Later we will have a proper ceremony, but for now both parents whisper the name. And then step back, because it may grow again."

Nathan kissed Nadine on the forehead. His eyes were wide with wonder as he gazed at the new life they held between them. Nadine had suffered so to help the hatchling emerge from the egg. He knew of no greater sacrifice than for a mother to suffer so for a new life. Although this hatchling was not of their kind, Nadine had been the mother figure it needed to live and it honoured Nathan to be part of the circle of love that now formed on this wondrous day.

"May I hold the hatchling?" he asked Nicolous.

Nicolous looked down at the pages.

"Yes," he smiled. "The hatchling has already formed a bond with Nadine. You may hold it."

Nadine handed the hatchling to Nathan, who gazed curiously at him.

"Hello," Nathan dropped his head for the forehead greeting that he has seen Nadine do so many times.

The hatchling returned the forehead greeting and spat out a little fish onto Nathan's arm, and pushed it with its face.

"I think it wants you to eat it," laughed Nicolous.

"Um… he regurgitated it." Nathan grimaced.

"Go on, it won't kill you. It is a great honour," said Nicolous.

Nathan's forced smile made Nadine laugh. He picked up the fish, closed his eyes and swallowed hard. His stomach lurched as the fish slid down his throat.

"That was… revolting… but thank you… I think," Nathan told the hatchling.

The hatchling's sharp, small talons pierced Nathan's skin as it scurried up his arm and onto his shoulder.

"Ouch. Now I know why falconers wear leather coverings on their arms."

Nathan knelt, with the hatchling still gripping onto his shoulder. He was grateful for the leather shoulder detail on his tunic. He reached into his pouch and pulled out the berries he had collected for Nadine.

"Oh Nathan, you found my favourite," she cried as she reached for one. But the hatchling jumped off Nathan's shoulder and devoured them all. Its tiny tongue licked the last drops of juice from the tip of its snout as it greedily sniffed the ground for more.

Nadine's mouth hung open. Nicolous laughed, "Now you know how your mother and I felt when you were a child."

"Funny," huffed Nadine.

"Do you feel strong enough to walk," asked Nathan.

"I may faint with hunger," said Nadine, "but I think I can."

"Well, the berry bush is quite close by. Shall we walk to the stream so you can bathe? We can grab some berries along the way. I can make a small fire and make us breakfast."

Nicolous and Nathan helped Nadine to her feet. Her legs

quivered a bit. But they steadied her as they led her outside the cave.

"I can't believe that Maimi did that three times. It was awful." Nadine rubbed her arms as she stood, absorbing the sunshine.

"One moment, please," said Nicolous as he moved back to the cave.

He brought a shawl. "Cover your chest with this."

Nadine looked with horror at the slow dark spread on her tunic. "It can't be."

"What is it? Is she injured?" asked Nathan.

"No. She is not injured. It is milk."

"But how can that be?"

Nicolous leafed through the pages.

"It says here that when a female Dragon Whisperer goes through a hatching, the hormones of her body react in the same way as a normal birth."

"But dragons don't suckle, do they?"

"They don't. It says here that it will pass in a few days, but that there is a risk of milk fever to the Whisperer. So, we need to get back to Elizabeth soon. There is another purpose for the milk, though," said Nicolous.

"What is that?" asked Nathan. Nicolous looked at Nadine. She could feel the intensity of their stares.

"What are you not telling me?" asked Nathan as he looked at their faces.

Nadine gazed at the two men she loved. The silver in her father's hair and the strength in Nathan's body. Time stood still in this circle of love that had helped bring the hatchling into the world. They were bonded together forever. The hatching's arrival had changed everything.

"I am ready Father."

Nicolous nodded. His eyes were bright with tears as he pulled her close and kissed Nadine on the forehead.

"Will someone please tell me what just happened?" asked Nathan.

"I think, Nathan, that Nadine just accepted your proposal," smiled Nicolous.

"What? Nadine, is it true?"

"Yes," she smiled. Nathan grabbed Nadine and swirled her around.

"Argh," screamed Nadine. He stepped away in horror.

"Did I hurt you?"

"Nathan, it is the milk. It hurts my breasts," she said, as her face turned scarlet.

"The milk makes the breasts swell, Nathan," explained Nicolous. "They will be tender until the supply is gone. Be gentle with her."

"I am sorry," said Nathan as he drew her face towards his. He kissed her cheeks "I love you."

"And I love you." Nadine picked up the hatchling which had slid to the ground when Nathan grabbed her.

It gave Nathan a reproachful stare as it settled on Nadine's shoulder.

"What? Don't look so cross. We are going to be a family." Nathan grinned. "Now let's get that breakfast sorted."

ⴰ

A cry of silent rage filled the Masked Man as he cleared his table in a single furious swipe. He had failed to reach them in time, and now the egg had hatched. Nadine had bonded with another. And he had nothing. Nothing at all to show for all his planning.

A look of hatred spread over his face. His brother's camp was winning yet again. There had to be a way to trap that girl and stop her before she found the other eggs. With each bonding she grew stronger, because love was indeed a powerful force.

There had to be a way of luring them in. His reports were becoming harder to complete. He had to keep one step ahead of the King, but always the spies found some new form of intelligence that forced him to change plans. Nadine grew stronger with each day, and the love bond she had now formed made it almost impossible to read her. Except for the moments when the pain of the… He stopped and stared at his scroll collection. The young Whisperer had milk. Without a babe to suckle, she faced the risk of milk fever. Which meant that she would seek the help of the Medicine Woman. He drummed his fingers on the table as his mind recalculated his course of action. Elizabeth was the woman that his brother loved. Perhaps there was another way. He rummaged through his scrolls. Somewhere there was a map for an abandoned Copper Fire Dragon Whisperer's lair.

A knock on the door startled him. He grabbed the mask and covered his face. The members of the King's council were being summoned to meet. He knew that the King's spy was in Lord Logan's territory. He would have to get there as well. There were two places that he needed to visit.

FORTY-SIX

Remembrance

Nadine slipped out of the Sanctuary Cave into the cool night air. She inhaled deeply. Since she had come to this place, there was a peacefulness in her spirit. She wondered if this is what Elizabeth felt as she walked through the land of the Ancients. In the night's silence, she could hear the trickle of the water of the stream in the distance. She had never had this level of sensory sensitivity. Nadine felt as if the constant chatter in her mind reached a crescendo of penetrating sounds she could not block out. As if even a whisper was a scream. The Dragon Whisperer had told her that in time she would learn to manage them. An Emerald Forest Whisperer was the best tutor for this. But so far there was no evidence of the other Whisperers surviving.

Nadine infuriated her father by insisting on walking alone at night. She would wait until she saw his forehead drop forward and his chin rest on his chest before she snuck out. He had not been the same since his captivity in the Dragon Tunnels. She knew he loved her, but his worry for her felt like a cage that held her spirit captive. In the dark, her spirit could soar. A call of a wolf in the distance sent a quiver through her. The slow call of a pack mingled with the whistle-like hoot of a solitary owl. There was a rustle in the leaves ahead. Nadine shivered at the intrusion and pulled her Emerald Forest Dragon cloak a little closer. The young Whisperer looked up at the moon, framed by a circular cluster of branches. In the night sky they looked stripped of leaves, but the daylight would reveal the tiny first buds of spring. The night lights changed in intensity as a swift progression of clouds drifted by, covering and uncovering the full moon in their path. She felt as if her thoughts were sailing on the clouds to their sanctuary.

Nadine knew, too, that soon Nathan would wake and come to find her. But for now she could be alone with no words, no instructions, just her heartbeat. The Whisperer honing her mind by concentrating on one sound at a time. She tried to listen to the shrill bursts of the beetles' call, but could only sustain this honing for a few seconds. Soon the frogs and crickets' sounds penetrated her focus, and she felt her thoughts run wild again. There was the snap of the twigs again - and something burst through the trees. Panic rose in Nadine, but to her relief, it was only a hare.

The clouds cleared for a moment, and the creature stopped and looked at her. It lifted onto its hind legs and held up its front paws. Its nose twitched and its bright eyes flickered in the moonlight. The hare seemed mesmerised.

In a sudden flash of fur and ravenous jaws, it was gone, and Nadine gasped. A wolf turned to face her with the hare, limp between its teeth.

Its silver fur was thick and lifted gently in the breeze. Nadine felt a prickle of fear as the wolf stepped over the fallen branches that lay between them. Its paws danced over the surface of the ground and bridged the distance between them. But Nadine could not bring herself to move. With just an arm's length between them, the wolf stopped and dropped its prey at Nadine's feet. Then it raised its head and howled.

A return call startled Nadine, and her gaze snapped to the

side to see a group of younger wolves emerge from below the trees.

"Nadine!" Nathan called. He ran out towards her, and the glint of metal shone in his hand. The wolf snarled at him, looked at Nadine, and then ran back through a cluster of bushes.

It turned again to look at her and its gaze returned for a second to the hare it had left at Nadine's feet. Nathan tried to pull Nadine away, but she broke loose and bent down to pick up the hare.

She bowed to the wolf, and it turned and disappeared into the night.

"What happened?" asked Nathan.

"I think a mother just returned a favour," replied Nadine. "Feel like making wild hare stew for our meal?" Nathan looked back in the stream's direction.

"Yes, but only if you promise not to go off like that alone again."

"Sorry, that is not fair trade."

"Why do I even bother?" Nathan shook his head and marched off towards the cave.

Nadine smiled when she saw the first sparks ignite into a flaming dance. Soon Nathan would prepare the warming drinks that she so loved.

FORTY-SEVEN

A Time to Rise

In the Tunnels of History, Adira, the Guardian, checked the vessel. There was only one scoop of the precious powder left. Her eyes followed the lines of carved shelves. She snorted. "Why did I think that I, as Keeper of History, would not have misplaced a jar?"

She mixed a paste with a mixture of berries and herbs according to the recipe in the book. Emuna looked up from her harp. Adira marvelled that her small, aged hands could still pluck out the beauty of the knotted cords. She looked at the man that lay on the stone. Arpachshad's peaceful face remained unmoved.

"Your music makes me feel as peaceful as your great-uncle looks," said Adira as she handed Emuna the bowl and drinking vessel.

Emuna glanced at the contents and then looked up at Adira.

"It is the last of the baobab powder," said Adira. "The tunnels that lead to the row of trees have collapsed. I can no longer travel there to harvest it for you."

Emuna nodded in silence as she swallowed the mixture from the vessel carved from the outer shell of baobab fruit.

Adira lifted Arpachshad's head for Emuna to scoop the mixture into his mouth. They turned him and massaged his body. Adira lifted his limbs and began the rhythmic movements to exercise his muscles. Then she pulled the lever that opened the top of the cave. Emuna lifted her face to the warmth of the sun's streaming light. The surrounding plants seemed to smile as they welcomed the nourishing rays that illuminated their leaves.

"The warmth eases my joints," sighed Emuna.

Adira placed her hand under Emuna's arm. "Let's walk off some of that stiffness."

"Emuna, is it not time to plant some herbs from the seeds in the pouch? I know there are plants there that would ease your suffering."

"Do not tempt an old woman," Emuna scolded. "They are his to protect."

Adira nodded. "I know, but time has moved slowly, and I have no other ways to help you now."

Emuna patted her hand. "You have been a faithful companion all these years. I am grateful for your care. I do not know how we would have managed without you."

The word "we" made Adira turn to consider Arpachshad.

Each day Emuna had cleaned the old carvings of history, as she and her family for generations had done before her. Many of the carvings were by Emuna's own hand and some by her mother's hand.

Adira had tirelessly pursued many of the anti-aging plants and herbs that Emuna's body needed to be strong enough to keep caring for Arpachshad - a task that was passed to her by her mother. But her withered body could not endure forever. Immortality was not a gift for the Custodians. Emuna's life force was like a candle flame in a breeze. Its light reached into the darkest spaces, but too strong a wind could extinguish it in a moment. And then what would become of Arpachshad?

To record history, Adira had to travel. The Keeper of

History had always prepared Emuna for her absence, but her return showed that the lack of support added extra weight to the ravages of time. Adira was reluctant to go on this next trip. But she knew she could no longer delay. There was an uprising, and she was the closest Custodian to witness and record. She could not let her love for the old woman detract her from her purpose.

Ͼ

As nations collided in their plans to rule, in the forest there was a unique energy and for the first time in over a hundred years Arpachshad's eyes flickered open. Adira would return to find Emuna's body curled up in her favoured patch of yellow tulips with an eternal peace etched on her withered face. But there was no trace of Arpachshad.

ổ

Arpachshad stepped into the clearing. He searched for the cluster of oaks near the rivers. The Emerald Forest Dragon Whisperer hoped that the dark ones had not burned them, as they had destroyed so many of the sacred oaks. He could not yet locate the dragon, but knew it must have hatched for him to have awoken. The life force was not strong enough, but he could sense the Silver Wing Whisperer. Her energy clashed with the forest, and in doing so, she placed the hatchling at risk.

There was an enemy searching for the young woman. He felt the urgent probing of a force that meant them harm. Below the tree lay his marker. Arpachshad used his dagger to cut away the overgrowth until the carved root revealed itself. The root appeared connected to the tree, but he had hollowed it out before the end of the last war and inside lay Arpachshad's weapons: a whip woven from a blend of hair and vines, his dragon claw stars and his walking staff. Although his great-niece had meticulously cared for him, turning and exercising his muscles, Arpachshad still felt stiff. He stretched his neck and rolled his shoulders and then stood for a moment, absorbing the forest sounds. The hatchling was of Ciommed's own line. Once the Silver Wing Whisperer had matured, they would search for another together. But for now, she needed his help. He opened the leather pouch and breathed in the sacred herbs that he had blended together so long ago. They revived his senses, and he felt at one with the earth again.

Without a dragon he would have to make his way through the forest unaided, but the river would help him. He looked for the largest tree. Wrapped around it was what appeared to be a large hunk of bark. It was, in fact, a River float that would take him to the waterfall and from there he could climb the trees and move through the intertwined branches until they got to the cluster of caves where he sensed the Silver Wing Whisperer. It was best not to travel on the ground. Too many predators of dragons used the roads, and he needed a good vantage point.

It took him several days to pinpoint Nadine's location, but when he arrived, he could feel the ominous energy of the forest. Something other than the normal cycle of life had disturbed its creatures. He crouched on the thickest branch of the oldest tree. It would take ten grown men to encircle its massive trunk.

This ancient friend of the forest was one of the last of its kind. Man had harvested far too many of the ancient oaks. Arpachshad saw a young woman walk out of the cave. He watched a man tap her on her shoulder and dart away. The Emerald Forest Whisperer smiled at the playful exuberance of youth.

Then he saw it… the hatchling. A mischievous sparkle gleamed in the hatchling's eyes. He had the male jealousy of a hatchling besotted with its mother figure, and he strutted with the pride of a fine peacock, showing off the width of his speckled green wings. The trio seemed to have the bliss of a young family, unaware of the impending danger. Arpachshad sniffed the air. The predators were already there, but as yet he could not spot them.

ϭ

A web of rope fell from a tree… a net. To his horror, he watched the net ensnare the hatchling. The Silver Wing Whisperer screamed, but Arpachshad did not move. He scanned the treetops to find the attackers. There were five in the underbrush, making their way towards the female Whisperer and the hatchling.

He needed the forest's help, but he was unfamiliar with the plants as he had last travelled these parts more than 100 years before. Then Arpachshad saw the fine column of dragon-silk hanging vines. He knew that this plant had fine needle-like reverse barbs on the stem. Arpachshad jumped from branch to branch until he found them. With a stroke of his whip, he propelled the plants into a swaying motion. They were almost invisible to the naked eye, but swung into the faces of three of the men, painfully ensnaring the skin of their eyelids and cheeks. As the fine thorns were reversed, victims would try to pull the barbs backwards to release their grip, but these men did not know that and the more they struggled, the deeper the barbs penetrated.

The young Whisperer's screams had alerted a man who now came running out of the cave. The Whisperer showed signs of training, but her instincts were immature and without weapons she was just another thrashing woman struggling against the worst kind of man.

He saw one attacker step out from behind a tree and take aim at the older man, whom he assumed was the Whisperer's father. With a flick of his wrist, Arpachshad released a dragon-claw star, severing the attacker's jugular. Blood erupted from the wound, and the man's body crumpled and crashed to the ground in front of the older man. The dead man's blood tarnished the earth and Arpachshad sighed at the loss of life. He designed his weapons to save life, never to take one.

He threw two of his remaining dragon-claw stars at the ropes that had trapped the hatchling. The creature broke free and Arpachshad whistled, signalling the Emerald Forest Dragon to climb. The hatchling's eyes searched the trees for the source of the sound, but could not resist the Whisperer's call.

Two men grabbed hold of Nadine and threatened to kill her if Nicolous or Nathan came any closer. From the forest, Arpachshad saw a flash of white as a solitary wolf rushed out of the shadows. Without a sound, the creature pounced on one man and pulled him down. Her teeth sank into his shoulder as she dragged him, thrashing and screaming, towards the trees.

Outnumbered, the final assailant released Nadine and tried to escape into the forest. Arpachshad stepped out of the way, but Nathan ran after the assailant and ended his life by throwing his dagger at the escaping man.

FORTY-EIGHT

No Turning back

The servant inside Lord Zayne's manor could no longer ignore what was happening; the child was hot to the touch. She called Meira's head attendant.

The older woman did not even need to feel Meira's brow; the angry red glare of the wound told her everything she needed to know.

"You were meant to change the dressing every day. They sack servants for less, and if Lord Zayne was a flogging man, I for one would offer you up. You are a lazy and reckless girl. Now take these sheets and get out of my sight before I flog you myself." She left the room and gave instructions to call for the Medicine Woman. Now she would have to tell Lord Zayne.

C

Lord Zayne stood on the balcony, staring into the distance. It disturbed her that in the last few days he had missed his meals. He seemed trapped by a growing melancholy. What was he waiting for? He had not even been in to check on his ward for two days, as if he was distancing himself from her.

"Lord Zayne, you must come. It is Meira... She is... unwell." She drew to the side and indicated with a gesture that he should follow.

Lord Zayne smelled the putrefied flash before entering the room. He shot a stern look at the servant.

"Who is responsible for this?"

"I am, Lord Zayne," she said with lowered eyes.

"I doubt that. You are covering for someone you delegated the task to. Have you called for the Medicine Woman?"

"I have."

"Good. Now bring me some boiling water and fresh linens. I will remove the bandages myself and clean up as best I can before she arrives."

Lord Zayne felt the heat of the wound before he even touched Meira's skin. The soggy bandages stuck to the pus filled skin. It had expanded so that small blisters had formed as the festering contents oozed from the skin. He tried to remove a bandage from her chin, but it seemed stuck to her skin.

He soaked a strip of linen in the hot water and added it to the messy mass on the girl's chin. The water soaked through the bandages, releasing the hold of the underlying bandages and allowing him to pry them off. As the last of them came away, Elizabeth entered the room.

A look of shame came over Lord Zayne. Elizabeth saw his vulnerability, and it tugged at her heart. She realized he cared for the child - but now was not the time for reproach. They had to focus on healing Meira.

"Your servant has explained the circumstances. I see you have already prepared the wound for me. You have done well. I have no urgent cases. I suggest I close my rooms for a day or two and remain close to help her."

"I have a guest room that adjoins this one, you may stay here."

Teafa's words "Be careful, Elizabeth," haunted Elizabeth now.

"It is just a suggestion. The servants can bring you keys and I am happy to stay at the inn tonight."

"I… Perhaps that won't be necessary."

Lord Zayne placed his hand on hers. "Please… Elizabeth, I do not know what would become of me if anything should happen to her."

The Medicine Woman cleared her throat noisily and removed her hand from his.

"Forgive me," he said, and looked away.

Elizabeth busied herself with her instruments, laying them out on the table. She put her leather apron on and took out a fine bone slither, sharpened to a point.

"I would be grateful if you can keep her still - and perhaps you should change; this may get messy."

Lord Zayne called for his manservant to fetch his work shirt. Then he reached back and pulled his own shirt off in a single swift movement, leaving the skin of his back exposed. A few aged scars formed a light pattern on his back. Elizabeth recognized them as flogging marks, but instead of pity she felt an odd stirring. Lord Zayne had a vibrant energy that flowed through him. She felt curious about his history, but drew her thoughts back to her patient. Lord Zayne turned as he put the fresh shirt on, and the glimpse of the muscular lines of his stomach stained her cheeks scarlet. He saw her looking at him, but diverted his eyes to Meira.

"What do you need me to do?" he asked.

"I need her to keep still, while I lance this wound. Sometimes it trickles and sometimes it explodes. I can not say which, but I am hoping to drain it gently."

Lord Zayne's eyes filled with pity at the sight of Meira's face, but he steeled himself to the task at hand.

Elizabeth pressed on either side of the angriest part of the wound and touched the tip of the bone slither against the wound. An angry eruption of pus and blood splattered against her apron. She mopped up the mess with fresh strips of linen. Lord Zayne remained unflinching, although some mess had landed on him.

"Is it cleared?" he asked.

"Not yet. No. I will draw it out with more hot strips of linen. The heat will bring the infection to the surface. But after that, I will need to apply pressure to purge all of it. For now, let us clear up and let her rest for the hard work is yet to come."

Lord Zayne called for his servant.

"Please open the guest room for the Medicine Woman and bring her hot water to freshen up. I would be grateful if you could bring us a meal here in Meira's room."

Elizabeth stepped into the side-room. She found a new dress lying on the bed and boiling water infused with jasmine blossoms in a bowl on the table. There were fresh-cut flowers in the corner and a small flask of wine. She wondered how many women had found themselves in this room. Although the whispered gossip between some of her patients had revealed that Lord Zayne did not entertain any guests at his home.

Elizabeth had not thought to bring a change of clothing. At first she did not want to wear this new garment, but despite her apron, her dress was still coated in filth. This dress was ideal for a woman of her calling. Practical yet flattering, with simple embroidered green flowers along the seams of the neckline and shoulders. The shoulders had thin leather epaulettes sewn into them and the entire length of the shoulder had the same soft leather reinforcing the garment. Men seldom got the size of a woman right, but this dress appeared to have been made specifically for her. The green brought out the colour of her eyes, and she blushed as she looked at herself in the polished mirror on the small table.

Elizabeth fidgeted with the panelled seams as she entered Meira's room.

"Thank you for the dress. She saw he had also changed his garments. Lord Zayne reached beside him and held out a leather garment.

"The artisan designed this to fit into those leather epaulettes. May I show you?"

Elizabeth nodded, but words would not come. He threaded the leather through the epaulettes. It created a full length apron that covered the entire length of the front of the dress. The leather was pliable, unlike her own rigid apron. Elizabeth had received many beautiful gifts from her male patients over the years, but most of them were to show off their wealth or knowledge. This gift was specific to her calling and so well thought out that she felt seen for the first time.

He motioned towards the small table. His servants had set it with grapes, berries, and fine goat cheese.

"Forgive the peasant softened bread, but I prefer the taste." There was a small ceramic bowl with a flickering flame in it.

"What is this?" she asked.

"You see this metal grill?" When I put this over the flame, I can add another bowl over it. He put some of the cheese in the bowl and picked up a thin dagger. As the cheese softened over the heat, he placed a crust of bread on the point of the dagger and plunged it into the bowl of bubbling cheese. He pulled it out, dripping with the rich melted cheese, and handed it to her.

"Careful, let it cool slightly."

The gooey richness of the bread blended with the goat's cheese had filled her mouth with a sensation unknown to her. Her eyes lit up, and he watched her expression fill with wonder. Elizabeth's intellect would intimidate many men and they would not see that beneath her efficiency as a healer lay a sensual woman whose senses were waiting for a man who could celebrate all the facets of her personality. But Lord Zayne saw Elizabeth for who she truly was. Her ageless beauty did not just lie in her eyes, but in her youthful curiosity to embrace new experiences. "That is what made her an excellent healer", he thought, "Because she strives to experience new techniques and master her own mind." He sipped his wine as he watched her expressions.

"Do you think Meira is ready for the next phase?"

His question threw Elizabeth off guard. She had managed to for a moment step out of the world of healing and into the world of pleasure.

"Yes, of course."

Meira's guardian opened the door and called for the servants to remove the meal and bring the fresh linen and hot water. Lord Zayne and Elizabeth completed the painful process of purging the wound of the infection, and afterwards Elizabeth settled in the chair to watch over Meira.

Lord Zayne excused himself and went to the balcony. He had sent out a pigeon several days before, but had not yet received word back. Lord Zayne thought of his mother and sister. He could never go back. But perhaps there was a way of getting the girl to them.

It had been many years since the fateful day that he had left home. His father had been a merchant. The young boy was bored with his father's constant business prattle. When he was of age to learn, his father had taken him on his first trade route trip. Bored with the idea of being a merchant, he had begrudgingly checked the wares and not even paid attention to the route they took from home.

A sudden flash of swords was the first sign that they were being attacked. The bandits had taken everything and left him half naked with his dead father lying in his young arms. The boy had wept until exhausted and with no idea how to get home. It was only when a kind traveller stopped and offered him food and clothing in exchange for delivering a message that he felt anything.

The promise of more food and the ability to earn a wage had added speed to his errand. He delivered the message, and received another handed over in exchange. He still remembered the sly look that passed over his rescuer's face.

"I thank you, boy. Delivering that message has made you guilty of treason and now, I own you and you will do my bidding when I ask or I will hand you over to the king to be drawn and quartered."

And so the boy was unwittingly recruited to be a spy. He could never go home again. The years had been brutal with several beatings, but eventually he had embraced the dark hidden world of spying.

Each recruit had a special talent. His had been sensing a woman's soul and her deepest yearnings. But a child… there could be no forgiveness for manipulating a child. If he could get but one message that there was a safe sanctuary for them, he would leave this place and bury them so deeply into a new life that no one would ever find them.

As the sun set, Lord Zayne returned to the room. He found Elizabeth asleep on the chair. He carried her to the guest room and covered her with a fur. As promised, he packed a bag and paid for a room at the inn for the night. However, he was sure to return home before sunrise.

Elizabeth awoke to find herself in the guest room. There was food, wine and fresh water on the side table, and another dress draped over a chair. After freshening herself, she walked to Meira's room and found a servant keeping watch over Meira.

"Where is Lord Zayne?"

"He returned a few minutes ago from the inn. He is on the balcony."

Elizabeth checked on Meira. The child's fever had broken,

and the wound held no signs of infection. She felt confident that Meira would awake soon enough and be in good spirits.

The Medicine Woman stepped through the balcony entrance. Lord Zayne seemed troubled. She lingered awhile, watching him. Meira's guardian stretched out his hand and a pigeon settled into his palm.

"Hello friend." He stroked the bird and placed it on the table next to him. On the table lay scattered seed which the bird pecked at. Lord Zayne removed the tiny roll of parchment secured to the bird's foot.

He stared at the message for a moment and then held it in the flame of a candle next to him. None of his plans had materialized, and he had run out of time. He had a hunted look that frightened Elizabeth. She turned to leave, but felt his hand on her shoulder. He had silently bridged the distance between them.

"Good morning. I trust you slept well?" Elizabeth felt a chill up her spine.

"I did, thank you."

"Shall we go and check on Meira?"

"Yes." Elizabeth thought of Teafa and her words of caution.

When they arrived at the room, Meira was awake. Lord Zayne's eyes were bright, and his hand trembled as he touched her cheek.

"Pappa Zee!"

"You gave us quite a fright there, little one. Are you hungry?"

"Yes, very!"

Elizabeth smiled. "She speaks. When did that happen?"

"Only recently. I will get the cook to bring up some broth for her. She must strengthen herself now."

The three of them sat eating their meal in silence. Lord Zayne's thoughts seemed to have carried him to some distant land. After the servants cleared the room, he excused himself, telling Elizabeth he would not be long.

Downstairs, the head servant had locked the doors and moved away, followed by all the other servants. Lord Zayne had paid handsomely for their next six months with bonuses and letters of references. Each of them carried a parcel with furs, a new set of clothing, beeswax candles and a sack of flour.

Lord Zayne returned to Meira's room, bringing wine and milk. Elizabeth had changed the dressing and looked pleased with her findings.

"A toast," he proposed. "To Meira's good health."

Meira downed the warm milk with honey.

"What is this wine flavoured with?" Elizabeth looked puzzled, but the taste was pleasant and she eagerly sampled the new sensation.

Lord Zayne stood close to Elizabeth, ready for when the drug took effect. She slumped into his arms just as Meira's eyelids drooped.

Meira's guardian lay Elizabeth onto a plush dark fur. With any luck, she would awaken in safety and escape. He carried her down the stairs and left through the servant's entrance. He had already positioned the carriage at the door. He put Elizabeth on the floor of the carriage and covered her with more furs, making sure that she could breathe. Then he returned for Meira.

Some weeks before, he had paid handsomely to have a key duplicated for Elizabeth's rooms. He stopped the carriage at the rooms and stepped in to leave Meira's wax tablet on the table and a note on the door.

Carved into the tablet were the words… "*miss maimi - must find her - Going to the hunt hut then walking to my home.*"

He put out some slivers of pork and a saucer of milk for the kittens and after leaving the cottage, paid a messenger to go to Lady Christine.

Lady Christine was preparing for the council when the message arrived.

"Dear Lady Christine,

One of the women in a neighboring village is having a difficult birth. The babe had not turned. I will be there for a day to assist with the birth. I have prepared a fresh batch of oils for your skin. I cooled them with the essential oils and they need time to fuse with the carrier oil. They will be ready about midday. I have left a key for you under the pot with the lavender to the side of my rooms. I shall be back on the morrow for our tea.

Blessings to you.

Your friend Elizabeth."

ὃ

Lord Zayne pulled on the reins, and the cart shuddered to a halt. He turned to look over his shoulder at the criss cross tracks of the horses' hooves on the ground. One set of hoof prints was much larger than the rest. The King's warhorse was in every way as powerful and fearless as his monarch, as if the devil himself lived inside its eyes. King Radolf, armed with his poleaxe and thundering towards an enemy, had caused terror in many a battle-hardened man. He was ruthless, and the spy had no illusions about the level of danger he was putting himself and Meira in.

Lord Zayne's mouth felt dry, and he closed his eyes for a moment before he turned towards the cottage. Picking up Meira, he slung her over his shoulder and forced his body forwards. He dared not carry her in his arms. That would be a sure way to show that he had compassion for the young child. If there was a God in heaven, He would allow the girl to remain asleep during the rendezvous. But if there was not, he hoped the opium drops would comply with his will.

Although there was no one in sight, he knew they would be watching. His breath was sharp, and a tremor ran up his spine when the floorboards creaked beneath his first step. Despite his many missions, he was not immune to the effects of adrenaline. Lord Zayne had felt it surge through his veins countless times when he was in pursuit of his latest conquest. There was always the thrill of the chase. But this feeling was different. It stirred recessed memories of when he was a boy on that fateful last day on the road with his father as he watched with terror the flash of the bandit's swords dance before him.

His fingers tightened over Meira's small body. Lord Zayne exhaled slowly to calm his body and focus his mind. With his free hand, he pushed the door all the way open before he stepped inside. An eerie silence emanated from the room, as if the cottage itself was holding its breath. He wondered how long the cottage had been vacant, as the musty smell of rotting wood filled his senses and he glanced at the barren hearth filled with old damp ashes.

There was an age cot with a rolled up moth eaten fur on it. Lord Zayne shuddered at the thought of it touching Meira's skin. But now was not the time to get sentimental. He had a small oilskin rolled with a sling strapped over his shoulder. He moved the girl's body and cradled her head with one hand while he balanced her over his knee as he bent down to unroll the oilskin with his free hand. It was a clumsy job and the bed was not at all like her bed at the manor, but comfortable enough. As he saw no one he risked going to the cart to get a fur. It took only a few seconds but when he returned, he found Lord Teebald sitting on the bed next to the girl stroking her hair. Anger rose in him like a jealous lover's caress. But his face remained blank.

"Lord Zayne, it has been too long," smiled Lord Teebald. "I see that the girl has blossomed under your care."

Lord Zayne pushed past him and covered the girl with the fur.

Lord Teebald brought a bag of dried meat out of his

pouch and slid one piece slowly into his mouth. He chewed for a while, his eyes never leaving Lord Zayne's face. It was not uncommon for a spy to say very little at a rendezvous.

"Our spy has told us that Lady Christine is on her way. You have done well," remarked Lord Teebald.

Lord Zayne knew that Lord Teebald sometimes sent a backup spy, but now this knowledge filled Lord Zayne with dread.

"Lady Christine's reputation of caring for children is common knowledge. If I had not given this child the best care, I would have given away my cover," explained Lord Zayne. He realised his mistake in showing too much concern for the girl, when Lord Teebald raised one eyebrow. He ran his finger across the sleeping girl's cheek and scrutinised the spy's expression.

Lord Zayne deliberately turned to look somewhere to sit. He prodded at the cracked frame of a chair near the fireplace and sat down.

"I need to gather a few sticks and make a fire. My note said that Meira had run away. In this cold the child would surely have tried to warm herself," said Lord Zayne.

"Very well," said Lord Teebald. "That is a logical thought, and I know that as one of my students from the District there are few men so adept at sensing the fairer sex's needs, even if they are still saplings."

The thought of it repulsed Lord Zayne, and he twitched as if to shake off the feeling. It was fortunate that there were already a few dry twigs next to the fireplace, so he would not need to leave Meira unattended with the King's spymaster. The twigs ignited easily under his practiced hand.

Lord Zayne had impressed enough virtuous maidens with his firemaking skills. The heat of the flames always seemed to soothe their nerves when he was about to claim their virginity. And what little resolve they had after weeks of playing on their emotional needs were soon enough erased with a combination of heavy wine and gently blowing on their earlobes with whispered promises of sweet seductive pleasures. Most of the women were begging him to take them, even if it was just with their eyes.

It was all a game to him. A testing of his skill against the clutches of their moral upbringing. The foolish parents and clergy who had threatened these girls with eternal damnation of their immortal souls were no contest to the promise of earthly pleasure to girls who were starved for love.

Only one had ever thwarted his pursuits - a young woman so confident in her self-worth that she had seen right through him. Her own father had taught her of the power of her feminine charm and that the love of her God was like that of a King's love for a Princess. She did not need to satisfy her needs with those of a man who offered mere charm and only the hint of marriage. Sometimes her eyes flashed before him. The one who got away.

Looking at Meira, he remembered that young woman. Her father had with his words created a confidence that no seduction could toy with. But little Meira was too young for such games. None of his training could have prepared him for this moment.

A tremor shot up his spine as he heard a heavy boot stomp on the creaking stairs outside. The door opened and Lord Zayne's heart thundered as he found himself looking into the dispassionate face of King Radolf. The King leaned his poleaxe against the wall and sat heavily on one of the weathered chairs. His penetrating stare suddenly made Lord Zayne very afraid for Meira. Lord Zayne looked across at the fearsome weapon and resisted the urge to check on Meira again.

"It is best that I sit with her. Should she wake and cry out and Lady Christine hears that, it will alert her to the girl's plight," said Lord Zayne. "We are too close to Lord Logan's castle, and whatever patrols he has will storm down on us."

"King Radolf has enough men watching for us not to be concerned about that," said Lord Teebald.

"Lady Christine is with child and she has with her Beatrice, who is in charge of training the women for battle. I would not underestimate her."

"While we wait, let us have a meal," said Lord Teebald, ignoring the comments and offering a disdainful shrug.

"There are no cooking utensils here," replied Lord Zayne.

"We prepared the meal ahead of time," smiled Lord Teebald. "Carrier pigeon makes an excellent stew," he added, watching the other's expression very closely.

Lord Zayne's expression remained blank as he stared back at Lord Teebald.

"Good. Best we give the girl some. She cries when hungry and we don't want to alert Lady Christine, should she be close by. He leaned over the girl, even though it risked turning his back towards Lord Teebald. The Spymaster reached over to claim a bowl of the stew that his squire was heating over the fire. He ignored Lord Zayne's fussing over the girl.

Meira stirred as the drug wore off. Her eyes were wide with fright. Lord Zayne placed his hand over her mouth and whispered in her ear.

"Be still Meira, Pretend to sleep. When the time comes, I will call for you. Take this mason's nail, Meira, and strike any man that comes near you in the face - and if you can, right in the eye and then run, as fast as you can. I will prepare the way for you." He placed the heavy mason's nail under the fur and positioned her hand over it.

"She will be asleep for a while yet," he said. Lord Teebald sat eating his stew quietly as he stared at the floor. The silence was oppressive and Lord Zayne felt his world slow down while the inner working of his mind calculated his moves. Lord Teebald placed the empty wooden bowl on the floor beside his chair.

"Did you think we would not find out about your betrayal?" he asked.

Lord Zayne wiped the traces of sauce from his mouth. He did not bother to deny the Spymaster's accusation. He slowly rose from his seat. But the King was not as patient as the two spy veterans.

King Radolf lunged forward, aiming to bring the poleaxe down onto Lord Zayne's head, but Lord Zayne deftly stepped away, drawing his hands close to his body. The weight of the axe propelled King Radolf's body forward. Lord Zayne stamped his foot in front of King Radolf's leg, causing the monarch to stumble. The spy struck his elbow into the crook of King Radolf's elbow and the king's forearm dropped, allowing Lord Zayne to grab the handle of the poleaxe and claim the weapon.

Lord Teebald came in from the side with a sword. Lord Zayne spun around with his elbow, struck Lord Teebald's elbow and twisted his arm down, causing him to drop the sword. But King Radolf had regained his footing and pulled a dagger from his belt. Lord Zayne stumbled over a loose floorboard and fell with his head close to the fireplace, knocking over an urn full of ashes. Grabbing a handful, he flung them at King Radolf's face, blinding the king. Lord Teebald ran toward Meira.

"You will back down," he snarled.

"Now Meira!" called Lord Zayne. The frightened girl thrashed at Lord Teebald with the mason's nail as he tried to grab her wrists, but Meira's panicked movements were erratic. Then, as he moved in closer, she fell forward, driving the point into Lord Teebald's eye.

Lord Teebald screamed with pain, and his hand flew up to his face, clutching for the end of the nail. But it had lodged deeply, pressing against the bone of his nose. The impact had forced the other eye closed and Lord Teebald stumbled forward once more. Meira recoiled in horror as the eye bulged and angry red ooze filled the socket.

"Jason, help me!" Lord Teebald screamed at his squire, his eye socket throbbing with pain. Lord Zayne lifted the poleaxe he had claimed from King Radolf and flailed at the remaining men.

The door was bolted, but Lord Zayne kicked savagely at a wall panel to his left. The panel fell away, giving enough space for Meira to flee. But the space was such that an adult man would need to bend to use it as an exit.

"Go Meira, run!" he roared.

Lord Zayne reached forward and grabbed a shovel from next to the fireplace and flung some of the burning logs out towards the centre of the room. The aged wood quickly ignited and the smoke rose. Holding the shovel in one hand, he flung the poleaxe into the flames and ran after Meira. Lord Zayne pulled a dagger from his boot and severed the ropes securing two of the horses and then pressed the red-hot edge of the shovel against the two horses' flanks. As the pain seared through the animals, they bolted, then he untied the last horse and mounted it. The King's war horse was nowhere to be seen.

Meira ran blindly, fueled by terror, and stumbled over the loose earth in her haste to get away. Lord Zayne stayed low on the horse for fear of arrows. He had to get to Meira to protect her. The spy needed only to catch up with her, and they would be home free.

As he gained on the girl, he put out his hand to grab her, but at that very moment Beatrice entered the clearing with Lady Christine. She saw Lord Zayne grab for the girl and hurled her spear. The spear penetrated his chest. Lord Zayne released his grip on Meira's arm, and his body slid from the horse in a death dance that seemed in tune to a slow waltz.

"Pappa Zee!" screamed Meira.

His body crashed down next to her as his lungs filled with his deep red life force. Lord Zayne looked in disbelief at the spear and then turned to Meira.

"Run, Meira, run," he gurgled as his mouth erupted with a flow of crimson. The earth flowed red as it drank in his life force.

"No, Pappa Zee, no," cried Meira. Blinded by her tears could not stand up, and pummeled him hard in the shoulder.

"Get up, Pappa Zee. Get up. Don't leave me," she cried, "I love you. I am your ward. You must take care of me. You promised."

Beatrice rode hard towards the girl. She dismounted and over her shoulder in the distance she saw a black war stallion rear.

"It is King Radolf. Come girl, we must leave now." She ripped Meira away from Lord Zayne, but Meira screamed and kicked.

"You killed him!" she screamed. "He was trying to protect me." Beatrice grabbed the girl by the wrists and bound a cord over them. She had seen this before. When an enemy had formed a bond with their capturer. The girl would hinder their escape and Beatrice had to get Lady Christine back to the safety of the castle.

"Beatrice, untie that girl at once," cried Lady Christine when she saw Meira bound on the horse.

"I cannot. She is a hindrance to us getting back to safety. You can coddle the girl all you want when we return. But King Radolf has been using this girl all along to lure you in. We must go back to the castle now."

ó

Elizabeth moaned in her sleep. Although a warm fur covered her, the surface she slept on was hard and her limbs felt sluggish. In her dream, she felt as if her body were floating. She dreamed of Meira and imagined she heard the girl screaming for her guardian. The terror in the child's voice gripped her with fear. But then the sound disappeared and everything was dark.

FORTY-NINE

Taken

Lady Christine had called for her servant to prepare a room for Meira. The child had cried all the way back to the castle and Beatrice had added a guard to the room. They feared she would try to run away to find her parents. Lady Christine had dispatched men to locate the girl's parents, but for now they would keep Meira under a watchful eye.

C

Beatrice stood near the doorway of Lady Christine's chamber. The fire crackled in the hearth as the last rays of the sun trickled through the coloured glass windows. The Spymaster observed her employer's hands tremble as she touched her belly and stared into the distance. Beatrice watched the flickering light play over Christine's furrowed brow. Lady Christine turned as she heard Beatrice cough.

"You have news..."

"Lady Christine, we brought Lord Zayne's body to stronghold inspection cells. I asked Teafa to check the corpse."

"Teafa… What for?"

"She came to me after we rescued Meira, to share her suspicions. Teafa worked in the District's training camp for spies. She has identified the scars on Lord Zayne's back and a few other markings. Although he grew a beard and fashioned his hair differently, Teafa has identified Meira's guardian as Zaccheus." Lady Christine held her breath for a moment.

"I informed Lord Logan, just moments ago. He is on his way to speak with you. I will give you time to prepare." Beatrice turned to leave. Her fingers lingered on the bronze handle of the door and she looked at the bear head carved on it and back again at Lady Christine. The Spymaster closed the door behind her and returned to the shadows to wait for Lord Logan.

Lady Christine tried to calm her mind, turning over the facts again and again, trying to make sense of them. They now knew that Lord Zayne was Zacchaeus, the man who had kept her and Mary captive in the castle. Her servant had fallen prey to his seduction and endangered Lady Christine and the future heir because of the love affair. Lady Christine knew she had almost handed herself over to King Radolf because of this one trip. If it had not been for the girl's escape, she might well be on her way to the King's castle. She stretched out her fingers. Her trembling frightened her, but if she could rest for a while, she could settle her heart.

Lady Christine jumped as the door opened without a knock.

"Husband, you startled me."

Lord Logan's eyes burned with anger. She had never seen him like this. He sat on the chair next to the bed and fixed his eyes on her. Lady Christine felt a sudden chill. He had the look of a lion - like those she had seen with the exotic animal traders - ever watchful for an opportunity to attack. She looked away, her hand holding her belly where the babe nestled.

"Oh, now you fear for the babe?" His voice seethed with rage.

"I was planning to tell you."

"When, Christine? Were you planning to send me a note? Under lock and key in the Northern Kingdom? 'Come quickly'?"

"It was not like that. I got a note from Elizabeth and when I went to her rooms, I found what I thought was a note from the child. It was just meant to be a quick ride to the hut to fetch her."

"Could you not have sent Beatrice?"

"You know how intimidating she is, even to trained warriors, let alone a small child. She did accompany me."

"Christine! Woman, I am at the end of my tether with you. I have indulged your every whim. You wanted to start a school for the children and I provided for that. You wanted to start a camp to train female warriors, and I endorsed it. You wanted to make a sanctuary for prostitutes escaping their captors, and I helped you with that."

"And I am grateful."

"Silence! I will not hear one more word from you. I am not finished. Today you put not only yourself, but our child in danger. The child we have waited years for. One that in a heartbeat King Radolf could have taken from us." He got up and paced the floor.

"I…" Lady Christine wept.

"Your tears will do nothing to silence me now. You are to remain in this castle and you are not to put one foot outside these walls without my permission. Do you understand? If I must, I will have guards outside this room, and if you still do not comply, I will lock you in the tower. Is that what you want?" He turned to look at her.

"Christine, have you ever thought about my position? These lands… were bequeathed to my father under the feudal system. Need I remind you that legally I am bound to my knight's service to the Northern Kingdom?"

"I did not think of that..."

"Of course you did not. If they captured you, I would give my dying breath to rescue you and it would be my dying breath because to rescue you I would stand against King Radolf, and that would be an act of treason. Do you know what the penalty for treason is?

King Radolf uses treachery because he can not make a direct attack against me. We pay our taxes and we have prosperous trade routes. By wronging me, the Lords would be fearful of him taking their lands without cause and would rise against him. But if he baits me to come for you... well, then that is a direct attack. It would appear that you do not care enough about me or this babe to even think of consulting me."

"That is not true; you know that I love you. You know that I want this child more than anything."

"Then act like it, damn you." He slammed his hand on the table.

"I am sorry..." she approached him.

"Don't!" He held up his hand. "I am too angry with you now..."

Christine gasped at the rejection. He had always been so forgiving. She sobbed and sank down to the ground. A pain shot through her and she cried out. Her face contorted. A pang of guilt erupted through Lord Logan.

"Christine. Oh dear Lord, what have I done?"

"Beatrice!" he shouted. "I need you." Beatrice raced into the room.

"Send a messenger for Elizabeth. Now!"

Beatrice summoned Lady Christine's messenger. Reginald looked at the white face of the employer, who he and his wife both loved and raced out of the door without needing instruction.

Lord Logan soothed and rocked Lady Christine as a series of cramps washed over her. Beatrice's face was calm, but Christine's face filled her heart with dread. This was the last remaining heir of King Frederick's line.

Time seemed to stand still, and every few minutes Beatrice would peer down the passage. After a while, Lady Christine fell asleep and Lord Logan covered her with a fur and stepped outside into the passage.

"I did not mean for this to happen," he told Beatrice.

"Lord Logan, your reaction was understandable. I warned her against leaving the castle, but she would not listen to reason. With children and the weak, her mind does not obey logic." Reginald hurried up the stairs with an unknown woman.

"Who is this?" asked Lord Logan. His eyes were full of suspicion.

"Forgive me, Lord Logan. This is a midwife from the lower districts. It is the best I could do. The Medicine Woman, Elizabeth… she is missing."

Elizabeth's head pounded. She knew she was in a dark place. It was not just the absence of light that she surrounded her. It was something else. The thread of humanity that connected all living souls seemed to hang in tattered layers in the air. The dark banished the enlightenment that the Ancients had pursued, had fled from this place. She looked up at the shadowy walls.

"He has never seen you, you know. He won't realise that the one they have in the stronghold is not you," said an unseen voice.

"Who are you?" said Elizabeth. "Show yourself."

"I am not sure that is what you want." The voice had an

aged richness to it. Elizabeth felt a wave of fear cross over her. But she knew she could not show weakness. She heard the strike of tinder as a spark of light burst into the darkened room.

"It was in a room much like this one that Helena buried her cries," said the approaching voice.

"Who is Helena?"

"Ah, he has not told you." Elizabeth felt a hand trace the outline of her face. Her hand lashed out at her unseen capturer.

"Told me what?"

"I thought true love has no secrets. But then I doubt he has any genuine love. He is too weak to give himself over to another." Elizabeth heard the scrape of a chair moving closer to her and with it came the flicker of a candle light.

"Ah, in the flicker of the flames, I see what he sees in you. It is said that red-haired beauties have a fire in more than just their crowning glories. They say it lives in their souls. Yours is a beauty that with age matures into a regal quality that men would pledge their dying breath for. It is the passion that a Copper Fire Dragon Whisperer would pledge his soul for. Do you think that is why my father betrayed the dragons? I was told that my mother Helena had mesmerising green eyes with flecks of gold that danced in the firelight. Do you think that is why my brother loves you? Because you remind him of the mother we lost… Helena.

Would my brother betray his precious dragons to find you? History records Gadriel's betrayal of the dragons as the most severe. Tamyss called my father a brother. It is why, despite the bitter pain of losing his mate and hatchling, he heeded my father's call to save the babe and rear it in the Copper Fire Dragon colonies." Elizabeth's eyes widened in fear.

"Ah, I see you now understand," smiled the man. He concealed his face, but she sensed him smirking.

"I am the forgotten twin. The one that no one came for. I trained the darkened dragon. My power was strong, even from a young age. If Gadriel understood the methods behind darkening a dragon's heart or that of the Whisperer, he would have fought harder to keep me. I found a friend in the stolen hatchling, Arucroth. It did not take long for him to see what I felt, that the Whisperers were on a path to destruction. They controlled the hearts of dragons. And the Whisperers had betrayed his kind. I planted the locations of the colonies in his mind. I tracked down each Whisperer and destroyed them through Arucroth. My body was too weak to make the trip. The warlords kept me caged with the dragon, feeding me only enough to keep me alive. The bond the hatchling and I formed was the tool that the warlords used against us.

They sought to control the neighbouring kingdoms. I sought to destroy the Whisperers. But the dragons blocked me from finding the child they had raised as their own. Their chosen one," sneered the man. "They taught him to communicate with all the dragons, just like a Silver Wing Dragon Whisperer."

"I thought Gadriel trained the darkened dragon," said Elizabeth.

"You thought what I planted in the minds of the dragons. They passed my message onto their kin and in time Gadriel's legend became what it deserved to be. He tried to reach Arucroth, but he could never break our bond. Gadriel watched from the warlord's stronghold as Arucroth destroyed the land he had once tried to protect. In time, Arucroth took revenge on Tamyss, the father who had abandoned the search for him, as Gadriel had abandoned me," said the Masked Man.

"How can you blame your father or your brother?" They were both victims of their circumstances."

"They could have tried harder to find us," replied the dark

whisperer. "The path to turning a dragon and a Whisperer is one of unimaginable cruelty. One that the warlords willingly pursued."

The Masked Man stepped around the room, lighting torches until the room brought his face into focus. Elisabeth's expression changed as pity filled her. His face was pitted and scarred like that of a leper.

"No, do not pity me," shouted the Masked Man. He grabbed her face and brought his face close to hers.

"You see this scar," he said, turning his face... "They branded me. This is the symbol for the name Amat-ul. Do you know what it means?" he asked as he released her face.

"It means 'slave of'," replied Elizabeth, forcing herself to keep looking at him.

"Correct. I was their slave. They gave me this when I was sixteen. It was when I fell in love with the servant girl who brought meals to the prisoners. She was the only person who showed me kindness. They branded me so that no free woman would ever want to be with me."

"What happened to the girl?" asked Elizabeth.

"That is none of your concern," said the Masked Man, turning away.

"I see," said Elizabeth.

"Do you now? What do you see when you look at me?" he hissed.

"I see a man who is..."

"A man, is that what you see? Not a thing of hideous proportions... a slave worthy only of pity," he interrupted.

"This mask that King Radolf forces you to wear, it is an act of cruelty." The Masked Man's laughter echoed against the walls of the room.

"I wear the mask of my own choosing," he said.

"But why?"

"It was my path to escape. For over a century I was passed

on and traded by men who wanted the power of a Dragon Whisperer. Over fifty moon cycles ago a warlord used a dragon to raid a Kingdom. I found gold hidden beneath the King's throne. I commissioned a blacksmith to fashion this mask. No one would have thought that a man would choose this for himself. It allowed me to escape undetected."

"But I don't understand why if you had the ability to escape, you did not do it earlier?" asked Elizabeth. "Unless, the girl you said that you fell in love with…" She looked into his eyes and saw a glimmer of pain die as quickly as it had surfaced. "... They kept her captive to hold you."

"I can see why a Whisperer would love you. You are learned, wise and beautiful, and you have empathy. These are good qualities for the mate of a Dragon Whisperer. We Dragon Whisperers can live for hundreds of years. The silly nature of frivolous young girls can do little to sustain our souls. We need a woman of more substance. We are the most passionate and loyal of all the Whisperers. But the love of a Whisperer brings only pain. It is that pain that I wish to extinguish. When the last of the dragons and their Whisperers slip into the eternal sleep, the pain will end," explained the Masked Man.

"You plan to kill your brother…" said Elizabeth.

"It is what must be," replied the Masked Man.

"And do you plan to kill me as well?" asked Elizabeth.

"No. If I had planned that, I would have let King Radolf have you," he said.

"I do not understand. How did I come to be here?"

"The spy, the one you know as Lord Zayne, drugged you and left you in the carriage, when he took the girl you call Meira," he said.

Elizabeth stared unseeing at the wall. Teafa's words came back to her. "One of Lord Teebald's men has been in this room."

Elizabeth quivered as she felt as if the room was closing in around her. The Masked Man had hinted that he had brought her here to protect her from King Radolf. But that did not imply that she was safe. He planned to extract some information from her in order to lure the Dragon Whisperer.

"I have to leave for a while. You are probably hungry and I will need to make sure that you are strong enough to remain conscious long enough for my brother to track you should he not heed my call. If he comes for you quickly, you will not be harmed. I want him, and I want the Silver Wing Whisperer. I know she has found eggs and plans to hatch them. If we can track the remaining eggs, then no one else needs to be harmed. But if he fails to reveal the location of Nadine, and the eggs, then I am afraid I will have to resort to more drastic measures."

"Why do you want Nadine?"

The dark Whisperer turned to look at Elizabeth. His eyes lost all expression and Elizabeth knew that Nadine was in great danger.

The Masked Man extinguished all the torches. Elizabeth heard the shuffle of his feet. There was a sliding, grating sound of stone against stone. Elizabeth's heart hammered in her chest, and she felt her breath quicken. Although there was a swirl of fear that threatened to overtake her, she kept her eyes fixed ahead. She knew that he had not left. The Medicine Woman had felt the rush of air as he had opened the passage. But no change came, and she knew that he was waiting for her to move.

She willed herself not to take the bait. Although every one of her senses screamed at her to move, she knew she could not underestimate a man who would exterminate an entire species for his twisted sense of justice. Elizabeth tried to imagine the polished mirror in her home. She had taught countless patients to look into their own eyes in one of the polished surfaces to calm themselves. The Medicine Woman imagined that the pounding in her heart was one of the drums that she kept in her cottage. It was an instrument that one of the musicians with the coffee-coloured skin from a far off place had gifted her in exchange for her treatment. The rhythmic pace soothed her into a trance. It was a matter of reframing her experience.

At some point the Masked Man would have to leave, and then she would be ready. A sudden gust of wind extinguished the flames. Elizabeth heard her captor's footsteps. His face was so close to hers that she could smell the pungent aroma of raw onions from his breath mingled with a putrid smell like rotten meat. She guessed it was from one of the festering sores on his face. Elizabeth heard him exhale close to her and felt his finger hover just short of her cheek. But he did not touch her. Instead, he straightened, and she heard the gentle scraping of the softened sound of his boots glide over the stone floor.

Elizabeth recognised them from the boots of the Dragon Whisperer. They designed them to silence the footsteps of a Whisperer. Whisperers had no magic; they merely had the power to communicate with dragons and other Whisperers telepathically. They needed natural methods to move undetected when separated from dragons.

Elizabeth held her breath and waited for a change in the sounds. The sliding stone door did not shut. Was he still there? She did not think so. Was he waiting for her to attempt to escape? Escaping now would be foolish. He would never risk leaving her completely unattended. But she needed to know what her surroundings were like. Elizabeth kept her back straight.

Using only her feet, she worked her shoes off. She did not have the silent boots of a whisperer, so her feet would have to be bare to be silent. She felt the cold stone of the ground and tried to recall the position of the furniture. Elizabeth slowly widened her arms with her fingers outstretched, ready to probe her surroundings. She inched forward, using one foot at a time to feel her surroundings. The stone was smooth and cold. As she moved, she felt the change of the air as she grew closer to the opening. Elizabeth pushed her arms forward, and her hands collided with the edge of the passage. She slid her arms along the sides. It was slightly wider than one person, and she would have to bend forward to get through it. The Medicine Woman sucked in her breath as she heard a soft thud in the distance. She stepped back and felt her foot touch something like a thick layer of dust. "Flour," she thought. It was an old spy tactic she had heard Beatrice speak of. When wearing boots, it was undetectable and would leave prints alerting a spymaster to the presence of an intruder.

Elizabeth bent down and with her fingers tried to explore the breadth of the flour. It was not wider than the width of her skirt. She lifted her skirts, bent down and blew hard on the surface, close to where she had stepped. "No. it is not enough," she thought. Elizabeth knew the heaviness of the flour would not spread evenly with only a breath. Bunching her skirt in her left hand, she squatted and rubbed her other hand lightly over the flour. Then she lifted each foot and rubbed whatever flour residue she felt. "Oh Lord, help me," she thought, as she inched her way back to the chair.

Elizabeth felt as if she might weep, as her fear travelled across her skin, making her hair stand on end. But she reminded herself that he would expect fear in any case, so it would not give her away. The Medicine Woman prayed that she had blown hard enough. Elizabeth found the chair and used her feet to locate her shoes. As she slipped her feet into her shoes, she heard the shuffling of the Masked Man's soles. It was the merest whisper of a sound, but every sense in her body quivered in heightened awareness. In the dark she exhaled and closed her eyes and eased back on the chair. The chair scraped on the stone and Elizabeth held her breath. But still no sound or light emerged. Elizabeth quietened her mind, trying to sense him. She knew he was drawing her fear from her. But she would not let him claim it. She focused on her breathing labouring over each breath, willing her airways to pace each breath so that her thoughts remained rational. An assault of light pierced her eyes as the Masked Man lit the first torch. Elizabeth cried out as his face emerged just millimetres from her. How had he sneaked up on her?

"Our kind train all Dragon Whisperers to cloak their minds," he said. His gaze travelled across the lines of her face that seemed to quiver in the flickering light. He watched as a stray strand of her flaming locks shimmered in the light's glow. She wore her hair in a long, tight braid down the centre of her back. He wondered what it would be like to run his fingers through the silkiness of the strands. In an instant, he felt the sharp pain that haunted his dreams. The one brief, sweet moment that he had felt the warmth of Helena's maternal embrace as she had cradled him to her breast. The guards had let him suckle just that once. Enough to form the bond. And then the guards tore him away from her. He could still feel her screams inside his head, boring into his soul.

All Copper Fire Dragon Whisperers were born with this heightened sense of relational memory. He no longer called her mother. To do so would pick at the scab of the wound that deadened his heart to his kind. But something in this woman called to the memories he wished to bury. She was strong and like Helena had stood like a queen even in the face of certain danger; he saw in Elizabeth the steady, rhythmic wave of her emotions as she sought to control them. The merest glint of fresh tears remained contained in her eyes, and her jaw was set like that of a rebellious child. The sudden fright of seeing his face had ignited her emotions, and her eyes shone brightly in the light. He watched the erratic heave of her bodice, and he wondered if her flesh was soft or firm. She seemed ageless, almost youthful, and yet he sensed a wisdom, which stretched across decades.

The Masked Man opened the sack he had brought back, and produced a round of cheese, bread and two shredded pork pies. He also took out a leather pouch containing a skin of wine.

"On those shelves, you will find some bowls. Get two small ones and two larger, for our meal," ordered the Masked Man. The Medicine Woman stared at him.

"Elizabeth, I mean you no harm. When the time comes to summon my brother, then things may change. But that is up to him. For now, know that you are safe and I will care for you. Do not be the author of your own suffering when it is unnecessary."

Elizabeth got up and moved to the shelves. She found the bowls and several jars of ointment. She guessed they were for the pustules on his face. The Medicine Woman felt his gaze on her form and it sent a shudder up her spine. As she turned, his intense stare startled her, and she dropped one of the bowls, which fell with a crash. The Masked Man bent down to pick up the fragments and saw a fleck of flour on the hem of her skirt. He looked up at her but said nothing. Elizabeth swallowed hard and sat back down.

She could not escape his penetrating eyes. The Masked Man sliced through the cheese with a flint blade and placed a portion and a pie into the new bowl he had taken from the shelf. He poured the wine into the smaller vessels. Elizabeth glanced at the blade on the table. It reminded her of the blades that the ancients had fashioned to harvest herbs. The handle had the same symbol on his face carved into it.

"I would rather not," she said.

"Rather not have wine. I imagine you want to keep your wits about you. In case you get more flour on your skirt," he said as he held her gaze.

"You would not have gotten far," he added. "I left explicit instructions for my great nephew. But I wanted to test what sort of woman you are so that I know how to secure you."

"It won't work, you know. Your brother will never betray

the dragons. He is not sentimental. I am his physician and nothing more," said Elizabeth.

"I can see he has not bedded you yet. If he had, you would know how deep a Dragon Whisperer's loyalties and passions lie. A Copper Fire Dragon Whisperer is too loyal to partake in frivolous infatuations. They bide their time in courtship. Because they can not afford the error of letting their manly desires bond with a woman inferior to the role of a Whisperer's wife. You may find that he has withdrawn from you should he accidentally have touched you or you have touched him." Elizabeth blushed.

"Ah, he has touched you. When was it?" Elizabeth thought back to the night that they shared a meal when Zairdenth had taken Nadine and Nathan to the ruins. Her hands trembled.

"You touched his hands. Did you feel the power flow through them? A Copper Fire Dragon Whisperer's hands are strong. They need big hands to ride a dragon as powerful as a Copper Fire Dragon. Yet, they are capable of indescribable tenderness. I could never ride Arucroth as a free man. I was always a slave." He drank deeply of the wine. She could see his body relax as the strong drink reached his senses. The Medicine Woman had never seen his brother drink heavy wine. Elizabeth relaxed a little herself and nibbled on a piece of cheese. Despite her captivity, she enjoyed the flavours of the meal. Her captor had chosen well.

"Does anyone ever use your name?" she asked.

"It has been many years since anyone has. When I escaped, I chose not to reveal it," he replied.

"Would it cause you discomfort if I did?" she asked.

"Within these walls, I suppose not," he replied. We pronounce it A- maat- ool - Amat-ul," he explained.

"Do you know your brother's name?" she asked.

"So he had not shared it?" he smiled.

"Another example of his feeble fear. If I were not on this quest, if I were not so disfigured, I would claim you for myself.

I can see it in your eyes that you have already flown on a dragon. The experience never fails to leave a mark. There is a special awakening that only comes when you have seen the world disappear into tiny specs below you." He walked to a dark ebony kist and lifted out a book.

"I took this from Tamyss's cave after Arucroth killed him," said the Whisperer.

"He killed his own father," recoiled Elizabeth.

"Tamyss gave up his right to be called a father. The bond was severed before it even started. Arucroth darkened soon after I arrived. A Whisperer's suffering can drive a dragon mad. In a trained dragon it takes far longer but for a hatchling separated from its mother before the naming ceremony the process is swift," he explained.

"Who did the naming ceremony?" she asked.

"Gadriel… did it," he replied.

"Did you see him?" she asked.

"I did… that is when I realised that the alliance between dragons and mankind had to end." He placed the book in front of her.

"In this you will learn more about my brother, and somewhere in those pages, I imagine you will find his name."

"You have not read this?"

"No. It would hinder my mission. But it may answer some of your questions. When you have learned my brother's history, your bond with him will grow and then it will fuel his desire to come for you."

Elizabeth pushed the book back. His scars stretched as he smiled. The shrunken flesh pulled taunt and she could see that he could not sustain the crooked expression for long.

"Elizabeth, you are a woman of learning. You studied with the ancients, and you fill your home with treasures from around the world. I know you will read this book. You know you will. Like I said, I do not want you to suffer. I do not want to harm you.

Who knows, maybe someone in our family may be able to save the woman he loves."

Elizabeth stared at the book in silence. The aged leather cover showed the pock-marked skin of an enormous flightiness bird that a patient with coffee-coloured skin had once drawn for her. He told her that the marks were where the massive wings of the bird had been.

There was a crest branded on the cover. She recognised it from a small tapestry that she had once seen her Copper Dragon Whisperer unroll. Perhaps by reading this book, she would be able to help him heal his past traumas.

Amat-ul got up.

"I have to prepare a report for King Radolf. It will take me an hour or so. There are some shards of charcoal and parchment, should you wish to write, and I have some scrolls on the far side which have some of the teachings of the Emerald Forest Whisperers. You may find those beneficial to your studies."

He chose a few beeswax candles and placed them in an arch pattern on the table. "This formation gives the best light for studies. When I am done, I will create some privacy for you to sleep, bathe and change."

Elizabeth ran her fingers over the scrolls on the shelf. On the edge of one of them she saw a glimpse of a marking that seemed vaguely familiar. Amat-ul turned to see her peering intently at it, and he smiled and turned back to his work.

Elizabeth was torn. The scroll she had discovered had an illustration of one of the outer thorns on the dragon egg that they had uncovered. She wanted to know what was in it, but at the same time she wanted to read the book. The Whisperer had said that he needed to make a report to the King. Galdolf, King Radolf's former Prison Master, had told Lord Logan's war council that King Radolf always wanted reports delivered in person. That meant that Amat-ul would leave to attend the private war council. King Radolf usually held two councils.

One with a Bishop who reported to the church, and another where matters that were not intended to be discussed by the church were mulled over. But the Friar had confirmed that Father Stephen had been appointed the new Bishop and that as long as his purse was filled, the church would not receive accurate reports.

The Medicine Woman ran her fingers over the raised surface of the leather cover. The book was quite slim. She was confident that she could read it within an hour.

"Elizabeth, I neglected to tell you… behind that curtain is a chamber should you need to relieve yourself. It leads into a sewerage system. But one that is too small for humans to climb through. It is however effective in drawing waste away. This lair belonged to another Whisperer who had no surviving relatives. I found the plans in his cave after I sent Arucroth to slay him. Each Whisperer has their own hidden fortress, which they pass down to their family. My brother has no doubt claimed our family hideout, so I have made this one mine."

He turned back to his report.

Elizabeth felt her mind slide into action. But she steadied herself and opened up the book first. The words were penned in an ancient form, but one that her studies with the Ancients allowed her to interpret. It would just take longer than anticipated. But she settled in the chair and began to read:

Helena smiled in blissful exhaustion at the tiny red-faced infant that had nuzzled itself against her breast. His ravenous slurps and tugs showed that he was strong and would grow to be a fine Whisperer. Helena smiled at Gadriel, her husband, who had been her only midwife. Despite the misery of their captivity, the infant's fragile frame was a light that seemed to block out the darkness of their captivity. The warlord had assured Gadriel and Helena that he sought only the hatchling and so they needed only to complete the naming ceremony and then make their way back home and rebuild their lives. They had been well fed and until a few days before. Even though their lodgings had been basic, they were comfortable and Helena's physical needs well taken care of. When she displayed signs of the babe coming, they had moved to a more sparse room, which they were told would give them more privacy and not disturb the rest of the occupants in the stronghold.

Helena gave birth to her son with the ferocity of a glorious hunting cat. She was a vision to Gadriel whose heart burst with pride as he caught the bright red, squalling infant. Even drenched in perspiration and her hair in complete disarray, Gadriel thought that Helena was the most exquisite woman that the Creator had ever fashioned. After the babe had emptied both breasts, the door opened, and the warlord entered to see the infant.

'You have done well, Helena,' he said as he touched her cheek. Gadriel's fury burned in his chest and his eyes flashed with venom. The warlord nodded at four guards stationed at the door. Two of them held Gadriel face down on the floor. One secured his arms and the other with his boot on the small of Gadriel's back, and the other two secured Helena's arms. The warlord yanked the startled infant away from Helena. He smiled down at her naked chest and sniffed at the babe.

"I can smell your milk upon his breath. I thank you for your service."

Two additional guards entered the rooms armed with spears. After the warlord left, the guards backed away. Helena's screams and sobs echoed through the corridor as the warlord hurried to the wet nurse who he had assigned to the babe. Moments after the babe had been ripped from her arms, her body convulsed as another birthing pain slammed into her. "Twins," thought Gadriel. His heart and mind raced. He had to act quickly. Gadriel clamped his hand over her mouth.

"We have a chance to save this one," he whispered. "Hush now, my love." Helena swallowed her screams and sobs for her stolen babe and with Gadriel's love, she had fought for the infant that wracked her body with pain as it demanded to be set free from her flesh. Her husband could feel her deep etched anguish for the babe she would never again hold. But Gadriel blocked out his own sorrow to be Helena's strength. He had torn his robe and knotted it into a rag that he had placed gently into her mouth. She bit down hard and swallowed her screams. Gadriel tied another strip of the robe on the bars of the window and lifted her already exhausted body up so that she could hold onto the rope to use the pull of the ground to ease the infant more easily out. Helena already knew what

he planned and her tears flowed unchecked as she bore down to release the babe.

If the guards heard her, they would know that there was another Whisperer fighting to enter the world. Together the couple had a chance to save at least one of their children from the evil of the warlords. Helena's body rocked as her silent moans tore at her soul. As the sorrow threatened to overtake her, Gadriel locked his gaze with hers and willed strength into her. They did not need words. She knew what he wanted and recommitted herself to the task. Even as a babe the first born could feel their bond and the plan emerging that would drive a wedge between the twins and thrust them into different worlds. Gadriel had opened his mind at last to Tamyss.

"Old friend, no words can ever take away from what I have done. But now I ask you to save my son and together we will fight to rescue the hatchling and my firstborn. Take this babe, I implore you. If not for me, then do it for my wife Helena, who Undor, your mate, loved." Tamyss roared in pain. He had lost so much. His beloved mate, his hatchling, and his friend. He felt the heavy cage of guilt and sorrow around Gadriel and pulled up his massive body off the stone where he lay. Gadriel was right, Undor would have willed this. She would have given her life to protect Helena and her offspring. He had glimpsed the memory of the night of Undor's death in Gadriel. He knew that it was the guard that killed her, and his heart ached for the Whisperer. As his body lifted into the sky, he called for his own stolen son's nurse.

"Prepare the cave for a human hatchling. Go to the sanctuary and leave a token and a single gold coin under the second oak. Someone will find it. Then light the torch outside the cave and leave another token and gold coin underneath. There must be cooked salmon, fruit and fresh spring water in the cave for the wet nurse who will arrive. Undor kept human bedding and clothes in her section of the cave. Find these and lay them out for the woman who will come. Send a message to the elders. We will have a council meeting when I return.

Helena felt the head of the babe pressing against the opening of her womb. Her muscles gripped the babe's body, pushing it in a painful burst, squeezing it through her passage of life. She could feel it twisting through her to find its way to the world. Her breasts dripped with the flow of nourishment that the first babe had stimulated, and the unchecked flow brought fresh waves of sorrow.

Gadriel felt it drip onto his hands, but he could not think of that now. He gritted his teeth and blinked hard against the tears that demanded release. But he could not allow them to make him waver in his strength for Helena. He reached under her body to wait for the drop of the babe. As the last grip of pain erupted through Helena, the babe slid out. There was no time to wipe off the slimy residue of the blood and water that encased the child. Gadriel pushed his finger into the infant's mouth, forcing it open. He pulled Helena's bodice open and thrust her nipple into the infant's mouth. Then, securing the babe with one hand, he used his free arm to ease Helena down. She sank into an exhausted pile. There was no food or water to replenish her. But in the corner of the room there was a slow trickle of water where a root had burrowed its way through the walls. Gadriel found a loose stone with a small hollow in it. He positioned the stone under the root to collect some of the water. Helena shivered, the shock of the long birth and the loss of her first son had begun to seep into her consciousness.

Gadriel felt Tamyss approach as the dragon's powerful wings beat down into the night air. Copper Fire Dragons could not cloak in the ways that Silver Wing Dragons did. Gadriel knew he had to have the infant ready when the dragon arrived. He ached as he watched his son's mouth greedily tug at Helena's breast, and he knew the bond had formed. Her face shone with a mixture of joy and sadness. The babe's little curled fist pressed into the swell of her ripe breasts. When the babe had emptied the first breast, she moved to the other. Gadriel smiled at the strength of his son. He knew the child would need every bit of survival instinct the Creator had allocated to the babe.

Tamyss swooped down over the lake and scooped up a single fish for Helena. He knew she would need it for strength. It was a few minutes' delay, but he knew without proper nourishment she would not recover from the birth.

The stronghold came into view. The room Helena and Gadriel were in was covered in vines on the outside. It almost looked like a pretty human dwelling from the outside where he flew, but inside lay destruction and hate. He watched the guards patrol, and he hovered in the distance. Two of them exchanged words.

Tamyss looked past the stronghold and saw a small enclosure with horses. He moved in closer and saw the horse's feed. The dragon threw a small controlled blast of flame and ignited the feed. Tamyss made sure it was small, so that the guards would not suspect a dragon. Hearing the cackle of the flames, the guards raced to the other side of the stronghold. Tamyss called to Gadriel.

"The time is now, old friend."

The Copper Fire Dragon lifted the fish to his mouth and flung it into the narrow slits of the window. Gadriel plucked the replete infant from Helena's breast. It made a noisy suction as it released. The babe opened its eyes in surprise and Gadriel thrust it into his travel sack. Then, closing his eyes, the Whisperer threw the babe out of the window. Tamyss swooped down to catch the sack in his claw just moments before the babe hit the ground. He could not stop to look for Gadriel. He had to leave before the guards spotted him.

A moan erupted from Helena as her grief slammed into her. As both babes cried out for the mother they had already bonded with, Helena's breasts responded with fresh floods of life force. Her wail could no longer be contained, and she screamed in anguish.

"Stop that row," shouted a guard, banging on the door.

"Hush, my love," whispered Gadriel.

Helena's angry eyes bore into Gadriel. She knew he had done the best he could for their offspring, but she had no one else to bear the burden of her grief. Gadriel grabbed her hand and bunched it into a fist. He pounded his chest with her hands. Again and again until she responded by pummelling his chest with all her strength until exhausted, she clung to him with her breasts still dripping.

"The babe casing," whispered Gadriel. "Helena, you must expel it."

"No, I will not. It is all I have of them," she retorted.

"You know if it remains in you, you will get sick and die," he said.

"Death is better than sacrificing my sons," moaned Helena.

"Helena, Tamyss has the second twin. He will care for it as his own

until we return. We will find out babes, Tamyss will help us. Now I need you to fight. Stand up Helena!"

Helena looked at him with fury in her eyes. She gritted her teeth and her breath came in hot, angry snorts.

"That's it. Let's get some of that fire in you, to ignite. Now lget that babe casing out. Helena's thighs quivered as she stood. Gadriel tore off a piece of the fish that Tamyss had thrust through the window. He chewed it a bit and then spat it out and pushed into her mouth so that she could swallow without chewing. He pressed down onto her stomach, massaging her belly to help the passage of the babe casing. Helena pushed as hard as she could, but her body-strength waned under the prolonged ordeal of the day. Finally, as her eyes closed, her body released the babe casing into a heap on the sacred cloth that Gadriel had placed. A Whisperer who was waiting for a child always had one with him. It was a specially treated silk cloth that the Emerald Forest Dragon Whisperers wove to catch the babe casing. It was carried in a watertight pouch that was never opened until the babe had come. The Emerald Forest Whisperers would feed part of the babe casing from the mother to her, replenishing the mother after the birth, and the other portion would be buried under the seed of an oak. (Each passing Whisperer was also buried beneath an oak.)

Gadriel carried Helena's spent body into the corner of the room and laid her down on the straw bed. He kissed her on the forehead and then cleaned the room. He used rags he created from his own cloak to wipe the fluids off the floor. As he had no way of disposing of them, he merely threw them out of the window. "Let the warlord find a way to dispose of them," he thought.

Gadriel settled down next to Helena. He draped his arm over her carefully to avoid touching her breasts. He would find a way to restore his family. His first son was within the stronghold walls. He could feel him. The babe's cries shredded through the Whisperer. But he could not let Helena know. Gadriel closed his eyes and called to Tamyss. The grieving dragon sat up in the cave. He had lost his own son and now he had Gadriel, the betrayer's son. Gadriel and Tamyss opened their souls to each other. Their sorrow gripped them in a way that made it impossible to use words. Undor's cries as Tamyss reached for her son clawed at him. He never expected the panic of the guard that thrust the sword into her chest. He felt as if the warlord taking his son was the Creator's way of punishing him for her death and stealing the hatchling. Now Helena was suffering for it. Tamyss felt Gadriel suffering. In some way, Undor's death had spared her the pain that Helena now felt. It was Tamyss who spoke first.

"My son, is he there in the stronghold?"

"I feel them both, but their pain makes it too hard to track either of them. The babe has the strongest call I have felt in years. But it is unmanageable. He is almost overshadowing the hatchling. I am sure that when I am called to do the naming ceremony, I will counsel them. What of my boy with you? How does he fair?"

"He, too, is strong. The wet nurse is in the cave and already he drinks every turn of the sandglass. I have spoken to the elders. They are willing to train him, and we have sent for trainers from all the dragons to visit. Your son will learn to communicate with all dragons so that we can warn them of the danger of the evil doers before it reaches the others."

"Thank you Tamyss, I do not deserve this kindness."

Tamyss was the first to break the bond. He was helpless to protect his son. He loved Gadriel as a brother, but to feel his pain reminded Tamyss too much of Undor. Tamyss looked down at the child nested in the wet nurse's arms. He felt the rise of flame in his belly that reached up to his throat. Just one moment of weakness was all it would take. He would avenge Undor. But he knew she would have given her last breath to defend Helena's child and so he swallowed his flame and walked out to search the stars.

In a few days, the Silver Wing Delegation would arrive. He had heard of the newly appointed Megadeus. He had been eager to meet the young dragon. He was still being groomed, but it was said that he was a dragon far beyond his years in wisdom. The Silver Wing Trainers were the best Whisperer trainers that there were. He needed their spiritual guidance now. He did not know if he had the strength to contain his rage at the death of Undor. Not with the infant who served as a constant reminder so close to him.

"Tamyss," called his son's nurse. He turned to stare at her. "The elders are calling for the human's name."

Tamyss looked at the boy... Technically as the boy's rescuer, he had naming rights. It made the boy his son now. The dragon thought of his precious Undor. He looked back at the sky. He could see the star formations. When a Silver Wing Dragon leader died, their bodies atomised and formed star formations. But his Undor, lay under a pile of rock that he himself had melted to form lava that flowed over her form. The rock was still bare, but in time the seeds that the Emerald forest dragons had planted would sprout and she would become a beautiful grassy hill that the human children would climb one day. No one would look to her guidance as they did with the Silver Wings.

"Menashe. The boy's name is Menashe,"

"What does it mean?"

"It is a Hebrew name, meaning causing to forget. It was the name Joseph gave to his son, saying that the Lord caused him to forget all his troubles. Joseph had to forget the pain that his brothers caused him when they betrayed him."

Gadriel heard Helena moan in her sleep. His head throbbed. He could feel the babe crying for her most of the night, and the hatchling's energy was at a dangerously high fever pitch. The Whisperer could almost feel it screaming as well as the clatter of its claws trying to escape the cage with the terrified infant.

There was a strange heat in the room. He reached out his hand to his wife and realised that the heat was emanating from Helena. He scanned her body. Then he saw them, grossly big breasts straining against the fabric of her bodice. Dark stains spread across her chest. Gadriel touched her breasts. They felt as though they were on fire and they were rigid and hard as melons.

"Milk fever," he thought. He had heard the midwives warn against it. When a babe died, many women succumbed to it. They could not get the milk out and it so engorged the breasts, so much so, that sometimes the

skin would blister and crack. Infection would wrack the body and if not treated, its poison would carry her to the internal sleep.

He tried to massage her and ease the milk out, but the breasts were unyielding. Gadriel banged on the door.

"I can hear the babe crying. Where is the wet nurse?"

"She ran off in the night," replied a guard. "It seems like there are not too many wet nurses willing to be in a cage with a hatchling.

"Then bring the boy here, his mother has milk."

"No, our orders are to await another wet nurse."

"You can't be serious. The child will die without milk. If you want to claim the boy, you have to give him a chance of life."

ó

Tamyss heard the frantic shouts of Gadriel as the whisperer beat against the door until his hands were raw. Since the fire, the warlords had stationed a band of Dragonslayers around the castle with dragon spears. They scanned the skies every night for the dragons. The Silver Wings had sent the first delegation to scout the castle. They were the only ones who could cloak. Once Gadriel had named the hatchling, he might be able to communicate with it through Gadriel, but until then, all he could do was feel Gadriel's pain.

ó

Gadriel turned away from the door and tried to massage Helena's breasts again. Fever had begun to snake its way through her. Helena's body trembled, and she cried out about the cold, and every time he tried to massage her breasts she screamed in pain. He felt around the tissue and for the hottest area. The part that burned the most would be the site of the infection. He had seen some of the Emerald Forest Whisperers treat it. But he had none of the herbs that they used, and he did not even know the names of what to use. He heard the lock of the door slide open and a guard entered. It is time for the naming ceremony.

"My wife, she is not well. She needs a midwife's help."

"Well then, best you get moving."

Gadriel looked down at Helena as she was sleeping. Her face almost looked peaceful. Gadriel walked down the corridor flanked by the guards.

They led him to the cage. In it lay his son on a bed of straw and he saw the infant's face was bright red from screaming.

The warlord stood in the centre of the room.

"The naming ceremony, if you please."

"I will not do it unless I can hold my son and take him to his mother. She needs the release of the milk."

"You are not in a position to give orders."

"Yes, I am. You have no other Whisperers to do the ceremony. I need only give the hatchling the wrong name and he will perish. I have already betrayed the dragons to save my wife. Do not think that I will not do it again."

"Very well, we will do the naming ceremony in your cells."

"You may hold your son when we get there."

"No, I will hold him now!"

Gadriel picked up the infant and inhaled his scent. The babe stopped fussing as he held it close. He walked to the cell and knelt next to Helena. Her breast was so swollen that the infant could barely grasp her nipple.

Tears clouded his vision.

"Helena, help me. Our son is here. Fight for him. Come back to me." He pressed and prodded until one nipple yielded and he clamped the child's mouth over it. The boy developed a rhythm, and Gadriel panted out his gratitude. The breast slowly subsided. But the effort exhausted the boy who was already weak from the night's crying. The babe had already fallen asleep.

"The naming ceremony Gadriel," demanded the warlord.

"Wait…"

"No! Now!"

Gadriel placed his outer cloak under Helena's arm and placed the babe in the crook of her elbow. He pressed his son's mouth against her breast. Helena stirred and pulled her arm closer.

Gadriel stood up and turned to face the warlord.

He put out his arm to the hatchling. He could see its fear. Its limbs twitched and the stunted creature beat its flightless wings. Gadriel lowered his forehead to do the greeting. But it did not respond. Gadriel glared at the warlord.

"I name you…"

Helena's arm slumped, and the babe rolled away, uttering a frightened squall.

Gadriel's face disintegrated into an expression of horror. He lifted Helena's arm and let it drop. She was unresponsive. He knew… knew she was gone.

"No," he roared as he pulled her limp body close.

Still on the floor, the boy began screaming again. It enraged the hatchling, and the warlord motioned to the guards who held a spear pointed perilously close to the boy.

"The naming ceremony!" spat the warlord.

"Arucroth. I name him Arucroth."

The hatchling blew a single flame across Gadriel's face, rejecting the Whisperer. It was too late, it had already turned.

"Thank you," said the Warlord.

As he turned to the guards, he gave the command to throw the woman's body to the beasts in the moat.

"They can do with a good meal. We don't want her corpse stinking up the place."

ǒ

Tamyss felt the hatchling turn. One moment he was a frightened hatchling and the next he was dark. The dragon had nothing to live for. Undor and Arucroth were gone. Gadriel was too late to save any of them. But Tamyss would not allow Helena's body to be claimed by those vile beasts. He was already hovering, and no longer cared if the dragon spears reached him. He would rather die than allow her to be ripped apart.

As he swooped to grab her from the moat, a single spear ripped through his wing. Tamyss glided through the air. The rushing wind pulled through the torn section of the wing. But he had only a short flight to the cave.

The Copper Fire Dragon landed with a thud. The body bearers carried Helena to the cave where her body would be washed. They would make an incision and drain the swollen breast and then prepare her for the stone burial. Tamyss would never fly again. The wing was too damaged, and he was too old and broken in spirit to care. He felt Gadriel's despair.

"Friend, I can not come for you anymore."

"I know, and while there is still life in my body and my first boy is trapped here, I must remain. Take care of my second boy."

"Gadriel, he will now be my son. It will be my gift to you. And I will write this story, in the Book of Secrets for both your sons to read when the time is right."

ό

Elizabeth's head seemed to outweigh her strength. She heard the drone of a voice that drew the fog of her thoughts into consciousness. Her tongue felt thick and sluggish, and her joints stubbornly resisted her efforts to move.

The Medicine Woman's eyes widened to reveal the iron rod of silence that adorned the Masked Man's face once more. She wondered why he had put the mask on after all this time.

Then she realised that her wrists and ankles were bound to the chair. Although she tested the ropes with short discrete tugs, she knew that he had been methodical. His former threat now morphed into reality as he lifted the mask just enough for him to speak.

"He isn't coming. Is he?" The Masked Man's voice was sad. He breathed out a sigh that filled her with dread.

"This means we have to take it a step further."

Her captor took out a jar, and some thinly stretched whitish membrane, and smoothed it out on the small table next to her.

"This is a sheep's intestine. But I suspect as a healer you already knew that. It is as pliable as human skin. It makes the perfect substance for my associates to help me draw my brother out."

Elizabeth watched in horror as the Masked Man placed a small ceramic jar on the table. He drew a sword from his writing desk and pierced the leather covering. A cloud of tiny yellow legs scrambled up the blade. The glint of the steel flashed in the candlelight as the Masked Man dipped the sword into a small glass jar that contained a piece of raw meat no larger than his thumb. The spiders responded by climbing over each other in an attempt to reach their meal.

"This will satisfy their appetite for a few moments, but not for long. They will seek a fresh supply. I think you know this species, don't you?"

Elizabeth tried to speak, but her tongue seemed fused with the top of her mouth. She knew her fear would help ward off whatever herb he had given her off faster, but not fast enough to escape a clutter of Yellow Spike Spiders. Just one bite would produce a blinding pain, but who could endure so many of them? The pain would only last until the venom reached the victims' heart. And then… it was too horrible to think of.

Sensing the meat, the spiders scrambled over each other, frantic to seek the source of the life force. The Masked Man pulled the membrane tight and secured it with a leather thong.

"They inject their venom to liquefy the meat, so they can feast. But there is not enough for them to lay their eggs in."

He lifted the jar so that the light of the candle illuminated the angry captives.

"When they reach the top of the jar, they will attempt to escape. Their venom will liquefy the intestine and they will be free to explore."

He ran his finger over her face. She shuddered as his finger brushed over her lips.

"I am sorry, Elizabeth. I enjoyed your company. I had hoped that my message would initiate contact with my brother. He has closed his mind to me, just like my father did with Tamyss. But the lock of your hair and the note should have enraged him enough to come to your aid. He did not take the bait. But even my brother cannot deny the passion and loyalty of a Copper Fire Dragon Whisperer forever. For your sake, I hope he yields before it is too late."

Elizabeth could no longer contain the strain of her confinement. She closed her eyes as her tears escaped down her face. Salty drops flowed over her lips and dripped onto her chin.

"An Emerald Forest Dragon Whisperer learned that if you pierce the skin of a victim, it excites the spiders and they escape their jar faster. I don't believe a Forest Dragon Whisperer has ever turned. But they should have been like the ancients and not penned any of their teachings. That kind of knowledge in the wrong hands is deadly, don't you think?"

Terror filled Elizabeth, but the Masked Man cupped her face and hummed the tune of an ancient dragon lullaby. "I would not harm you. I don't want you to die. It is only the dragons and the other Whisperers I seek.

"Why…" Elizabeth choked out the words

"Why would I do this? Have you learned nothing while you have been here?

"You cannot wipe out an entire species, it is wrong.

"I see your courage has returned. You would have made a fine Whisperer, if you were born with the calling. I am not the villain, Elizabeth. I am the saviour. Without dragons or their Whisperers, there will be fewer tools to hurt mankind.

Elizabeth remembered what Friar Watt had told her when he shared the story of his injury at the hands of the King's men. "Beware of false prophets, which come to you in sheep's clothing, but inwardly they are ravening wolves." The Masked Man was such a man. Although in his case he really believed that his calling was true. She could never reason with such a man.

Elizabeth thought of the corpses in the ruins. The spiders would find her, and their venom would paralyse her. Their spikes would burrow into her bones to make a cavity for their eggs, and when the eggs hatched, the offspring would erupt and begin to feast on her flesh while she was still alive.

FIFTY

A Teacher Will Rise

Nicolous approached their rescuer in the forest. The man was not much taller than Nadine. His clothing was not like any of the locals. The Emerald Forest Dragon Whisperer's tunic was loose at the shoulders and arms, but tapered from the elbow to the wrist and his leggings were loose at the thighs but had leather strips wrapped around his calves that tapered the garment to his feet. His shoes seemed more like the slippers of some women at court, pliable leather soles and fabric like uppers. His skin had an almost olive colour, and his warm brown eyes lacked the deep furrows of the Copper Fire Dragon Whisperer. His wrists were adorned with bracelets of resin and leather. The Whisperer's shoulder length hair was black, except for a few strands of silver. It was tied back in a bun at the back with a few strands that hung down his back.

"I thank you, friend, for coming to our aid. My name is Nicolous."

"Arpachshad, Emerald Forest Dragon Whisperer, at your service," the Whisperer smiled. "This must be the young Silver Wing Whisperer? I have waited a long time to meet with one. And this fine young hatchling is yours, I presume?"

"Well," blushed Nadine. "I don't look much like him. But yes, I hatched him."

Nathan entered the clearing with the hatchling perched on his shoulder.

"I am Nathan. I, too, am grateful, but I have to ask. You are a skilled warrior, so why did you not stop that last man?"

"It is not our way. We protect life, we do not take it. Our weapons are always used to save a life."

"So then, you killed the man who would have killed my father, but the last man was trying to escape, so you spared him."

"Correct."

"And what do we do with those three?" asked Nicolous.

Arpachshad smiled. The men had ceased to struggle.

"I would untangle them, remove their weapons and shoes and set them on their way without horses. We have to leave in any case; the darkened Whisperer seeks to find you, Nadine. These men know this location, so we have to leave immediately. You still have a long way ahead of you if you are to learn what I have to teach, but before I train you, I must meet with your Copper Fire Dragon Whisperer."

They packed their belongings, while Arpachshad checked his weapons for damage.

"What is this?" asked Nicolous, picking up the circular hand thrown weapon.

"It is a Dragon Claw Star. We make them from Dragon's teeth. Copper Fire Dragons and their artisans make them. A Copper Fire Dragon Hatchling has fine flames that can cleave through smaller items. They slice through a dragon's claw and sculpt it into this circular shape with the barbs that can cut through most things. Copper Fire Wing Hatchlings also make the dragon rods."

"You can help Yakhal with his wing," exclaimed Nadine.

"Who is Yakhal?"

"He is a Silver Wing hatchling. He has an injured wing. A

tree shredded it and the Copper Fire Dragon Whisperer used splints to restructure the wing."

"How many moons has it been?"

"I have not counted. But it happened at the end of Winter."

"It is possible. Where is he now?"

"He and his mother Muquin, are hatching an egg we found."

"How many of Ciommed's protection eggs did you find?

"Only two. But we have found a carrier egg with clues on how to find the remaining eggs."

"So you can not summon your dragon."

"No."

"Makes sense. You need to protect the new eggs. This youngster is too young to fly, so we must travel by horseback."

When they arrived at Holly Hill Cave the Whisperer and Zairdenth were nowhere to be seen.

"It is best we set up camp outside here," suggested Nadine.

"Why?" Arpachshad raised an eyebrow.

"He is a complicated man. And he values his privacy."

"He is a Dragon Whisperer who lives in an open cave. This is not his private lair. No Dragon Whisperer may deny another Whisperer who seeks sanctuary."

"Sanctuary? And from whom do we seek sanctuary?"

"You know from whom. The Fallen Whisperer is searching for you. This Whisperer's twin. I know them both well." He frowned as he looked at the table.

"Does something seem a bit off to you?"

"What do you mean?"

"Your trainers have honed you in self-discipline and warfare. But your intuition… you have to reconnect with yourself. For women, this is usually easier. But you have faced too much too soon, and so you doubt yourself. Try again."

"Perhaps…" Nicolous tried to assist.

"No, do not help her. You will hinder her. Nadine, close

your eyes and pretend you were not with us and had just walked into this room. What is out of place?"

Nadine took a deep breath. She closed her eyes and slowly opened them, and then she saw it. A piece of parchment in the centre of the table. The Copper Fire Dragon Whisperer leaves no documents lying around. He always packs them into the chest."

"It is a message."

"Perhaps he left it for us."

"What does your intuition tell you?"

"Someone left a message for him..."

"Very good. Now read it."

Nadine's face fell as she scanned the contents of the parchment.

"What is it?" asked Nathan.

"The Masked Man, he has Elizabeth."

"I take it that this Elizabeth is someone important?"

"They love each other," whispered Nadine. "I must warn him."

"No, you must not. Post-war hatchling protocol forbids it. Amat-ul wishes to lure him the way the warlords lured their father. We must find this woman ourselves. From this moment, you will close your mind to the Copper Fire Dragon Whisperer, and you must do so now. You cannot lead him to this woman. We must break the bonds of the past."

"Wait, who is Amat-ul?" asked Nathan.

"Amat-ul is Taildriecren, The Redeemer's twin."

"Now you are just speaking in riddles," said Nathan. "Nadine, who is Taildriecren. The Redeemer?"

"You don't know who Taildriecren, The Redeemer is?" asked Arpachshad, turning to raise a questioning eyebrow at Nicolous.

"No." Nadine scowled at this game. She wanted immediate answers.

"Nicolous, did you not teach her about her lineage?"

"I left home at six years of age to become a page. I never saw my family again."

"That explains a lot. When did Nadine find out she was a Whisperer?"

"A few months ago."

"Ah, so Taildriecren, the Redeemer, has concealed his identity by lingering alone in this cave. Gadriel, father to Amat-ul and Taildriecren, betrayed the dragons to save his wife Helena from the warlords. She was with child at the time and the warlords held her ransom for a hatchling. Tamyss named him Menashe, which means to forget. He had hoped that in time his bond with the boy would help him to forget the loss of his family. But the Whisperers call him Taildriecren or just Taildri. Taildri is a bit easier on the tongue.

The warlords set a trap for Gadriel. They never intended to release Helena or the child. Helena bore two sons; the Warlords took the first to do their bidding. That child was Amat-ul, the name means 'a slave of.' But the Warlords did not know that Helena carried two sons. Gadriel called his dragon to rescue the second boy.

The dragons reared him in the colony as one of their own.

You know Amat-ul as the Masked Man and Taildriecren, the Redeemer as the Copper Fire Dragon Whisperer.

Amat-ul turned while in captivity. He is trying to recreate history by baiting his brother to come and find this Elizabeth."

"How do we even find her, without The Copper Fire Dragon Whisperer?" asked Nathan with a shrug of his shoulders

"Copper Fire Dragon Whisperer's are Keepers of Secrets. Taildriecren was part of the inner circle of Elder Dragons. Each Copper Fire Dragon has a secret lair known only to him, but the location is lodged in the sanctuary library. Only an Elder Keeper of Secrets would have access to it. Some time back, Amat-ul went on a campaign to destroy all the Whisperers. But there was one in particular who interested him.

Cymreg was a lifelong friend of Taildri. He met his first wife through Cymreg. He had a special love for architecture and for exquisitely crafted lairs. Many of the Whisperers would commission him to forge their lairs. He gifted a lair to Taildri after the birth of his first child. But when the child died, Taildri never returned to the lair. Legend has it that the lair was close to the Northern Kingdom. For Amat-ul to move from the castle, it would have to be a location close by.

If we can find the ancient ledger with the lair's location, then we stand a chance to find Elizabeth."

The group searched for the scrolls, but there was no sign of the ledger. Arpachshad looked carefully at the carved walls of the cave. Above the kist were more carvings showing a woman with her arms outstretched. And on either side was a babe. Around her neck was an amulet.

"There..." smiled Arpachshad. "When Gadriel found out that Helena was with child, he gave her an amulet as a sign of his undying love for her. The symbol on that amulet is on that wall.

"But how do we get all the way up there?" asked Nadine

"Stand on my shoulders."

Nadine reached up and pressed on the amulet. It slid away from the wall, revealing a slim scroll with a map showing two pairs. One which was close to King Radolf's castle. Burn marks pitted some of the text and concealed the exact location.

"It's a start," said the Emerald Forest Whisperer after inspecting the map. "But we must be quick, if we are to find your friend before the Masked Man finds out that Taildri is not coming."

FIFTY-ONE

Elizabeth

"I see nothing," complained Nadine.

"Isn't that the purpose of a hidden lair? It is meant to be a secret." Arpachshad looked up at the rock, his eyes searching for clues.

"The lair would have to have two things. A way to let sewage out and a way to let fresh air in."

"Shouldn't we be travelling along the line of the tunnels? Wouldn't it make sense to link the lair to a dragon tunnel?"

"In the beginning, some of them had access to the tunnels. But after the second dragon war, Amat-ul hunted down the Whisperers using the tunnels. Cymraeg started constructing them away from the major lines and away from the sacred oaks. He made them from many types of rock but favoured rocks which grew plant coverings quickly."

"It could be anywhere."

"Did you bring the jasmine?

"I did."

"Give it to the hatchling. It does not grow in these parts. If Elizabeth perfumed herself with the jasmine, the hatchling would find her. The scent may be faint, but he can smell an out-of-place scent."

The hatchling, whom Nadine and Nathan had named Bliant, sniffed the flower. He sneezed as the new and powerful fragrance tickled his sensors. Arpachshad sat down with a handful of berries and coaxed him into responding to his commands. Bliant jumped into his lap and pushed his snout against the Whisperer's arm.

The Emerald Forest Dragon Whisperer laughed as the little dragon frantically tried to get to the berries.

"You won't get them by knocking me over. That's cheating." He placed three of them on the ground. Bliant slurped them up and began licking Arpachshad.

"No, your tongue is too rough. Now be still and breathe in the land. Nadine, sit with us. This is part of your training to learn to tell the differences in your surroundings. Bliant is like any human toddler, their energy is all over the place. We must train them to be still and centre their thoughts. I will reward him with his favourite treat when he has completed this exercise and again when he has picked up Elizabeth's scent."

C

The warmth of the sunshine on her back lulled Nadine into a soothing sleepiness. She watched as the hatching scurried over the rocks and foliage and disappeared over the ledge that jutted out over the top.

The sound of rustling leaves yanked her from her feeling of calm. Her head turned, and she tried to steady herself; she strained to discern what the sound meant.

Horses moved unseen near the trees. She stepped away from the clearing and moved closer to the rock face. Nadine peered around the hanging foliage that covered the rocks that the hatchling had scaled. She heard the crunch of the pebbles that lay scattered between the trees and the rock. Whoever it was, had dismounted, and their slowed footsteps did little to conceal their movements.

The intruders were too close for her to use her bow, but a dagger would do. The Emerald Forest Dragon Whisperer's code did not apply to her. Isa taught her to eliminate threats and she would shed blood if it meant protecting Elizabeth or any of those she cared for. Nathan was too far away for her to call without giving away her location, and she could not call to the Whisperer without opening her mind to the Masked Man.

From the sound of it, one intruder was walking towards Nadine. She slid the dagger from its sheath and slowed her breathing. The intruder paused for a moment, and then the footsteps resumed, but slower this time. This could not be a casual traveller. Someone was searching. She felt confident that it was not the Masked Man. The footsteps were of a lighter man. Could it be one of the king's guards?

Nadine crept closer to the edge of the foliage and bent her knees in preparation to lunge forward when the intruder came into sight.

But the intruder stopped again. The pause in the movement caused Nadine's heart to pump adrenaline into her and the thrill of the hunt ran through her. Her breathing raced ahead of her mind's efforts to control it, and the quivering blade in her hand revealed her struggle to regain control. Just one overzealous movement and she could destroy all their efforts to rescue Elizabeth.

Nadine silently stepped out from behind the foliage. The intruder was facing the opposite way and was unaware of her edging closer. The stranger was of similar height and Nadine could now see a way to immobilize the intruder without a kill.

The Silver Wing Whisperer jumped out and hooked her arm around the intruder's neck, blocking the airflow as she pulled the intruder backwards. She eased the body down and bent to inspect the unconscious intruder.

"What are you doing so far from home?" thought Nadine, as she recognised the girl as the bully from the village school.

Nesta's mind felt foggy as she adjusted her eyes to the

light. The glint of Nadine's dagger loomed dangerously close to her chin.

"The fear in your eyes now, convinces me more than ever that bullies are cowards." Nesta scrambled backwards.

"I am no coward."

"You ran away from the village after you saw the injury you inflicted on Meira. When I went looking for you, your father told me that you ran away leaving your mother to do your share of the chores alone."

"My father is a maggot. You know nothing of my life."

Nadine said nothing, but searched Nesta's face for answers to questions she could not express.

"What are you doing here? Are you one of the King's spies?"

"No. I am one of Lord Logan's spies."

"Now, I know that you are lying. Lord Logan would not recruit someone like you. His followers are brave, loyal and defend the weak. You have none of those qualities."

"There was a notice that all seeking sanctuary could go to the training camp. I did not run away, I volunteered."

"Then why are you here?"

"They needed volunteers to scout this area and gain knowledge of the patrols. I saw your group from a distance and came to investigate." The sound of Nathan's footsteps interrupted Nadine's next interrogation question before she could voice it.

"Who is this?"

"This is Nesta, she claims to be a recruit from Lord Logan's training camp for women."

"Great, we could do with an extra set of hands. The Emerald Forest Dragon Whisperer asked me to fetch you. He thinks the hatchling has found something."

Nadine did not reply. While having extra hands would help, she disliked the thought of Nesta being the one to save the Medicine Woman. Especially after Elizabeth had to stitch Meira's chin when Nesta tripped the child.

"Did you hear me? Nadine, what's got into you? Let's move." "Whatever has agitated Nadine will have to wait. She is as stubborn and as unyielding as a slab of granite," thought Nathan.

The Whisperer glanced at the new girl.

"This is Nesta," said Nadine. Her eyes defied him to ask any further questions. The Whisperer looked at Nathan, but Nathan shrugged and said nothing.

"We need to get up there," explained the Emerald Forest Dragon Whisperer, looking up at the rock.

"That is awfully high." Nadine stared at the mass of foliage that contrasted with the grey rock.

"From what your father told me, you have the strength to do it."

"I will help you," offered Nesta.

"I don't need your kind of help. Stay here with the others and look out for danger." She glared at Nesta and turned towards Arpachshad. "Which way do I go?"

"You can start here. These vines will help carry some of your weight. But test each of them before putting your full weight on them. I will guide you from here and then follow. We are looking for a shaft that carries air into the lair. There will be overgrowth, but he would have added a woven dome-like structure to keep the plants from growing over the opening. It won't be vertical, but rather will come in from a slight angle which would allow the Whisperer to collect drinking water inside the cave when it rains. So the plants may be raised above the rest of the foliage."

Nadine gripped the vine. It felt sturdy and stayed true, so she pulled herself up.

"Look for hand grips inside the rock and be careful of rock spiders."

"Thanks for that. I feel really safe now."

"Careful of rock spiders," thought Nadine. "Who says that kind of thing?" she muttered.

Nadine tried to centre her mind. There was no way to tell if there were any grips.

"Use your feet to feel the stone. You will find pockets of it in between the foliage, but you must search for it."

"If it is so easy, why don't you climb up here?"

"I will join you, but from here I can guide you and see where the obstacles are. Besides, where is the fun in doing what you have a natural talent for?"

Nadine growled under her breath. She did love to climb, but the circumstances were different. Elizabeth was in danger, and time was of the essence. Instead of prolonging his long 'nap', why did he have to wake up after she had already hatched the egg? He could have trained her for this beforehand. The way that Isa had. Nadine rolled her eyes. She realised she had become loyal to Isa.

"The best training is on-the-job training."

"What?" Nadine knew that her mind was not open. Was he reading her thoughts? "It is a kind of hard to do this with all your talking," she panted as her foot found a jutting rock, no bigger than the length of her toes, but it was enough for her to catch her breath.

"Careful of areas where there are a lot of roots, they tend to weaken the..."

Nadine screamed as a handful of vine ripped from the rock, raining pebbles onto her. She now hung by one arm, frantically looking for a place to grab onto. She should have asked her father to climb with her, but he was somewhere on the other side.

"Nadine... to the right! Swing to the right, there is another stronger vine. Nadine felt as if she might cry. The strain of hanging on was unbearable and her fingers ached, but she swung her legs in the direction of the vine. It held true.

"In the centre between your feet is a small rock, test it." Nadine moved her toes. She almost wept with relief as her foot held firm.

The Silver Wing Whisperer edged her foot in deeper and her muscles relaxed for a moment. But as her foot edged in deeper, she felt something yield and then a weight on her foot. Nadine froze, and her throat closed over a silent scream. She licked her dry lips as she dared to look down. A brown-grey-coloured snake with dark stripes running from its neck slid silently over her foot.

Her eyes were wide with fright, but she tried to focus on what Friar Watt had told her "And I am certain that God, who began the good work within you, will continue his work until it is finally finished on the day when Christ Jesus returns." She hoped that was true.

"Relax Nadine. It is a bat boa. It is not dangerous unless you are a bat or a lizard. Some villagers believe that its oil helps with joint pain. Just wait for it to pass and then keep moving."

Nadine watched as the snake wrapped itself around a vine and went in search of another hiding spot.

"Can we keep nature lessons for another time?" she called down.

"Why? I bet you won't forget the name of that snake, its habitat and diet for the rest of your life," the Emerald Forest Dragon Whisperer chuckled.

"I am on a quest with a Jester Whisperer," thought Nadine, and she turned to look for the next vine to hoist herself up with.

"The top is just a few footholds away. I will follow you once you reach the top." Arpachshad turned to Nesta. "Come Nesta, let's move. I will climb with you and show you how to get to the top."

"I have never climbed before."

"Don't worry, we will do it together."

Nadine could not believe what she was hearing. "I will climb up with you…" while he watched her struggle.

"It is about time you arrived," said Nicolous from the top as he reached down to give her a hand. Nadine snorted and pushed past her father. It was like some sort of conspiracy against her.

"How did you get up here so fast?"

"Arpachshad told me that the eastern side of the rock had the least vegetation and the most visible foot holds, so it would be easier to climb."

"Oh, did he now?" Nadine flexed her trembling fingers. She shuddered as she remembered the snake sliding over her foot.

"Where is Nathan?"

"He is searching for the air vent. Here, he asked me to give you one of his honey cookies." Her father sat down next to her.

"Why is everyone so hard on me?"

"It is because we can see what lies inside you. Even as a child, you would find clever ways to get out of work or try to do things differently. But when you apply yourself, you grow. Those people who know you, push you hard to draw out what is inside of you. You have the gift of leadership, Nadine, but you have to have some struggles to earn the respect of others. When you try to find the easy way, you miss the learning."

"I think we found it!" called Nathan.

Nadine felt her muscles protest at the thought of getting up. She gulped down the last of the honey cookie and brushed off her hands on her tunic. If Elizabeth was in this cave, there was no time to lose.

She smiled at the hatchling as he tried to balance on Nathan's shoulder.

"You are getting too big to do that," she said, tickling the Emerald Forest Dragon under the chin. He pushed his chin upwards to allow her hand more space to stroke his neck. She smiled and ran her hand over the soft scales on his chest. The dragon wriggled its back in pleasure

"Ouch," cried Nathan. It's full of thorns. Bliant jumped off Nathan's shoulder and licked his hand. "Not now." Nathan tried to push the hatchling away.

"Don't push him away," cautioned the Emerald Forest Dragon Whisperer. Those thorns are a deliberate sabotage. They can not kill, but their poison produces a slow healing wound. The hatchling has enzymes in his saliva that breaks down the poison, allowing the human body to expel it easier. We should not try to move these thorns ourselves. Once the hatchling has treated the wound, he will move them. Nathan, let him lick for as long as he wants. He will stop as soon as he is satisfied he has removed all the toxin."

The hatchling glanced at the dome and back at Nathan's hand. He licked for a bit and looked at Nadine and back at the dome.

"There is something wrong." Nadine frowned. She wished she could open her mind to communicate with the hatchling. "Is there no way of moving these thorns ourselves? He seems agitated by something down there."

"Can't we just chop them down?" asked Nicolous.

"I wish we could. If we chop them, it will do two things. One, it may alert the Masked Man. And the second thing is that the chopping will release the sap from the thorns. The sap is very slippery, so this forms two layers of defence. In this case, slow is steady and steady is fast. When we find Elizabeth, we will have to hurry and then we can not afford injuries."

The hatchling felt as if everyone was watching him as he hurried to remove the sap in the cut. Nathan flexed his fingers and felt the burn of the sap had stopped spreading. He made the forehead greeting and stroked Bliant on the back of his neck. The Emerald Forest hatchling blinked and sniffed the wound. Satisfied, he turned to the thorns. The pliable thumb sized stems had rows of thick razor-sharp curved white thorns that almost completely covered the stems.

"This plant is not a vine, but Amat-ul has trained it to curve around this woven basket," explained Arpachshad, upon examining the spot more closely."

"Trained… what do you mean?"

"Usually this plant grows upright with the leaves and these red flowers positioned at the very end of the stem. But these are curved over and see here, they are connected by cat's whisker threads."

"Cat's whiskers? The wound-stitching intestines?"

"Yes. He has used them to pull in the stems just below the leaves to cover the basket. He has been planning this for months. This was painstaking work, as he had to avoid being cut by the thorns. Some say that this was the plant used in Christ's crown of thorns."

"Is that true?" asked Nadine as she watched the hatchling place its claw under the first red flowers.

"I don't think so. There is no evidence of this plant in that area," said Arpachshad kicking away two thorns close to their feet. The hatchling sliced through the end of the stem and severed the cat's whiskers. The trained stem moved a mere two fingers breadth away from its position, but it was enough for the hatchling to position his claw between two of the thorns near the base of the stem and slice through it.

Nadine felt as if her mind was caged. It was like watching a snail move across a branch. She rubbed the heel of her hands against her eyes.

"I can't watch this. Somewhere inside there is Elizabeth and we are just standing around."

C

The female Yellow Spike Spiders had devoured the last of the meat in the jar. Their abdomens were swollen with eggs, making them anxious to burrow. But without a host, the females felt trapped. They first devoured some of the males. Driven by the desire for a host, one of the females scrambled over the writhing bodies of the males, as they fought off their ravenous mates. Her spike quivered as she tested the intestine with one of her front legs. Once she had located the thinnest part of the membrane, she sank her spike into it releasing the toxin that would dissolve the covering to their prison. Soon the other females followed, and together they released a combination of poison that would hasten their escape.

Elizabeth watched with horror as a small hole emerged at the top of the membrane that stitched over the opening of the jar. Her wrists were raw from her attempts to release her bonds. As the hole widened, the first spider tested the size with her forelegs. The Medicine Woman could see the yellow tips of the spider's leg reach out through the opening. Her breathing grew rapid as she searched frantically for something, anything, to use in her escape. The Friar had used a herb on a burning stick to stun them. But she had nothing. There was a candle on the table which would provide fire. But with her hands secured, she had no way of reaching it.

*

"Let's send in the hatchling," suggested the Emerald Forest Whisperer.

"No, you can't. What if the Masked Man is in there? He could kill the hatchling," protested Nadine.

"Do you have another plan?" Arpachshad searched Nadine's face to see if she would attempt to answer.

"It is natural for you to be afraid for the hatchling. But we must all live according to purpose. Amat-ul has lived in fear his whole life. That is why he uses methods to instil fear, and fear stops you from growing and taking action. I have waited many seasons for this hatchling, but I cannot let that stop me from fulfilling my purpose to help mankind. When you are afraid, you must use that fear to help you gain knowledge. It is the unknown that makes us afraid. All children fear the dark, but that is when we must learn instead of cowering. Do you understand?"

"Yes." Nadine nodded. But it did not settle her heart. She had suffered through the hatching, and her bond with him was strong. Bliant turned his head and chirped at Nadine. His green eyes blinked at her in expectation.

"Show courage, Nadine. He feels your fear."

Nadine nodded again. She picked up the hatchling and gave him a forehead greeting, letting her head linger as she fought to settle her mind. Then she walked with him to the air vent.

The hatching looked down into the dark depths of the air vent and back and Nadine. She smiled at him and tapped her hand at the opening.

The little dragon chirped and waited for the sound to echo back to him. He stepped into the shaft and stretched out his wings. to touch the sides of the tunnel. The initial drop was sudden, but once he was inside, its slope angled to a steep descent, but it was no longer vertical and the hatchling could spread his wings to give him a little more grip. The stone was smooth with only a few jutting stones for him to find a grip, but the angle caused him to slip in several places and his chirp grew anxious.

"He is frightened; perhaps the angle is too steep. Do we have a rope with us? It will help secure him." Nadine looked frantic.

"Perhaps I should go down with him." suggested Nicolous.

"No, it is too narrow for you. Here, we will lower tie a vine to him and get him ease his wings over it. It will help secure him," replied the Emerald Forest Whisperer.

Nadine lay on her stomach and edged forward to secure the rope under the hatchling's chest and then tied the knot under his wings. She knew that the Masked Man would kill the hatchling if he saw him.

Nicolous and Nathan held onto the rope to offer the hatchling some security.

The creature edged forward and repeated the chirps to measure the time that the echo returned. Soon a faint glow emerged and the back of a tapestry that blocked the view of the room. He severed the rope with his claw and dropped to the ground.

The hatchling sniffed the air for signs of the humans. There was a female. The musky scent of her fear gripped his mind, and he blinked in the candlelight, trying to adjust his sight to the room to locate her. But there was something else… something terrifying. He had never seen a Yellow Spike Spider, but knew the human was in grave danger. Then he saw them, a wave of yellow legs scrambling over each other from a jar on the table. One of them scurried to the woman on the chair, and she pushed her foot to one side and stamped on it before it reached her skirt. The female wrestled with a rope of woven vines that secured her wrists to the seat. The hatchling bounded to her and with a flick of his claws, he severed the ropes. Elizabeth stumbled over the chair, trying to back away from the spiders that moved in a steady stream in her direction.

The hatchling backed away from the spiders and moved his head frantically, trying to calculate how many there were and if they were all moving in the same direction. He knew they could not harm him, but the woman… was only a host. She stood no chance against these venomous creatures. He knew he had to protect her, but was not sure how. There was something else he could smell; it was some sort of animal fat. The hatchling made short frantic sniffs, trying to locate the source. It was in a bowl on a small side table next to the cooking fire. He knocked the bowl to the ground and flattened the contents with his feet, spreading it into a line between the advancing spiders and Elizabeth.

Then he jumped onto the table and grasped the burning candle in his claws, and dropped it onto the fat, which ignited in a powerful burst

The others heard the blast from the outside.

"I am going in," said Nadine.

"No," said the Whisperer, "I will slide down. I know these caves and I will help find a way out."

The Emerald Forest Whisperer landed with a thud behind the tapestry. He blinked against the intense heat of blaze. Elizabeth crouched, weeping, on the ground. The hatchling shielded her body from the exploding spiders with his rapidly dehydrating wings. The Whisperer lifted the Medicine Woman to her feet.

"Elizabeth, I am Arpachshad. I am an Emerald Forest Whisperer. We must leave this place now. Where is the exit?

"I don't know."

"Where is Amat-ul, the Masked Man?"

"I don't know."

"When he leaves you here, in which direction does he go? Can you hear him leave?"

"Over there, by that carving. But I could never find the way out."

"I will find it. But we must move fast. The burning pig fat fumes will kill us as surely as those spiders." He closed his eyes and ran his hand over the carvings. A sudden explosion erupted near the scrolls.

"The scrolls," cried Elizabeth. "I must have them."

"Elizabeth, no, they are not worth your life."

"The clues for the location of the eggs are here…"

"The missing scrolls? Amat-ul, the Masked Man, does he have them?"

"Yes, and the true history of the Gadriel family line. I have to save them."

"Very well, but once I find the opening, we must leave, scrolls or no scrolls."

A crash of a beam from the oak ceiling made Elizabeth jump back. Some scrolls had already ignited. Her terror became overwhelming as she tried to find the map among the scrolls. In her fright, one of the scrolls dropped onto the floor and a spark flew towards the corner. Elizabeth stamped out the flames, but lost a section the size of her thumb.

She rolled the scrolls up and thrust them into her waist sash. Then she grabbed the book and pressed it into her bodice.

Arpachshad gave her a curious look. Despite the circumstances, he smiled. This was a woman worthy of a Copper Fire Dragon Whisperer's love.

Arpachshad felt a click, and the stone panel slid open.

"Come, we must slide the panel closed. The pig fat will soon cause another blast and the structure of this stone will weaken. We must warn the others."

They ran down the corridor of rock with the hatchling on Nadine's shoulder.

"I can't see a thing," cried Elizabeth.

"The tunnels have a structured pattern. It will be 100 footsteps at a normal pace. Running would be roughly 50 steps. But have courage. I suspect we will find Amat-ul somewhere close to the end. He would not have gone too far away.

ᐤ

An explosion from behind them shook the tunnel and at the top of the rock Nadine, Nicolous, and Nathan felt the stone beneath their feet rumble.

The Masked Man stepped onto the rock with his arm around the throat of Nesta.

"Silver Wing Whisperer, where are the others? Where is my brother and where are the dragons?"

"I came alone."

"You have been shielding yourself from me. You have grown more powerful. But it will not save you or the dragons."

"You know we will never let you have the dragons."

"You would not have left the new hatchling alone. No mother Whisperer would ever do such a thing. Bring me the hatchling and I will spare this girl. She is not part of our fight."

Nesta's lip quivered. She had been so afraid for so long, but now, seeing the courage of Nadine and her friends, she knew that she could no longer bear the thought of being afraid. Her tutor's words returned to her. "One day, you will make amends for what you have done."

"Nadine, get away. I am not worthy of your quest. My father always told me how worthless I am." Her eyes glistened with the memory of the shameful words. "Let him claim me. Save the hatchling and your friends."

"No Nesta. Do not say such a thing, we are all created worthy."

Nesta's eyes followed the trail of the Christ Crown thorns. There was a discarded stem near her foot. She crushed the stem with her heel, releasing the slippery sap, and moved towards it. The Masked Man's dagger nicked her skin as his foot slid on the sap. He slid backwards, but grabbed Nesta's tunic as he slid across the rock. Together they plunged over the rock face. A jutting ledge broke their fall. The Masked Man had landed on a bush, but Nesta groaned as her breath rushed out of her lungs with the impact of the raw rock.

A blast of rock erupted from the exploding lair, and Nadine looked away to shield her eyes. When she looked back, the Masked Man was gone.

The Silver Wing Whisperer climbed down the side of the rock and lifted Nesta's head onto her lap

"You did a very stupid thing there. But I thank you.

Nesta tried to smile. But the air she so desperately needed

would not find her lungs. She made a few pants, trying to re-inflate them. Her heart raced as she fought to breathe, and slowly her chest rose with the mercy of air.

"My life is not as worthy as yours." Nesta breathed out the words in a shaky whisper.

"You have lived in the shadows for too long, Nesta. You lived in fear for so long and could not tell anyone about it. But you are with us now. Friar Watt wants us to be the champion of those who live in the shadow of tyrants. He quotes this verse from Isaiah a lot. 'Tyranny will be far from you; you will have nothing to fear. Terror will be far removed; it will not come near you.' But we have to embrace those words."

Nesta's body heaved with sobs. "There is no excuse for the way I treated Meira. I was just afraid… afraid all the time. I tried to be a good girl. But always there were the beatings, no matter what I did. Then I got angry, angry that I could not make him stop Angry that I could not protect my mother. Angry every time he told me I am worthless and sometimes when I could not do the work the way the tutor wanted it done, I felt those same feelings, and I wanted to feel powerful. Then I would see Meira and then… then."

Nesta buried her face into her hands as the emotions raked through her. Her feelings burned through her just as her hot tears burned down her cheeks and her body felt weak. Elizabeth and Arpachshad watched from a distance for a while.

"Elizabeth, we can not stay here. It is not safe. We must move on. I feel the girl's suffering… but we must get you back home to Lord Logan's territory. You have been through a lot."

Elizabeth nodded. Her throat trapped her words; Nesta's sorrow had ignited the Medicine Woman's own emotions. Nadine looked up and saw the tear-streaked soot on the Medicine Woman's face. She looked at her father and then back at Nesta. Nicolous held out his hand to Nesta.

"Come Nesta, let's go home. You can come live with us until you find a new path."

"My mother…"

"I have some experience with bullies. Until you stand up to them, you will always be afraid."

"I can't…"

"Yes, you can, Nesta. You are not alone. You need never be afraid again."

Nadine reached for Elizabeth, and the two women clung to each other.

"It's good to see you, Nadine. But where is…?" She looked around, searching for the one person she really wished to see now.

"We had to come without him. Arpachshad said that…"

"I understand." Elizabeth looked away and brushed a tear from her cheek. She touched the book of Gadriel's family buried in her bodice.

"It is for the greater good."

She stared toward Holly Hill cave and sighed. A sad smile masked her disappointment.

"I have some more good news. I have found the scrolls that hold the clues to the whereabouts of the hidden eggs."

A Sneak-Peek At Book 4!

PROLOGUE

Zargor, the Emerald Forest Dragon, closed his eyes to the horror below as the flames devoured the trees. The charred stumps seemed to cry out to him as their sap bled into the earth. Zargor could not save them now. He thought only of his promise to his mate, Ciommed, as her silent screams pierced his heart while her egg ripped through her. She had to contain her pain to protect their egg from those who hunted her. The Emerald Forest Dragon knew that Nyla, their Whisperer's wife, was with her and would care for their egg with the last of her strength, but she could not save Ciommed from the suffering a hardened egg would produce. He should have been with his mate now, but they had taken an oath to conceal the eggs at all costs. It was too late to save his beloved Ciommed. They only hoped to protect their species with these chosen eggs.

If he made it through the war zones, he would go back for their hatchling and rear it himself. He knew the Crystal Water Dragon egg he carried with him would not survive long without a water source. Zargor scales were more pliable than the Copper Fire Dragon, and he suffered in the desolation of war. There was nothing green to lift his spirits. No water source close enough for him to quench his thirst.

Then he heard the soothing voice of Cemradoss.

"Zargor, you grow weary. Come, drink from the Itufil lake and rest."

"I cannot see. The flames, they cover everything."

"Follow my voice. I will be your guide."

Zargor squinted through the flames and smoke. His throat burned, and for a moment he forgot his sorrow as he strained to focus on the voice.

Cemradoss, the oldest of all the dragons, waited below the surface of the lake. Her large sapphire eyes watched the creatures of the lake dart from one rock crevice to the next. They too, felt the hatred of war. It unsettled the delicate vibrations of the water.

She could not keep the egg with her. It would be too dangerous. Cemradoss knew that her kind were being hunted. She would lead the Emerald Forest Dragon to the beginning of the life source. The place that birthed that first volcano. Man did not venture to its depths. Without a mother, the egg would not hatch and no human had ever climbed the steep sides of the volcano. Unless a Mother Whisperer had a dragon to help her, no one would reach the egg.

It had been decades since the volcano had released the last of its anger on the earth, and now its once ferocious mouth contained the healing waters of a thousand rain showers. Together she and her sisters had moved the clouds to heal the earth and silence the volcano's rumblings.

She felt Zargor's despair. It was too heavy a burden to carry another's eggs when your mate lay dying so far away. She felt her own heart tighten as his sorrow gripped her. So many things flowed through water, it was impossible not to be moved by them.

A Crystal Water Dragon's strength was to feel another's emotions, but it was also their curse. She had felt each of her sisters' death cries as the warlord's hunters had harvested their bodies from the layers of protective fat that lay beneath their blue grey scales. It was their insulation against the depth of the icy waters when they made their migration, but it burned brightly and the dark lords believed it had magical properties. Such slaughter for mere superstition was an assault against nature.

She would wait until he was almost over her before she would rise. She could not risk being seen.

Zargor's vision blurred as his strength drained. The Copper Fire Dragon egg was so heavy. He never imagined how much of his strength it would drain. His shoulders ached from the strain of keeping himself airborne. Zargor's once beautiful emerald wings looked dull as the heat of the inferno below him sapped them of moisture. He felt as brittle as the trampled autumn leaves that littered the rocks of the Caves of Desolation where the Copper Fire Dragons went to die. Cemradoss felt his depression weave around his soul and pull on his strength. She knew she had to reveal herself sooner than she had hoped.

"Zargor, do not give up, you are so close."

Zargor felt his mate's last breath leave her body, and it carried with it his will. The eggs no longer mattered. He was too tired, too thirsty, and too filled with sorrow.

Cemradoss separated her fin like wings and rose from the depths. She swirled around, creating a column of vapour until it swelled into a cloud. It was a risk. Her massive body would be visible from beyond the dying forest. But she had to bring the life-giving gift of rain to the carrier of the eggs.

Zargor glided blindly. His breath came out in short sharp pants as his lungs cried out for the sweet, cool air of the forest. He thought of Ciommed's gentle forehead greeting and reached for her in his tortured mind, but she did not return his embrace.

The Copper Fire Dragon egg was the first to fall. He did

not see its descent, but carried on gliding on the wind created by Cemradoss's efforts. She flew below the egg carrier, creating a pocket of air to support him, and then the first delicate drops falling from the clouds teased his wings with their gentle caress. His wings soaked up the life-giving force, but Zargor's eyes remained closed.

"Drink Zargor. Renew your strength."

His mind was closed to her, and she saw his neck droop again with the weight of the remaining egg. She could not keep him afloat and reach for the egg at the same time. The rain fell unchecked down his face and over his back, but while his body soaked up its cooling life force, he did not open his mouth to drink.

"Zargor! Zargor! Drink!"

Cemradoss could feel him slipping from her. His sorrow assaulted her like a tornado, whipping at her mind and crashing through her soul. She pushed some clouds past her to the burning forest, hoping they would release their mercy onto the earth.

The Crystal Water Dragon could not see where they went without breaking her rhythm and pushed hard to keep Zargor in the sky.

Cemradoss almost wept with relief as the Itufil Lake's soothing waters filled her vision. She folded her wings and dived in and watched how Zargor's body dropped from the sky and cascaded into the refreshing waters. The pouch with the egg slid off his neck and sank into the depths of the lake's embrace. The impact of his body against the surface of the lake forced his mouth open and the sweet waters filled his mouth. Cemradoss rose and lifted him, pushing his body to the edge of the water. She searched for the berries that the locals used to energise their sick with and carried them to him. Cemradoss pried Zargo's mouth open and dropped a few of the berries onto his tongue. She pierced them with her claw and the juice trickled down his throat. Zargor's body responded, but confusion still bound his mind.

"Ciommed… the egg, is it safe?"

"Yes." Cemradoss could not bring herself to correct him. She granted him the mercy of ignorance. "Rest now, renew your strength."

The Crystal Water Dragon pulled a few fallen branches and shielded his body with them, and then dove into the lake to retrieve the egg. Fish swirled around the egg, curious to see what had disturbed the bottom of their haven. The egg rested in the lake's bottom like a hatchling curled up next to its mother. Cemradoss smiled and thought of her own hatchlings. They had all grown and started families of their own, but now… She shook away the memories of the losses of war and allowed herself to fantasize about keeping this one for herself. But the protocols of war dictated that they would hide the eggs, unless it was a dragon's own offspring. The elders knew that a new mother and a hatchling were both vulnerable and that the warlords would seek them out. Cemradoss would have to carry this egg herself to the volcano. Zargor no longer had the strength. She would have him conceal the egg and come back to the Emerald Forest Dragon.

KIM VERMAAK'S STARTER LIBRARY

Building a relationship with my readers is the very best thing about writing. I occasionally send out newsletters with details of new releases, special offers and other bits relating to my book series.

And if you sign up to my mailing list I'll send you the Chronicles Of Nadine novella, A MOTHER'S WARNING, FOR FREE!

You can get this book **for free** by signing up at:

https://storyoriginapp.com/giveaways/27c4d176-52aa-11eb-b6c4-3f292efffb0b

You may unsubscribe at any time.

Enjoy this book? You can make a big difference

Reviews are the most powerful tools in my arsenal when it comes to getting attention for my books. Much as I'd like to, I don't have the financial muscle of a New York publisher. I can't take out full page ads in the newspaper or put posters on the subway.

(not yet anyway).

But I do have something much more powerful and effective than that, and it's something those publishers would kill to get their hands on.

A committed and loyal bunch of readers.

Honest reviews of my books help bring them to the attention of other readers. If you've enjoyed this book I would be very grateful if you could spend just five minutes leaving a review (it can be as short as you like) on the book's sales page.

Thank you very much.

Book Three Character List

ACACIUS

A guard at the monastery. Acacius is a Latinized form of the Ancient Greek which means thorny.

Pronounced: Uh-kay-shus

Adira

A Guardian of History.

A name of Hebrew origin meaning strong, noble, powerful.

Pronounced: ah-deer-ah

Alizah

Silver Wing Dragon hatching that Muquin hatched.

A name of Hebrew origin name meaning joy.

Pronounced: A-li-zah

Amat-ul

Also known as The Masked Man.

A fallen Copper Dragon Whisperer. Twin Brother of Nadine's Tutor.

Meaning: Arabic origin meaning: Slave of or Servant of: They typically give the name to females.

Pronounced: A-mat-ool

Gender: Male

Pronounced: Are-oo-croth

Arpachshad

The Emerald Forest Dragon Whisperer

Hebrew name meaning healer

Pronounced: Ar-pach-shad

Arucroth

A Copper Fire Dragon. This was the darkened dragon that the warlords had taken.

Gender: Male

Pronounced: A-Roo-Croth

Aisha

Galdolf's wife. She is an innkeeper.

Arabic, Swahili, meaning "living, prosperous"

Pronounced: Eye-Sh-A

Beatrice

Lady Christine's spymaster. She was the daughter of a Contron Warrior.

Meaning: The Bringing of Blessing

Pronounced: Beer-Tris

Bliant

An Emerald Forest Dragon Hatchling that Nadine hatched.

Gender: Male

Meaning of the name: Name: Healer

Pronounced: Bl-eye-ant

Captain Julian

Captain of the Guard in Lord Logan's Land. The man who rescued Lady Christine from King Radolf in the prequel novella.

English, Latin origin and means "youthful, downy-bearded, or sky father."

Pronounced: Jew-lee-ann

Captain Hucchon

A mercenary trainer of warriors. Originally from Lady Christine's lands.

Scottish form of French name Hugon, HUCHON means "heart," "mind," or "spirit."

Pronounced: Huch-on

Cemradoss

A Crystal Water Dragon. The oldest of all dragons.

Gender: Female

Pronounced: Cem-ra-doss

Ciommed

An Emerald Forest Dragon who died passing her egg. She was a carrier of the chosen eggs.

Gender: Female

Pronounced: See-oh-med

Cymraeg

A dragon Artisan: Architect for the Whisperer Lairs

From the Welsh meaning compatriots.

Pronounced: Cum-Ray-g

Dalila

A former child prostitute, rescued from the Dristrict.

Tanzanian origin meaning "delicate or gentle"

Pronounced: Da-lee-la

Deivdri

A dragon slayer

Prounounced: Dave-dri

Dorothea

Nadine's mother

Greek origin meaning "gift of God".

Pronounced: Dor-oh-thee-ah

Elizabeth

The Medicine Woman who lives in Lord Logan's Lands.

Meaning: "God is my oath" in Hebrew

Pronounced: E-liz-a-beth

Emuna

The great niece of Arpachshad (an Emerald Forest Dragon Whisperer). She cared for him when he was in The Long Sleep.

Meaning of the name: "faith" or "faithfulness”

Pronounced: eh-moo-nuh

Father Stephen

A priest planted by King Radolf to be appointed Bishop for the Northern Kingdom.

Meaning: Greek origin meaning "wreath, crown" and by extension "reward, honor, renown, fame.”

Pronounced: Stee- Vuhn

Friar Watt

Nadine’s spiritual tutor. He is also a healer.

Meaning: The Watt surname derives from ancient forms of the personal name Walter. Walter means "powerful ruler" or "ruler of the army,"

Pronouced: W-h-ott

Galdolf

Former Prision Master of King Radolf. He cared for Yakhal after Nabal captured the hatchling and brought it to the stronghold in the Northern Kingdom.

Pronounced: Gal-doll-f

Helena

The Masked Man and The Copper Fire Dragon Whisperer’s mother.

Meaning: Greek origin, and the meaning of Helena is "shining light".

Pronounced: He-leah-na

Lady Christine

Lord Logan’s wife. Lost Heir of King Frederick. She was betrothed to King Radolf, but escaped from his Kingdom.

Christine is a feminine name of Greek or Latin origin. Derived from the word Christ. It means a follower of Christ or a female Christian.

Pronounced: Kri-steen

Lord Teebald

King Radolf’s Spymaster

A name derived from the Old German Theudibald, from teut-bald, strong or bold leader.

Pronounced: Tee-ball-d

Lord Jefferson

Close friend of Lady Christine's Father King Frederick.

Jeffrey is a variant of Geoffrey, meaning "peaceful place,"

Pronounced: Jef-uh-suhn

Lord Zayne

A nobleman who is Meira's guardian.

Zayne is from Hebrew origin and means God is gracious.

Pronounced: Zey-N

Maimi

A term of endearment for a mother.

Pronounced: May-mee

Maireid

Nadine's sister

Pronounded: May-reed

Meira

An inntured servant taken by King Radolf's men as payment for outstanding taxes.

Meira is from Hebrew origin and means "light"

Pronounced: May-rah

Menashe

The name that Tamyss named Gadriel's second son. It is a Hebrew name meaning to forget. It was the name Joseph gave to his son, saying that the Lord caused him to forget all his troubles.

Pronounced: Meh-naa-s-haa

Mikael

Nadine's Brother.

Mikael is a boy's name, of Hebrew origin, and the meaning is "who resembles God?"

Pronounced: Mee kyl

Mıykaeel

A crafton warrior. She was responsible for the campaign to capture mother dragons with eggs.

Pronounced: Mee-kay-eel

Muquin

A Silver Wing Dragon.

Gender: Female

Leader of the Silver Wings Dragons

Pronounced: Moo-quin

The leader of the Silver Wing Dragons and Nadine's Tutor.

Megadeus

Former leader of the Silver Wing Dragons

Gender: Male

Muquin's fallen mate.

Pronounced: Meg-a-dew-s

Nabal

The Dragon Thief. The Copper Fire Dragon Whisperer's grandson.

A Hebrew name meaning of the name: Fool, senseless.

Pronounced: Nay-bell

Nathan

Nadine's friend. He is also Lord Logan's Trade Adviser.

The name Nathan is of Hebrew origin and means "gift of Go"d.

Pronounced: Nay-than

Nyla

An Emerald Forest Dragon Whisperer's wife. She helped Ciommed pass her egg.

Nyla is an Arabic name meaning one who achieves.

Pronounced: Ny-Lah

Nesta

A villager in Lord Logan's territory. She has an abusive father and she also bullies Meira

A name of Welsh origin meaning "pure".

Pronounced: Neh-stuh

Nicolous

Nadine's Father.

A name derived from the Greek name meaning 'victory of the people'.

Pronounced: Nick-O-lus

Nyla

The Emerald Forest Dragon Whisperer's wife who helped Ciommed pass her egg.

Nyla is an Arabic name meaning one who achieves

Pronounced: Ny-lah

Nullah

This is a Dragon Artisan Blacksmith.

The name merans club or hunting stick and comes from d from the Dharug language.

Pronounced: Null - uh

Peberra

Nullah's wife. She helps on the blacksmith

Pronounded: Peb-ear-a

Paeon

This was Elizabeth's tutor. He hwas named after Paeon the Greek physician of the gods.

Pronounded: Pie-ann

Pope Viktor

The head of the church, the first pope to be appointed who was not of noble birth.

A name of Russian origin meaning Conqueror

Pronounced: Vic-tor

Raguel

Captain of the Pope's personal guards.

A name derived from the Hebrew meaning "friend of God". Raguel is one of the seven archangels mainly of the Judaic traditions.

Pronounced: Rah-Guy-oo-ehl

Simcha

Silver Wing Hatchling

Gender: female

Pronounced: Sim-cha

Sophie

Captain Julian's Wife

A name of Greek origin, meaning "wisdom". Sophie is related to the name Sophia.

Pronounced: Soh-fee

Shuo

This is one of the female warrior trainers in Lady Chrstin'es Womans camp. It is typically a man's name of Chinese origin. The name Shuo means 'one who achieves greatness.

Pronounced: She-oo-oh

Tamyss

Leader of the Copper Fire Dragons. He had reared the Copper Fire Dragon Whisperer.

Mate of Undor, Father of the turned Copper Fire Dragon.

Pronounced: Ta-miss

Tagliyot

Birth name given to Bliant when his dragon mother, Ciommed, passed the egg.

Gender: Male

Pronounced: Tag-lee-yot

Teafa

A prostitute from Lord Teebald's spy training camp.

Meaning: Irish origin meaning place name.

Pronounced: Tea-fa

Zairdenth

A Copper Fire Dragon who lives with Nadine's mentor.

Gender: Male

Pronounced: Zay-r-den-th

About the Author

Kim Vermaak always had a pen in her hand. Whether doodling, crafting poems or writing letters.

Born into an abusive family, Kim's first heroes were her adoptive parents. Through them, she learned the gift of new beginnings.

She also learned a love of reading and how she could be transported to a place where ordinary people could find the courage to rise above insurmountable odds. Through books, she found her courage.

But it was not until South Africa faced its first series of power cuts, she found her talent for storytelling. In the dark with a frightened daughter, she began to create heroes that could tap into their inner strength and win.

Through her love of reading, history and young people, Kim crafts stories that embrace the true purpose of storytelling. To impart wisdom. But in today's fast-paced society, we often reduce stories to entertainment value. This leaves little room for us to grow and forces us to relive the painful lessons of the past. It is Kim's passion to see communities create a legacy that will empower future generations.

In her medieval fantasy series, "The Chronicles of Nadine" Kim weaves a landscape of characters all on the path their choices have carved. She welcomes readers who have learned lessons through these characters to share them with her and each other.

www.kimvermaak.com

Grab your free copy of A Mother's Warning

https://storyoriginapp.com/giveaways/27c4d176-52aa-11eb-b6c4-3f292efffb0b

Yakhal Publishing

Title: The Call of the Ancients
Series Name: Book Three | The Chronicles of Nadine
Author: Kim Vermaak
Cover Design: Concept: Author Kim Vermaak
Typesetting: Books by Bella
Illustrations: Kim Vermaak
Author Photo: Hush Naidoo
Edited by Judy Ward
Published by: Yakhal Publishing
First Edition: 2021

ISBN: 978-0-620-93263-9(print)
ISBN: 978-0-620-93264-6(e-book)

Cover Image: Tammy Bradbury
Cover Layout: SHAHRUKH HUSSNAIN
https://www.fiverr.com/shahrukhshah000

Website: www.kimvermaak.com
Facebook: https://www.facebook.com/thechroniclesofnadine
Instagram: https://www.instagram.com/kimvermaakauthor/
Linkedin: https://www.linkedin.com/in/kim-vermaak-a4682b1/

www.ingramcontent.com/pod-product-compliance
Lightning Source LLC
LaVergne TN
LVHW041104080826
845145LV00007B/1685
* 9 7 8 0 6 2 0 9 3 2 6 3 9 *